Across the Top of the World

Also by Wally Herbert

A WORLD OF MEN

Across the Top

THE LAST GREAT

FOUNDED 1838

GPPS

by WALLY HERBERT

of the World

JOURNEY ON EARTH

G. P. Putnam's Sons, New York

AUTHOR'S ACKNOWLEDGMENT

This story starts where the journey ends—an epic adventure that spans ten years. It is the story of one man's obsessive ambition to cross the Arctic Ocean and of those men who endured with him the hardships of the journey. To them, and to everyone who helped and encouraged me, I offer my warmest thanks.

WALLY HERBERT

Bishopstone, Wiltshire
September, 1970

Contents

Illustrations appear following page 128

Foreword

by HRH The Prince Philip, Duke of Edinburgh

As our knowledge of this planet grows, so it seems to shrink in size, and when we saw the pictures of it taken from the moon it became almost insignificant. Yet it has always been the same size to men, and its mountains and deserts, oceans and ice caps still pose the same problems and challenges to men with a feeling for adventure and discovery.

This book is a graphic account of the first surface crossing of the Arctic Ocean and the longest sustained journey in the history of polar exploration. It is an achievement which ranks among the greatest triumphs of human skill and endurance.

Buckingham Palace
January, 1971

Prologue

The Hunter of Moskushamn

A BLUE–GRAY fog was tumbling softly round a dead campfire when I awoke cold and stiff on the morning of June 18, 1960, rolled out of a depression in the spongy tundra, launched a canoe and resumed my journey along the fjord. In the past three days I had paddled eighty miles through breaking seas along a coastline aproned in scree and scarred by rushing melt streams; under towering, fluted cliffs and curtains of nesting birds; and through the ice-choked waters fronting the Von Post and Tuna glaciers. It was a race against time—a race to catch the *SS Lyngen,* which was due to sail south on the morning of June 19 from the Norwegian mining town of Longyearbyen, the largest township on the Arctic island of Spitsbergen.

My stay on the island had been a short one. During the past four weeks, I had been a member of an expedition whose object had been to carry out physiological experiments to see if the human being could adapt to an abnormal length of day. It had been a pleasant and relaxing period, without isolation, great stress or hardship, or time for discontent. For a month I and my companions, Dr. Hugh Simpson, Myrtle his wife, and Fred Bruemmer had lazily watched the birds fly to and fro, or lay their eggs while the sun baked their backs and the tundra steamed around them. We had watched the eggs hatch out and heard a symphony of birdsong rise in pitch and volume. Snow-bed plants burst into bloom; melt pools that had teemed with larvae became dance floors of gnats, black midges and mosquitoes; warmth drew the vegetable matter, and the odor set the insects humming. Warmth had melted the surface of the glaciers; water, perspiring down the smooth green creases, trickled in streams which joined up and became torrents, boiling and cascading with a roar into crevasses which filled up and overflowed. Huge blocks of overhanging ice, eaten loose by the flow of melt water and the ambient pressures in the glacier, had broken and crashed into Tempelfjord—the fjord in which, without then knowing it, I would one day plan to end a transpolar journey of 3,800 miles.

Fog muted everything that morning; even the plunging canoe made only a dull thud as I hugged the cliffs which rose sheer from a thin line of froth. Often during that day they drifted away into the mist, and by evening, as I drew in to the coast alongside a cluster of derelict shacks on the opposite side of a small tributary fjord from my destination, I was fatigued and frozen to the core. Though it was only two miles across from there to Longyearbyen, I had no reserves of energy to cover that short distance and stay the night in the mining town. In any case I had been far too depressed by Longyearbyen—its sense of dereliction, its covering of dust—to feel inclined to spend another night in that godforsaken spot where aerial coal tubs, like wingless buzzards, gently swayed in slow procession above barrack blocks and sheds. Instead I had elected to doss down in some sheltered nook among the deserted mine workings of Moskushamn.

A wiry, strained-face man appeared, strode down to the water's edge, greeted me in English and lifted the canoe high above the beach. We picked our way through the debris of broken-down buildings, rusted engines, and abandoned mine workings toward a warped three-storied warehouse. Most of its windows were shuttered and the groaning door flapped gently on its hinges. Inside the warehouse it was dark. Pit props supported a sagging ceiling. The whole building seemed to be listing, and the rotting staircase creaked as we climbed to the attic.

My host was the only inhabitant of Moskushamn, a recluse who had spent the two previous winters on the north coast of Spitsbergen hunting polar bear. He was at that time gathering stores and equipment for another winter, and the squalid attic was his temporary retreat until autumn, when he would ship by sealing vessel up the coast, occupy his tiny hut, bait his traps, set his fixed guns and wait for the bear to come. He was a man with a stare in his eyes; a man who wintered alone by choice—a nocturnal man who awakens at sundown and prowls around in polar darkness.

Several hours passed before I felt at ease in his company, for surprisingly he was intense; a nervous man, a man of great intelligence—enigmatic and yet in some ways very simple. Not for him the expedition with its snug comforts and scientific programs. We came from different worlds, he and I, and yet we spoke a common language, and while the wind moaned past the windows we talked away the hours of sleep.

We talked about the life he led and about his techniques of hunting. We talked about the polar bear and about the polar basin.

"Why is it," he asked, "that no one has ever attempted to sledge across the Arctic Ocean?"

"Because it is not feasible," I told him, without giving it much thought.

1

'Dark, Dark, Dark . . . '

THREE YEARS were to elapse between my meeting with the hunter and the realization that the journey we had talked about was not only feasible but probably the most challenging journey left to man on the surface of this planet. I cannot claim that during those three years I nursed a dream of crossing the Arctic Ocean; on the contrary, half that time I was obsessed by an ambition to reach the South Pole, and not until some eighteen months after I had been stopped two hundred and fifty-five miles short of that goal had I felt compelled, as had Amundsen just over half a century earlier, to switch my attentions to the other end of the earth.

I had been thumbing through a past number of the *Polar Record*, with its notes on the Antarctic activities of the British expeditions of 1955–56 (of which I had been a part), when a map of the Arctic Ocean caught my attention. On it were plotted the tracks of several Russian drifting stations. I added to that same map the tracks of the American drifting stations T-3 and Arlis II, Nansen's ship the *Fram*, and Russian station SP-6, and was intrigued to find that the ice circulation formed a pattern which broadly divided into two currents. One, evidently a slow-moving current, drifted clockwise in the western half of the Arctic Ocean; the other, a faster-moving current which seemed to originate north of the New Siberian Islands, flowed over the North Pole and out of the Arctic Ocean between Spitsbergen and northeast Greenland.

The more I studied that map, the more reasonable it seemed to me that a party of men and dog teams could set out from Point Barrow, Alaska, and sledge via the North Pole to northeast Greenland. Calculating rapidly on the basis of four men and three teams of dogs, I felt they would so benefit from the drift of the pack ice * that they would be able to maintain an average of fourteen miles a day and complete the trans-Arctic journey in 130 days. I had not taken into account in those first rough calculations that the 1,850-mile airline route from Barrow to northeast Greenland would, over the polar pack, be increased by thirty percent or more; nor had I at that time studied the records of previous explorers who had attempted to reach the North Pole, to say nothing of giving thought to how I might raise the money for such a venture. Perhaps it is just as well, for had I realized how much hard work, frustration and disappointment lay ahead I might never have become involved in a project which, to the exclusion of all else, was to occupy seven years of my life.

Within a few days of entering the literature I became completely absorbed in the subject. Here were examples of ruthless greed, pride, conceit, courage, foolishness, and heroism in a setting more colorful and far more hazardous than I had found in the Antarctic. Here was the story of man's struggle to master the polar environment—a struggle that even in recorded history reached back over two thousand years.

Where in the short history of the Antarctic, for example, is there a hero to compare with Pytheas—the Marseilles Greek who sailed north in 325 B.C. in search of tin, and returned with stories of people (the British) who "live miserably and like savages on account of the severity of the cold"? [1] It was Pytheas

* For a glossary of Arctic environmental terminology, see p. 323.
[1] Strabo (first century B.C.): *The Geography,* Book 2, translated by H. Hamilton and W. Falconer (London, 1854).

who brought back an account of a land he called Thule, where there was no night in summer and "where neither earth, water, nor air exists separately, but a sort of concretion of all these, resembling marine sponge, in which the earth, the sea, and all things were suspended, thus forming, as it were, a link to unite the whole together." [2] Was this a description of a fog bank off Iceland, and was his ship stopped from making further progress north by ice which "could neither be traveled over nor sailed through"? [3] Where is there a figure in South Polar history as colorful as St. Brendan?—the Irish abbot who, as the saga goes, together with a crew of monks sailed north from Ireland in frail skin-covered coracles in the sixth century A.D.; or his disciples, who set up a colony on Iceland and encountered the "curdled sea" when they sailed north of their new home in 825 A.D.

There was still a small colony of Irish monks on the island in the middle of the ninth century when the Norseman Rabna Floki found his way there across the North Sea by periodically releasing ravens and watching in which direction they flew in search of the nearest land. Other Norse noblemen, evading taxation, followed Floki of the Ravens and colonized the island. Ohthere (Ottar, as he is sometimes known) in A.D. 870 penetrated the Arctic, rounded the northernmost point in Scandinavia and sailed east—the first recorded voyage into polar waters. Eric the Red sailed west and founded a Norse colony in the southern part of Greenland; and Eric's son, Leif the Lucky, discovered America and voyaged north up the west coast of Greenland to a point beyond the eightieth parallel.

The colonies flourished during the eleventh, twelfth, and thirteenth centuries, but then mysteriously died out, and by 1400 A.D. all that had been discovered by the Vikings, except Iceland, was lost. Even the sagas that told of their voyages came to be regarded merely as recitals of pious lies. But Viking blood with its heritage of courage and its seafaring tradition, had helped create England; and five centuries after the Vikings had discovered their Arctic world, the English had taken to the sea.

[2] Strabo: *op. cit.*
[3] Strabo: *op. cit.*

They went north in search of a sea route to the Orient, for news of the immense wealth of Cathay brought back by Marco Polo's desert caravans had dazzled the merchants of England. They went north because they had no choice; the Portuguese were in command of the sea route around Africa, the Spanish in command of the route around South America. They saw incredible sights: "mountaines of yce tenne thousand times scaping them scarse one ynch . . . and they were brought many times to the extreamest point of perill. . . ." [4] They saw infernos and fortresses of moving ice and sustained miracles of light in seas wherein "nature breeds, perverse, all monstrous, all prodigious things, abominable, inutterable, and worse than fables. . . . " [5] Their tales fired the imagination of their sons, and the poets Shakespeare, Milton, Keats and Coleridge added their magic to the imagery of floating ice.

But in this first period of polar exploration, men were in such fear of the North that even the boldest dared only brief summer excursions into the ice-strewn seas. Polar darkness was dreaded like the torments of hell, and those forced to spend the winter in the Arctic had found that it was "dark, dark, dark . . . without all hope of day" and had died miserably of scurvy. Their diaries told of suffering and hopeless courage; of storms, disease, and intense cold. The Elizabethans, however, were not so easily put off. Their Queen approved of the search for trade routes to the Orient which promised wealth for her kingdom and the command of the northern seas, and with the exception of the temporary distraction of fighting off the Spanish Armada, the Elizabethan polar explorers—notably Frobisher, Davis and Hudson—became almost obsessed with their search for the illusive passage to the East.

It was the age of discovery. The age of undreamed-of wealth, that gave birth to the great trading companies whose profits were

[4] King Alfred's description of Europe, translated by Richard Hakluyt and contained in his *The Principal Navigations Voyages Traffiques and Discoveries of the English Nation*, vol. 7 (Glasgow, Hakluyt Society, 1903–5).
[5] John Milton: *Paradise Lost*.

used to promote further exploration—an investment which paid dividends in plenty, for at Henry Hudson's reports that the Spitsbergen waters were teeming with whales, there developed a piratical battle for oil. Under successive waves of men, each six-week midsummer saw hundreds of ships of several nations and sixteen thousand men engaged in the looting of the coastal waters and the extermination of the great sea mammals. The rivalries, the hazards, and the slaughter were soon over. Within a couple of decades the wildlife that had teemed in the waters and abounded in the valleys was wiped out and the rape of Spitsbergen was complete. Only the shallow graves of a thousand men on Deadman's Island and some of the terms they used for the ice that had harrassed them remain, for what they discovered they jealously guarded and seldom if ever logged.

Hudson's farthest north latitude, 80°23′, a record he set in 1607, remained unequaled until 1773 when Captain the Honorable Constantine Phipps RN surpassed it by twenty-five miles in Spitsbergen waters with a well-appointed naval scientific expedition that, like Hudson's voyage, was attempting to reach the North Pole directly by sea. But the Phipps expedition is remembered less by the British for its record northing than for the adventure it offered a mischievous midshipman by the name of Nelson, whose destiny it was to lead his country to many a naval victory.

Mistress of the seas after the Battle of Trafalgar, the Royal Navy looked once again to the Arctic, but this reawakening of interest was freshly motivated; it was now no longer the Northwest Passage they were seeing but the exploration and extension of British Arctic territory, and as an added incentive to explorers an Act of Parliament was passed in 1818 offering a reward of £20,000 for the discovery of the Northwest Passage and £5,000 for attaining the Pole. Naval expeditions responding to this challenge no longer fled the Arctic with the setting sun; instead, following the example of Edward Parry, they hibernated beneath a canopy of canvas covering the decks of their ships.

Parry had served as second-in-command of John Ross's expedition in 1818, when an attempt had been made at the Northwest Passage, and his first command at the age of twenty-nine had had the same objective. But on that voyage Parry penetrated deeper into the maze of channels than anyone before him, and in its record of good health and high morale this first wintering of naval ships in the Arctic was a remarkable success. He was lionized in England and given the command of two other naval expeditions in search of the Northwest Passage; expeditions that, although not as impressive as the first, were rich enough in experience to enable Parry to reach conclusions that were to revolutionize polar-travel techniques.

All previous attempts to reach the North Pole had been shipborne, for it was believed that once through the belt of pack ice at the perimeter of the Arctic Ocean there would be open water beyond. Parry did not wholly accept this theory of the open polar sea, and "proposed to attempt to reach the North Pole by means of traveling with sledge boats over the ice, or through any spaces of water that might occur." With a ship to transport him to a base on the edge of the Arctic Ocean, and advancing from his ship over the ice on foot, Parry inaugurated a technique that was to become common procedure for almost all later attempts at the Pole.

In his ship, the *Hecla*, he reached Treurenberg Bay on the north coast of Spitsbergen in early June, 1827. From there, with twenty-seven men, provisioned for seventy-one days, they set out to reach the North Pole dragging boats shod with steel runners. They suffered inexpressible hardships, advancing blindly through fogs, rain, and slush over hummock ice and pressure and along leads of open water. They toiled throughout the hours of evening, then took an hour off for dinner and resumed their labor until "dawn." Hauling their boats up onto a safe floe, they would spread the sails for a canopy, congregate for prayers, then suffer the hours of inaction until the bugle called them to another night of toil. It was a hopeless struggle—the drift of ice was against them. Almost a thousand miles they covered on a treadmill of drifting floes without getting further from their ship than 172 miles. But Parry had set a record at 82°45′ N which was unbeaten for half a century, and in originality of plan his attempt at the Pole has been unequaled by any Arctic explorer with the exception of Fridtjof Nansen.

The advancement of polar technique took a further step forward a few years later. Though far less dramatic than Parry's attempt at the North Pole, John Ross's voyage in the *Victory* in search of the Northwest Passage (1829–34) distinguished itself on three counts. The expedition discovered the north magnetic pole, spent four consecutive winters in the Arctic without loss of life, and brought Europeans for the first time into close association with the Eskimos.

There were of course retrograde steps from time to time, and the biggest of these undoubtedly was Franklin's expedition of 1845. But the tragedy and subsequent search for that ill-fated expedition, which involved some forty ships and more than two thousand men, accelerated the discovery and exploration of the Canadian Archipelago, solved the long-drawn-out question of the Northwest Passage, and introduced new men to the north—men who, through the pioneering example of Leopold McClintock, had taken to the Eskimo methods of travel. This brought a surge of freedom to polar exploration, and it was but a short stride from there to the Pole. The heroic age had begun—a strange mixture of incompetence and courage; of honor and dignity in death and glory in defeat.

Goaded by the growing competence of such men as the Americans Elisha Kane, Isaac Hayes, and Charles F. Hall, who had suddenly become rivals to the Royal Navy's hard-won place in the forefront of polar endeavor, the Admiralty in 1875 sent out Captain George Nares to bring back the Pole for Britain. To his credit he navigated his two ships to the very edge of the Arctic Ocean; to the honor of his country his men, under the leadership of Lieutenant Albert Markham, by sheer grit and patriotic fervor planted the Union Jack north of the previous record. But in the light of history it seems inexcusable that he had his men suffer, hauling their heavy boats across the ice, when lighter and faster techniques were known to exist. The American military expedition of 1882–84 under Major Adolphus Greely was an even greater disaster; only seven of the twenty-five men were still alive when rescue eventually arrived, and of those only three properly recovered. Nor was the suffering that marked this period of Arctic history confined to the so-called American route to the Pole in the vicinity of Northern Ellesmere Island. The American, Lieutenant George Washington De Long, a sailor already toughened by Arctic experience, had sailed his ship, the *Jeannette,* through the Bering Strait at the end of August, 1879, in the hope of finding an open polar sea beyond the peripheral belt of pack ice. The *Jeannette,* beset off Herald Island, drifted for sixteen months before being crushed by the pressure of ice. Only one of the three boats' crews survived the struggle to shore and the long trudge across the Lena Delta to the outposts of civilization; but at least history can say of De Long that his idea was original.

Nansen's epic drift in the *Fram* followed—an expedition that has no equal in the whole history of polar exploration. It was the perfect balance between adventure and science: an expedition inspired and conducted by a man of greater vision and adventurous drive than any other explorer the world has known.

Fridtjof Nansen was a Norwegian scholar, and only twenty-three years of age when in 1884 he read a newspaper article describing some debris of the *Jeannette* which was found embedded in ice that had washed ashore in southwest Greenland. It occurred to Nansen that "if a floe could drift right across the unknown regions, that drift might be enlisted in the service of exploration." His plan was born: He would build a ship which would ride up on the ice as pressure squeezed the hull—a small stout vessel it had to be, with sail and auxiliary engines, a vessel provisioned for five years which would be driven into the ice in the vicinity of the New Siberian Islands and drift with the currents across the Arctic Ocean toward the Greenland Sea. Many problems of the Arctic basin would be solved by such a voyage. It would settle once and for all whether there existed a continent or an open polar sea; the nature of the currents; the depth and temperature of the water; the nature of the drifting ice, and whether there was any animal life in the Arctic Ocean.

His plan was not put into immediate operation, and many years passed, years during which Nansen tested his mettle by making the first crossing of Greenland; but his theory of the polar drift was seldom far from his mind, and in November, 1892, he traveled to London to lay his plans before the Royal Geographical Society. At that historic meeting, the simplicity and revolutionary daring of his plan alarmed practically all the polar pundits; but despite the condemnation of so many of its members, the society, with an English illogicality, contributed £300 toward his expedition. On June 24, 1893, nine years after he had first read the article that inspired the venture, his ship, the *Fram,* with thirteen men on board, set sail to put his theory to the test.

The *Fram* performed perfectly, rising above ice floes that would have crushed any other ship, but as time went on it became apparent that the *Fram* would not drift over the Pole but would bypass it by about three hundred miles, and the adventurer in Nansen compelled him and Lieutenant F. H. Johansen to attempt to reach the Pole by a dash across the ice floes with sledges and dogs.

Leaving the *Fram* and her crew in the command of Captain Sverdrup, Nansen and Johansen had set off with three sledges and twenty-eight dogs on March 14, 1895, from latitude 84°04'N, longitude 102°E, and in just under a month had reached latitude 86°14'N. From there the northern prospect was "a veritable chaos of iceblocks" and the nearest land some four hundred miles to their southwest. They reached Franz Joseph Land after a hazardous journey about 130 days later, more by chance than by good navigation, for shortly after turning back from their farthest north both Nansen and Johansen had carelessly let their chronometer watches run down with the result that all their longitudinal calculations were out by several degrees. Nor were all their troubles over on making land. They had somehow to survive the winter and continue their journey the following summer, but they were now without dogs, for it had been part of Nansen's plan to feed dog to dog in order to increase his range, and he and Johansen had killed the last two dogs on August 7. They now had to make their way back to civilization by sledge and kayak some six hundred miles westward to Spitsbergen, where they hoped to come upon a whaling sloop that would take them home to Norway.

Nansen's account of his fifteen-month's journey from the *Fram* to the historic meeting with the English explorer Jackson on Franz Joseph Land on June 17, 1896, and its epilogue of his reunion with the *Fram* a few days after his return to Norway, I read, as so many other explorers have done, with profound admiration. Clearly, in the light of his vast accumulation of scientific data and the record of his drift as a whole, it was of little consequence that Nansen failed to reach the Pole; and yet even before his book *Farthest North* was published in 1897, the adventurers were back on the scene: a Swede by the name of Salomon Andree had set off in a balloon from Spitsbergen with two companions in an attempt to reach the Pole—a voyage from which they did not return. The Pole, still unconquered, was now seen as the summit of a supermountain and attacked from a base on Franz Joseph Land by the distinguished Himalayan explorer, the Italian, Prince Luigi Amadeo of Savoy (the Duke of Abruzzi).

Incapacitated by frostbite, the Duke had delegated the command of his assault party to Captain Cagni, and in three detachments a total of nine men, thirteen sledges and a hundred and two dogs set off across the pack ice. Cagni's detachment sledged north for forty-five days, reaching their farthest north on April 24, 1900, in latitude 86°34′N—beating Nansen's record by twenty-two miles; but their return journey was hazardous in the extreme and one of the detachments failed to reach the base. The Duke's conclusions from the experience of his men was that the Pole would never be reached from a base on Franz Joseph Land, and that future attempts should be made from the north of Ellesmere Island. This had already occurred to that most assiduous of all explorers, Robert E. Peary.

Peary, an American naval officer, was obsessed by the ambition to reach the North Pole and strove for twenty years until he saw attaining the Pole not only as his patriotic duty but as his divine right. This very remarkable, even fanatical man devoted meticulous attention to the planning of his campaigns. He developed and refined a technique of polar travel which enlisted whole villages of Eskimos as part of his military-style assault. He adopted Eskimo methods of sledging but used Eskimos as an integral part of his plan based on divisions. Each division was a complete traveling outfit; in fact, except for a cooking stove and cooking utensils, each sledge was an independent survival unit which carried food for the driver and dogs for fifty days. The leader of each division was a white man, and the purpose of each division to carry out implicitly the moves planned several months or years in advance by the leader of the expedition. Indeed, Peary himself was fond of likening his campaigns to a game of chess—with, of course, the obvious reservation that "in the quest for the Pole it was a struggle of human brains and persistence against the blind brute forces of the elements of primeval matter, acting often under laws and impulses almost unknown or but little understood by us, and thus many times seemingly capricious and not to be foretold with any degree of certainty." [6]

His deployment and use of his divisions was a complex mathematical maneuver, in which his relay parties were sent back to land at carefully calculated stages of the journey. He argued: "Supporting parties are essential to success because a single party, comprising either a small or a large number of men and dogs could not possibly drag (in gradually lessening quantities) all the way to the Pole and back, some 900-odd miles, as much food and liquid fuel as the men and dogs of that party would consume during the journey. It will be readily understood that when a large party of men and dogs starts out over the trackless ice of the polar sea, where there is no possibility of obtaining a single ounce of food on the way, after several days' marching the provisions

[6] Robert E. Peary: *The North Pole*, p. 18 (London, Hodder & Stoughton, 1910).

of one or more sledges will have been consumed by the men and dogs. When this occurs, the drivers and dogs with those sledges should be sent back to the land at once. They are superfluous mouths which cannot be fed from the precious supply of provisions which are being dragged forward on the sledges. Still further on, the food on one or two more sledges will have been consumed. These sledges also, with their dogs and drivers, must be sent back, in order to ensure the furthest possible advance by the main party." [7]

Peary set out from Cape Columbia, his land depot on the north coast of Ellesmere Island, on February 22, 1909, on what was his last determined effort—his last chance to reach out and grasp at glory, for he was then fifty-three years old. His party consisted of twenty-four men, nineteen sledges, and one hundred and thirty-three dogs. Strictly according to plan, one by one, his divisions had turned back toward land until finally only Peary's division remained. He claimed to have reached the North Pole on April 6, 1909, and, as every schoolboy knows, to have returned home safely; but a few days before he sent his triumphant message— STARS AND STRIPES NAILED TO THE POLE—a more dramatic announcement had astonished the world. Dr. Frederick A. Cook, an experienced and respected American explorer, had declared that he, accompanied by two Eskimos, had reached the North Pole on April 21, 1908—a year before Peary.

It was on July 3, 1907, that Cook had set out from Gloucester, Massachusetts, northward bound on a mission whose real purpose he had kept secret from all but his closest friends. He was a highly experienced polar explorer. He had been the medical officer on board the Belgian Antarctic expedition of 1897–99, an expedition which had been the first to winter south of the Antarctic Circle, and on which Roald Amundsen (who was later to be conqueror of the South Pole) served as first mate. That expedition had brought Cook considerable fame as an explorer, a scientist, and a writer; and in 1907, after further increasing his stature as an explorer by making the first ascent of Mount McKinley, the

[7] Robert E. Peary: *op. cit.*, p. 189.

highest mountain on the American continent, he was easily persuaded by the millionaire sportsman John R. Bradley to organize
a hunting expedition in northwest Greenland.

At Annoatok, a small Eskimo settlement in northwest Greenland, he went ashore and set up winter quarters, sending back
with Bradley a letter addressed to the Explorers' Club of New
York, informing them that he would try for the Pole. He spent
that winter with a German companion, Rudolph Francke, hunting and trading with the Eskimos, and on February 19, 1908,
he and Francke, with ten Eskimos, eleven sledges, and one hundred and five dogs, set out across Smith Sound on a poleward
journey which was to take them in a northwesterly direction
across Ellesmere Island, through game territory discovered by
Sverdrup, to the northern tip of Axel Heiberg Island. After sending back all but four of his Eskimo companions, Cook claimed
to have set off across the pack ice in the direction of the Pole.
Three days later, and about sixty miles north of Cape Stalworthy,
he sent back two more Eskimos, and continued with his two Eskimo companions, Etukishook and Ahwelah, and twenty-six
dogs. He claimed to have reached the North Pole on April 21,
1908, and during his return journey to have drifted off course
and made a landfall one hundred and sixty miles to the southwest
of Cape Stalworthy. It was then too late to get back on course
and so take advantage of the caches of food he had left every
fifty miles along his outward route, and he was obliged to continue due south. At Cape Sparbo in Jones Sound he and his two
companions survived a miserable winter in a crude stone hut, and
in the spring of 1909 continued their journey, man-hauling their
sledges up the east coast of Ellesmere Island and across Smith
Sound to Annoatok. The journey had taken them fourteen
months.

Neither Peary nor Cook were able to produce conclusive proof
of their attainment of the Pole, and the controversy, now over
sixty years old, is no nearer being solved. Many millions of words
have been written on the subject and many reputations staked,
the Cook supporters arguing that the incredible distances Peary

claimed to have covered after the last of his support parties turned back were physically impossible; the Peary supporters, equally vehement, argue that Cook and his two Eskimo companions were never at any time out of sight of land. But controversial though the final attainment of the Pole was, at least it extinguished for a time the burning torch at the top of the world, and Arctic explorers could, for a while, concentrate on scientific expeditions undazzled by the lure of a geographic prize.

Ironically enough, the North Pole, after being the goal of so many expeditions, became in 1937 the starting point of one: a Russian expedition under the leadership of Ivan Papanin was landed at the Pole by aircraft, and there set up a scientific drifting station which they were to occupy for eight months before being picked up off the east coast of Greenland after a drift of just over two thousand miles. It was an expedition of outstanding scientific merit which led, after the second World War, to the establishment of several other drifting stations, both Russian and American.

From these drifting stations, manned by scientists in relays over the years, the nature of the Arctic basin became a specialized study and the logistic support of these stations a practiced technique. Regular commercial flights over the Arctic Ocean were inaugurated by Scandinavian Airlines System in November 1954 and were followed shortly afterward by others; the first voyage of a nuclear-powered submarine across the Arctic basin was successfully made in August, 1958, and by 1965 the Arctic basin had assumed considerable strategic importance as the center of the populated hemisphere—the middle sea of the twentieth century which separates the Eurasian landmass from the continent of North America. Facing each other across this frozen sea were the most sophisticated antennae of the two most technically advanced nations; classified charts of the Arctic Ocean were webbed with the flight paths of possible missile attacks and peppered with strategic targets; beneath the drifting ice pack cruised submarines with their lethal cargoes, while above patrolled the nuclear bombers.

On what grounds could anyone argue the need for a journey by dog sledge across such a hostile environment when from any licensed travel agent one could purchase an airline ticket across the top of the world? The skills of sledge travel had slipped into disuse, and hardships which for so long had been a factor in polar exploration had come to be regarded as an indication of fool-hardiness in the field or incompetence on the part of the organizing committees. As for the physical act of walking across the Arctic Ocean, it would almost certainly be regarded by most polar experts as unfeasible and by scientists as a waste of time and money. Only from among such men as the hunter of Moskushamn who had the vision to see a journey across the Arctic Ocean in its historical setting as a culmination of four centuries of polar endeavor—a journey which had been only half completed with the attainment of the Pole—could I expect to receive encouragement, advice, or sympathy.

2

An Adventurous Pioneer Journey

ON July 20, 1965, I completed a thesis of 20,000 words—the result of two full years' work and a tour of the major centers of polar research in the United States, Alaska, Canada, and the Scandinavian countries, where I had discussed my rough plans with many of the world's leading polar authorities. That thesis was in the form of a proposal to the Royal Geographical Society for the first surface crossing of the Arctic Ocean—a plan which had matured considerably as a result of my research. I had abandoned all thought of a dash and now saw the expedition as a journey by dog sledge from Barrow across the longest axis of the Arctic Ocean to Spitsbergen via the North Pole—a journey that would take sixteen months, during which, throughout the period of continuous darkness, while the four-man party was drifting northward, a program of scientific research would be conducted.

My theme was that "there is only one ocean left uncrossed—a challenge to which man must respond." Admittedly, the theme was not original. In 1913, Sir Ernest Shackleton had proposed the first surface crossing of the Antarctic continent for basically the same motives. He had argued that a trans-Antarctic journey was the last great journey that could be made, now that the South and North Poles had both been reached by sledging parties; as for the crossing of the Arctic Ocean, it was considered impossible by all but one man, Alfred H. Harrison. Shackleton's proposal was a natural step in polar exploration, at the same time giving hope of action for his restless spirit and vent to a nation's patriotism.*

Shackleton had outlined his plan for research but had concluded by insisting that primarily his expedition was a "sporting feat"—a phrase which, not surprisingly, had alarmed the officers of the Royal Geographical Society who considered themselves, to use Shackleton's words, ". . . the keepers of the conscience of the geographical world." Nevertheless, his expedition was supported by that society, for any expedition which is a pioneer journey is, by its very nature, an exploration. By the same argument, I was now claiming that the first surface crossing of the Arctic Ocean was an exploration. Until as late as 1918, I argued, it had been universally believed that the Arctic Ocean was a desert— that "nothing could be obtained from the ice but water, and to get that, fuel had to be carried for melting it."[1] Nansen when he had set out from the drifting *Fram* on March 14, 1895, was convinced that the only certain supply of food to be found on the Arctic Ocean was either carried on the sledges or was pulling

---

* Speaking at a meeting of the Royal Geographical Society in February, 1914, he had stated that ". . . first and foremost, the main object of the expedition is the crossing of the Polar Continent from sea to sea. Some people condemn this object as being spectacular and of no particular use, and consider that no expedition should set forth without the one object of being purely scientific. Until the South Pole had been reached, deep in the minds of every explorer who penetrated the Antarctic, was the desire to reach this goal. My desire is to cross the Antarctic Continent and in undertaking this expedition, the members of it are agents of the British Nation. If I said differently, I would be untrue to my convictions. I have put the crossing of the Continent as the great object in this expedition and there is not one person in this room tonight, and there is not one individual under the Union Jack in any part of the Empire, who does not wish the British flag to be the first national flag ever carried across the frozen wastes."

[1] Nares, Capt. Sir G. S.: *Voyage to the Polar Sea,* vol. 1, p. 277 (London, Sampson & Co., 1878).

them.[2] Cook and Peary had based their plans on the same conclusion. Indeed, with the exception of Stefansson and Storkerson in 1914–18, no explorers had intentionally sledged great distances over the polar pack until Bjørn Staib led an abortive attempt to cross the Arctic Ocean by dog sledge in 1964 from Ellesmere Island via the Pole to Severnaya Zemlya. It was my hope that by sledging with dog teams from Alaska to Spitsbergen via the North Pole I could vindicate or prove false Stefansson's theory that the central polar basin supports sufficient wildlife to sustain the skillful hunter and his dogs over an indefinite period. But since I was more inclined to believe Nansen than Stefansson, I based the logistics of my proposed expedition on the assumption that no game would be found during the sixteen months' journey.

I had arrived at other conclusions as a result of my historical research which were strongly to influence my plan. I had noticed that the pyramid of support—the formula by which practically all expeditions in the preflight era had sought to solve the problems of penetrating a desert beyond the limit set by the weight of food, fuel, and clothing they were obliged to carry—had one major limitation: range. In the heroic age of exploration there was, of course, no alternative but to use the pyramid of support, a structure up which the leader (or the man he had delegated) climbed toward the summit. Scott of the Antarctic was the summit of a pyramid; Peary was another; so too were Tenzing, Hillary, and, more recently, Armstrong and Aldrin—all of them summit-party heroes, elevated by a structure that, by its very nature, left room for only one; for you cannot have more than one *first* man to set foot on the summit of a mountain, or more than one *first* man to plant a boot on the surface of the moon. The partner in each case is part of the structure, and the height climbed or the distance reached depended on the number of explorers, sherpas, Eskimos, or computers that went to form that structure.

[2] Nansen, Dr. Fridtjof: *Farthest North,* vol. 2, p. 87 (London, Constable & Co., 1897).

Peary's critics maintain he did not reach the Pole, but fell short of it by some sixty miles or so. This had set me wondering: assuming they are right, would he have reached the Pole if he had had a larger support party? Diagrammatically it would seem so. If the number of four-man divisions had been increased, he ought to have been able to extend his range from Cape Columbia, the point where he set out. The trouble is, by increasing the number of supporting parties you numerically increase the problems and the party becomes unwieldy.

Hunt recognized this, and avoided the temptation to load the mountain when he was planning the assault on Everest in 1953. The factors which influenced his planning were surprisingly similar to their polar counterparts: he had to allow for a physiological deterioration in the party at high altitude and for physical exhaustion; to assess the amount of stores and equipment which could justifiably be carried up the mountain; to ensure that his climbers were equipped with enough suitable food, clothing and shelter, and to provide adequate support in the form of backup parties that would enable his summit party (spared the heavy work at the early stages of the buildup) to make the most of their opportunity when eventually it came. Hunt's plan of campaign was meticulously calculated: the pyramid of support which made it possible for Tenzing and Hillary to reach the summit of Everest on May 29, 1953 (thirty-five sherpas and twelve Europeans), was exactly the right size. But had Everest been a thousand feet higher, Hunt's plan might well have failed, and had the North Pole been more than five hundred miles from Peary's land depot, his 1909 expedition *certainly* would have failed.

Any plan for a crossing of the Arctic Ocean therefore had to be based on some formula other than the pyramid principle that the summit party would return by the same route they had taken out—a route kept open by the supporting parties. The first alternative suggested, however, proved mathematically even more complex: instead of the pyramid of support which would provide food and fuel enough only for the summit party to reach its goal, Alfred H. Harrison, an American with somewhat limited polar experience, had put before the Royal Geographical Society in June, 1909 (a few weeks before news of Cook's attainment of the North Pole reached the outside world), a proposal for a continuous journey across the Arctic Ocean which would take two and a half years to complete, during which the staple food for men and dogs would be oatmeal. His plan for the crossing was based on the principle that a pyramid of support, if reformed into a column, would reach further. "I intend to start out from Pullen Island," Harrison had told the officers of the Royal Geographical Society, "with nine Eskimos and one hundred dogs to cross the Arctic Ocean to Spitsbergen, where I expect to arrive 912 days later."

The plan was never put to a practical test, and, like so many plans that have failed to get off the ground, it was subsequently ignored by the historians. This I find surprising, for the biggest flaw in Harrison's plan was not arithmetical; his error in applying such a plan to the Arctic Ocean was in not allowing for the vicissitudes of traveling over drifting sea ice. In his calculations he assumed a total distance for the journey of 1,550 miles. The shortest possible route from the northernmost tip of Alaska to the northernmost point of land in the Spitsbergen group is 1,670 nautical miles (1,920 statute miles)—a route which I calculated would work out in practice to be 3,800 statute route miles, for it is seldom possible to travel more than a mile across pack ice without having to make a detour to avoid some form of obstruction. The ice of the Arctic Ocean is in constant movement, drifting sometimes as much as ten miles a day, fracturing, pressuring, gyrating.

I concluded that the technique of hauling heavy boats across the ice, as Parry had done in 1827 and Nares in 1876, was impracticable; a surface crossing of the Arctic Ocean by Peary's system was unfeasible; Harrison's plan was suicidal. The ocean at its longest axis could be crossed, in my opinion, only by a marriage of the oldest techniques of Arctic travel with the most advanced form of logistic support: radios, homing beacons, and satellite information on the weather and ice concentration. Moreover, from a broadly scientific point of view, I believed that by walking across the top of the world the four members of the expedition—Allan Gill, Fritz Koerner, Roger Tufft and myself, a party whose polar experience totaled twenty winters and forty-one summers—would learn more about the environment than we would by flying, submerging, or stationing ourselves in a heated observatory on the ice.

Mine was a five-phrase plan: there would be three periods of sledging, when we would be able to counter any adverse drift of ice, and two periods—the height of summer, and the long polar night—when we would be completely at its mercy: the success or failure of the expedition depended on how accurately I could predict the drift and how closely we could keep to the schedule.

Sixteen months was not a period casually prescribed. The earliest date on which the expedition could set off from Point Barrow was February 1; the latest, February 21. Those are the only three weeks of the year with a chance of the wide belt of fractured young ice along the coast being quiescent and packed tightly enough to form a "bridge" between the land and the heavy polar pack drifting slowly past the coast about eighty miles offshore. This ice bridge we would have to cross at the coldest time of the year when there was very little daylight: it would have to be a dash with light loads; if necessary, we would have to be resupplied by a single-engined aircraft operating out of Barrow. Our landfall on Spitsbergen would be equally hazardous and could be made only at the end of May (by the first week in June of an average season, the ice pack has begun to loosen its grip on the islands), and only by an approach from the northeast. Between those two dates we had four hundred and eighty days in which to cover a minimum of 1,920 statute miles; but for some two hundred and forty of those days our only progress would be drift. How much drift? Until this question was answered with a reasonable prediction, I could not begin to calculate how far we would have to sledge during the three sledging seasons and compare this figure with the records of previous explorers to see if it was feasible. Even then, the rate of drift would depend on what part of the Arctic Ocean we were in, the extent of the ice cover, the direction and force of the surface winds. . . .

Often problems that seem complex from one angle are simple when seen from another. So it was with the projected track of the trans-Arctic expedition: by working through each phase of the journey in reverse it all fell into place. Beginning my calculation with the date we would make our landing on the north shore of Spitsbergen—the last day of May—I plotted a rough course across the Arctic Ocean (in the opposite direction to the way we would travel) to a point three weeks before sunrise. In the vicinity of the Pole that date would be March 1—which would give us only three months of sledging in the final phase of the journey; but it was evident from the tracks of the *Fram,* and those of the Soviet drifting station NP–6 in 1959, that we would have the benefit of a strong and fairly consistent drift on our port quarter. I could see no reason therefore why we should not comfortably reach Spitsbergen from somewhere in the vicinity of the Pole, providing we abandoned our winter quarters on March 1.

The transpolar stream drifts across the Pole. Several Soviet floe stations have been carried by it and its rate and direction seemed reliable enough for me to predict that a five-month drift in that vicinity was worth about three degrees of latitude, or about 207 statute miles. The drift would not however be toward Spitsbergen but in the direction of the Greenland Sea—the main exit point for pack ice carried by this current. Retracing that winter drift I was able to select a location in which we should establish our winter quarters if we were to benefit to the full from the transpolar stream and climb steadily toward the Pole and perhaps cross it during the period of continuous darkness. That vital point was latitude 88°10′N, longitude 170°E. It should be reached by October 1 at the latest, for at that latitude, by that date, barely any daylight would remain.

So far, the predictions had not been difficult and I had accounted for eight of the sixteen months; but in terms of distance I had covered less than half the route. The earliest we could set out from Barrow was February 1; however, I could see from the tracks of the drifting stations that by sledging on a bearing about ten degrees west of north we could receive some small benefit from the currents that circulate in a clockwise gyral in the western part of the Arctic basin and, providing we had reached a high latitude near the confluence of the two major drift streams by the time we were stopped by the summer melt about June 12, we would, during the summer, drift due north about one degree. This would leave us only about three degrees, or about 200 statute miles, to travel in the autumn to reach the ideal point for the start of our winter drift.

From these predictions I found that the net drift gain during the summer and winter drifts totaled four degrees of latitude, or about 276 statute miles. The shortest route along the proposed track from Barrow to Longyearbyen via the Pole would be 2,200 statute miles; we would therefore during the eight months of sledging have to make good an average of eight statute miles a day. This average I checked against the most reliable records and found that while it was greater by about two miles a day than Nansen's average across polar pack, it was a mile a day less than the average maintained by Cagni, during the period when he was finding the conditions good for traveling, and that part of Peary's 1909 journey when Bartlett was breaking trail. The journey therefore, on the face of it, seemed feasible; but there was a factor I had as yet not included in my calculations—the additional mileage we would have to cover in detours and against the treadmill of adverse drift.

There were marked differences in the records of previous explorers on this subject, no doubt because of local differences in the nature of the ice pack. Nansen deviated from his straight line by 40 percent; Cagni by 20 percent. Peary does not mention deviations in his account of the journey he made in 1909, but assuming that he met exceptionally easy going and made no deviations at all on the unwitnessed stage of his journey from Bartlett's farthest north (latitude 87°47′N) to the Pole and back, he must have averaged forty-four statute miles a day for eight consecutive days (which I found extremely difficult to believe).

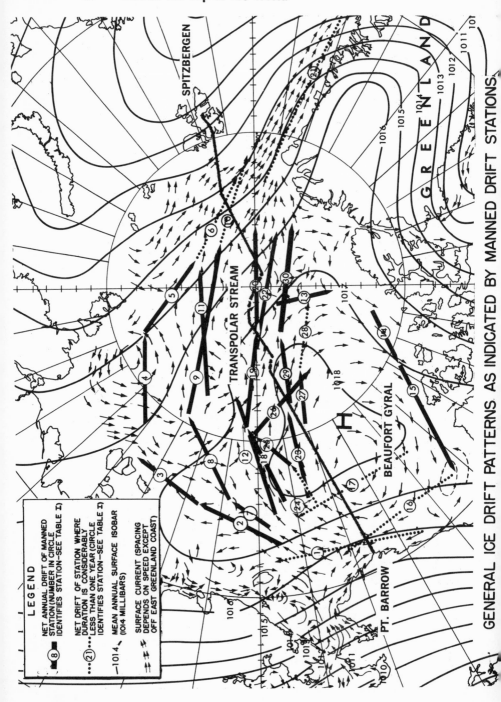

GENERAL ICE DRIFT PATTERNS AS INDICATED BY MANNED DRIFT STATIONS.

FIGURE 1

Circulation and sea-ice drift patterns within the Arctic basin have been under scrutiny since Nansen's historical drift in the *Fram* between 1893 and 1896. Considerable information was added by the drifts of the *Karluk*, 1913; the *Maud*, 1922–23; and the Soviet-manned ice station North Pole 1 (Papanin) started at the north geographic pole in 1937. But continual observation and study of the Arctic basin did not begin until 1950, when the Soviets launched an accelerated program of aircraft landings and a comprehensive and continuing survey using one or two drift stations.

In Figure 1, the general patterns of the pack-ice drift are indicated by the trajectories and net annual drift of manned stations. These are set on a background of mean annual surface isobars based on 15-day surface-pressure values, and on surface current circulation patterns obtained from Soviet sources. All this information was made available to the expedition by Walt Wittmann of the U.S. Naval Oceanographic Office.

On the chart (from Pt. Barrow to Spitsbergen) is plotted the *proposed* route of the Trans-Arctic Expedition which was based on predictions arrived at from a study of the tracks of previous drifting stations and long-range weather forecasts.

INDEX TO FIGURE 1

No.	STA-TION	DATE Begin	End	No.	STA-TION	DATE Begin	End
1	Karluk	12 Aug 1913	11 Jan 1914	16	T–3	2 Jly 1959	25 May 1960
2	Maud	24 Sep 1922	24 Sep 1923	17	Arlis	10 Sep 1960	16 Mar 1961
3	Maud	24 Sep 1923	8 Aug 1924	18	N.P.4	8 Apr 1954	17 Apr 1955
4	Fram	25 Nov 1893	24 Nov 1894	19	N.P.4	17 Apr 1955	19 Apr 1956
5	Fram	24 Nov 1894	22 Nov 1895	20	N.P.4	19 Apr 1956	20 Apr 1957
6	Fram	22 Nov 1895	27 Jne 1896	21	N.P.1	19 Nov 1937	19 Feb 1938
7	N.P.6	19 Apr 1956	19 Apr 1957	22	N.P.3	9 Apr 1954	20 Apr 1955
8	N.P.6	19 Apr 1957	8 Apr 1958	23	N.P.3	12 Apr 1950	11 Apr 1951
9	N.P.6	8 Apr 1958	12 Apr 1959	24	N.P.8	8 Apr 1959	15 Jly 1959
10	N.P.6	12 Apr 1959	14 Sep 1959	25	N.P.8	15 Jly 1959	15 Jly 1960
11	N.P.5	16 Apr 1955	16 Apr 1956	26	N.P.8	15 Jly 1960	15 Jly 1961
12	T–3	July 1950	July 1951	27	Alfa	9 Jne 1957	10 Jne 1958
13	T–3	1 Jne 1952	4 Jne 1953	28	Alfa	10 Jne 1958	3 Nov 1958
14	T–3	14 Jly 1957	14 Jly 1958	29	N.P.7	23 Apr 1957	13 Apr 1958
15	T–3	14 Jly 1958	2 Jly 1959	30	N.P.7	13 Apr 1958	11 Apr 1959

My eight-mile-a-day average had now been increased by deviations to almost fourteen miles a day—an average that would be impossible to maintain if we were obliged to carry heavy loads. We would therefore require seven airdrops of supplies: four during the first traveling period; one large supply drop which would take us through the summer melt period; one massive seven-months' supply drop which would provide us with enough food and fuel to see us right through the winter and the first traveling stage of the final phase; and one forty-five day resupply at a point some 430 miles from Spitsbergen, which would take us through to the landfall. On the north shore of the island we would collect supplies that had been laid there for us the previous summer by surface vessel. We would then sledge overland to the mining town of Longyearbyen. The budget for the entire program, including a nine-months' workout in northwest Greenland, I estimated at £37,000.

Almost three months were to elapse before the Royal Geographical Society was able to consider that proposal, for most of the members of the Expeditions Committee were away on holiday; however, a subcommittee of polar experts was convened, and on October 11 I was thoroughly interrogated. The result was a resolution couched in sympathetic terms ". . . that the Expeditions Committee should recommend support of the British Trans-Arctic Expedition as a well-planned and feasible, adventurous, pioneer journey though with only very slight scientific content." But this resolution, after being thoroughly debated by the full Committee on November 1, was rejected on the grounds that expeditions supported by the Royal Geographical Society should show some scientific or technological dividends, and that the society would not be justified in backing a purely adventurous enterprise, more especially as doubts had been expressed about my ability to raise sufficient financial support in the short time available.

The support of the Royal Geographical Society was to have been my certificate of competence, from which the financial backing of the venture would have received its initial impetus. Had I sought the support of private patrons I might have raised the backing independently of the Royal Geographical Society; indeed, I had been strongly advised to do so by several sympathetic friends, but I had been confident that the society would support my proposed expedition. Why I did not give up there and then I am not sure; perhaps it was in an effort to salvage three years of wasted work that I went back to my office and began typing hundreds of letters.

Slowly I amassed a private army of supporters from among the world's foremost explorers, travelers, and adventurers, all of whom recognized in my plan the vision and daring which is the vital characteristic of the pioneer, and were prepared publicly to say so. Eight of the most eager of those supporters were later to come together to form a fund-raising committee under the chairmanship of Sir Miles Clifford, a former Governor of the Falkland Islands and its Antarctic Dependencies; but at the time of my next meeting with the Royal Geographical Society's Expeditions Committee on April 18, 1966, this closely knit and very select "club" had not joined forces, and I was obliged once more to propose my expedition without the backing of an organization—let alone the financial backing of £53,000, the figure which I now estimated was required to launch the venture.

There were a few modifications to the original plan: We would, during the winter drift, live in a prefabricated hut, rather than in a clutch of snow houses which had been my original intention. This change of heart had come about when I discovered that there was on the market a padded tent weighing 1,400 pounds known as a Parcoll Housing Unit. The makers claimed it was easy to erect and dismantle, would provide comfortable shelter in temperatures as low as —90°F, and was specifically designed for transport by aircraft. This hut I proposed to test out in northwest Greenland during the winter of 1966–67. If it proved to be as good as the makers claimed, I would arrange for it to be shipped to Resolute Bay in Canadian Northwest Territories during the summer of 1967, and stored there until October, 1968, when it would be flown out and dropped to the expedition in the vicinity of the North Pole.

The training program in northwest Greenland had by this time become a vital part of the plan, for not only was it necessary to test thoroughly all the items of gear we would take with us on the trans-Arctic journey; it was also prudent to test ourselves over a course that would exaggerate any weakness in our resolve. It was not enough that we would, in terms of sledging experience, be one of the strongest parties ever to have set out on a polar expedition from Great Britain; clearly there was much that could be learned from the Eskimos. I had proposed, therefore, that three of us would live and hunt with them during the winter of 1966–67 and make a 1,500-mile journey the following spring with dog sledges from Qanaq in northwest Greenland to Resolute Bay in Canada. The route would be a tough one. We would follow the first part of the journey made by Dr. Frederick Cook; historically, this would be a more interesting route than any alternative in that part of the Arctic. And with a strong incentive to follow a predetermined track and a definite objective, Resolute Bay, it would be a more positive journey and a far tougher test of men and equipment than any aimless wanderings over pack ice in the vicinity of some scientific station. Moreover, any gear that was still serviceable when we reached Resolute Bay could be left there in storage, for Resolute was to be one of the staging depots for the support flights out over the Arctic Ocean during the even more arduous and protracted journey we would begin the following year. By then the crossing party would have amassed a total of twenty winters' and forty-one summers' experience in the polar regions.

Of the four of us, only Roger Tufft was not, professionally speaking, involved in polar work. He was a teacher. We had sailed together on the Royal Research Ship *Shackleton* way back in 1955, spent our first year in the Antarctic at separate bases, and reunited at Hope Bay during the second of his three years in the south. We had been in our early twenties then; keen young men, recently released from our military service in the Middle East. But I had seen little of Roger during that year; my journeys had taken me in a different direction, and the impression I had formed of him had been very superficial: lean, muscular, intellectual, a prolific reader of historical biographies, a man of positive opinions. Over the years, however, we had corresponded from time to time and I had followed his exploits with interest. Shortly after his spell in the Antarctic, he had joined the crew of Major H. W. Tilman's pilot cutter *Mischief* and sailed with him 21,000 miles, visiting the sub-Antarctic Kerguelen and Crozet Islands. He later sailed 7,000 miles with Tilman in the Arctic, visiting the west coast of Greenland and Baffin Island; made a number of trips to Lapland, and joined Hugh Simpson on Spitsbergen shortly after I had set out by canoe on the first leg of my journey back to the Antarctic.

Our paths crossed again some six years later in a climbers' hut in the English Lake District on a black, wild night in the spring of 1964. Fritz Koerner, a glaciologist with whom I had spent a month at the end of my first spell in the Antarctic, was there too; and I remember telling them, on our way back to the hut from a pub along a deserted road, of my ambition to cross the Arctic Ocean. I did not ask them to come with me—there was no need; the invitation was in the tone of my voice, the setting, the secrecy to which I had sworn them. Fritz being a recently married man, there was clearly little hope of his interest in my plans taking priority over his own in the near future; but he had not said so directly, nor had Roger, and by the end of 1965—by which time Roger had man-hauled across the Greenland ice cap with three companions, and Fritz had spent a successful summer in the Canadian Arctic with his wife Anne and Allan Gill working as his assistants—I had my team for the trans-Arctic journey.

Allan, like the rest of us, had started his polar career on British bases in the Antarctic. He had gone south at the same time as Fritz, and joined him at Hope Bay for his second year. The pair of them had been together on many expeditions to the Canadian Arctic, and it was on Fritz's recommendation that I called at the

Arctic Institute of North America when I was in Montreal in April, 1965, to meet Allan, who was at that time in the final stage of preparation for an expedition to Devon Island in the Northwest Territories. I remember very well my first impression: a deeply creased, parchment-faced, wiry individual—the scruffiest man in the institute.

A master of temporary repair and ingenious contraptions, Allan at the time I met him already had an impressive polar record of three winters in the Antarctic—one in the Canadian Arctic, and two on the Arctic Ocean at the American scientific drifting station T-3. Much of his work on T-3 had been in connection with the geophysical program conducted by Lamont Geological Observatory; but in addition to gravity measurements and magnetics, he had been involved in several other pioneer projects for Lamont which had had their teething troubles, and to which he could apply the infinite patience for which he was renowned and his self-taught knowledge of mathematics and physics. He had made seismic measurements of waves transmitted through the ice, and experimented with a lethal piece of apparatus for measuring the sub-bottom strata of the ocean bed. He had taken core samples of the mud and dredged the abyssal plain with a bucket for ooze and microscopic shells. He was also a competent photographer, and had spent much of his two winters on the Arctic Ocean perfecting a technique of photographing, in color, the ocean bed and the turtlelike tracks of some unidentified creatures at a depth of twelve thousand feet. (The triggering mechanism of the camera shutter and Strobe light, which sank into the ooze at the end of a thousand-pound cable, had presented the sort of problems which Allan found intriguing.) He did not know, nor was he too concerned about, what happened to his various samples when they were sent south. Here was a man who clearly was at home in the Arctic and in his element puttering, far from the pundits who would give him the answers to his problems in chalky formulae or a more expensive piece of equipment. Here was a man who clearly was ideally suited for the sort of expedition I was planning—a tough man of placid temperament who loved the polar environment and could make an invaluable contribution as a trained geophysical observer.

With a glaciologist of Fritz's experience as the scientific leader of the expedition, ably assisted by Roger (who in the Antarctic had been a meteorological observer) and Allan, whose versatility was truly remarkable, I had the basis for an expedition of considerable scientific value. There was no question of fitting in a scientific program; the two drifting periods of the five-phase plan would have to be occupied with some useful project even if the work were of benefit only to the crossing party. With a full scientific program, the journey as a whole, like Nansen's epic drift in the *Fram*, would be much more than an adventure; it would be an advancement of knowledge which might greatly benefit mankind, for the variable extent of the Arctic pack ice was seen by many scientists as a sensitive climatic lever—one of the key links in the chain of atmospheric circulation (the mechanism by which heat shifts from one region of the earth to another).

Soviet scientists in the late fifties had established that a decrease of only ten percent in the summer albedo of the Arctic pack (the amount of solar radiation that is reflected back into space from the snow surface) would destroy it completely in eight to ten years; yet until even as late as 1965, systematic measurements of albedo had never been conducted by U.S. investigators on the Arctic Ocean. This is a vital component of the heat budget; so too are ice-thickness measurements and the rate of growth and decay of Arctic pack. Much work had been done on the drift patterns of pack ice, and on these studies I had based my calculations of course and rate of drift for the crossing; much work also had been done on the properties of sea ice, but the amount of ice exported from the Arctic Ocean could only be guessed, since no one had ever made an ice-thickness profile over any appreciable distance that took into account the age of the ice. Nuclear submarines with topside fathometers have collected invaluable data, and the whole ocean has now been webbed with subsurface profiles of the pack. Ice-observation flights are made regularly by the U.S. Oceanographic Office, and the polar-orbit-

ing satellites provide an excellent system for observing the movement of cyclones over the area; but at the time I presented my
new proposal to the Royal Geographical Society, there was still
much that a glaciologist could do to extend our knowledge of the
pack-ice environment—if one could be found who would be prepared to walk right across the top of the world, observing and
measuring as he went; and we had just such a man in Dr. Koerner.

Our target, once clear of the fracture zone off the coast of
Alaska, would be the Pole of Relative Inaccessibility, which we
would aim to reach before the summer overtook us and the floes
became flooded with water: this would be about June 14. In that
stage of the journey, Fritz would keep a meteorological log and
a log of ice-thickness measurements.

During the summer-melt period we would camp on hummocks,
and as the floes drifted northward we would occupy ourselves
with a study of the environment. By the end of August, light
frosts would set in and grease the leads with a film of ice; snow-
falls and heavy fogs would blanket the icescape. Traveling conditions at this time of the year would be treacherous, but some
sledging would have to be attempted in order to adjust our course
and get ourselves into a better position before the long polar night
began. It was my intention to get across the dateline into the influence of the transpolar stream before calling for the winter supply drop, which would include a prefabricated hut (the Parcoll
Housing Unit). Providing our winter quarters were set up in the
right position, we would, during the period of continuous darkness, drift across the Pole. Fifteen hours a day, every day throughout the winter, we would devote to a program of scientific work
and to the preparation of our equipment for the final stage of
the journey.

Three weeks before the return of the sun, we would abandon
our winter quarters and set off on the final stage of the journey,
carrying with us all exposed film and copies of all scientific data.
I aimed that the crossing party would reach Spitsbergen at the
end of May, 1969, and made provision for a ship to be on standby
in Spitsbergen waters to pick up the party should we be carried

off course by the currents on the final approach to the island and be drifted into the Greenland Sea.

I remember entering the conference room of the Royal Geographical Society on April 18, 1966, in a truculent mood. But the atmosphere was sympathetic, and by the time I left I was almost certain that I at last had the approval of the society; my hopes were later confirmed by the pleasant expressions and in some cases even the smiles of the members of the committee as they walked in threes and fours to the gentlemen's cloakroom. Two days later the official letter of confirmation arrived.

The first meeting of our own committee was held six weeks afterward, when my plan and I were the subject of close scrutiny; for of the eight men who had gathered to help me I had previously met only four. In less than two hours my advisers had the measure of the situation and resolved that we should form a company limited by guarantee, and that the memorandum and articles of association should be so worded that the expedition would be eligible for the status of a nonprofit company.

In Great Britain at that time the climate for raising money was against the expedition. As a result, the expedition had no access to hard cash until a few days before the departure for Greenland of Allan Gill and Roger Tufft. Fritz unfortunately could not join us, for he was already committed during this period to an expedition in Antarctica with the U.S. Antarctic Research Program.

Neither Allan nor Roger were personally involved in the affairs of the expedition during this period; Roger was teaching at a school in the Lake District, and Allan was in the Arctic. Even Fritz, with whom I had always talked over the problems of the expedition on my short visits to London, had left the country as part of the "brain drain" to take up the post of Assistant Professor of Glaciology at Ohio State University.

I was therefore obliged to operate on my own, from a base in my parents' home. Every letter ordering food or equipment had to be carefully composed, for I still was without sufficient funds, and crises of one kind or another came thick and fast during those last few weeks. Suppliers would telephone to say they could not meet their deadlines; airline companies could not fit the sledges into the aircraft; and, of course, there were the usual invoices stamped FINAL REMINDER and other financial embarrassments too painful to recall.

Allan flew back to London from the Arctic in September to do a crash course in filming, and on October 17 I drove him and Roger at eighty miles an hour out to London Airport to catch a flight to Copenhagen, where they would transfer to a charter aircraft bound to Thule in northwest Greenland. It had been a desperate rush, and so many last-minute snags had occurred that I had been obliged to cancel my flight.

I had chosen October 17 as the deadline for leaving London to reach the settlement of Qanaq (eighty miles north of Thule, the American strategic airbase) before October 24, so that we could erect the hut before the sun set for the last time that year. As for the choice of location: I had wanted to spend the winter with the Polar Eskimos. There are very few of them left these days, probably no more than four hundred spread around the five settlements in northwest Greenland. The biggest one, and the administrative center in the Thule district, is Qanaq. There, from what I could gather from the Ministry for Greenland and the Royal Greenland Trade Department in Copenhagen, were a few Danes, a radio station, and a hospital.*

All our heavy equipment, such as the prefabricated hut and the fuel supply, had been sent from Montreal to Thule earlier in the year on the Canadian Coast Guard icebreaker *John A. MacDonald*. The rest of the gear had been divided into two freight loads

---

* I knew far more about the settlement of Siorapaluk, for the inhabitants of that settlement had been the subject of a book written in 1955 by a Frenchman, Jean Malaurie. His book *The Last King of Thule* was a most readable account of a winter he spent among them, and in my earlier plans I had intended to winter at the same settlement. What finally dissuaded me from doing so was simply a matter of logistics. Siorapaluk is visited by only one ship a year. Unless there is an emergency, no visits are made by the helicopters of the air rescue detachment based at Thule except for a Christmas courtesy call; whereas Qanaq is served by frequent helicopter visits from Thule Air Base throughout the winter—a gesture of goodwill from the Americans much appreciated by the Danes at Qanaq.

and sent to Thule via Copenhagen on a charter aircraft of the Scandinavian Airlines System. By the kind cooperation of the Americans at Thule, it had been arranged that the entire mass of expedition equipment would be flown by helicopters of the air rescue detachment to Qanaq; and there, with the permission of the Danish government, we were to set up our winter quarters.

My thirty-second birthday passed unnoticed, and my new deadline of October 31 came on at a breathtaking pace. I went everywhere at frantic speed, but there were no more committee meetings during that period, for I was officially away on the expedition and in every sense living on borrowed time. By Friday, October 28, I had transferred my filing cabinet from Lichfield to the Library of the British Antarctic Survey in London, and on Monday morning in a daze I drove alone to the airport.

I slept all the way to Oslo, and on arriving was told over the public address system to go immediately to the chief customs inspector. He warned me to speak to no one but the deputy director of the Norsk Polarinstitutt when I passed out of the customs hall; and when I was safely hustled into a car and on my way to town, Kaare Lundquist told me that a young Norwegian by the name of Fløtum, who was himself planning a trans-Arctic journey, had been trying to get an exclusive face-to-face interview with me for which he would be paid handsomely by one of Norway's leading newspapers. Dr. Tore Gjelsvik, the director of the institute and an old friend of mine, knowing that I was hoping to keep my plans for the trans-Arctic journey secret until after the successful conclusion of the Greenland training program, had taken immediate action. He had been one of the leading figures in the Norwegian underground movement during the war, so forestalling Fløtum was to him a relatively simple task. But the incident set me wondering, for Fløtum was only one of many who, if he could raise the money, might succeed in crossing the Arctic Ocean and so claim to have forestalled me. True, Fløtum's proposed route across the Arctic Ocean was by the shorter axis; I believe he was then thinking of setting out from Spitsbergen and making for Ellesmere Island via the Pole—a route which subtends an angle of only 95 degrees of longitude. Nevertheless, I recalled uncomfortably the words of Scott on reaching the South Pole and discovering that he had been forestalled by the Norwegian explorer, Amundsen: "Great God! This is an awful place and terrible enough for us to have labored to it without the reward of priority."

I flew on to Copenhagen and from there to Thule, feeling uneasy in spite of Dr. Gjelsvik's encouraging remarks that only he who plans a long slow journey stands any chance of success. I had heard too of an American expedition which, during the summer of 1967, was going to make an attempt at the North Pole with Bombardier Skidoos (motorized toboggans); and a German expedition, also using mechanical vehicles, which planned to set out for the Pole from a base in northeast Greenland. The five million square miles of the Arctic Ocean for the first time seemed too small and the Pole too absurd a goal.

3

Winter with the Polar Eskimos

WHEN we arrived at the U.S. Air Force base the sun had set, and at midday Thule was in twilight. The lights of taxis, trucks, and heavy plant were pricks of yellow in a blue-gray scene that was raw cold and very depressing. There was a metal Christmas tree outside the HQ—its lights had been switched on ceremonially the day the sun officially set—and recorded bells of a country church played hymn tunes at regular intervals from a rosette of amplifiers on a chapel roof. Men muffled in enormous parkas shuffled from one warm building to another, each building connected to its neighbor with high-voltage cables and insulated lifelines beneath which white foxes scampered.

Roger and Allan, together with some of the fuel and our hut, had already been flown to the settlement of Qanaq by the helicopters of the air rescue detachment.

My own turn came on the morning of November tenth. The helicopter settled gently at the edge of the village and was soon surrounded by Eskimo children. There was just enough twilight to see our hut before I was led off across the snowdrifts to meet Inspector Orla Sandborg. In his cosy office I found the "king" of

Qanaq, informally but neatly dressed in a gray shirt and match-
ing gray trousers. Orla, a man of about thirty-eight, had spent
most of his life in Greenland, held several positions of influence,
and had the reputation of being a strong but scrupulously fair
administrator. He had long since grown out of the idealistic and
slightly patronizing attitude which the less experienced Danish
administrators have toward the Greenlanders; his was a doctrine
influenced by his genuine love of the Eskimos, his subjects, whose
language he spoke fluently and whose ways and attitudes he
understood.

The Thule District which came under his jurisdiction is a remote one and the last outpost of the polar Eskimos, whose fore-
fathers had come from North America some thousand years previously. Socially cut off from the west-coast Greenlanders by Mel-
ville Bay, an area of inclement weather and treacherous icefloes,
the Polar Eskimos have in a way been isolated from the changes
which have occurred in the south. They know of these changes,
of course, for contrary to general belief they are a literate people,
and newspapers in their own language are eagerly read. They
have their own radio program, too, and few Eskimo homes are
without a radio. Moreover, there are always a few Polar Eskimos
who will visit the Greenland settlements of Upernavik and
Umanak, and bring back reports telling of a changing way of life
where the traditional hunting economy is giving way to a more
lucrative fishing industry. In the Thule District, however, the
Eskimos are encouraged to hunt, although it would seem they
need little persuasion.

They are also a proud people. This traditional pride we at first
mistook for arrogance, in spite of being amply warned by such
writers as Peter Freuchen that the Eskimos regard white men who
winter among them as irritable children; but once we had become
established in the village, they visited us on any pretext at all.

The Danes, whose curiosity equaled that of the Eskimos, were
more discreet. We had literally landed among them without
warning—the crates in which our hut was packed, like carrion
carried in slings below the helicopters, had been gently dropped

at the edge of the village in the last grazing rays of the setting sun and quickly erected. Only Orla Sandborg had known we were coming and his instructions from Copenhagen had been to keep our plans confidential, for we had no wish to be forestalled on the trans-Arctic journey while we were preoccupied with testing out our equipment and technique in northwest Greenland. It was important that we should use during that winter the cruder form of lighting, heating, and cooking that we would be obliged to use on the Arctic Ocean in two years' time; the electrician who offered to lay electric cables to the hut had therefore been told politely by Roger and Allan that they preferred to use kerosene lanterns, and rumors had soon spread around the village that the two men were sleeping on packing crates and cooking on primus stoves. My two companions were somewhat embarrassed by this setup, which to all the Danes except Orla must have seemed most mysterious, and during the period before my arrival had therefore seldom ventured abroad during the day. It was rumored that occasionally, after it got dark, they would wander out on the sea ice and along the coast with bundles of rubbish under their arms and bulging from their pockets, light a small fire about a mile away, and an hour or so later sneak back to their hut. The villagers not surprisingly concluded that Roger and Allan were antisocial.

This was an unpleasant period for my companions. By nature both of them are reserved, and the ordeal of buying provisions at the store from a plump Eskimo girl who shook like a jelly every time she laughed—and laughed every time she looked at them— was evidently disconcerting. Neither could summon up the courage to ask for each item boldly in English, and their attempts at Danish or at thumbnail sketches had all the Eskimo ladies in stitches. My two companions therefore were ravenous by the time I arrived and bored by their routine, for not until the helicopter flight which brought me in did the bulk of our equipment arrive.

We set up beds and a cooking table, at one end of which I allocated myself space for an office. We built shelves for the food and our small library of books, and pitched a tent outside in which to store experimental food which had been donated by the U.S. Army's Natick Laboratories. Around the walls we hung our ropes and gear and in no time at all the hut took on the appearance of an expedition base. By thus exposing our goods and chattels, however, we laid ourselves open to criticism. Some of the Danes thought it was some form of expensive joke, but the Eskimos in their criticism were more robust, and with macabre delight marked the map on the door (which showed our proposed sledging route from Qanaq to Resolute Bay) with crosses where they predicted we would perish.

The word had gone out from Orla's office that we needed twenty dogs. The timing of this had been carefully considered. The Eskimos would be eager for a few extra kroner for Christmas and would be more likely to come forward then than immediately after their hangover, when they would begin thinking of the hunting trips they would make in the spring. But once the Eskimos began responding to Orla's notice, we found it hard to distinguish a dog seller from a casual visitor, for all the Eskimos that came to our hut looked and behaved alike to us; and judging from their private jokes in a language full of glottal stops and grunts, they thought we too were indistinguishable from one another, and our behavior equally odd.

A soft crunch in the snow outside was usually the only warning we had that our privacy was about to be invaded. The tin door handle would rattle, the door fly open, and plowing through the cold mist that slid into the warm hut ahead of them they would stagger, their bowlegs clad in polar-bear fur, their stocky upper half in grubby anoraks; two or three of them—sometimes half a dozen. The creeping death, as we called the floor fog, would dissipate as the door was banged shut behind them, and as they sat themselves down on a packing crate the pressure on their buttocks would split their faces with embarrassed grins. For the next half hour we would go through the routine of showing them various bits of gear and Jean Malaurie's book *The Last King of Thule,* in which there were photographs of many of their friends and relatives. Eventually, after a couple of cups of tea, we would get round to the miming of dogs pulling a loaded sledge.

If the motive of the visit turned out to be mere curiosity we would release the muscles that held our smiles in place, and allow the tea kettle to go off the boil. If on the other hand they had some dogs for sale, we would perform a weird arm-waving dance around the hut, bumping and tangling with each other as we struggled into our parkas.

In a long column we would stagger down to the sea ice and, holding up lamps which bathed the hunter's dogs in a pale yellow light, would make polite gestures of amazement at how big they were and how strong they looked. More often than not it was obvious that the dogs we were being offered were the outcasts of the pack, but since we knew that there were few if any useless dogs in the Thule District, we accepted gratefully any we were offered that did not cower or respond with a snarl as we approached to examine them more closely for bites and harness sores.

The price we paid for the dogs was reached by negotiation. These negotiations were conducted in the hut over a brew of tea. We paid according to the size and age of the dog (120 kroner being the top price) and by mid-January had bought twenty-six, from which we had selected the best twenty for the journey and given away the remainder.

Our problems increased the more dogs we bought, for they had to be fed. Unlike the hunters who throughout the winter would wait for hours at the lines of fracture in the sea ice for the seals to come up for air, we were obliged through lack of time and skill to buy frozen carcasses of seal and walrus meat from our Eskimo neighbors. The meat could not be cut up and fed to the dogs until it was thawed out, which meant that for several weeks we shared our hut with seals whose expressionless bulging eyes seemed to watch our every movement; dead seals that once unzipped released their odor and a mucous mass of gut. The floor of our hut was greased with blubber and blood, and our sleep disturbed by dreams of our seals slipping their hitches and plunging into the drums of intestines above which they hung perspiring. For weeks we were visited by no one, for there was not a crate or box on which a visitor could sit, and to keep his footing on the floor was impossible for even an Eskimo.

We had been accustomed in the Antarctic to doing everything ourselves; but at Qanaq we were living in a community of two hundred Eskimos and twenty-five Danes—very different from a community of twelve men in isolation where there were no social strata and no need to dress for dinner. We had come to Greenland prepared for a polar expedition and had found, much to our embarrassment, that we were frequently invited to parties at which the Danes formally and courteously entertained one another. We felt unclean in their presence no matter how much we scrubbed, and yet overdressed in the presence of the Eskimos with whom we had hoped to spend the winter. Reluctantly we allowed the Eskimos to help us.

A few of them we knew by name, but for convenience we gave them nicknames that were easier to remember: Warm Inner Glow; Mrs. Cutpurse; Little Worried Frown. The seal and walrus carcasses, for a small charge, we arranged to have thawed out and cut up in the home of Limpy, one of our Eskimo neighbors, and every second day we collected and fed to each of our twenty dogs four pounds of warm meat. The dogs' harnesses were made up for us by Mr. Okeydokey and our rubbish collected and water delivered in milk churns by Nut and his good friend Crackers. Electricity we eventually accepted when we discovered that there was insufficient light from the kerosene lamps to do any filming, and we were given a key to the shower over at the power house. "Now you are being sensible," was the chorus of the Danes. "Now you are just like all the other white men," said the eyes of the Eskimos.

After a month or so, our Eskimo neighbors had mellowed enough to give us some advice. By that time the object of our sojourn in Greenland had become common knowledge in the Thule District: We were there to learn what we could from the Eskimos and test out our equipment. They would sit for hours in our hut and with crude diagrams and drawings show us how they hunted seal during the winter night. They shook their heads sadly, however, when they saw us assemble our two sledges. One was an exact replica of a sledge which had survived Peary's last journey over the polar pack ice—a replica based on a set of photographs and measurements that the National Geographic Society had had specially made for me from its exhibit in the Explorers' Hall of the society's beautiful building in Washington, D.C. The other was modeled on one of the sledges used by Stefansson during his long journeys on the polar pack between 1914 and 1918. Each sledge was about twenty inches wide—too narrow for the heavy loads we would be carrying, the Eskimos said. They predicted that neither sledge would survive the journey to Resolute Bay and urged us to use three-foot-wide Eskimo sledges instead; but we found it unthinkable to exchange our two beautifully constructed, English-made sledges for the crude Eskimo counterparts, and ignored their advice.

An Eskimo suggestion we were to adopt, however, was the use of fur clothing. Furs had not been used on Antarctic expeditions for over fifty years, for though it may at first seem odd they are not really necessary there. The Antarctic explorer seldom spends more than a few minutes outside during the winter when the air temperature is below minus fifty Fahrenheit; he does his traveling in the summer when the weather is generally calm and the air temperature is seldom below minus twenty. Lightweight windproof anoraks and trousers worn over thermal underclothing and woolen shirts and sweaters is perfectly adequate in such conditions, provided a man keeps moving. In northwest Greenland and on the Arctic Ocean, so we were told, caribou parkas and polar-bear pants are essential, for a traveler there must do his traveling in the winter and early spring when the air temperature is below —50°F.

The traveler needs an outer garment that not only is warm but breathes. We would also need kamiks—Eskimo footgear made from reindeer with the fur side outside, and soles made of walrus skin. The inners for the kamiks are dogskin, fur side inside—a separate piece of footgear, the same shape as the outer but smaller. We were measured up by the Eskimo women who, chaperoned by their menfolk, felt free to roll their eyes and make crude jokes as they performed the fittings. They taught us how to plait the grass which was sandwiched between the inner and outer kamik as an insulator, and how to turn the kamiks inside out to dry them at the end of the day. They fitted us out with dogskin mitts which were trimmed at the top with polar-bear fur, and stroked their handiwork with admiration and a few coy giggles while their menfolk rolled on their buttocks, laughing at our embarrassment.

Both our sledges and our furs we tried out during the winter night on sledging journeys to the neighboring villages, and by the New Year, 1967, the two teams of dogs we had bought were settling down. It was on one of these runs that Roger and Allan met Cali Peary, the Eskimo son of the American explorer Robert E. Peary and the father of Peter, who was to be one of our guides up the coast of Greenland and across Smith Sound to Canada. The Eskimo son of Peary's Negro servant, Matthew Henson, also lives in the Thule District, and although there are no Eskimo offspring of Dr. Frederick Cook, the brother and children of Etukishook (one of Cook's two Eskimo companions) often came to visit us. It would have been fascinating, had we been able to speak their language, to discuss details of the stories told them by that famous old hunter, for in spite of the language barrier we were able to gather from gestures and rude noises that they considered Cook a faker. Most of the Eskimos with whom we discussed Cook's claims in sign language believe that the doctor and his two Eskimo companions, after having crossed Ellesmere Island, went southwest instead of northwest; and instead of sledging up Nansen Sound to the northern tip of Axel Heiberg Island (from where he set out across the polar-pack ice toward the North Pole), spent the summer of 1908 hunting in the region of Hell Gate off the southeast coast of Ellesmere Island. The Eskimos are excellent map readers—we could see this from the way they ran their grubby fingers over the map on the inner door of our hut as they vividly described some hunting anecdote, or traced the route we planned on taking, up to the point where they predicted we would perish. They must have known Cook and his Eskimo companions had sledged northwest —the stories handed down over the years could not have been so far distorted. We can only assume, therefore, that the Eskimos told us (as their fathers had told Peary and MacMillan) what they thought we wanted to hear.

With the route we ourselves proposed taking and with the techniques we intended using, there was much more honest criticism from the Eskimos, and some straight talking from Orla Sandborg too. It was, he felt, his responsibility to see us safely out of his territory. The U.S. Air Force at Thule airbase I suspect felt a similar responsibility.

The final weeks before our departure from Qanaq were every bit as hectic as the period immediately prior to our departure from London. We were by then familiar figures around the village, and many of the more famous Eskimos had developed the habit of dropping in to see us. This was all most encouraging, for with their friendship and (provided that we completed our present journey) a small measure of respect, we stood a far better chance of persuading them to provide us later with dogs for the trans-Arctic trek. We had also by that time become socially acceptable to the Danish community at Qanaq and the personal friends of Orla Sandborg, without whose help we would have found it extremely difficult to carry out our program.

Through Orla we were introduced to Kissunguak, a well-built, cheerful, but superior Eskimo who accepted more as an obligation than a pleasure the task of guiding us safely out of the Thule District and across Smith Sound to Canada. As a dog handler and a hunter he was renowned; he was also very ambitious. One day he would represent the Thule District on the Greenland Council, for "his dogs are lions and his wife is a goddess." Several times I invited him to visit our hut, but he had neither the time nor the inclination until early in the new year, when, with Peter Peary and Peter's wife, he came to look us over. He had by then decided to stand for election to the Greenland Council, and he had nominated Peter to take his place on the trip to Canada.

We were delighted with this arrangement, for Peter was already familiar with the ways and strange ambitions of explorers. He had accompanied the Norwegian Bjørn Staib as far as Alert, the point from where Staib had launched his attempt at a trans-Arctic crossing in 1964. That Norwegian assault, which had been sponsored by the National Geographic Society, had aimed at crossing the Arctic Ocean in one headlong dash. It was an expedition which had failed not through lack of courage or financial support (as far as I can gather), but because the start was made too late in the season from a point on the edge of the Arctic Ocean where there was a tremendous buildup of pressure. By good fortune, the American scientific drifting station Arlis 2 (which has long since drifted out of the Arctic Ocean and melted) was at that time drifting across Staib's route about halfway from Greenland to the North Pole. He located it and from there was flown out. Peter Peary's part in that "sporting challenge" had been to build Eskimo sledges to replace those of Staib's which had broken up in the first few miles of the journey—and Peter was to witness the breakup of more sledges before his career was much older.

Peter and his wife, Imanguak, were delightfully relaxed and lacked—or, at least, concealed—any doubts that we would be ready to start on February 26. Much more characteristic of the Eskimo in features, build, and temperament were Kaunguak and his woman, Nivikinguak, who were to join us at Siorapaluk, a village two days' journey to our west. It had been arranged through Orla Sandborg that the four of them would accompany us as far as Alexandra Fjord on the west side of Smith Sound where there was an abandoned Royal Canadian Mounted Police post; they were to be our guides and hunters and were to carry on their sledges some of our provisions. For their help we were to pay Peter and Kaunguak ninety dollars each—not an unreasonable sum, considering that they were going to cross Smith Sound anyway on their annual polar-bear hunt. But the spring hunting trip is the one time of the year when Eskimos become impatient, and Kaunguak was no exception.

The date I had originally set for our departure from Qanaq was February 8, ten days before sunrise in that latitude; but we had to postpone it for a couple of weeks so that we could film the rituals and orgies we assumed would mark the end of the winter night. It was very disappointing. We saw not one Eskimo leaping in the air as the sun climbed over the southern horizon for the first time in four months, and to the best of our knowledge not a single Eskimo lost more sleep that Saturday than he usually did.

We started dismantling the hut in earnest about 2 P.M. on February 25 and had it flat on the ground in less than two hours. There was no lack of assistance or of scavengers, and there were a good number of sightseers too; but by 7 P.M. the Eskimos had all gone home to their little wooden huts.

Early the following morning they turned out again, to see three white men dressed up like Eskimos in their polar-bear pants and kamiks and enormous parkas made of reindeer skin—an occasion not to be missed. Trying hard to be inconspicuous, we moved out onto the sea ice with our two sledges, each loaded with nine hundred pounds of gear. We had cameras, tape recorders, radio transmitters, dog food, man rations, a large quantity of fuel—for we were expecting temperatures well below —50° Fahrenheit during the crossing of Ellesmere Island—camping gear, and a variety of clothing so comprehensive that we were equipped for any climatic condition likely to be met north of the tropic of Cancer.

Seldom before had we set out on a sledging journey with such enormous loads. In addition to what we carried on the sledges, a sizable amount of gear belonging to us was being hauled by Peter Peary's superb team of dogs. We had little or no alternative. The journey ahead of 1,500 miles was a long one by any standards, and there were only two places along our proposed route where we could collect a prearranged supply of provisions: the weather station at Eureka and the deserted hut on the Meighen Island ice cap. We were committing ourselves to a journey tougher than any we had previously experienced, a journey from which there could be no turning back, for the whole point was to test our mettle, our technique, and our equipment over a course that would either break us or prove we had the measure of ourselves and our methods. If we failed we could not hope to convince our sponsors that the longer and more hazardous journey across the Arctic Ocean was feasible. This was a test of singlemindedness. The route would at only one point touch an outpost of civilization—Eureka. We could, if our situation was desperate, call for assistance by radio, but since the object of the journey was to simulate as closely as possible the dire stress and isolation we might meet during the trans-Arctic journey, there could be no question of calling for help; exhaustion would not qualify, neither would hunger—only a definite risk to human life.

4

Neck or Nothing

THE sound of a creaking sledge had been so soothing and the surface of the sea ice so smooth that for several hours after the last boxlike huts of Qanaq had slid out of sight I had been sledging in a daydream in which the past winter seemed like a pantomime of colorful characters in situations too absurd to be taken seriously. Now I felt the overwhelming relief of being once more on the move. A frozen sea stretched out ahead eight hundred and sixty miles to the still point of a spinning world that had been the goal of so many men before me.

The teams turned into the coast and stopped. There were two fishing boats on the beach leaning against their props, and beyond, a wooden shack, in which we were to spend our first night of the journey to Resolute Bay in the company of the Eskimos Peter, his wife, Imanguak, and the politician Kissunguak, who by chance was there when we arrived. Roger seemed happy and relaxed for the first time in several weeks. He had not enjoyed the winter at Qanaq, nor for that matter had Allan. They felt too much time had been spent being entertained by the Danes and in returning their hospitality; too much time housekeeping; not enough time out with the Eskimos hunting, so that the winter, by and large, had been wasted. I disagreed. We had lived for four months in the hut which from October 1968 to March 1969 would be our winter quarters on the Arctic Ocean, and had proved it satisfactory; we had got together two teams of dogs, been fitted out with furs, and made friends among the Eskimos in a district from which we would need to buy more dogs the following year. We could not have done any of these things had we not wintered over. All this, Roger felt, could have been done by me, and he could have flown up to Thule in early February in time for the start of the journey. He felt he had an obligation to justify any leave of absence from his school, for he had spent so much time away from his profession in the past ten years; as far as Allan was concerned, he would rather have been on T-3 somewhere on the Arctic Ocean doing something useful. These were men of action who had come through a tedious winter and were now at last on the move. It was good to see them joking and wrestling with the Eskimos on the sleeping platform as we all curled up for the night.

The following morning we set off for Siorapaluk into the wind. The sea-ice conditions were good, the going smooth, and we made steady progress with our strong, fresh teams; but we were three men with two teams of dogs, and I was bored and found myself wondering whether or not it would be wise to increase the strength of our party by an extra team. I tested this idea on Allan who was jogtrotting alongside me at the back of his sledge. As a cameraman, mightn't he find it easier to be free of the responsibilities of handling a dog team? "I'll manage all right somehow," he assured me. I then suggested, since I had no team and was bored stiff, that I might from time to time take over his team. To this he thoughtfully agreed and suggested that perhaps I could share the driving of Roger's team too. I had my answer. In the nicest way possible, Allan had told me his team meant a lot to him; Roger I felt sure would have responded the same way. I was now quite sure that it would be essential on the much longer and tougher trans-Arctic journey for each of us to have his own sledge and dog team. And in view of the great weight we had to carry on our present journey on the two frail-looking sledges we had brought with us from England, we would be justified in taking on an extra sledge at Siorapaluk and more dogs, even though the supply of dog food we had with us and the depots of supplies which had been laid for us in advance were provision enough for only two teams. These extra dogs we would feed by gun if possible.

We reached the village of Siorapaluk feeling very hungry, but were given nothing to eat. We were given nothing the following morning either, and when at last evening came and our host Kaunguak warmed up some seal meat, there was hardly enough of it to feed one healthy adult, let alone a hut full of inquisitive Eskimos and three ravenous Europeans. For fear of offending and embarrassing Kaunguak, I decided against buying a seal from another hunter to feed our host and his household; but it occurred to us later that perhaps he had had more contact with white men than we thought, and expected during his employment with us to be fed royally on European fare.

That first day in the village at which I had originally hoped to spend the winter we spent in checking our gear and dividing it into three loads. Roger felt I was making a mistake. He believed that on a journey planned carefully for two teams of dogs, their number should not be increased unless provision was made to feed them. Such a change of plan he saw as a repetition of Captain Scott's greatest error—that of taking on a fifth man in his pole party when he had catered only for four. I considered inflexibility a greater risk; that we had a good case for increasing the number of sledges; and that there was no similarity between the journey we were making through game country and Scott's journey across the Antarctic ice cap. We therefore went ahead, bought an Eskimo sledge, increased our dog strength of twenty-two animals by three and divided them into three teams, two teams of eight and one of nine.

On the morning of March 1, Roger and the Eskimos Peter and Imanguak set off ahead of Allan and me with the understanding that we would meet them further up the coast at a nest of three

huts called Neki. Allan and I recorded the preparations and the
start of their journey on two movie cameras and spent the rest
of the day making ready the third sledge. By lunchtime half the
village was tipsy.

I had seen drunken Eskimos three times before—on December
1, January 1, and February 1. On a points-rationing system, the
inhabitants of the Thule District (Danish administrators and
British expeditions included) are allowed as a monthly allowance
per person: one bottle of spirits, two bottles of wine, or twenty
small bottles of beer. The Eskimos invariably buy a bottle of
whiskey and finish it off in one lurching tour of the village. At
Qanaq our hut had been bypassed by most of the Eskimos and
so we had not become involved in the drunken sprees on the
first of each month; but at Siorapaluk, Allan and I were right in
the thick of it and the focal point of interest.

With the exception of Inutasuak, an old hunter of great dignity
who had traveled in his youth with Edward Shackleton (now
Lord Shackleton), every Eskimo in the village by nine o'clock
was rotten. Men were squaring up to each other and then falling
over, old crones screamed like stuck pigs or sobbed, and wide-
eyed children cowered in the corners or hid beneath thin blankets
on sleeping platforms on which their elders were wrestling in a
stupor of fornication. From each hut in the village came the roars
of lunatics and the thud of falling bodies. Doors were wrenched
open and, framed for a moment in the light of a lantern, bowlegged drunks lurched out into the night.

At midnight I followed the old man through the village. He
was in a hurry and the thin shaft of light from his torch did not
for one moment change its angle, nor did he once look up. He
was disgusted with his fellow villagers and ashamed that I had
witnessed the Inouit (the men *par excellence*) in their weakness.
"Drink and the Eskimos no good—no good, NO GOOD," he kept
saying. Inutasuak had admired Edward Shackleton's determination and enjoyed his company, and in a little hut set apart from
the village—a hut so drifted in with snow that I had stumbled
into the tunnel leading to the door before I had realized we were

there—he showed me his treasured possessions: an autographed copy of *South,* the story of Sir Ernest Shackelton's *Endurance* expedition, and many snapshots taken during his journeys with Shackleton's son.

He told me, too, of the Sverdrup Pass, and his sketch-maps confirmed Dr. Cook's account of a long easy climb from the head of Flagler Bay along a frozen riverbed. He told me I would have to make a detour to the north after I had passed a watershed, for a glacier blocks the river valley which descends into Irene Bay. This same glacier had been mentioned by both Sverdrup and Cook, but by none of the Eskimos we had met at Qanaq—why, I do not know.

We got away to a late start the following day. Kaunguak and his woman, Nivikinguak, set off first, followed by Thomas and Maktok Kiviok and the cousin of Peter Peary, who were also going across Smith Sound after polar bears. Allan and I, each with a sledge, were last of the line—six sledges in all—and within a quarter of an hour they were out of sight and we were creeping along on our own.

By nightfall we were still four miles from the huts at Neki, on ice that was like a frozen sea of ink. The sledges slid over it without vibration, and had we not spotted the torchlights of our Eskimo friends when we were still two miles from the huts, we would probably have had to feel our way along the coast until we literally stumbled upon the six teams of dogs and the eight cheerful, fur-clad figures who were busy chopping up walrus to feed them.

The following morning, for the first time since leaving Qanaq six days before, we set off with our full party plus our three additional traveling companions—a total of eight sledges. We made good progress across the first bay, but at the second point the sea ice was not strong enough to bear our weight. Farther on we could see open water. We had no alternative but to clamber over the pressure ice and sledge along a snow-covered ledge sloping toward the sea. Several times the sledges rolled over or crashed against boulders. At one point the ledge was only two feet six inches wide. This was a difficult place to get past with the Eskimo sledges, which were three feet or more in width. On one side of the ledge was an overhanging rock, on the other side a drop of twenty feet to the sea, which was beating a fine cold spray over the ice cliffs.

It was in a situation such as this that the Eskimos excelled. The technique of negotiating the obstacles was simple enough, and had we not been accompanied by Eskimos we would no doubt have got round it in the same way. Where the Eskimos differed from us was in their attitude to the problem. They took it all in their stride and evidently enjoyed the whole operation of roping up the sledges one at a time and manhandling them, still fully loaded, across that precarious ledge. We were to learn a great deal from the Eskimos during the next few weeks; some of these lessons were simply tips on technique, but more important was their attitude as a whole. Unlike most Europeans, they do not regard the Arctic as a setting in which to test themselves. They are the Inouit, the real men, and never in a hurry.

Allan and I did not catch up with the rest of the party until we reached the foot of the glacier, which, we understood from the Eskimos, led up to a high, windy route around the edge of the ice cap—a route which we would be obliged to take in order to detour the open water around the coast. By then our sledges had taken a beating and it was beginning to look doubtful if Allan's would survive. To the Eskimos, the breakup of our sledges was inevitable. Huddled together over a brew of tea in one of their flimsy tents, they amused themselves for half an hour with sound impressions of sledges splintering.

We set off into a biting wind over the rough windswept surface of the glacier. Our loads were heavy and our dogs, unresponsive to whips that did not crack like those of our stocky native companions, were disinclined to work. By the time we had climbed 500 feet we were soaked in perspiration which froze the moment we stopped to catch our breath. When we had pushed the sledges up to 800 feet the Eskimos themselves were beginning to feel cold and were tired of waiting for us. At 900 feet and some six miles inland they came back to give us a hand, but by then they were losing interest in the inland route; clearly it was going to be a long hard slog. They turned and headed back down the glacier, sweeping past us, each Eskimo riding his sledge sidesaddle and cracking his whip fore and aft in a superb show-off display of brilliant sledge and dog control. We in turn followed them, thankful that at the back of the column they could not see the pathetic attempts of the three *kraslunas* (the men from the south, inferior to the Inouit, the real men, the Eskimos) to master the native technique.

The sledges as we made that descent took a tremendous hammering over the blue ice (ice that had been swept free of snow by the wind) and the hard, wind-packed snow. At the back of the column, following in the tracks of Allan's sledge, I passed so many torn strips of wood, bridge members, and screws that I expected at any moment to overrun him, standing alone with nothing left to show of his sledge but the load it once supported. His sledge however was not the only one cracking up. Two hundred yards off Allan's tracks to the left I spotted the cousin of Peter Peary sitting on his broken sledge smoking his pipe, and about a mile further on the runners of my own sledge folded in and the sledge ground to a halt. It was a beautiful evening; not a breath of movement in the air; not a sound save for the occasional clink of a clip hook as a dog stretched or kicked in his dreams. I, like the Eskimo I had spotted, sat on my broken sledge and lit my pipe, and in a short while slipped into a soothing daydream from which I did not awaken until, disturbed by the crunch of footsteps, I turned to see two Eskimos approaching. I felt annoyed. Here was I trying to adopt the Eskimo philosophy of smoking a pipe whenever there was a problem to solve; there were they unloading my sledge and getting on with the repair which I could quite easily have done myself.

With a penknife they cut some holes in the runners and lashed them back into a vertical position with a strip of hide. The lashings they tightened by banging wedges of wood between them and the runners, and in less than half an hour we were, all three of us, riding a bucking sledge on an exhilarating descent to sea level where we rejointed the rest of the party.

We camped that night for the first time with three men in a two-man tent, and the following morning, cramped and miserable, I told Roger and Allan of the decision I had reached during my meditations the previous evening: Allan and I would return to Siorapaluk, taking with us two teams of dogs, two broken sledges and two sleeping bags, leaving the rest of our gear where it was. In Siorapaluk we would buy two Eskimo sledges to replace our broken ones and five more dogs, for we would need ten dogs to a team with the heavier Eskimo sledges. Roger was to set off with Peter Peary and Peter's wife as soon as the ice reformed and continue up the coast to the deserted village of Etah, where they would wait for us. Kaunguak and Nivikinguak were to wait for Allan and me to return; there was enough hunting to keep them occupied during our absence. The rest of the Eskimo circus were free to do as they pleased.

I have seen many happy Eskimos, but never have I seen them as enthusiastic as when they were given the job of chopping the broken rear half off Allan's sledge. They went to it with hand axes, roaring with derision as they hacked away and hurling the broken parts with shrieks of delight as far as they could from the remaining six feet of what was once a beautiful thirteen-foot sledge.

The 38-mile journey back to Siorapaluk was without incident, and with two light but somewhat fragile sledges the distance was covered by the dogs at a fast trot in just under eight hours. It was dark by the time we arrived; nevertheless within minutes we were surrounded by fur-clad figures fussing over us. They led us off to Kaunguak's house, lit a fire, made us a meal of boiled walrus and then, to our surprise, left us in peace. The following morning, accompanied by the dignified Inutasuak, we made a tour of the village in search of sledges and dogs. Most of the menfolk were off hunting and among the few sledges we saw on the racks there was none that looked stout enough for the journey we were contemplating, nor did there seem to be any dogs for sale.

It looked for a while as though Allan and I would have to sledge all the way back to Qanaq to get the sledges and extra dogs we needed, but a radio conversation with Orla Sandborg solved part of the problem; and by that evening Orla himself appeared, after a two-hour drive on his motor toboggan, with a fine new sledge in tow. A second sledge, and the five extra dogs we needed, we had managed eventually to pick up in Siorapaluk after involved negotiations which occupied us all that day; and by the time we turned in that evening I had paid out $180, and, with Orla, Inutasuak and Allan, finished off two bottles of whiskey.

We spent most of our last evening trying to rid ourselves of two old crones who had parked themselves ceremonially in our bedroom, and on March 7, for what was to be the last time, we set out, and just before nightfall reached the camp at the foot of the glacier. Kaunguak seemed well pleased with the sledges and the additional dogs, and told us over the evening meal of boiled walrus that the rest of the party had set out the day before after a few days of good hunting.

We were at last well and truly on our way; even the impasse we met about eight miles up the coast did not dispirit us. The others evidently had got around the Cape before the ice had gone out, or they had gone out with it—we would not know until we reached Etah, the place of rendezvous. We retraced our route for a couple of miles before turning into a bay and driving up to the snout of a steep glacier. We spent the next twelve hours in getting the three sledges over the rocks and up the icefall to a height of 300 feet. "Who said the Eskimos are the men *par excellence?* Listen to old K—he's round the bloody bend." I grinned at Allan as we put our shoulders to the man's sledge. God, it did us good to see and hear him screaming at his dogs. Sure enough it was a tough haul—three teams of dogs to a sledge, one sledge at a time: altogether thirty-five straining dogs, two Englishmen, an Eskimo woman and a fury fiend. "He's a tough old bastard though, you've got to admit."

The long haul up the glacier the next day was crippling: Allan's knee was giving him trouble; my ankle was swollen. Our Eskimo companions were way out of sight. We set off early on the morning of March 11 and came upon the Eskimos' tent in the lea of a rocky outcrop at the top of the glacier. Two round, cheerful faces poked out of the door flap, steam escaping from the tent past their faces—grotesque; it looked as though the faces were on fire. Their tent was a sheet of lightweight canvas propped up with a couple of harpoons, stretched out and pinned down around the sides with heavy blocks of snow. It stood no more than three feet above the surface of the glacier, and I wondered how we would all get in until they opened the flap. "The crafty old bastard—look at that, Allan; he's dug himself a pit." His stoves were on the floor of the pit. There was no groundsheet. The slops he just tipped onto the snow. Their bed platform, cut out of the hard-packed snow, was about two feet above the floor of the pit but was itself about two feet below the surface of the glacier. It was covered with reindeer skins. Hanging from the ridge of the shelter was all their footgear. "A real snug little hovel you've got here, old bugger." Kaunguak grinned at what he guessed was a compliment from Allan and rolled his laughing woman into the back of the tent to make room for his two guests.

After a brew and a smoke we got out, and while Nivikinguak broke camp, Kaunguak iced the runners of his sledge. Allan and I were watching him out of the corners of our eyes as he ran a cloth soaked in tea slops smoothly over the steel runners several times until a thin film of ice built up on the runners. He turned the sledge over, loaded it up and glided away effortlessly from the camp site.

By evening we had sledged fifteen miles, caught up with the Eskimos, and begun our descent of the glacier above Etah. It got steeper and steeper until even Kaunguak was obliged to stop and twist steel chains around his sledge runners. We did likewise, but within minutes of setting off again were careering down toward the sea ice and the five derelict huts of Etah. Roger and the five Eskimos who had gone around the coast had arrived the day before, and over the next two days, while we checked our gear and

fed the dogs on as much walrus meat as they could take to prepare them for the journey ahead, we swapped stories.

The Eskimos had some good ones about Roger. He had fallen
through thin ice on one occasion and been immersed up to his
armpits in the sea. Never once did they mention that on the same
day one of the men *par excellence* had also broken through thin
ice. The nonswimmer had splashed around for several minutes
on his back, kept afloat only by the air that was held captive in
his voluminous fur parka and polar-bear pants. That Eskimo was
a lucky man. He would have drowned, as so many Eskimos do
each year, had there not been men nearby to throw him a line.

On the morning of March 13, just before setting off, Roger
discovered that one of his dogs had a broken leg. The dog had
been limping for a couple of days. We thought of shooting it, but
for some reason the Eskimos insisted on hanging the poor creature from the eaves of a hut. It was still swinging gently when
we set off with a strong wind on our port beam down the long
fjord. The ice was so polished by the wind that it was almost impossible for the dogs to keep a footing, and sledges and dogs were
blown for nearly three miles before we reached ice that had a
rougher surface and were able to check our course.

We were in historic country; on the shore not two hundred
yards to our right was the site of the old Eskimo village of Etah,
which until 1937 had been the northernmost settlement of the
Smith Sound Eskimos. They had first encountered white men in
1854, when, according to the American explorer Dr. Elisha Kent
Kane, they had swarmed aboard his ship and regarded as theirs
any object that could be lifted or dragged. Kane was later obliged to teach them the laws of possession by abducting the
womenfolk of the thieves:

> ". . . the women were stripped and tied; and then, laden with
> their stolen goods and as much walrus-beef besides from their
> own stores as would pay for their board, they were marched
> back to the brig. The thirty miles was a hard walk for them;
> but they did not complain, nor did their constabulary guar-

dians, who had marched thirty miles already to apprehend them. It was hardly twenty-four hours since they left the brig with their booty before they were prisoners in the hold, with a dreadful white man for keeper, who never addressed to them a word that had not all the terrors of an unintelligible reproof, and whose scowl, I flatter myself, exhibited a well-arranged variety of menacing and demoniacal expressions." [1]

A treaty resulted from this, from which in turn there developed a working relationship between the white men and the Inouit that was mutually beneficial. Dr. Hayes, Commander Peary, Dr. Cook, MacMillan, Dr. Humphreys, and MacGregor all wintered their expeditions in the vicinity of Etah during the period 1860 to 1938. Every foot of that coastline along which we were sledging must have been known to those men.

We were obliged to turn inland shortly after rounding Sunrise Point at the northern entrance of the fjord in order to avoid open water along the coast. The Eskimos had taken this decision over a brew of tea—which seems to be the way all their decisions are made; either that, or sucked audibly from a pipe. They set up their brew box whenever they feel thirsty, tired, or meet other Eskimos on the trail. At the sight of open water, a broken sledge or a white man suffering from the cold, out come the primus stove, pot, tea caddy and mugs. Not for them the vacuum flask, for the very act of preparation would mean they anticipated the need for a hot brew on the trail.

What a grueling struggle that climb was, ten yards at a time; collapse against the sledge, hearts thumping, throats dry as an exhaust; all over the hills curses, cracking whips, whining dogs, yapping dogs. The hills are being stormed: eight men, two women, a hundred and three animals straining their guts out, tongues dragging in the snow, ground drift twisting through their legs. Daylight is draining from the sky, dripping blood on the hills of Ellesmere. The northern horizon, furred with drifting snow, is barely visible.

[1] E. K. Kane: *Arctic Explorations,* p. 219 (Nelson & Sons, 1882).

The stars are out now. We're on a plateau. Can't see the others, can hear them only when they call.

"Why don't those bloody 'skimos stop?"

"I suppose they know where they're going."

"Do they hell—the silly bastards are lost!"

We're losing height; sparks fly off the steel runners as we scrape grit and scratch over unseen rocks. There's a moon, but it's too low to light the scene; it merely bleaches part of the sky and makes the drop to sea level look even blacker than the throat of hell.

"What have they stopped for now?"

"I dunno."

"They sit on their arses till the sun gets tired, then spend all night striking matches to see where they're going!"

"They're lighting their pipes I suppose."

"No they're not—they're bloody well lost."

The ground falls away from under the sledge. The dogs are overrun and dragged. I can't get the chain under the runners. I can't reach. We're plunging. A heavy sledge plows into the mucus of soft drift snow; dogs are tumbling all around me, whining, snapping, whining. It's quiet now—dead still. The moon's skidding upstream against a current of clouds. Its weak light bathes my pit for a moment and fades. It comes and goes. The sledge is a sullen, heavy bitch; I heave at it for half an hour, and in a rage which boils the blood in my neck I right it and fall on it, spent.

The dizziness has gone now, and the dogs, dug out of their nests, are working the sledge down a snow trough to the sea. It's 5 A.M. The tents are a soft smudge of light. I can hear the murmur of conversation—the Eskimos are tired but contented; I am bruised inside by a pounding heart and sore and angry with myself.

Three hours later Kaunguak was up and puttering. We were not out of the tent until 11:30 and didn't get going until 2 P.M. Allan's sledge broke a runner; the Eskimos fixed it and we went on into a cutting wind alongside the ice edge, across a bay, and

up onto the ice foot at Cape Hatherton. By early evening Allan
and I were so cold we could barely move. Had we been traveling
by ourselves we would have put up the tent and crawled in out
of the wind. Suddenly the women came over to us, gave us a hug
and started beating us with their fists. In no time the whole tribe
was chasing us up and down the slippery ice foot, twenty feet
above the cold, black, frost-smoking sea, in a game of tag. We
could have the women if we could catch them, their eyes seemed
to say. Perhaps we misunderstood them; the object of the game
was in any case to restore the circulation, and this we succeeded
in doing long before the chase was abandoned and we continued
on our way.

We camped that night farther along the coast on an ice ledge
just broad enough to take a tent and not 200 yards from the
southern edge of a floating ice bridge spanning the entire thirty-
five miles across Smith Sound. The following morning, March 15,
we lowered the sledges onto the sea ice. The bridge was about
four miles wide at its widest point: the most chaotic ice pack I
had till then ever seen. Fortunately, however, there was a strip of
smooth sea ice on the southern edge, a strip in places no more
than a few hundred yards wide, which provided good smooth
sledging all the way across to Canada. Only once in the last
twenty years has the ice in that strait not held during the months
of February, March, and April. Every year except one it has
provided the Polar Eskimos from the Thule District with an ice
bridge to their hunting grounds on the east coast of Ellesmere
Island. In fact, so traditional had this route become that the
Royal Canadian Mounted Police set up and for several years
occupied a station in Alexandra Fjord to intercept the Greenland
Eskimos on their way across and drive them back to Greenland—
for the polar bears that freely roam along the east coast of Ellesmere Island are regarded by the RCMP as the preserve of the Canadian Eskimos, the cousins of the Thule people. Our traveling
companions were obviously in fear of the RCMP and illustrated
their stories of encounters with the Mounties with much grunting
and arm-waving. Small wonder they were so excited when that

morning, while still in their own territory, on a day dead calm and cold, we saw against a backdrop of blue-gray clouds three blurred and distorted yellow forms miraged above the horizon, moving in slow procession across our path. Without a word louder than a whisper, five sledges were hastily unloaded and in less than a minute were skidding away from us after the bears. They were the first polar bears I had seen in their wild free state. We were to see many more over the next few years and at far closer quarters, but on that day in Smith Sound they looked magnificent as they shuffled across the skyline.

It took us two days to cross Smith Sound to Cape Sabine, the eastern extremity of Pim Island (near which all but seven of Greely's party of twenty-five men had died of hunger before relief had arrived on June 22, 1884). We would have sledged around the north coast of Pim Island and past the site of Greely's camp had the ice been passable, and no doubt out of a macabre curiosity would have stopped for a while to look around that desolate spot where the rescuers had discovered among the dead in their shallow graves six mutilated bodies. Instead, we had made a two-day detour south: past Payer Harbour (where the *Alert* and *Discovery* of Nares' expedition had secured on July 30, 1875), up the narrow strait which separates Pim Island from the mainland, and past the small bay in which Sverdrup had wintered the *Farm* in 1898–99—a journey during which I had cause on several occasions to be grateful to our Eskimo companions, who were always ready to lend a hand and cheerfully encourage us when we were feeling cold, frustrated, or exhausted.

By white man's standards, Allan, Roger and I were highly competent dog sledgers, but we were still regarded by the Eskimos as children. We had not yet learned to relax in a polar environment, for on all our previous expeditions we had been competing with one another (without ever admitting it) to establish the reputation we thought befitting an explorer—that of being intrepid. For the first time in my polar career I began seriously to question my motives: was I attracted by the rigors and privations of expeditioning, by the romance and adventure of exploration, or simply by a love of the environment? Was I bound to conclude, as it had become evident that Allan and Roger did, that the attraction for me was a complex mixture of romantic ambitions in a setting that was coincidental—that any desert would have done, the Arctic Ocean being merely a convenient chart across which I had drawn a line? If this were true, what was it that motivated Allan and Roger? If they loved the Arctic as much as they professed, why would they ever leave it?

Eventually we came in sight of the cluster of neat boxlike huts at Alexandra Fjord at nightfall on March 18. Over the next two days we carefully checked and sorted our gear. We had come about two hundred and fifty miles from Qanaq, and three of our Eskimo friends had already left us to go in search of bears. Peary and Kaunguak urged us once again to change our plans and not take the route across Ellesmere Island by the Sverdrup Pass— the riverbed that had brought Cook across from Flagler Bay without much difficulty to the other side of the island. Inutasuak, the old hunter we had met at Siorapaluk, had confirmed Cook's report that this was a long easy climb, but had cautioned us that we would have to make a detour in order to bypass a glacier that blocks a portion of the river valley. Peary and Kaunguak warned us that if there was little snow in that valley we would run into trouble, and suggested that we go over the ice cap to the south side of the pass; but I was adamant. Allan and Roger, although impressed by the good sense of the Eskimos' argument, were more concerned, in view of the lateness of the season, about our chances of completing the journey, and suggested that we should head south when we reached Eureka Sound and make for the Eskimo settlement at Grise Fjord by a route along the southwest coast of Ellesmere Island. I was strongly against this suggestion, but spent much time thinking about it as I puttered about checking gear and watching the Eskimos knock the back teeth out of the heads of two of the dogs in my team; an operation which they said would put an end to the habit of harness chewing. The operation in fact nearly put an end to the dogs, for in order to hold them still and keep their mouths open while the Eskimos broke the teeth with a hand axe, the two hunters anchored the dogs to the ice by a noose which passed around the dogs' necks and through a small tunnel chipped through the ice with a knife. It took us several minutes to resuscitate the animals, and it was some ten hours before the dogs had recovered sufficiently to stand.

We spent almost three full days at that abandoned RCMP post in the cheerful company of our remaining four Eskimos, who, although still rating our chances of completing the journey as slim, needed little persuasion to drink to our good fortune from a bottle of rum we had secreted in our sledge load for the occasion.

Our camp on the first night out from Alexandra Fjord was about seven miles from the huts, and on the morning of March 22, our four friends one by one poked their heads through the sleeve entrance of our tent to say good-bye. Peter had been first as usual, a more energetic Eskimo I had never met. He had inherited more from his illustrious grandfather than his famous name. He had attributes of leadership uncommon among the Eskimos, and a lively interest in the outside world; a lively sense of humor, too. Often, throwing some article of clothing on the floor, he had ordered his wife to pick it up; then, as she had done so, roared with laughter. He had the gait of a polar Eskimo—a bowlegged lurch; but his facial features were European enough. I would not go so far as to say that one could mistake him for an Englishman in the foyer of the Waldorf Astoria; but the carpets of the Waldorf Astoria are probably the last soft surface on earth he would wish to tread, for he is a hunter, one of the finest of the Thule District, and his wife, Imanguak, one of the most attractive, full-blooded and moody women of the north.

Even as Peter shook hands with us, we sensed the urgency of the hunter's pulse. It had been in the firm handshake of his wife too. I can see her now, dressed in polar-bear pants and a flimsy pale-blue anorak; and Kaunguak, his full brown face split with a grin not quite sincere—for we were to him, even after sharing so many adventures, still the *kraslunas*. He had been annoyed with his woman Nivikinguak, whose eyes were full of tears. She was the only one showing emotion, the only one of them who seemed genuinely sad at the moment of parting.

The Arctic suddenly seemed very empty; our Eskimos had sunk into the mist. We were alone, adrift, more than a thousand miles from "land"—I could think of Resolute, our destination, in no other way—and we were to test our equipment and our endurance over a course not much more than a quarter the distance we would be obliged to cover if we were to cross the Arctic Ocean. To my way of thinking, there could be no question of shortening our route to Resolute Bay; as for the depots of supplies that had been laid in advance at Eureka Station and Meighen Island, I regarded them as equivalents of the air drops we would receive during the crossing of the Arctic Ocean, not as an excuse to stop. We were already twenty-six days behind schedule; for men and dogs we had only food enough on half rations to reach Eureka. I had expected to leave Alexandra Fjord with a fit party, but hunting had been poor and already we and our dogs were weak. The trans-Arctic journey was going to be a longer and tougher journey than any we had ever made; possibly more hazardous than any journey made in the polar regions since the heroic age. Now was the time to develop the right mental attitude toward such a journey; an attitude as relaxed and optimistic as that of the Eskimos, and yet determined almost to the point of obsession.

We traveled all that day into a biting wind and all the next through mist, reaching the head of Flagler Bay at about 5 P.M. on March 23. The prospect ahead up the valley looked ominous. The only snow to be seen was in the beds of frozen streams which braided the valley floor. Allan and Roger made a foot reconnaissance the following morning in a blizzard to a point some three miles up the valley while I assessed our situation. They reported some four hours later that the going would be extremely difficult; I in turn reported that according to my calculations we could complete the journey provided that we maintained an average of thirteen miles a day, killed the four weakest dogs on reaching Cape Stalworthy (the northern tip of Axel Heiberg Island), and

arranged for the depot on Meighen Island to be split so that part
of it could be shifted by aircraft to some point on the Grinnell
Peninsula. On this schedule, the dogs would receive one pound of
pemmican a day instead of the full ration of one and a half pounds
a day throughout the journey—except for a big feed which they
would receive at Meighen Island and Devon Island, when they
would get six extra blocks each. Both Allan and Roger were worried about working the dogs on short rations; I argued that we had
no option.

March 25: A black day. By relaying the sledges with double
teams, we reached the point where Allan and Roger had turned
back from their reconnaissance yesterday, but Roger's sledge was
torn to shreds over the rock and has had to be written off. If only
we had left the steel runners on that sledge instead of replacing
them with bakelite—a hard, strong, synthetic resin which has a
low coefficient of friction but, alas, wears out over rock. Roger is
now without a sledge and obviously very upset. I know exactly
how he feels; I felt that way at the start of the journey.

March 26: Pinned down by a blizzard most of the day, but
managed to get out on a reconnaissance of the valley late in the
afternoon. The valley floor is deeply cut here by two main streams
and the watercourse is steep. I must have covered several miles
looking for a route. Arrived back at the tent in an exhausted state.

March 27: Our breakfast of porridge this morning would
hardly have been adequate for a child. We all feel very hungry,
cold and sluggish. It seemed to take hours to sort the gear into
two sledge loads. The morale of the party is at a low ebb: I sense
resentment at my decision that Roger's team should join Allan's
in hauling the larger sledge, but whichever way the loads are split,
it would be the same, for the root of the resentment, I suspect, is
that I took on a third team of dogs having planned on two. Was
glad to see the last of that campsite. Hard haul up the frozen rap-
ids; we were obliged to relay the loads as far as the point I reached
yesterday, where I set up camp while Allan and Roger went back
down the falls to collect the rest of the loads. A blizzard blew up

shortly after they had set off—one of the worst I have seen in the Arctic with visibility at times less than three yards; but they got back okay. Wouldn't say morale is high, but it is better tonight than it has been of late.

March 28: Today was the worst since leaving Qanaq. Fumes from the primus practically finished us off this morning: we guessed we were being poisoned and at one time all had to fight our way to the tent door for air. Fell back and for a long time were incapable of moving; in fact, we did not get moving until 4:15 P.M. Took a long time to dig out. Violent headaches all day. Badly sprained my knee and had to rest every few minutes. Made about two miles.

March 29: Visibility one mile, temperature —28°F. All very weak and dizzy, but made some progress by keeping to the south side of the stream on a narrow strip of snow for a couple of miles before running onto gravel and getting stuck. Dogs are very hungry now; they ate the sleeve of my reindeer parka which I had carelessly left on the sledge while I was away on a reconnaissance. Eventually managed to move the sledge by using all thirty dogs; rest of the day was one long torture. Have ten days' full rations left.

March 30: The poisoning is getting worse. We all felt drunk last night and very sick. The poisoning seems to be cumulative; we can't shake it off in spite of sleeping with the tent door wide open and spending all day in the open air. We are very worried about cell damage and are beginning to wonder if we will get through. Have thoroughly checked the primus but can find nothing wrong with it; all the pots and pans are spotlessly clean. Made very little progress. Desperately hungry. Cut down to half rations.

March 31: Felt too weak to move until midafternoon when I managed to get the aerial up and contact Eureka by radio. Allan and Roger went off on a reconnaissance at about 4:30 P.M. Shot three hares and devoured two of them for dinner, but still feel dizzy and very weak.

April 1: Too weak to move.

The following day we advanced one mile before meeting an impasse and setting up camp on the watershed of the pass. Roger insisted that all three of us should make a foot reconnaissance ahead, for if I did not accompany them I would not believe them if they brought back any report less than glowing. All three of us set off and after a mile of rock found a snow-filled river bed that meandered for another four miles before it fell into a narrow canyon. On April 3 we moved the sledges forward in a blizzard to the head of the canyon, and, totally exhausted, set up camp.

In February, 1908, Dr. Frederick Cook had entered the canyon at this point in an attempt to escape from the cutting wind, but had found the air so full of blowing snow that they could hardly breathe. The temperature was —78°F: "Two dogs had frozen during the storm. All were buried in the edge of a drift that was piled fifteen feet. An exploration of the canyon showed other falls and boulders impossible for sledge travel. A trail was picked over the hills to the side. . . ." [2] They made a descent by a tributary stream bed farther down the canyon at a point about halfway along its course. They had camped on the night of February 28 on a glacial lake; the temperature by then was —79°F. Otto Sverdrup, who in April, 1899, had been the first white man to attempt a crossing of Ellesmere Island, had at this same point recorded that ". . . the river fell in a steep waterfall into a canyon. We made an attempt to get down here, and crossed a large drift of snow into a fissure with perpendicular walls on both sides. The fissure became deeper and deeper the farther we went, and at last we saw nothing but a small strip of daylight above our heads. Suddenly it became narrower than the breadth of a sledge, and all further progress west by that way was cut off. We were obliged to turn and laboriously work our way back up to camp. . . ." [3] The route taken by Cook down into the canyon beyond the first narrow fissure had been taken by Sverdrup nine

---

[2] Frederick A. Cook: *My Attainment of the Pole,* p. 166 (New York, The Polar Publishing Co., 1911).

[3] Otto Sverdrup: *New Land,* vol. 1, p. 131 (London, Longmans, Green & Co., 1904).

years earlier, but Sverdrup had not taken his sledges down into it. The ice of the glacial lake Sverdrup had found to be crystal clear: ". . . the clearest I have ever seen."

I went into the canyon alone on the afternoon of April 4 and was at first enchanted by what I saw. As Sverdrup had said, there were places where the fissure was narrower than the width of a sledge; there were many frozen waterfalls and giant windscoops with knife-edged ridges which we would have to cut a passage through, but although it was photogenic, I did not at first sight consider it as a route worth the effort while there was still a possibility of an alternative. I scrambled out of the canyon at a point which I later discovered was about a quarter of the way along it, and returned to camp along the "plateau." Neither Allan nor Roger was keen to spend time on what might prove to be a fruitless search for an alternative route; neither was I prepared to commit the party to the canyon until we had thoroughly reconnoitered it on foot to a point beyond the last obstacle met by Cook. At 1 P.M. on the following day, after a good deal of discussion, the three of us set off on a crippling walk that was to take eight hours. But it released some of the tension that had developed between us over my insistence on sticking to the route and taking on extra dogs to haul the heavy sledges; for although the canyon promised to be one of the most difficult obstacles we had ever encountered, we had at least satisfied ourselves that there was, that year, no alternative route across the bare ground of the plateau.

For the next four days we were pinned down by blizzards, fatigue and lethargy. We felt so weak we could barely move. On April 9 I killed the first dog. There was hardly enough meat on it to feed four of its teammates, let alone a pack of twenty-nine ravenous "wolves."

I thought we should kill two more dogs; Roger thought we should kill four; Allan was of the opinion that we should jettison all inessential gear, such as the Bell and Howell movie camera and the reserve radio. He wanted to cut the end off his sledge to lighten it, and ditch his furs, now that the weather was getting warmer; but on further discussion we agreed that the saving in weight would not appreciably alter our situation, and we decided to postpone the killing of the dogs for a couple of days.

We talked during those four days a good deal about our chances of completing the journey, for we were by now so far behind schedule that, even had we and our dogs been in perfect condition, the original goal seemed beyond our reach. In spite of this, however, I remained strongly in favor of going on, arguing that to call for rescue at this stage—or even the less humiliating alternative of turning south on reaching Eureka Sound and making for Resolute Bay by the shorter route—would be regarded by our sponsors as failure. Roger did not agree: to press on stubbornly, he argued, and lead the party into a hopeless mess from which we would have to be plucked by helicopters flown all the way from Edmonton or Montreal, was an even more certain way of losing the respect of sponsors; it was far better, if it was the confidence of my sponsors that I was concerned about, to show them that I had as a leader experience enough to know when to give in. "You should take a lesson from Shackleton," Roger said. "Because he had the courage to turn back he never lost a man. It takes more courage to admit one's plan has failed and give it up than it does to press on and confirm the failure." Roger had put a good argument, but as I saw it the whole point of the journey we were making was to find out what we were made of. How should we know we had the guts to attempt a trans-Arctic crossing unless we proved it to our own satisfaction, and to the satisfaction of our sponsors, by completing this journey against heavy odds? We must go on.

We entered the canyon on April 10 and got as far as the first fissure before camping at 11 P.M. The ten hours of shoveling, cursing, and straining had advanced the two sledges only three hundred yards. It took us four and a half hours to get the tent up and prepare a weak stew. It took an additional four hours to get up and have breakfast next day. The temperature was only —20°F, but over the last few days, weakened by fatigue and starvation, the cold seemed to be slowly seeping through the skin. It could be only a matter of days before the warm core inside each of us would seize up and our bodies become frozen monuments to our folly.

On the eleventh we worked for eight hours, back-packing to and fro along the floor of that fissure like ants, scrambling up and down waterfalls, and wriggling the emptied sledges through— lifting, twisting, scraping them through on their sides.

On the twelfth we made a couple of back-packing trips the full length of the narrows to a point about halfway along the canyon, returned to the camp and collapsed. For over two hours we were unconscious and woke feeling even weaker; but we got out, loaded up the pack frames once more and set off along the canyon, this time filming as we went. Seldom have I felt colder or more miserable and frustrated than I did during that carry. Each camera angle Allan set up laboriously—each shot required a tripod, a careful light-meter reading, and a rehearsal. Two hours it took us to shoot about a hundred feet of film; over two hours to change the film in the tent, for the camera had to be thoroughly dried out each time. The hand warmers that Allan had secreted inside a duffle bag tailored to fit the camera had to be primed and relit each time; we even went to the trouble of setting up a mountain tent halfway along the canyon (between the camp and the forward campsite) in which we had set up a primus to heat it, as a staging post in which Allan could change films. We had not then learned the technique of filming in cold weather, and, with what in retrospect seems unbelievable devotion to the task, spent a total of eight hours in capturing on film a few sequences that together would run through a projector in three minutes. By the end of that day we had moved one sledge through to the for- ward campsite and most of the gear; by the end of the next day we had moved the second sledge through and set up camp at the forward site and had only the dogs to fetch. By then we had on film a total of six minutes, each frame a painful record of two men in furs staggering under heavy loads or manhandling sledges down frozen waterfalls and along the snowdrifted bed of a black- walled gorge. How we suffered to get those few feet of film, and how bitterly disappointed we later were to find that the camera, affected by the cold in spite of the hand warmer, had been running at the wrong speed!

On our last morning in the canyon we had returned from the forward camp to collect the dogs and film them as they ran loose along the floor of the fissure and slid over the iced waterfalls. I had taken along a tape under my furs to keep it warm; but the dogs were too quick for the cameraman and the tape recorder developed a mechanical fault. Wearily we loaded the sledges and hitched up the dogs for the first time in three days. The canyon here was wider and the walls were less perpendicular. Sunlight almost reached the frozen stream on which we were now skidding. The canyon widened still more as it twisted and turned until it was as wide as a road. The walls fell back into hills, the road opened up, and we slid out onto the frozen lake which both Sverdrup and Cook had crossed so many years before. Nine days earlier when we ourselves had first crossed this lake, the ice had been so clear and polished that we had barely been able to keep a footing; now it was covered with glacial clay deposited by the wind of the last few days, and the four miles of crystal ice we had seen on the fifth took nearly three hours to cross. We camped that night within a hundred yards of where the glacier tongue lolled across the lake and almost touched the rock wall on the northern side of the valley.

That glacier had evidently retreated quite a bit in the past sixty years. When Sverdrup discovered it, the glacier had blocked the valley; now there was a narrow, boulder-strewn passage of rock and ice between the rock wall and the ice face. This passage we negotiated the next day, back-packing, as we had done in the canyon, every item of gear save for the sleeping bags and the tent. These we man-hauled on the sledges, filming as we went, and in twelve hours of almost continual hard labor we advanced the camp half a mile and cleared the last obstacle that lay between us and the sea ice of Bay Fjord. We were by that time in a very bad way, and had left only a few hares' heads and six days' rations for ourselves, and four days' food for the dogs on quarter rations.

From this point Cook had sledged down a highway of ice which he had called the Greely River. "The air had just a smart of bitterness," Cook wrote of that day fifty-nine years before. The temperature was —78½°F but the day was beautiful, and for the first time he felt the heat of the sun through the thick fur. "We fed our internal fires liberally with warming courses, coming in easy stages. We partook of superheated coffee, thickened with sugar, and biscuits, and later took butter chopped in squares, which was eaten as cheese with musk ox meat chopped by our axes into splinters. Delicious hare loins and hams, cooked in pea soup, served as dessert." [4] How we envied him as Roger read aloud that passage of his book on the morning of April 16, and how encouraged we were by his account of the romp he and his Eskimos enjoyed as they covered the twenty-five miles down to the sea ice!

The air temperature on the sixteenth was only —15°F, but we were frozen to the core, and the highway of ice on which we eventually found ourselves was so polished that we descended by sliding helplessly from one rocky patch to another and jamming on each. It was a hard, frustrating day. The next day was even harder and more disheartening, for the riverbed braided into several hundreds of small streams, few of them wider than a sledge. Many times we thought we would have to unload and back-pack forward, but by exerting ourselves to our last ounce of strength, and by hitching all twenty-nine dogs to one sledge at a time, we managed to keep going in relays and reached in due course an area where there was snow cover. At last we rounded a projecting spur of high ground onto a flat lagoon which opened onto smooth sea ice. We stopped for a smoke, sledged on another hour and camped. On the sledges there was two days' food left for the dogs on quarter rations, for we had fed them nothing on the sixteenth; we ourselves were in a better position, for by making five days' rations last for nineteen days we still had five days' rations left to get us to Eureka.

I set up the radio on the morning of April 18, not expecting to

[4] Frederick A. Cook: *My Attainment of the Pole*, p. 169.

be heard, for the co-ax cable connecting the aerial to the set had fractured, and the repair job Allan had performed, using a spoon as a soldering iron, we had not thought would hold. I had missed the prearranged radio schedules through bad radio conditions and it was three weeks since I had reported our position. We had at that time been thirty days behind schedule; we were now forty-seven days behind schedule, and by the calculations of the men at Eureka Station should have run out of food several days ago.

The voice of Hans Keiner came over loud and clear: "Traction, Traction—Eureka, Eureka; how d'you read?" He was as surprised as we were when we got through to him by Morse code. "Perhaps I ought to tell you that Ralph Plaisted is on his way to find you—the aircraft took off from Eureka some time ago. They have food on board for you; they also have a film crew and newsmen on board. Do you want me to tell them where you are?" I have never been asked a more difficult question. Ralph Plaisted's party with motorized toboggans (Skidoos) was making an attempt to reach the North Pole from their base at Eureka Station. I had heard that the expedition was lavishly equipped and lacked for nothing except possibly experience. I had heard also that the ice party had made hardly any progress on the Arctic Ocean and that it was only a matter of days before the expedition would be folded up. The film crew was a CBS outfit under Charles Kuralt, a well-known face to viewers of CBS News. Why were they flying this rescue mission to us with their own aircraft? Was it one last attempt to get some exciting footage out of an abortive expedition? I discussed this with Allan, for Roger was at that time off in the nearby hills looking for hares.

"Don't you think we should give them the benefit of the doubt? After all, we could do with food."

I had already told Hans in a short burst of Morse what I thought of "rescue"—but Allan was right; if we didn't accept Plaisted's food, we should have to kill and eat dogs unless Roger was lucky enough to see a few hares. I called Eureka again, gave Hans our position, and within five minutes the aircraft landed on the smooth ice of Irene Bay and taxied up to our camp.

Any misgivings I might have had were dispelled as soon as Ralph and his companions tumbled out of the colorful twin-engined Otter, for even though they were bristling with cameras and portable tape recorders, their grins were not those of men about to deceive us. On the contrary, they seemed so impressed by the fur-clad and gaunt-looking men who were giving them a conducted tour of the dog teams and battered sledges that it was almost with embarrassment that they offered us assistance. For men whose staple diet at their base consisted of T-bone steaks, fresh vegetables, fruit and beer, it must have come as a surprise that we had been able to survive during the last twelve days on two days' rations. It evidently surprised them too that we were, in spite of our furs, small men; I overheard Weldy Phipps, the pilot, pass a comment to Kuralt: ". . . if you shaved him he'd probably be something of a runt."

Roger had returned by that time and for the next half hour we bustled around the camp sorting out gear which Weldy Phipps could take back to Eureka to relieve us of some weight, while Ralph Plaisted's men snapped us, filmed us, and recorded us on their expensive apparatus. We invited them to stay for a cup of tea, but the idea did not seem to appeal to them—perhaps just as well, for I discovered later that we had none left.

Grateful though we were, we felt a great relief when our neatly dressed and sweet-smelling friends scrambled back aboard their aircraft and took off, leaving behind them two boxes of their sledging rations (five days' rations for three men), a duralumin sledge, a jerry can of kerosene, and all the loose bars of chocolate they had in their pockets. We were as excited as kids at Christmas digging into the many cardboard boxes scattered about the camp. The sledge, although small, was for Roger a tremendous boost to his morale; we could now once again run three separate teams of dogs and would, we thought, surely reach Eureka within a week, for it was only 150 miles. The lack of dog food was our only problem, but as we tucked into the biggest meal we had ever eaten, even this did not seem serious: there would be good hunting in Bay Fjord and Eureka Sound, the Eskimos had told us.

The Eskimos were right; during the next three days we passed several blowholes in the ice and occasionally, in the distance, seals lying on the ice basking in the sun. Never in my life have I felt as useless as when the dogs, excited by the scent of seals, would look around at me as if to say, "Well, why don't you do something?" Nor have I ever seen a sight more pathetic than a team of starving dogs lying on their bellies around a hole in the ice that was reeking with the smell of seal and stained with its juice, each dog dipping its paws into the water in an attempt to scoop out a seal that was not there. Those dogs that had once been owned by Eskimo hunters were now dying in the harness of men who had not acquired the skill.

The poor creatures were by now so weak that they would break into a trot only when they smelled seals, and a mad rush only when they caught sight of the feces of the team ahead, or hares. On those occasions they were capable of the most fantastic output of energy: I recall when Roger, who had been off hunting along the coast, came within sight of the dogs carrying two hares over his shoulder. The dogs, seeing the white downy bunnies bobbing up and down against his back, went crazy. Allan and I flung ourselves on the sledges as they flew past, and Roger, who saw the teams coming after him across the coastal pressure ice, set off up the hill. The dogs pursued him, dragging the sledges over angular rocks and boulders up to a height of nearly forty feet above sea level before the sledges eventually jammed. By that time the dogs' energy was spent, and the only way we could get the sledges back down to the sea ice was by completely unloading them of what little gear they carried and manhandling them.

We were ourselves in a weak state, for although we had Ralph Plaisted's rations plus what was left of our own, we were now being obliged to haul the sledges along with the dogs. We were in fact burning up more energy than we were replacing with our diet of 5,800 calories a day, and in a desperate effort to increase our daily mileage, we were averaging only four hours sleep a night. By April 22 we were all three of us feeling weaker than at any stage in the journey; the dogs we were feeding butter and what few scraps of meat Weldy Phipps had been able to take on board at Resolute and drop to us the day before on his way back to Eureka. We had hoped he would be able, through the RCMP at Resolute, to purchase a seal carcass from the Eskimos there; but this arrangement had not worked out. Had there not been dog food depoted at Eureka, or had we been less optimistic about finding game, we would that day have killed three or four dogs and fed them to the others; as it was, we blindly kept going, driving our dogs and ourselves to within a breath of complete exhaustion. On the twenty-fifth one of my dogs collapsed and had to be carried on the sledge. The next day he suffered a spasm, ran round and round in a small circle, dropped, and died during the last three miles along the fjord and within sight of Eureka Station. The men of the station who came out to greet us were shaken and silent, for we were burned the color of parchment, scabbed and raw with frostbite sores, and our dogs were fragile frames; but we had got through with the loss of only two dogs, and could now give them as much food as they could consume in three days, and take on with us as much feed as they could haul.

Still dressed in furs we were led into the station and sat down at a table. We gorged ourselves on everything that was put before us, snatching each plate as if afraid that the man who offered it might change his mind and take it away from us. We ate until our stomachs were tight balls of compressed food as hard as solid rubber and as heavy to carry to bed.

I had originally considered Eureka merely as a depot; indeed, my intention had been to camp out in Eureka Sound and go in with empty sledges to collect the food and fuel that had been left there for us. My reason for this was that any break in the journey at this stage would upset our concentration on the goal, and ruin any effort to simulate the sort of psychological stresses we would encounter during the final hard dash to Spitsbergen after a winter spent in the cramped quarters of our hut. The state in which we and our dogs had arrived at Eureka, however, left us no alternative but to rest up until either the dogs were fit enough to haul heavy loads, or until I had found some way of lightening the loads, whichever was the sooner. Roger and Allan felt the dogs needed at least a week of resting and feeding if we were seriously to consider going on. As far as I was concerned, there could be no question of not going on.

Dennis Stossel, the officer in charge of the weather station, had found some dog meal which had been left at Eureka many years before and very kindly offered it to us, together with any meat that could be dug out of a snowed-in food store, provided the meat was found to be unfit for human consumption. The meal was in powder form and took a long time to prepare; uncovering the food store required twelve man-hours of hard labor, and these jobs fully occupied Roger and Allan on the twenty-seventh while I was sending telegrams or talking on the radio to anyone in the Queen Elizabeth Islands who might be able to help us.

Dr. Hattersley-Smith, who was at his base camp in Tanquary Fjord, about 140 miles to our northeast, offered us six boxes of dog pemmican in exchange for three from our depot of eight 20-man/day sledge-ration boxes at Eureka: these were to be exchanged in a couple of days when an aircraft would visit them from Eureka. Dr. Fred Roots, coordinator of the Canadian Polar Continental Shelf Project, who at that time was at Isachsen Station on Ellef Ringnes Island, told me over the radio that he had some days before arranged for a surprise to be left with the depot of supplies his aircraft had left for us on Meighen Island: 400 pounds of seal meat for our dogs. To meet the urgent need for red meat I asked the RCMP constable at Resolute Bay to arrange immediately for 500 pounds of walrus meat and seal to be purchased from the Eskimos at Resolute Bay and sent up to us at Eureka in Weldy Phipps' plane. The Plaisted Expedition, which had taken over the old weather-station buildings at Eureka as a base, generously came forward with an offer of spare meat— frozen chickens, meat hash, and sausages. I made an arrangement with Weldy Phipps for a resupply of food and fuel at the northern tip of Axel Heiberg Island (in order that we could travel as lightly as possible during the first hundred and fifty miles of the eight-hundred-mile journey which still lay ahead), and arranged

over the radio with one of the polar shelf project's scientific investigators, who was just about to pay a flying visit to the
Meighen Island ice cap, to take aboard his aircraft half of the
depot of food and fuel that had been left there earlier in the season and shift it down to the isthmus at the head of Arthur Fjord
on Devon Island.

By these arrangements we would have three depots of food
along the route instead of one, and I had brought Resolute Bay
once more within range—providing we forced the pace up to
twenty miles a day. The season was already far advanced. Already the Plaisted party was seriously considering calling off its
expedition—all of them without exception were anxious to get
home. Roger and Allan I suspected had felt a similar inclination
when we had first staggered into Eureka, but I had ignored this
and concentrated on the ways and means by which we might continue. The fact that the original plan had not worked out to the
letter did not disturb me, but Roger, I now sensed, harbored
doubts about committing himself to my leadership on a journey
five times as long; he had seen too many changes of plan and suspected that I was determined to go on somehow, anyhow, and regardless of the feelings of my companions. As an assessment of
my attitude toward the training journey this was true, for it was
the only way I could measure the loyalty of my companions and
their confidence in my leadership. This was a test, to some extent
contrived, to see how we would react under the stress of a far
longer journey where, presumably, things would not always go
according to plan no matter how carefully that plan was laid. We
were all very tired and still very weak after the ordeal of the first
half of the journey, and on April 28, even as I was outlining the
new schedule and explaining how I had arrived at my figures,
Roger fell asleep. Allan, however, accepted the plan. We would
move off as soon as possible.

The following day a blizzard struck and visibility over the next
four days seldom lifted to more than fifty yards. Working outside
shifting sledges and gear was a misery, and I was beginning to
wonder if we would ever get away. There was more anxiety in

the Plaisted camp. They had made no radio contact with their ice party for several days, and on May 4 their expedition was officially called off and the ice party picked up by Weldy Phipps. We were by then in the final stage of repairing Allan's sledge, converting two sledges which Plaisted had kindly lent us into dog sledges, and making a final check on our gear in preparation for the eight-hundred mile forced march to Resolute. In this work, as in everything else we needed, the residents of the weather station could not do enough for us, and it was no surprise, when eventually we moved onto the ice on May 6, that all nine members of the station were there to wish us well.

The ten days of resting and feasting had put new life into the dogs. Roger and Allan were in good shape too; but so time-consuming had been the problems of readjusting the schedules, arranging for extra meat for the dogs to be flown in from Resolute Bay and Tanquary Fjord, that I was traveling in a daze. The whole of my last night, I had spent writing reports, memos and letters, and drafting telegrams concerning the expedition, for in less than six weeks I would be back in London and in less than nine months we would be setting off from Barrow on the trans-Arctic journey. Small wonder the obsession I felt toward our goal when you consider what for me as leader was at stake: To that ambition of making the first surface crossing of the Arctic Ocean I had already devoted four years of my life, all my savings, and as much borrowed money to launch the training journey alone as I had in total earned during my whole working life. If this training journey failed to acquit itself well in the eyes of our sponsors, the trans-Arctic expedition would miscarry and all those years, with the vision, the agony, optimism, and frustrations that had been crammed into them, would be wasted. Neither Roger nor Allan would ever fully realize this; my only hope was that they would make allowances for their leader's shortcomings and stick with him through all the hazards and hard times that lay ahead.

The snow cover of the fjord in places now looked like brown sugar—the temperature only a few degrees below freezing. Summer was already upon us. We ran all day on our first day out and made thirty miles. We covered thirty-five miles the next day, twenty-eight on the eighth, and by the end of our sixth day out had reached Cape Stalworthy—the point from where Dr. Cook had set off for the Pole across the polar pack. Here, for the first time since leaving Greenland, we were to divert from his route; here we had reached our farthest north. We must now head south with all the speed we could muster. We had cut it fine over those first one hundred and fifty miles since leaving Eureka by taking with us only enough food to last six days. On the twelfth as arranged, Weldy Phipps landed at our camp and resupplied us with the dog food which had been flown down to Eureka from Dr. Hattersley-Smith's camp at Tanquary Fjord; on the thirteenth I shot a reindeer, but the carcass hardly whetted the appetites of the dogs. There would be more fresh meat at Meighen Island, I had been told, so we doubled the dogs' ration of pemmican and over the next four days made good steady progress in perfect weather down the northwest coast of Axel Heiberg Island.

Somehow we sensed that those four days would be the most comfortable of the whole journey; we were more relaxed, more observant, more appreciative of the beautiful, wild scenery through which we were passing. The rugged grandeur of Ellesmere Island had been seen through the eyes of starving men and trodden by cripples; Eureka Sound had been so many tortured miles; Nansen Sound a headlong race against time. Now we were on skis, swishing along beside sledges that were gliding smoothly behind teams of dogs that for the first time since leaving Greenland were leaning into their harnesses. It could not last.

On May 18 we drove through the thundering echoes that rained all around us off the cliffs of Cape Northwest and headed out in mist across the Sverdrup Channel toward Meighen Island, a weak sun serving as our guide for the compass was useless. We stumbled into the island at the end of a long weary march on the twentieth and drove the teams up 900 feet to the ice cap the following day. The depot that had been laid for us was about thirty yards from a collapsed hut that had once been Fritz Koerner's base, but we found there only three boxes of dog pemmican instead of ten, three gallons of kerosene instead of five, one box of sledging rations so badly damaged that it was useless, and no trace of the 400 pounds of seal meat for the dogs. We had only enough dog food to last fourteen days on half rations. What had happened we could not guess, nor was there anything we could do but feed as much of our own supplies to the dogs as we could afford and carry on. I remembered Fritz telling me there was a squalid little hut at the south end of the ice cap, and on the morning of the twenty-second we sledged to it and found there a parcel of three T-bone steaks and a couple of frozen loaves of bread; stuffed them into the sledge bags, drove off the cap, and at about 500 feet altitude, sank into cloud which like a sea washed against the lower slopes of the island. For the next three hours we wound our way down to sea level in fog along a narrow stream bed. We had been lucky with the weather at least: Meighen Island has the reputation of being the most miserable spot along the entire periphery of the Arctic Ocean. Cook on his way south had passed within a few miles of the island on June 13, 1908, without seeing it.[5] Vilhjalmur Stefansson had made quite an issue of this, arguing that Cook could not have gone the way he said or he would have discovered the island; although it is clear from Stefansson's account in his book *The Friendly Arctic* that he did not himself discover the island until he was fifteen miles from it—the date, June 13, 1916.[6] It was foggy, as usual, the day after we left the ice cap; in fact, we sledged fifteen miles along the coast within fifty yards of the coastal pressure and only once caught sight of the island, from which we couldn't have been more than a mile! We traveled in fogs, mists, and whiteouts for the next eleven days, and at one time traveled for an hour or more before we realized we were sledging over land.

The surface by now was soft and sticky and the dogs weaken-

[5] Frederick A. Cook: *My Attainment of the Pole,* p. 330 (New York, Polar Publishing Co., 1911).

[6] Vilhjalmur Stefansson: *The Friendly Arctic,* p. 518 (London, Macmillan and Co., 1921).

ing by the day. Traveling for nine hours we would, if we kept working, cover eighteen miles. We could not travel longer without giving them at least a four-hour rest. We desperately needed food for them, but saw no seals until the morning of twenty-seventh when we were about to break camp. I set off with a rifle, but it was too windy to use the hunting screen we had been given by the Eskimos—a white screen behind which they can crawl unobserved by the seal until they are within range—and was obliged to stalk the seals patiently and with infinite care. For almost an hour I crawled forward until I had closed the gap to a hundred yards, a range at which I considered I could not possibly fail to hit the brain; but I was just taking first pressure with the cross hairs of the rifle 'scope steady on target when the two seals caught scent and slid into their hole. I got up and as I did so noticed Roger coming straight toward me with his team of dogs. It was an hour before I returned to the old campsite, hitched up my dogs and set off after the others; and several hours before I had got the incident off my mind—by which time the weather had closed in and it was snowing. By midafternoon a blizzard was blowing and I had lost their tracks. I pressed on for a while in the hope of stumbling upon the tent, and perhaps would have done so had not my bitch chosen that time to have a pup.

She had delivered it in a matter of minutes—time enough for the rest of the team to curl up into furry balls to get some protection from the wind. I watched her for a while as she carried the squeaking pup in her mouth from one dog to another, trying with each in turn to push it into the warm pocket of their laps; none of them would take it. Clearly I could not continue the journey with a whelping bitch. The pup had to be killed before it started taking milk from the mother. Allan's bitch a week before had produced four pups and each of them had been eaten alive by the hungry pack. The bitch had not seemed unduly upset by this, but my bitch was different. She wouldn't let me get anywhere near it after my first fumbling attempt to take it off her, so I was obliged to resort to trickery to separate the two. All would have gone well had she not waked the rest of the team with the anguished noises she was making. They spotted me sneaking away into the blizzard with something in my hands and broke loose. I took one look over my shoulder at that pack of ten hungry dogs coming for me and pitched the pup into their midst, expecting it to be killed instantly and so save me the trouble; but to my surprise they veered away from it as the screaming bitch plunged into the pack and scooped it up in her mouth. Visibility by this time was less than twenty yards and setting up the mountain tent was a wrestle that took almost an hour. I dispatched the pup in due course; but without pots and pans and a primus stove I was unable that night to make a hot meal and spent a miserable six hours in that flapping tomb, considering the many changes that would have to be made in our equipment and technique before we could set out on the trans-Arctic journey with any degree of safety. I thought a good deal too about how I was going to organize such a major project in six months without assistance; I had asked Roger three days earlier if he would be prepared to work with me in London, but the proposition had not appealed to him, and Allan could not help me for he was already committed to spending the rest of the summer as station leader of the Arctic Institute of North America's expedition on Devon Island.

I knew that I must get back to London as soon as possible and look around for a keen young man—the sort of man I had been at the age of twenty-four would be ideal, for he would have all the enthusiasm needed to work long hours at a low wage merely for the satisfaction of being part of the team that helped launch a pioneer journey. Also, I must take back to London with me a film—we must shoot it over the next two weeks, and must pass through Resolute without delay. What we needed was someone in Resolute who had our interests at heart; someone who could sort out and pack gear that had been flown there from Eureka; someone who could arrange in advance of our arrival for the hand-over of the dogs and for their transport to the Eskimo settlement at Grise Fjord.

I fell into a fitful sleep, and without anything to eat or drink, set off early on the twenty-eighth. I found the tracks after a long search and came upon the pyramid tent after an hour's run. The wind was still blowing but the blizzard had abated, and all that day and for the next seven days we sledged through mists and fogs. We fumbled our way forward, often without any idea in what direction we were going, for without the sun for a guide in an area where there seemed to be no tide to lift the ice into a ridge along the coast; and in such close proximity to the north magnetic pole that the confused compass needle spun as though trying to escape from its pivot, there was no way of knowing south from north or snow-covered land from snow-covered sea ice until we found ourselves climbing steadily up onto Slime Peninsula. The dogs were so slow now and so weak that they could move the sledges no faster than one mile an hour, and yet the sledges were so light that we could haul them over short distances with one hand. In order to make miles we sledged now on a forced-march routine, traveling for eight hours, resting for four, and sledging on for another eight—on and on until a blizzard struck us on June 3 which did not die out for five days.

For those five days we were pinned. We dared not move for we had no way of knowing if there was ice cover to our south. I spent most of the time recharging the batteries with a hand generator and trying to make contact by radio with Resolute Bay to arrange for an aircraft to supply us with the small reserve of dog food that was held at Resolute. Eventually I managed to get this message out and was told over the radio on the eighth that one of Fred Roots' aircraft would come out to us as soon as the weather improved. Even with the few boxes of dog pemmican this aircraft would bring out there would not be enough food to put the dogs back onto full rations for the final stage of the journey. We had seen no sign of game during the past ten days and could not guarantee that we would be successful in the hunt during the dash to Resolute across breaking ice. One obvious way to make the best use of what dog food was being brought out to us was to send one man and six dogs back to Resolute in the aircraft, if they had space enough, and to spread the food they would have consumed among the remainder of the dogs. There were other advantages in sending a man on to Resolute by aircraft. He could arrange for the quick hand-over of the dogs, pack up and make ready for a quick getaway south to civilization, and coordinate any further air support we might require, while the two men in the field on the final stage of the journey concentrated on filming, as a safeguard against the possibility that I might have to pay off the expedition's debt in this way. Allan as the cameraman obviously had to stay and I as leader felt it was my responsibility to complete the journey. I felt miserable at having to ask Roger to help us in this manner for very naturally he wanted to complete the journey, having suffered so much to get within striking distance of our goal. But when I did put the proposal to him, he flatly refused to go. The aircraft landed at 1:15 A.M. on June 9, and as it turned out, there was not enough room on the aircraft anyway, for it was carrying three passengers and some cargo. We had no choice now but to cut the dogs' rations right down and drive them harder than they had ever been driven.

The pilot reported that the ice in Belcher Channel was still holding, but that there were a few long leads penetrating from the west. We sledged for fourteen hours on the tenth and again on the eleventh. Twenty-six seals I saw on that day, and polar-bear tracks crisscrossed the ice like cracks in a shattered pane of glass; but the dilemma now was whether we could afford the time to stalk them, for the pilots who knew this area well were predicting that the ice of the Belcher Channel would go out any day. I shot two seals on the eleventh but the shock of the bullet's impact in both cases was just enough to set them sliding on the slippery ice, and they slithered into the hole before we could get up to them with a harpoon. That night however, while we were eating our evening meal of meat-bar stew, a polar bear came right into the camp after the dogs and there was enough meat on him to give the three teams one good feed.

Whether we would have reached Devon Island without having to kill some of the dogs I cannot say; that one good feed certainly put a few extra miles into those dogs, and over the next five days we made steady progress. By the sixteenth we had reached a small lake on the isthmus between the Grinnell Peninsula and the main body of Devon Island, and there I received the shattering news by radio that the ice of Wellington Channel had gone out and that our route across to Resolute was cut off. We were 143 miles short of our goal after a journey of 1,200 miles. It was heartbreaking, but at least we had the consolation of knowing that the Eskimos in Qanaq would be surprised by the news that we had got so far, and that our failure to complete the journey was not for want of trying.

At that small lake there was a depot of food that had been laid there at my request by Fred Roots' aircraft, an arrangement which I had made by radio from Eureka, but our problem now was to let Resolute know that we wanted an airlift from that point. My radio signals were so weak that it took three full days of battery charging and transmitting before I was able to get a message out, and with time slipping away from me, time I should have been spending at an office desk in London, I was worried. Would there be enough time to raise roughly £50,000, order and ship all the equipment we would need up to the staging depots, arrange to buy and collect a new batch of dogs from Qanaq and fly them over to Alaska and complete all my writing commitments?

On the morning of June 19, Roger told me what for some time I had suspected—that he had no wish to remain with the expedition. He felt he could not afford to jeopardize his career by committing himself to an expedition which he frankly doubted I would get going. Six months was not enough time in which to raise so much money and organize, without a single error, such a complex operation. There were flaws in the plan which, in his opinion, there was not time enough to iron out: The radio transmitters were not powerful enough and without reliable radio transmitters it would be suicidal to set off on such a journey; we had come through the nine-month training program without reaching a definite conclusion on what type of sledge would be best suited to the conditions—indeed, we had not even set foot on the polar pack; the lack of sufficient dog food he felt was irresponsible leadership, and dogs in any case were not necessarily the most efficient form of traction. Roger had often argued the case for man-hauling to the North Pole from Northern Ellesmere Island; he had man-hauled in the Antarctic and across the Greenland ice cap and was of the opinion that a strong man-hauling party would make faster progress across the pack ice; moreover, by taking the shorter route from Ellesmere Island to the North Pole the journey could be made in one season. There was no point in arguing or trying to persuade him to change his mind, for even though all his criticisms could be answered, I could not for one moment consider taking any man on the trans-Arctic journey who lacked complete trust in my judgment and confidence that under my leadership we would succeed. Allan made no comment, but clearly was shaken by Roger's decision, and the two of them went off for a long walk together while I stuck by the radio and tried every half hour to make contact with Resolute.

The aircraft came in that evening to a bumpy landing on the tundra and I flew out with a small amount of gear and eight dogs. There was room for more dogs once they had settled down, but by that time the aircraft was taxiing across the tundra. Within an hour I was in Resolute, and for the next six days slept only in snatches.

What had I learned from this ordeal? I had learned what I had set out to discover—the weaknesses in the equipment, the plan, and in my companions and myself. A short, pleasant journey would have discovered nothing. It had had to be hard; neck or nothing; a gamble where everything was at stake, for if there was a weakness that this training journey was not tough enough to uncover, the trans-Arctic expedition would certainly find it. The journey had convinced Roger that the whole concept of the plan was weak, and its equipment and technique suspect. Equally convinced had I become that the trans-Arctic expedition was feasible, and would succeed provided the party was made up of men who were by temperament relaxed and yet possessed of exceptional resolution, courage, and confidence in each other. We must have so much dog food that they couldn't eat it all; we must leave a trail of dog food all the way across the Arctic Ocean. We must have enough aircraft support so that in spite of feeding the dogs double rations we were traveling light. We must use the Eskimo-type sledge, but they must be made of the finest oak: they must be stronger than the Eskimo sledges but as flexible. We must each have a dog team; there must be reserve sledges on hand at Barrow and Resolute, our two staging depots, that could be flown out to us; reserve tents, sleeping bags, primus stoves, food—re-serves of everything. Each sledge must be a completely self-con-tained unit down to the smallest item of essential gear. We must have lightweight, robust radio sets with power enough for ranges of up to 800 miles. We must have furs, but not caribou; they must be wolf and must be made up for us by the best furrier in Alaska from pelts that had been properly tanned. But most im-portant of all, we must think like Eskimos, move like Eskimos, relax like Eskimos, but drive ourselves with the spirit of white men obsessed by their goal.

For six days I critically examined every piece of gear we had used and every entry in my diary, and for six days tried every possible argument and inducement to get the pilots to make a flight out to pick up Allan, Roger and the rest of the dogs. They were uneasy about a landing at that site after the experience they had in taking me off, but eventually one of them took on the task and collected my companions. There was a flight about to take off for Allan's summer camp on Devon Island, and time only for him to have a quick shower and a change of clothes before he was bundled aboard. He had had six days in which to think over what Roger had said and to decide for himself whether or not he would stick with me. I knew, and I guess he knew too, that if he joined Roger and backed out, the trans-Arctic expedition would fold up; for it would be impossible for me to convince my com-mittee, sponsors, and many supporters that the plan was still vi-able, and that I as the leader was competent, if two of my chosen companions, after a nine-month trial in the Arctic, had lost con-fidence in my leadership and in the feasibility of the plan. He, like me, had had six days in which to assess postoperatively what had been the hardest journey any of us had ever made; but it would have been impossible for him not to be influenced to some degree by Roger's feelings, for Roger and he were very close friends.

He was about to board the plane now. I had not had an opportunity to talk to him, no chance to put my point of view, during the whole nine months we had been together; I had only twice had a chance to talk to him in private and on neither occasion had we talked seriously of the doubts which I secretly harbored. I caught his eye. There were men all around us and the propellers of the aircraft were thrashing the air; he had just shaken hands with Roger; I could not speak. He shook hands with me and said only, "I'll see you in London in September."

5

Moment of Decision

WEARING a sun-bleached beard which I had had no time to trim, a pair of khaki slacks and an anorak, I arrived at London Airport on June 30, 1967, suntanned and more fit than I had felt for years.

After a long private interview by three representatives of the *Sunday Times,* a half-page spread which presented my plan appeared on July 9 under the title "The Longest, Loneliest Walk in the World." The *Times* followed this up on Monday with a front-page article.

Eleven days later, well-scrubbed and more neatly dressed, I reported to the committee of management at a meeting held in Sir Vivian Fuchs' office. The usefulness of the Greenland training program I assessed in terms of the lesson learned, and listed the items of gear which would have to be modified or replaced.

"All right, Wally—now what's this about Tufft resigning?" Briefly I explained Roger's views.

"And what about Gill and Koerner; are they likely to back out too? Have you been given their assurance that they are still keen to go?" They could see from my hesitation that I was embarrassed by these questions.

"You had better send them a telegram right away and get a firm commitment; we can't announce the names of the party until we have their replies. Now then, finance. . . ."

The bankers were worried men: although literary contracts could be expected to yield £48,000, £7,000 of the £8,000 received to date had already been spent. I needed an imprest account, an office, a secretary, a car, and an interest-free bridging loan of £50,000; but the financial climate in Britain at that time was not very healthy. The banks were being squeezed hard and the rich were surrounded by private armies with instructions to keep at bay all beggars with bright ideas. Nor, the chairman explained, could there be any question of seeking royal patronage until the financial situation of the expedition became a little clearer.

To add to our problems, we were informed by the Royal Geographical Society that their support of the expedition covered only the Greenland training program, and that I would have to submit yet another proposal and present myself again for questioning.

The proposed journey across the Arctic Ocean was regarded by our sponsors as a fine feat but a financial gamble; it was regarded by me as a journey that could not be launched if there was any hesitation or delay in ordering equipment, any penny-pinching, or any relaxation on my part. I considered that the function of the Committee was to guide, counsel, encourage, and temper my enthusiasm; to use their far-ranging influence in the City to ease my work load, and to check at our fortnightly meetings the progress of a project which I had been planning for four years on my own, and was now erecting on the foundation of their wide and varied experience.

During the nine months I had been away in Greenland, Squadron Leader Freddie Church of the Royal Air Force had attended several meetings of the Committee as an adviser on radio communications. I had first met him at the Ministry of Technology. I remember very well the first words exchanged between us: he had sat listening intently as I expounded my plan to a small gath-

ering of technical experts in a room full of gray filing cabinets
and inexpensive furniture. Even before I had finished he had
expressed himself keen to join in the expedition. "You're too
bloody old," I had said jokingly, giving it no more thought. Evidently Freddie did not share my view, and in preparing his brilliant communications plan had in effect written himself into the
scheme as a radio-relay operator who would be stationed initially
at Barrow, Alaska, the starting point of the crossing; then transfer
his equipment at the appropriate stage to the American scientific
drifting station T-3 on the Arctic Ocean, and finally to Spitsbergen keeping at all times within 500 miles of the crossing party.

Freddie was duly seconded to the expedition for its duration
by the Ministry of Defence, and a man more devoted to his job
or more loyal to his colleagues I have never met. For sixteen
months he was the expedition's link with the outside world—our
friend, agent, adviser, secretary, and keenest supporter. He was
to become the most respected man in Barrow, and his voice as
familiar to me as the Redifon man-pack radio set which I tuned
up every night. His calm assurance and diplomacy were responsible for American and Canadian friends never losing faith that the
expedition would ultimately succeed, despite the many setbacks
we faced during the crossing of the Arctic Ocean. But by the end
of July the radio equipment, like practically all the other gear we
would require during the crossing, had still to be bought or borrowed, and Freddie's task like mine was office-bound and hectic.

To the telegram I sent Allan and Fritz on Devon Island, I
received a short reply on July 12:

> . . . I WILL COME. NO CONTACT YET WITH FRITZ WILL GIVE
> YOU HIS ANSWER SOONEST.
>
> ALLAN

Fritz's reply, which was also in the affirmative, came through a
few days later, but it was not until August 18 when I received a
letter from Fritz that I had any hint of the anguish he and his
wife had suffered as a result of that telegram:

. . . Firstly, Anne is expecting a baby in late January. This means I must be with her into early February. I cannot budge on this as you will appreciate—I am already frowned on by everyone for leaving her at all!

Secondly, I must have a *written* agreement on pay, as Anna will be unable to work with one helpless child to care for. . . . Thirdly, how much money can the expedition fund spare for scientific equipment? I can buy it here or perhaps it can be "borrowed" in U.K. The programs depend on our schedule, *i.e.,* how long we wait in summer and winter. We must do some science. Your last trip was obviously enjoyable but left many shaking heads. The opinion was generally "well done, but what for?" In addition to this there was a strong feeling that you had begged and borrowed too much. People had the idea that you had pots of money for the main expedition but would not use it in Canada where you could rely on generous assistance. . . .

I am very disappointed Roger is not coming and worried about his reasons. I have gathered them in conversation with Allan and in a letter from Roger. He is not trying to sink you, by the way, but at last returning a letter he owed me. I respect Roger's opinions on Polar matters more than anyone's and his remarks on dog food and sledges are strong ones. Allan, I think, agrees with a lot of Roger's points and remember, they are both intelligent, experienced men who greatly enjoy sledging for its own sake and not for any kudos arising out of it. I would hate to break my career at this point and leave Anna at a crucial time to find myself sat amidst a litter of broken runners and bridges and only the nearby coast of Alaska as relief. It is beyond the capabilities of one man to organize everything and I would have liked to see Roger coming with us and in charge *carte blanche* of the sledge/dog side of affairs.

Sorry to continue in this vein, but I simply cannot abandon my work here and, more important, leave Anna on her own with a young baby and no freedom to leave it even for a few hours without calling for assistance, unless I know I am going on a trip that is worth doing and stands a reasonable chance of success.

At the time Fritz had received my message (or rather, part of it) he had been with Anna in a small snowed-in hut on the Devon Island ice cap, and Allan was in a small hut at sea level on the north coast of the island. For several days Allan had been unable to make radio contact with Fritz, but as usual at sked time Fritz had switched on the set. Through the static he could barely make out what Allan was saying. It sounded like:

". . . are you still interested? Roger isn't coming. . . ." What could have gone wrong? Was Allan going? Why was I asking him?

It was a traumatic decision Fritz had to make the next day, for after discussing it for hours with Anna before the sked, he had, in spite of Anna's encouragement, still not made up his mind what answer he would give when he switched on the radio; and Anna, now emotionally exhausted, had fallen silent. It was a decision he was to be called upon many times to justify over the next few months both to his closest friends and to newspapermen who wanted a "human story."

But Fritz not only was openly criticized for proposing to leave Anna and the baby, he was cold-shouldered by many of his scientific colleagues, who regarded as irresponsible his decision to abandon his career and join a crazy, useless adventure.

The fact of the matter was that, far from abandoning his career or joining a useless adventure, Fritz was proposing to conduct a very full and valuable scientific progam. Had his critics nursed a less hostile attitude toward the so-called adventure (sharing the strong, almost pathological antipathy toward the trans-Arctic expedition which we were to notice in England, too, among a certain minority group of polar scientists), they might have been surprised. Our contention that a scientist on foot could learn a great deal about the environment was enthusiastically endorsed by every scientist of note and we were warmly encouraged by them. Nevertheless, for a man of Fritz's sensitivity, the attitude of his colleagues at the Institute of Polar Studies was upsetting, and from London I could do little or nothing to support him.

Fritz and Anna had arrived back in Columbus, Ohio, about

August 7, and over the next few months, while I was in London trying frantically to organize an expedition, he was equally busy at the Institute, writing up the field data he had gathered during his previous summer season in the Antarctic with the U.S. Antarctic Research Program's operation at the southern Pole of Inaccessibility, and during his last northern summer on Devon Island. We corresponded frequently; it was his firm intention to take full advantage of the unique opportunity the expedition offered to conduct a scientific program, and he was encouraged to this end by the trustees of the Leverhulme Trust in England, who made a generous grant of £6,000 toward the cost of his apparatus and officially appointed him a Research Fellow. For taking measurements of pack-ice thickness, snow depth and density, and the height and frequency of pressure ridges he would require very little equipment; but for the heat-balance studies he hoped to make in the summer and winter he needed sensitive totalizing anemometers; thermistors and thermistormeters; solarimeters; psychrometers; a radiometer, several low-temperature thermometers, and a gasoline-driven generator.

One of Allan's projects during the journey was to be filming; and the BBC, which at first had withdrawn its offer to cover the trans-Arctic journey, had a change of heart and asked me to get him back from the Arctic as soon as possible so that he could take a short crash course in cinematography at the Royal College of Art in London. During the winter on the Arctic Ocean, as we drifted, he would conduct a geophysical program of ocean-depth soundings, magnetics observations, and gravity recordings. The ice drift would be logged by taking observations of the stars with a theodolite.

My responsibilities during the journey, apart from those of leader, would be principally radio communication and navigation, although it was becoming increasingly evident that I would be obliged to do a great deal of writing during the summer and winter drift periods. I was to complete a book on the expedition one month after returning to London, as well as articles for American and British magazines. Personally I might have preferred taking a ghost writer as the fourth member of the crossing party, but it was the consensus of opinion in committee on July 31 that we should try to find a doctor.

Major General John Douglas of the Royal Army Medical Corps told me that the RAMC was short of doctors; indeed, they had only two that might care to consider joining the Expedition, one a gynecologist, the other a captain in the Special Air Service. The latter (since his qualifications were more appropriate) was phoned by the general, who asked if he was interested. Captain Hedges said he would consider it. I later learned that once he put the receiver down, he called in his sergeant and asked what he knew about the Arctic Ocean. His sergeant remembered an article on the subject in the *Sunday Times,* retrieved the paper from the trash, and they read it with interest.

Ken Hedges, a granite-jawed, soft-spoken man, was a few months younger than I. Born in January, 1935, he had spent his early childhood in the Fiji Islands where his father was a government architect. At the age of fifteen he entered HMS *Worcester,* the Imperial Nautical Thames Training College. He served a short period at sea on the Far East run to Japan, but a spell in the hospital after a serious traffic accident had developed his interest in medicine. Soon after qualifying as a doctor, he joined the RAMC. The last three years he had spent as regimental medical officer of the Twenty-second Special Air Service Regiment.

Ken Hedges was an outdoors man. He had been a sailing instructor at a YMCA summer camp in Massachusetts, an instructor at the Outward Bound sea school at Aberdovey in Wales, and an instructor of the Duke of Edinburgh's Award Scheme. He was a military parachutist, a frogman, had seen active service, and was among the last half remaining of the forty or so applicants who had responded to a newspaper article about the expedition, headed: EXPLORER WANTED.

Naturally enough, every one of those twenty men believed he was capable of a 3,800-mile journey across the top of the world, but few of them had the right background. I had upgraded Ken for his obvious qualities as a good officer, his courteous and pleasant manner, and his enthusiasm, and had been advised to mark a few extra points in his favor because of his medical qualification. I did not consider it essential to have a doctor in the party. Very few small expeditions, isolated communities, or scientific outposts in the polar regions have a doctor; indeed, providing there is more than one man who understands first aid and the party is in radio communication with the outside world, it is often advantageous to be without a doctor, for a qualified medical practitioner without patients is a frustrated man.

The choice as it turned out was a very close thing, for among the final four interviewed by the subcommittee was Geoff Renner, a geophysicist who had a similar background to Allan, Fritz and me. He, like the three of us, had spent two and a half years at Hope Bay in the Antarctic and had dog-sledged many thousands of miles, but was at that time still writing up the results of his Antarctic work. Ken on the other hand could be released from the Army on paid leave almost immediately, but sixteen months would be a long time to be cut off from his normal society. The environment and its hazards would be a totally new experience for him. He would be under far greater stress than the rest of us. He would need to learn everything—a whole new way of life. But then, I had been in that position myself twelve years before, when at the tender age of twenty-one, I had gone on my first Antarctic expedition; Fritz and Allan had gone through it too; so had every other explorer who had been to the polar regions. In my experience, if a man is going to settle in at all, he slips naturally into the way of life and the work of a polar expedition within a couple of weeks. If for any reason he does not instinctively take to it, no amount of instruction or encouragement will help him see the environment or the objectives of the expedition through the eyes of his companions, and the best one can hope for in such a case is that his pride will help him stick it out and that out of a sense of self-preservation he will become a competent sledger. At most scientific outposts, a man who discovers he does not like the isolation can be airlifted out; on the larger polar expeditions, he has a wider choice of companions; but on a journey such as the one we were contemplating, there could be no let-out unless the relationship between the men degenerated to the point where life was in danger. It was therefore vitally important that the choice was right.

Geoff Renner was my instinctive choice, but it was extremely doubtful that the British Antarctic Survey would release him until his reports were completed, and it was politic not to press them for they had already offered to handle the affairs of the expedition from their office during the period we were on the ice. That left Ken well clear of the field, for his qualifications far outshone the remainder of his rivals. The following day over the phone I broke the news to him.

Meanwhile, I had other crises. The lowest ebb was reached on September 6, when it was tentatively suggested that it might be safer to postpone the expedition for a year while its finances were put on firmer footing; for no foundation could be found willing to underwrite the expedition and it was the general feeling of Barclays, the expedition's bankers, that it would be unreasonable for them to carry all the risk at that stage. The following day an emergency meeting of the committee was called: we had three months left in which to come up with £ 50,000.

Two hours before the meeting, however, I was called by Mr. Pirie-Gordon, the expedition's honorary treasurer, to a consultation with his banking colleagues at Glyn Mills Bank in Whitehall. He asked several searching questions, then announced that Glyn Mills Bank was prepared to advance up to £ 15,000 provided the expedition's bankers matched this with at least another £ 15,000. The expedition at that point in time was born. Four days later we received a letter from Buckingham Palace informing us that His Royal Highness the Duke of Edinburgh had graciously consented to be our patron. On September 18 I presented my strongest case to the RGS Expedition Committee, and was informed within minutes of the meeting's close that, subject to the approval of the council, the expedition had now the full support of the society.

Now, for the first time in four years, it seemed likely that the expedition might get off the ground financially. The more I considered the financing of this expedition, the more I came to regard our sponsors as friends. We had also of course our fair share of detractors and critics.

We had opposition of a more positive nature, too. We had heard rumor that an Australian, Mr. David Humphreys, was in New York organizing a joint American-Canadian Expedition which would set out with dog teams by the shortest axis to attempt the first surface crossing of the Arctic Ocean from Spitsbergen via the Pole to Ellesmere Island. Bjørn Staib was rumored to be planning another attempt at the Pole; so too was Ralph Plaisted, the latter once again with motorized sledges. There was also a German, whose name we never did learn, who we heard was having a running battle with the Danish authorities to set off from a base in Peary Land (north Greenland) in an attempt to reach the Pole with snow-tracked vehicles. We took few of these reports seriously, for we were far too involved in our own affairs and in ordering equipment to waste any time corresponding with our competitors.

In order to simplify the massive task of equipping and victualing the expedition we concentrated our orders in batches. All foodstuffs were handled by the ships' victualers, Andrew Lusk Limited, and both our sledging rations and our winter supply, which was far more varied and bulky, were based on the diet of the British Antarctic expeditions—a diet familiar to Fritz, Allan and me. The clothing (including that supplied by the International Wool Secretariat) and general camping equipment were handled by Graham Tiso of Edinburgh. The dog food—a concentrate of whale meat, dried yeast, skimmed milk powder, precooked maize starch, beef dripping, and various vitamins—was specially prepared and packed by Bob Martins Limited: 33,000 pounds of it, at a cost of just under £5,500. Four modified Eskimo-type sledges and four wider, heavier, and much stronger sledges based on the Nansen design were built by Skeemaster Limited of Great Yarmouth. Special sledge boxes were constructed, dog harnesses made up, medical gear selected and packed; cameras, film, tape recorders . . . the telephone was seldom in its cradle. There were crises all the time; deadlines to be met. The responsibility weighed heavily on Frankie Ryan and me, for we knew that, once on the Arctic Ocean, any item of equipment that had been forgotten would have to be improvised; and in spite of many long lists we were sure that something was overlooked (as indeed proved to be the case—we had neglected to take along a soldering iron).

Allan Gill arrived in London direct from the Canadian Arctic and started his course at the Royal College of Art. I flew off to Edmonton, Alberta, to talk with two commercial-charter air companies about the expedition's air-support requirements and to meet, in Ottawa, General John Allard, Chief of Defense Staff, and to enlist the support of the Canadian Forces.

Which part of my letter of September 25, 1967, to Sir Michael Cary (Permanent Under-Secretary for the Royal Navy) carried weight, I cannot say. I marshaled many arguments why the Royal Navy should participate in the enterprise, pointing out that Spitsbergen was a theater of operation in which the Royal Navy had for two centuries excelled:

> It was from Spitsbergen that Captain the Hon. Constantine Phipps in 1773 made his attempt at the North Pole, a voyage on which there was among the young gentlemen of the quarterdeck a Midshipman Horatio Nelson. It was from Spitsbergen that Edward Parry made his attempt at the North Pole in 1827, setting a record farthest north for the Royal Navy that stood for fifty years. Spitsbergen was the traditional British route to the Pole and it is therefore only right and proper that it should be a Royal Navy vessel that supports this expedition on its approach to Spitsbergen.

The Royal Air Force was already represented on the expedition by Squadron Leader Church, who, in addition to manning a relay station and passing the expedition's weather and general traffic, was to conduct a program of research for the Royal Air-

craft Establishment into extreme low-frequency radio propagation. Redifon and the Signals Research and Development Establishment were providing the radios. The Royal Aircraft Establishment's experimental radio station at Cove was to act as base radio
station in the United Kingdom. The Army was represented on the
expedition by Captain Ken Hedges, RAMC. The Royal Air Force
solved the biggest of our current problems—how to get all our
gear to the two Arctic staging depots. Two flights were to be made
by an RAF Hercules. The first, on December 28, would leave
from the RAF base at Lyneham and fly direct to Resolute Bay;
the second, on January 6, 1968, would fly with Squadron Leader
Church and the remainder of the equipment to Thule, where it
would collect Allan, Ken, and forty dogs and continue to Barrow,
Alaska.

Perhaps the most emotional crisis in which I was involved was
that which developed between the committee and Fritz just three
months before the expedition was due to set out from Barrow.
Anna still had not had her baby and Fritz did not want to leave
before he became a father and was quite sure that Anna was comfortable and well-provided for. When pressed hard for a date, I
said "sometime between the middle and the end of January." The
committee expressed alarm and reminded me that they had bent
over backward to meet Fritz's wishes regarding salary and marriage allowance, and they were adamant that Fritz should join us
in Barrow on January 1. They felt that the start of the expedition
would be seriously affected unless he had undergone with us the
period of acclimatization and training.

I was in this case the buffer between two irreconcilable points
of view: on the one hand, the older generation, most of whom had
seen wartime service and accepted as nomal the separation of
husband and wife when duty called; and on the other, the under-
standable concern of a young husband torn between his ambition
to make one last pioneer journey and anxiety for his wife. The
press was scarcely more sympathetic; hardly a day passed without
some unpleasant remark. For my own part, I admired Fritz for

his stand; surely, I thought, it was up to me as leader to decide whether or not we could risk the delay. I waited for him to come over to London with Anna as planned and talk it out.

He and Anna were due to arrive at Gatwick airport on November 18, and Allan, Ken, and I had driven out through the fog to meet them. Peter Dunn and Frank Hermann of the *Sunday Times*, who had been assigned to cover the expedition's departure from Barrow, were there too. In the airport cafeteria, Peter showed me the draft of an article he was preparing for the following day. The story was good newspaper material: Four men who were proposing to make the last great journey on earth meet for the first time as a group—three of them very different in background from the officers of Scott's last Antarctic expedition of 1911. There is Fritz Koerner, the athletic, fair-skinned son of a dockyard electrician—a scientist with a Portsmouth accent and a PhD from the London School of Economics, who had joined the brain-drain to the United States because the science of glaciology is poorly financed in Britain, and who is now, at thirty-five years of age, Assistant Professor of Glaciology at Ohio State University. There is Allan Gill, at thirty-seven the oldest member of the party. Son of a joiner, he holds no certificates of education, but is better read than his three companions. He speaks with a Yorkshire dialect, owns only one pair of slacks, four shirts, seven changes of underclothing, an old jacket, five pairs of socks and a pair of shoes; he has no time for social snobs, newspapermen, or any job which keeps him office-bound for more than one week in thirty. There's the leader of the expedition—last in line of a family with a military history dating back over six hundred years, who at thirty-three years of age has, like Gill, no paper qualifications. And Ken Hedges, the only one of the four who would have felt comfortable at a wardroom table in 1911—for Hedges is the only officer and Christian in the group. He believes there is a lot at stake, and that Christians ought to jump at opportunities to join expeditions such as this. For Gill, the proposed journey is a private adventure—a chance of a lifetime to drive dogs across an ocean on which he has already spent three winters; for Koerner, the last physical fling and an opportunity to do some valuable work; for Herbert, the culmination of an ambition toward which his whole career has been steered.

The aircraft arrived on time. We posed for pictures which appeared in the newspapers, and on Monday the twentieth I met the chairman of our committee in Sir Vivian Fuchs' office to talk over the problem of Fritz in private, before Fritz and Anna joined us, and a compromise was reached.

Fritz would join the party in Barrow four days after the birth of the child; if, however, on February first the child was still in the womb, the birth would be induced; at all events, Fritz was to join us by February 10 at the latest. The suggestion that the birth should be induced was Anna's: poor Anna, she was obviously embarrassed that she was causing us so much anxiety.

"You know what," I said after the meeting, "if we worry much more about this baby, it's going to stay right where it is."

For a moment I thought the comment had gone unnoticed; then Fritz shot Anna a flicker of a smile:

"Doesn't look as though the poor little creature will be given the choice."

The following day, with Allan dressed in one of my suits, and Ken and Fritz and Squadron Leader Freddy Church all looking very smart, we drove with Sir Miles Clifford to Buckingham Palace to meet our patron, His Royal Highness Prince Philip. It was a breezy, informal, stand-up meeting—all over in ten minutes, but his good wishes and our memory of that occasion we were to carry many thousands of miles.

Ken and Allan left for Point Barrow on December 12. I arranged to join them early in January. Seventy thousand pounds of food, fuel and equipment was assembled, sorted and packed in Britain and airlifted to Resolute Bay in the Canadian Arctic and to Point Barrow, Alaska, by crews of the Tactical Hercules Force of the Royal Air Force, Lyneham. The forty Greenland huskies had been purchased on behalf of the expedition by Inspector Orla Sandborg over a period of several weeks from the many isolated Eskimo villages which are in his care and jurisdiction in the

Thule District of northwest Greenland, and these were collected by Allan and Ken over the Christmas period of 1967.

In company with a few Eskimos, Allan and Ken had driven the dogs seventy miles in total darkness from Qanaq to the U.S. Air Force base at Thule, to a rendezvous with a Royal Air Force Hercules on January 6. It had been for Ken his first sledging journey—a tough initiation for the medical officer of our party, who, as a doctor with the British Army Special Air Service, had spent most of his time in the jungle and hot deserts. For Allan, of course, that winter journey was nothing unusual; he was an old hand at the business and knew by sight and name most of the regulars who spent time in the Arctic outposts. The air transportation of the dogs to Barrow via Resolute Bay had therefore gone without a hitch, and the Royal Air Force Hercules had been met at the airstrip by several of Allan's Eskimo friends.

I read about their arrival in Barrow in *The Times* on the morning of January 10, 1968, while the aircraft in which I was about to take off for New York was taxiing along the slush-covered tarmac of Heathrow. I read with interest Peter Dunn's report that:

> . . . usually at this time of the year, when temperatures are well into the minus 40's, the moving pack ice at sea brushes elbows with ice locked to the land, forming a hazardous though passable bridge to the ice cap beyond. But unusually mild conditions have tilted the Arctic's erratic weather balance against the four men who are to walk 3,800 miles across the Arctic Ocean to Spitzbergen.
>
> An Eskimo hunter, reviewing the situation with Allan Gill and Ken Hedges, the first two members of the expedition to arrive here, thought last night that they might have to trek fifty miles east along the beach-level coast before reaching a suitable stepping-off point. . . .

I read also (in another part of the same newspaper) that last night I had been

> packing hectic last-minute suitcases, passport, pocket sextant, sea-temperature thermometer and mukluks—the white nylon sheepskin-lined gumboots of the frozen north. More than

70,000 lbs. of equipment, including the sledges, the special lampwick dog harnesses, 6,200 cigarettes, and 60 lbs. of pipe tobacco, have been flown out ahead. Today he will step into his airliner, looking with his dark grey suit, briefcase, and two-toned beard, like an eager young businessman. And he will step out of the world of business and briefcases into the last great adventure, the long lonely trek across the frozen roof of the world.

The chief steward had been equally businesslike and had handed me three telegrams just before takeoff. The first I opened as the aircraft was roaring down the runway—it was from the girl who later became my wife:

I DO NOT KNOW BENEATH WHAT SKY
NOR ON WHAT SEAS SHALL BE THY FATE
I ONLY KNOW IT SHALL BE HIGH
I ONLY KNOW IT SHALL BE GREAT
MARIE

I had only one important call to make on my way to Barrow. In Ottawa I had to work out details of the support arrangements that were to be provided by the Canadian Forces. It was a very relaxed conference attended by about ten staff officers who were clearly as stimulated by the technical problems of the "Exercise" as I was by the physical challenge of the journey. The Canadian Forces agreed to provide five resupply airdrop missions to the crossing party. A communications plan was drawn up between Squadron Leader Freddie Church, RAF, and Air Transport Command which covered every possible eventuality. It was a complex circuit with its point of lowest power in the 15-watt HF/SSB transmitter which I would operate in the field. The radio link between the field party and all other stations in the circuit would be the IKW HF/SSB transmitter operated by Freddy Church, which would be moved from Barrow to the American drifting station T-3 as the crossing party drew out of range. There were to be a total of seven resupply drops; the first two would be carried out by the U.S. Office of Naval Research's Arctic Research Laboratory, Barrow; drops three and four by the Canadian

Armed Forces, also staged through Barrow; drops five, six and seven would be CAF missions staged through Resolute Bay, Northwest Territories. A set of operational orders was drawn up that ran into nine pages and covered every aspect of the Exercise; ninety-nine copies of these orders were distributed, one was put on file.

On January 19, suffering from a hangover, I was driven out to the airport at Fairbanks through an ice fog, clutching four wolf-skin parkas which I had collected from the Martin Victor fur factory. I had changed into warmer and more casual attire in order to be less conspicuous but had evidently been recognized:

"Alaska Airlines announce the departure of their flight to Barrow. Would the leader of the transpolar expedition please board his aircraft now. The best of luck to you, Wally."

At Barrow, I found that our cargo had already been moved from the airstrip to a huge warehouse a short distance from the laboratory, and the dogs to a site nearby—a disused but well-heated hut where we could thaw out and chop up walrus meat, brought by the Eskimos, as food for the dogs.

Over the next few weeks these buildings were to become scenes of great activity. Our massive supply of rations, dog food, equipment and fuel was stacked in four loads and every item checked and rechecked. Our dogs were sorted into four teams of ten, and two tracked vehicles were put at our disposal to enable us to visit them frequently and shift cargoes of seal carcasses and walrus meat out to our satellite station. Our sledges were modified in the carpenter's shop and relashed with the help of the Eskimos.

Our dog harnesses were adjusted and restitched by the Eskimo women, and our fuel decanted into jerry cans. Our radios were checked, tents erected, dog traces made up, and starshots computed to check our nagivational method. We made frequent short trips out onto the sea ice and camped out on a couple of occasions to shake down our equipment and wear the newness of our clothing. We worked at fever pitch to get everything ready; it was a period which, in retrospect, I now regard as the most testing thirty days in my life.

For Fritz and Anna in Columbus, Ohio, it was a period of anxiety and great emotional stress. They were by now frequently pestered by reporters, sick humorists, and cranks who would telephone them at any hour of the day or night. Fritz and Anna were of course disturbed by these phone calls, and I would have been too had I then known about it; all Fritz told me on January 31 over the radio telephone was that he was now the proud father of a baby girl, and that his mother was flying over from England to look after Anna. I sent a message that night by radio to Sir Vivian Fuchs in London:

UNTO US A CHILD IS BORN HALLELUJAH

His reply came back next day:

AS COLD WATER IS TO A THIRSTY SOUL SO IS GOOD NEWS
FROM A FAR COUNTRY.

PROVERBS

With Fritz's arrival at Barrow on February 8, the expedition was complete and all ready to set off, for in Fritz's absence his team of dogs had been worked by Robert Okpeaha, an Eskimo employee of the Arctic Research Laboratory; his sledge was ready and all the gear sorted out. But a start at that time would have been suicidal; during the last two weeks I had made many flights over the Arctic Ocean looking for a route across the fractured young ice that drifts along the desolate north Alaskan coast, and each time I had returned dejected, for what I had seen on those ice-reconnaissance flights was a belt of sea ice far more open and active than I had expected. In the laboratory's ski-equipped Cessna-180, I had flown over wave after wave of pressure ridges, and soared with the engine roaring as narrow leads had opened alarmingly into smoking seas of open water. We had circled and weaved high above sea ice impossible to traverse; ice that was drifting at two knots or more and working itself like slime on a pool into banks and lines of friction. It had been a deeply impressive and sobering sight; a tracery of light and shade, of complex fractures and unhealed wounds from which rose long plumes of gray sea smoke bent by the winds which drove the ice in confusion against the sea currents. The more often I flew, the more hopeless had seemed the prospect of finding a way. There was no alternative but to wait at Barrow for the winds and currents to work in our favor and jam the young ice in the eighty-mile gap between the coast and the polar pack.

On the tenth I wrote in my diary: ". . . read in a Fairbanks newspaper the other day that 'the sun may never rise on the British Trans-Arctic Expedition.' We are sledging off, said the paper, into the 'constant darkness of the Arctic night' where we must endure 'cold and howling winds that can embalm a man in seconds.' The sun rose seventeen days ago! As for the idea of the weather being some kind of spectral undertaker, I cannot but admire the imagery. Sometime during the coming week, I have to reach what will probably be the most important decision of the whole 3,800-mile trek—whether the time and the conditions are right to load our four sledges and head north across that treacherous eighty-mile belt of fractured ice. If the wind blows too hard inshore, it will pile up a chaos of ice walls and rubble that would be impossible to cross; if it blows too hard offshore, the ice will relax and within hours there will be more water than ice between us and the polar pack. We are waiting for the northeasterly winds—we need a wind just gentle enough to tap the ice floes together and form a single skin across which we can make our headlong dash. Or we need several days of calm, cold weather to cover the open leads with a film of new ice. No lodger tiptoeing past his landlady's door on rent day moves more timorously than we will have to do on this sort of ice—we won't have time to wait for it to thicken.

"I am not too worried at present—we have got sixteen months in which to reach Spitsbergen. Must be patient; it is wiser to wait for the harmony between the wind and current. We will pull back the time we are losing here at Barrow; meanwhile we listen to our many advisers—and there's no shortage of them up here. The laundrymen at the ARL don't give us a chance; most of the Eskimos think that if we survive the first three weeks we might go four months before being hauled off the ice. Robert Okpeaha has confidence in us, and he knows a damn sight more than most of the Eskimos in Barrow about the ice out there. He was telling us the other day about an Eskimo hunter from Barrow (many years ago) who traveled alone over the pack ice and discovered a tribe of friendly people. He is said to have brought back proof of his discovery by exposing a whale tattooed on his back. The only indication of the distance he traveled was that he had worn out four pairs of kamiks—that's not so far, in my experience! He probably went across the Chukchi Sea and met a Mongolian tribe. We have been warned about Hell Hole—it's about 200 miles out from Barrow; they reckon there is a hole in the ocean's floor and the whirlpool this creates weakens the ice cover. Then there's the hollow-earth theory of Dr. Raymond Bernard, an American who thinks that flying saucers originate from the earth's interior —a subterranean land with openings at the North and South Poles. Fantastic! And I don't mean the theory; I mean how a man can keep a straight face while propounding such crap?

"It has been difficult during these last few days when small things have gone wrong to think beyond the first week of the journey. I was very sick the other day—probably nervous stress; but I shouldn't really worry; the structure of the journey is there; the airdrops, the radio link, the sledges and equipment have all been checked out. What nags me is that we don't really know how well we will cope with the sheer monotony of the hard and continual physical toil. The horizon each day will look much the same. Hard though the training program was, at least we had some variety in the scenery—more landmarks to look forward to. I have done as well as I can to break the journey up into five separate phases: the first, a hard period of traveling when we must push north with every ounce of energy; the second, a period of rest and recuperation during the summer when the floes are flooded in melt water; the third, a short, strenuous and hazardous period of sledging; then the winter, the fourth phase—a long dark 'static' period when we must become completely absorbed in our scientific program and work fourteen hours a day; then the fifth phase—the dash to Spitsbergen. I have deliberately broken up the diet, so that with each change of phase we have a change of food to look forward to. I have made sure that we would at all times have a sledge each, so that we will meet up with each other only when we meet some obstacle or when we camp at the end of the day. In this way we will look forward to the company of a tent companion. The system I used in the Antarctic was crazy—I am not surprised we used to get irritated sledging with two men to a dog team. Couldn't possibly use that system on such a long journey as this. I have even taken the precaution of arranging for a changeover of tent companions at the end of each twenty-day period, so that we can get to know the workings of each man's mind and avoid the temptation of forming special friendships. There is nothing more I can do except hope that my three companions have got the staying power and the guts. They don't really know what they are letting themselves in for. Fritz and Allan have made long journeys before, but nothing like this. What about Ken?—he has never been on a polar expedition before."

February 20, 1968: "I signaled Bob Murphy with a nod. Our position at that time was about eighty miles ENE of Barrow. He eased the ARL Dakota into a turn. I took one last look to the north. The vast expanse of drifting ice was awesome—limitless. The sky was overcast and its black cloud base lay heavy on the horizon. No mush ice, floes or pressure fields could be seen; but to the south, weak rays of sunlight pierced the clouds and scattered the ice with light. Cracks and open leads caught the sun for a moment, darting around like molten silver before cooling quickly through tones of blue-gray to jet black scars that marked the white skin of the sea. It was a moment of profound relief— the moment of decision; a decision from which there could be no turning back. Tomorrow, four men and four teams of dogs will set out from Point Barrow on a journey of 3,800 route miles across the top of the world."

The date I had originally set for our departure had been February 1, 1968. On that date at the latitude of Barrow there is barely four hours of twilight. We had hoped, by starting early, to get to a position some sixty miles to the east of Barrow, and

Route of British Trans-Arctic Expedition. Drawing by Wally Herbert

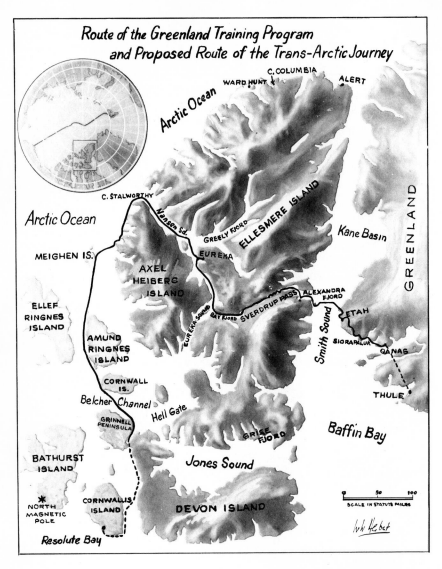

Greenland training program. Inset: proposed route of trans-Arctic journey.

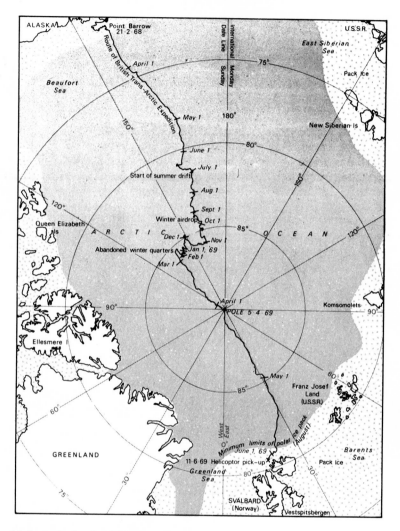

Major episodes in 1968–69 expedition.

Allan Gill and his
dog team on first
pressure ridge.

Wally Herbert,
during melt season.

Allan Gill and
Fritz Koerner,
a few days out.

Negotiating
pressure ridge.

At a line of
sheering—one sledge
has already crossed
the ice rubble.

Breath trails.

Air view of pack
ice off Barrow.

Leads in the pack
force party to
make many detours.

Sledging through
rough pack
(hummocks).

JOURNEY

Hacking through
pressure ridge.

Smashed-up floes,
heavy going.

Open ice conditions,
nearing land.

Wally Herbert with young Eskimo hunter and polar bear he shot at Barrow.

Allan watching narwhales in lead.

Polar bear interrupts
journey—at 15 feet
and still coming . . .

. . . shot. . . .

Dog inspecting
dead polar bear.

Winter airdrop. CAF C-130 Hercules makes low pass at camp.

View from rear cargo hatch as load drops by parachute.

QUARTERS

Airdrop seen from below.

Wally Herbert operating radio in winter quarters.

Fritz Koerner measuring wind and temperature profiles.

Fritz measuring solar radiation.

Intriguing glass spherule, embedded in epoxy, suggests possible lunar origin (see page 318).

Allan Gill operating hand generator (remains of polar bear in foreground).

Ken rescuing dog
from lead.

Allan repairing
broken runner
on sled.

At the North Pole.
Left to right: Wally
Herbert, Roy
Koerner, Allan Gill,
Kenneth Hedges.

Wally, Fritz and Allan—end of journey.

Ken Hedges.

Wally Herbert at end of day.

Loading sledges onto helicopter of HMS *Endurance*.

Camp on Little Blackboard Island on May 29, 1969—landfall was made from this camp next day.

Wally Herbert greets Captain Peter Buchanan of *Endurance* at journey's end.

from there make a dash for the polar pack eighty miles to the north the moment the ice ceased working. This moment we had hoped would come about forty-eight hours after a storm had died, leaving us two or three days at the very most to reach the relative safety of the thicker floes. We expected and were prepared for forced marches in darkness across thin ice and fields of pressure; we were keyed up, tense, and eager to get this dangerous phase of the journey behind us, but totally unprepared for the strain of delays and the irritation of critical comment.

For three weeks we had waited. We had listened to the Eskimos and sought the forecasts of weather experts. We had watched the sun rise higher each day and seen bets changing hands between the cooks and laundrymen in their rare moments of speculation on our prospects of survival. We had become a topic of conversation, most of it prophetic; but had also, during the last few days, been under new and more sinister pressures. Press agencies, puzzled by our delayed departure, were becoming suspicious, and it was evident from the number of radio telephone calls put through to us from London and New York that they had caught scent of a potential disaster and would be satisfied with nothing less.

For four years the expedition had been in the planning; for me, four years of full-time work from the first seed of the idea to the eve of our departure. To the north, not two hundred yards away, was the Arctic Ocean, its surface as unstable and perhaps as unsafe as any comparable area on earth. Our proposed journey along the longest axis would be a pioneer journey, a horizontal Everest that would dig so deeply into our reserves that it would mark each one of us for life. Our beds, most nights, would be on ice no more than two meters thick; ice which might at any time split or start to pressure. There would not be a day during the next sixteen months when the floes over which we were traveling, or sleeping off our fatigue, would not be drifting with the currents or driven by the winds. There would be no end to the movement; no rest, no landfalls, no sense of achievement, no peace of mind, until we reached Spitsbergen.

By midnight on the eve of our departure the pace of preparation had slackened. It was like the eve of a battle—still, clear, cold, silent, with no one sleeping; an atmosphere heavy with private thoughts. Fritz had spoken to Anna on the telephone earlier in the evening and had promised to phone her again the following morning. He was in his room now sorting through his papers and carefully packing his instruments. Ken and Allan were puttering with their gear. A mile away, in Freddie Church's radio shack, I was making my report to Sir Vivian Fuchs, who throughout the long preparations had been one of my strongest supporters. I was speaking to him in his London office through the expedition's United Kingdom radio headquarters at the Royal Aircraft Establishment experimental station; it was ten days short of ten years since the snow cats of the Commonwealth Trans-Antarctic Expedition, of which he was the leader, had rumbled into Scott Base at the end of their epic journey. I believe he noticed the excitement in my voice, for he, perhaps better than anyone, knew with what feelings we were struggling during those last quiet hours before dawn.

I had been through "last quiet hours" so often before during my long polar career, but somehow this was different. Alone in the warehouse, loading the sledge, I found myself thinking of the struggles and hard times of the past few years, the crises, the frustrations; and how, but for the faith of my parents and a few close friends and the encouragement of my committee and colleagues, the dream with which I had lived could never have become a reality. The expedition for me was already half over; for Allan, Fritz, and Ken, it was about to begin.

6

Across the Top of the World

I UNLATCHED the huge doors of the warehouse and spread them open. The night was almost over. It was calm, clear, and very cold. The sledge moved over the floor on rollers, bit the snow and slid forward, out into a deserted street smoke-gray in seeping twilight. I left it facing northeast at the end of two rows of day-bleached lights that pointed a perspective arrow southwest down the main street. There was not a breath of wind to dissipate the plumes of vapor that hung over each boxlike building; the camp was still and sleeping—the only sound the throbbing of warmth within each man-made shelter.

I shuffled up the street to the mess hall, where I met Freddie Church and the others. We ate breakfast leisurely, smoked and chatted for a while, then got up and left to make our round of farewells. Max Brewer and his staff were deeply moved.

By way of warehouse No. 37, we drove for the last time out to the hut we called the dog house in a snow-tracked vehicle with the four loaded sledges in tow. Already we could see a sprinkling of folk waiting at the dog house to see us off; these were the hardy ones who had walked the three miles from the laboratory. The majority, we knew, would be waiting at the rocket-launching site about a mile to our northeast. Whispering, those who stood around watched us hitch up the dogs and make our last-minute adjustments to the sledge loads. We took up positions in line ahead for the first stage of the journey—the one-mile run across the wind-chiselled snow cover of a frozen lake to the rocket-launching site—and set off. There was hardly time enough to feel any sensation other than that of a pounding sledge, and in no more than ten minutes we had drawn alongside a sizable crowd of well-wishers who had come out from the laboratory and the Eskimo village in relays of truck loads and private vehicles.

They were a motley collection, perhaps two hundred in all. Most of them were in khaki parkas with enormous fur hoods. Some had their hands in their pockets, others were gently pumping their arms to keep themselves warm. A mist of breath-vapor hung like a low ceiling over the whole gathering of curious spectators standing, it seemed, a respectable distance from a funeral cortege of four identical coffins.

When we moved away, they were still standing, silently, as they had stood on our arrival. Almost too late, they waved farewell like puppets; then their arms fell as if the strings had been cut, and in a moment they were lost in a pall of vapor created by our teams of dogs. I turned away and looked east. The wind bit into my face. I pulled the hood of the wolfskin parka across my line of vision and huddled deeply into a protective shell of fur.

By sundown we had traveled only five miles and the lights of Barrow were still in sight; but the black moment had passed. Released from all nagging doubts, I feared nothing now.

We headed due east and covered fifteen miles before nightfall on February 22, and sledged five more miles the next morning before turning north into a belt of ice rubble which separated us from a smooth "highway" I had seen on the ice-reconnaissance flights. It was important that we should locate that smooth stretch of ice, for it was the only route by which we could quickly reach a point some sixty miles east of Barrow—the point from which we would make our dash north across the eighty-mile stretch of fractured young ice that bridged the gap between the coast and the polar pack. Along the northeast coast of Alaska at that time of the year there is an apron of sea ice stuck fast to the land. The friction of the drifting ice past this landfast ice churns up the edge into a mush of ice debris that will not bear the weight of a man unless it is compressed or freezes solid. It seldom has a chance to do either, for the winds and currents keep the offshore ice in a state of almost constant movement. At that point sixty miles to the east of Barrow, the mush ice marking the northern edge of the landfast ice was at its narrowest—about half a mile wide. Elsewhere the lines of sheering, where two areas of floating ice had moved or were still moving past each other, were less distinct, for the whole vast skin of ice had been worked over and cracked open so many times that the lines of sheering, and the ridged walls of ice that form when two floes collide, were themselves cut to pieces. The only chance we had of crossing this fracture zone lay at that point where the mush-ice belt was at its narrowest. There was of course no certainty that the route we had chosen would hold together; but the omens were good—it was still calm and the air temperature was steady at minus forty.

Some three hours after turning north into the belt of ice rubble in search of the highway, night closed in on us. We had covered only a mile. No one passed any comment that night on the day's exertions, nor did anyone admit to feeling dispirited when we continued the slow, grueling struggle through to the highway at daybreak on the twenty-fourth; but that first two-mile belt of broken ice under its blanket of deep soft snow had us worried. Our sledges at that time were carrying only eight days' rations; they would seldom be lighter and the dogs never fresher. If so narrow a belt of rubble could cause us so much trouble, how could we possibly maintain an average of eight miles a day for the next sixteen months? True, once on the highway we made good progress eastward for the rest of that day but from what I had seen on the ice-reconnaissance flights, the rough country through which we had just come was more typical of the ice cover than the smooth ice on which we were now skidding east.

By midday on the twenty-fifth, by dead reckoning we had

sledged about sixty miles due east from Barrow. We were looking for a break in the massive 20-foot ice wall to our left when Bob Murphy, one of the Arctic Research Laboratory pilots, glided his Cessna in to a smooth landing on the sea ice, clambered out, and confirmed that we had reached the end of the road and must turn north immediately. He did not stay with us more than a few minutes . . . "you will want to be getting along."

We scrambled up the wall of pressure to get a better view of the ice to our north. The prospect was utterly depressing: As far as the eye could see there was chaos—no way seemed possible except the route by which we had come. It was like a city razed to the ground by a blitz or an act of God, an alabaster city so smashed that no landmarks remained. It was a desolate scene, purified by a covering of snow that had been packed down by the wind; dazzling bright and yet horrifying.

We took up our ice axes and went to work. In two hours we had hacked a bite out of the ice wall and with the debris built ramps up to it on either side. We worked the dogs one team at a time up the ramp and through the gap, three men throwing all their weight behind the sledge while the driver beat the traces with his whip handle and screamed at the dogs. Within three hours of stripping off our fur parkas and attacking the ridge we had got all four teams of dogs and the four sledges over the first of more than 20,000 ridges we were to cross during the next sixteen months. For the rest of that day and all the next we hacked roadways northward through the rubble of ice, across rafted slabs and over massive walls of pressure. On the night of the twenty-fifth we camped uneasily on ice only eighteen inches thick. On the night of the twenty-sixth, our two tents were pitched a hundred yards from a ridge which formed the south wall of a channel choked with pressure-ice debris and huge slime-green blocks of ice. There was no movement, no slush, no signs of water; and bathed in the pale pink glow of sunset, the mush-ice belt—the key we then thought to our chosen route—seemed tranquil enough.

Fritz was more relaxed that evening. His dogs had not been

working well during the last few days. Trained to run in the fan formation with traces of equal length, they had been upset at having now to run either side of a center trace—the method used by the Eskimos in Alaska. Robert Okpeaha, who had been exercising Fritz's team during his absence, had insisted that the center trace method was better, for by this method the dogs would be unable to spread out and snag their traces on the rough ice. Fritz, feeling that it would be impolite to change them back to fan formation until well clear of Barrow and beyond the range of the Cessnas, whose pilots or passengers might take photographs of us from the air, had persevered with the center trace system until that morning, when he had changed over to a modified fan formation where the dogs were on traces of unequal length. From the air, this change of formation would not be too noticeable if the dogs were at rest; and, as expected, the team was much happier. It was a compromise between a system they disliked and the pure fan formation—where they could rub against each other ten dogs abreast, drop back, and push in between any two they chose at any time, to the irritation only of the driver who would eventually have to unplait the traces.

Bob Murphy had in fact flown over us that day with Charles Stewart, the BBC cameraman on board. Whether he had noticed Fritz's change of trace I do not know, but he did mention over the radio that a floating ice island some ten miles in length (which we had first spotted on one of the reconnaissance flights I had made from Barrow) was now only thirty miles to our northeast and drifting at a rate of about three miles a day across our line of march. We were greatly relieved by this news, for that huge tabular iceberg, judging by the height it stood above the surrounding sea ice, might have been at least a hundred feet thick. Such a piece of ice would be an ideal haven for us in a storm. Ice islands are rare in the Arctic Ocean for there are very few glaciers that flow north and project floating tongues or shelves into the sea. The ice island we called "ours," like ice island T-3 on which the Americans have their scientific station, must have come from the Ward Hunt ice shelf north of Ellesmere Island. They were then, and probably still are, the only two ice islands drifting around the Arctic Ocean—an area of five million square miles. Because of the greater draught and the broader face they present above the surface, they respond differently from the floating sea ice to sea currents and winds, and sometimes plow through the sea ice leaving a wake of mush. More usually, however, they are beset by the surrounding floes and if they cannot be boarded from one direction, can be climbed aboard from another. For us that night, camped on a fragile skin of sea ice, the nearness of our ice island was a comforting thought, and the soft, magical beauty of the icescape as delicate as a fading dream.

There was a ball of fire burning its way through the ice on the southwest horizon which cast our shadows like flowing veils across the hummocks we had passed as we returned to camp. I remembered what I had written the first time I had seen such a sight, and imagined Ken must be feeling as I had then, twelve years before, at the other end of the world, and quoted: . . . "a curtain of low cloud drawn slowly across the sky, leaving only a chink of brilliant light along the western seaboard which caught the frayed cloud base in waves of crimson and purple, was reflected in the sea lanes between the ice floes. The faces of the beautiful bergs blushed a delicate pink. Shadows deepened and turned mauve, tarnishing the floes as they crept along like sin in search of a virtue to stain. To the east, night had already settled." Ken laughed. "A bit overdone don't you think—I mean, 'sin in search of a virtue to stain'? I suppose you have to describe things in that sort of way if you write a book."

Fritz and Allan were walking a little ahead of us. I knew them well enough to know that they would not at that moment be talking. I too fell silent. The three of us were here because we loved it—we loved the way of life, the isolation, the simplicity. the silent immensity and soft beauty of a polar setting. Ken was here for the adventure; perhaps in time he too would grow to love the environment.

Bad visibility all day on the twenty-seventh delayed us leaving that camp until midday the following day. After collecting a resupply of food and fuel from a nearby floe where Bob Murphy had landed, we set off eastward along the edge of the mush ice in search of the narrowest part of the belt. We were at that time about seventy-five miles ENE of Point Barrow. Several times we were forced to retrace our steps after long reconnaissance trudges. But except for the loss of one of my dogs (killed by the others in a fight while we were away on one of our many scouting trips), we were well pleased with what small amount of progress we had made along the southern edge of the mush-ice belt by the evening of the twenty-ninth. We seemed now to be in a good position for the crossing—from that point we had only to cross a small hummocked floe to reach the edge of the mush ice. Even the rumblings and groanings of the fifteen-foot wall of pressure ice (across which we had hacked a way a few hours before) drew no more than a few casual comments as we went about the task of pitching our camp.

It was a beautiful evening; a dead calm evening; the temperature was minus forty Fahrenheit. The rattle of pots and pans and the roaring of the primus stoves from the two tents was a soothing sound. Outside, Fritz and I were puttering with our sledges; the dogs were scratching nests for themselves out of the hard-packed snow and circling in a spiral, their noses pursuing their tails as they curled into tired balls and sank. The sun was still catching the tents and tinting the steam which poured from the vents. Fritz crawled through the sleeve entrance into his tent; I could hear him chatting with Allan:

"What's for dinner then?"

"How about meat-bar stew?"

"What's the alternative?"

"Nothing."

"Then I'll have meat-bar stew with nothing to follow."

I stretched out the radio aerial, found a dog in the way, eased him out of his nest with the toe of my boot and detected a growl; then four or five sounds like pistol shots.

"Christ—Fritz! Hey . . . the floe's split!"

It was as though several unseen blades had slashed the ice

straight through the floe in a movement quicker than the eye could catch; six parallel cuts, two on one side, four on the other, leaving the tents on a strip of ice no wider than twenty yards. Within seconds the splits had opened a couple of feet; by the time the others were out of the tents the fractures were over a yard wide and foglike clouds of frost smoke were beginning to rise from the water.

We hurriedly broke camp, but just as we were lashing up the sledges, the narrow strip of ice on which we were standing cracked at right angles to the two parallel leads, reducing the area in which we could maneuver the dogs and sledges to a rectangular pan of ice sixty feet by eighty. There was no escape route east, west, or south, for in those directions the floe had completely shattered. In the fading light the pans of ice appeared to be spreading out and slowly gyrating. Our only chance was the small hummocked floe to our north—a heavy-looking mass of ice with a profile so jagged that we were not too sure we would be able to get onto it. We persuaded the dogs by the whip to leap the first open fracture without difficulty but had trouble getting them over the second, seven-foot gap. Those that hesitated were picked up and thrown bodily into the cold black water and forced to swim across to the other side. The sledges all dipped their rear ends into the sea but by beating the dogs and keeping them moving the sledges rode out. By the time we had pitched camp about a hundred yards onto the floe, the night was pitch dark.

We slept fully clothed and kept watches for the rest of the night, and as dawn approached I ventured from the camp. Not two hundred yards to our north, where earlier that evening I had seen a narrow belt of mush ice, was now a vast area of open water; the compressed ice rubble and fragments of ice we called "brash" had floated off as the two floes had parted and were lost in the great expanse of the sea before me. To our west, about fifty yards from our tent, was a small north-south lead which linked up with the open water to our north and south. A precarious spot it must have looked to Bob Murphy when he flew over us that morning in one of the Arctic Research Laboratory's Cessnas. Several times he had flown over us in the past few days. Occasionally he had offered us advice over the radio on the best route out of some particularly confusing maze of pressure ridges and saved us many hours of hard and fruitless work; but on this day we needed more than a route—we needed some idea of the general nature of the ice cover to our north. What we suspected he later confirmed: We were still about forty miles south of the polar-pack ice edge and the whole area between the coast and the polar pack was breaking up. He passed us another piece of information, but that came as a complete surprise, for we had been unable to get a position fix. In the last forty-eight hours we had been carried by the currents fifteen miles to the west. We broke camp immediately and sledged due east.

By late afternoon we had covered two miles and reached a flat stretch of ice which had, that morning, been projecting like a prominent cape into the sea of open water to our north. The floes that had been on the northern horizon that morning had meanwhile closed in, but they were moving at about three knots and in opposite directions to the floe on which we stood, and at the point of contact a huge ridge of pressure was building. Great slabs of ice were creeping in jerks up the sides of a twenty-foot moving wall from the inside of which came groans and agonized muted screeches. Blocks of ice weighing several tons tumbling from its summit and shaken from its sides fell with roaring dull thuds and the sound of sliding shells as the ridge moved forward over the debris it was spreading. But the rate of movement and the direction seemed fairly constant, and at a point some two hundred yards farther east the wall of pressure that was building was only four or five feet high. It was a tremendous temptation to attempt crossing it while we had a chance, but by then it was dusk and would very soon be pitch dark so we moved two hundred yards south, away from the line of pressuring ice, and camped.

Within half an hour of pitching the two tents we were preparing our evening meal. We could hear no noise of pressuring above the roar of the primus stove, nor at first could we believe Fritz's shout of alarm that the pressure ridge was only thirty yards away and bearing down on us. The tent suddenly had become a tomb and the sleeve entrance our only chance of escape. We grabbed clothing down from the apex and dressed, stuffed our gear into bags, heaved them outside and plunged out after them into the night. Dimly lit by an auroral glow, the advancing pressure looked like an enormous breaking wave. Black sea was welling up at its base as though it was aboil. We could feel dull shocks through the ice as enormous blocks slid forward and thudded onto the floe. The noise was getting louder, the profile of the ridge climbing higher; we could smell the sea. Gear was thrown onto the sledges and lashed in a desperate hurry. The dogs were hitched up and the yelling, cursing procession moved off into the pressure hummocks of the rougher ice to our south.

I saw ahead of me the hurricane lanterns carried on the sledge, three pricks of yellow light bobbing and swinging. I could hear every word crystal clear. Behind me I could sense the nearness of the pressure ridge and hear it chewing up the small patch of smooth ice which had been our campsite. The aurora was brighter now and washing the sky with strokes of light, writhing, convulsing and radiating spears of brilliance. The icescape had taken on a green-gray magical quality, but it faded in time and turned black. *It cannot end like this—it cannot end now,* I thought, *so close to Barrow, so soon after setting out.*

For six hours we struggled, cursing our dogs and working the sledges over obstacles we could no longer see, for the batteries of all the flashlights had by then died of cold and our hurricane lanterns would stay alight only when the sledges were stationary. It was a fruitless effort to put ourselves out of earshot of the pressure. At times we seemed to be surrounded by the noises of grinding ice. Cold and exhausted, we pitched out tents and stood watches. It was dead calm, the sky was clear, the temperature was —41°F.

At the first light of dawn I took my rifle and set off to scout around. To my surprise and relief we did not seem at that time to be in any immediate danger; but Bob Murphy, circling over us in his Cessna a couple of hours later, could see that the floe on which we were camped was splitting and urged us to move in a hurry back along our tracks to a spot not three hundred yards southwest of the pressure ridge from which we had escaped the previous night. The ice to the north of the ridge was still moving west, but at a slower rate. There had also been a change in its appearance. In some places the floes screwing against each other forced hummocks of wet-ice debris high onto the floes' edges; crescent-shaped fractures were appearing and small "calves" off the mother floe were subsiding into the sea and being ground into mush. There was no chance of crossing over onto the northern floe; meanwhile the floe on which we were standing was reducing its size every hour as more and more fractures cut through it.

Bob, who had returned to Barrow to refuel, was out over us again by late afternoon and dropped me a message saying he had found a strip of ice on which he might be able to make a landing and would like to talk to me. It took considerable courage to land on such ice, which might at any time have split, and I drove the dogs over to meet him as quickly as possible without off-loading any of my gear in case I was cut off from the others. They meanwhile went southwest about half a mile in the direction he had indicated was the center of the floe and set up camp. It was nearly half an hour before I reached Bob, who was still sitting in the Cessna with the propeller still turning. I left the dogs about twenty yards away and climbed in beside him. He confessed he was feeling worried. "You probably don't realize it but I can tell you, from up there it looks bad. You've got the night to get through, and there's nothing anyone can do to help. Do you realize you are now only about thirty miles from Barrow? You're drifting fast toward a huge area of open water off the northwest of the Point. If you don't make any progress north over the next few days it will be all over."

I had never seen Bob as worried as this, and the way he shook hands with me and kept promising he would be out over us at the first light next morning profoundly disturbed me. He unloaded a couple of food boxes and some kerosene, and we parted company. I did not tell the others what he had said, and as the mist swirled around us all that night and all the following day we took it in turns to stand watch. As promised, he came out at first light on March 3, but we caught only a fleeting sight of the Cessna as it roared overhead; how he located us was a mystery. The following morning we found a message he had dropped. It was handwritten in capital letters on a couple of sheets of lined notepaper stuffed into a cardboard roll which had a piece of fluorescent bunting attached to it.

WALLY,   3.3.68.

WAS VERY GLAD TO SEE THINGS BETTER THIS MORNING. THE ICE TO THE NORTH IS BROKEN BADLY AND HAS MANY CRACKS AND LEADS RUNNING EAST AND WEST. IF THINGS SETTLE DOWN IT WILL BE SEVERAL DAYS BEFORE YOU CAN MOVE AND IF THIS AREA MOVES SOUTH, WILL CAUSE MANY PRESSURE RIDGES THAT YOU MAY NOT BE ABLE TO CROSS. IF YOU COULD TAKE YOUR SLEDS APART WE COULD MOVE YOU OUT TO AROUND THE ISLAND WITH THE CESSNAS IN ABOUT 4 TO 6 HOURS. THIS WOULD MEAN QUITE A BIT OF WORK TO FIX UP A STRIP WE COULD USE FOR TAKEOFF WITH A LOAD. WHY DON'T YOU GUYS THINK ABOUT THIS FOR A WHILE AND JUST GIVE ME A YES OR NO ANSWER ON THE RADIO. YOU ARE NOW ON THE ONLY SPOT LEFT NORTH OF THE PRESSURE AREA THAT CAUSED YOU THE FIRST TROUBLE AND IF THE ICE NORTH MOVES SOUTH FAST, THIS PLACE MAY GO. LET ME KNOW WHAT YOU THINK AND I WILL TALK TO MAX IF YOU WOULD LIKE TO TRY MOVING WITH THE AIRPLANES.

BOB

Such an operation would have been extremely hazardous, although no doubt less so than extricating ourselves. Those pilots would have done it too had we given them the slightest hint that we were losing our nerve—or beginning to see sense, whichever way you look at it. We passed the note around. Not much was said. We were all agreed that we should go on, and that one of these days, when it was all over, we would meet up with Bob again and have a bloody good laugh about it. Fritz was the one who really summed it up: "Good job we didn't find that note yesterday—we might have been tempted to accept the offer."

On the morning of the fourth, twelve hours after the movement had ceased, we drove our teams northeast and onto the mush ice. It now extended for three miles, a sea of debris and mush knit together by a thin film of ice. All that was needed was a five-knot wind from any direction, or for the big floes on either side to shift a few degrees, and the thin film of ice would have shattered; the whole lot would have relaxed and we would have sunk into it like trucks into quicksand. We spent a few tense hours on that treacherous surface and the sledges, men, and dogs broke through many times. I remember one particular situation when I was out in front and the other three were fully occupied with their own problems; five of my nine dogs started to sink through the ice porridge and in their panic started fighting each other and churning it up; the other four were on more solid ice but not at a good angle to haul the sledge, which then began to sink through the mush at the back. What stopped the sledge from going right down I don't know; perhaps there was a projecting root from one of the nearby blocks of ice on which the sledge was resting below the surface, perhaps it was my own unaided effort; I only now remember thinking, *if it sinks another inch I will lose it.* God knows how I got the dogs out.

Over the next three days we sledged due north and covered, at a guess, about fifteen miles; but it was like being on a treadmill, for the distance we made each day we lost overnight in a drift that was carrying us southwest. They had been three hard, miserable days, and the camp we set up on the seventh we had been obliged to shift in a hurry when the floe split that night. It was the nights we dreaded; those black nights when there was no auroral glow and the torch beam died as we plodded wearily around the camp sniffing the air, listening for the slightest sound, and wondering if, while investigating the floe in one direction, a crack like a black snake might be creeping toward the tents from a different angle.

On the morning of March 8, Allan, Fritz and I made a short

foot reconnaissance but no way could be found, and by that night our position fix showed we had drifted to within only seventeen miles of Point Barrow. Sixteen days we had been fighting the ice and losing; it was heartbreaking and alarming, for we could now smell the sea. The sky to the southwest was black. We knew we must be very close to the vast expanse of open water off the northwest of Point Barrow. By the following morning we could hear waves lapping against the floe and broke camp in a hurry at first light. All that day in desperation we weaved and hacked our way northeast, and camped that night with leads all around us. There was now nothing we could do but reconnoiter and wait. The strain was beginning to tell. We were averaging only four or five hours sleep a night, and our sleep, even with a man on watch, was fitful.

This period was tough on Freddie Church, too, for ever since our first difficult passage he had been maintaining a continual listening watch on the radio and sleeping out at his radio shack, an isolated hut about two miles from the laboratory. I had missed only a couple of skeds (scheduled radio contacts) with him since leaving Barrow. As a rule, he would take my position and sitrep (situation report) as soon as we had established contact, just in case the floe split within seconds of starting the sked; he would then pass me his important traffic, then the weather forecast, and finally wind up with a bit of local news. After we had closed down, he would write up his log, change frequency, and call the Royal Aircraft Establishment's experimental radio station at Cove (near Farnborough in England) and pass on the expedition's traffic. Cove in turn would phone the crossing party's position and sitrep, together with any other urgent message, through to Sir Vivian Fuchs' office; and any messages coming back from Sir Vivian, from my secretary in London, or from our committee would be passed on to me the next day through Freddie. We were kept fairly well informed of what the newspapers were saying, and from time to time Freddie would phone Anna in Columbus to let her know that Fritz was all right.

There was very little local movement on the tenth and eleventh, and with temperatures still in the minus forties, the leads were freezing over. The only movement we ourselves were able to make was a shift of campsite that put us nearer to a half-mile-wide lead that ran east-west across our line of march. On the twelfth I sent out a message via Freddie addressed to the chairman of the London committee, based on information Bob Murphy had given us on his return from a reconnaissance flight.

> This morning we crossed the only big lead within eighty miles of Barrow that was still frozen. We thought we would reach the ice island but were stopped seven miles short as the ice all around us opened up. Tonight we are as usual standing watches and are prepared to move at a moment's notice. But tonight our situation is precarious. The floe on which we are camped has been cut off from the safer ice to our north and with the steady drift set in motion by several days of northeast winds we stand a good chance of being taken for a long and sleepless ride westward.

The lead to our north which separated us from safer-looking ice widened about sundown, and a short walk with Allan and Fritz confirmed that we could not stay at that campsite, for on closer examination of the floe we found several hairlike cracks. The floe might at any time relax and shatter like a pane of glass. We returned to camp, shouted out to Ken that we were going to have to move and started packing up. It was a wise decision as it turned out, for on the way back along our tracks to safer ground we had to cross several fractures that had not been there on our way north. We pitched camp for a second time that night in an area of hummocked old ice, standing watches as usual; and visibility being less than a quarter of a mile the next day and for part of the fourteenth, we had time to rest up and think. My assessment of our situation I sent out over the radio to Freddie in the form of a letter to Dr. Max Brewer:

> At our present rate of progress, it may be several days before we reach safer and presumably faster going. By then we will be over four hundred miles behind our scheduled position and out of phase with the five phases of the expedition. It seems, at its very worst, this slow progress of ours could mean

that we will not reach the right latitude for our summer camp and in consequence drift in an unfavorable direction. We would be thrown even farther out of phase by not making enough northing during the autumn, and this in turn would leave us with such a great distance to cover during the spring of 1969 that we would fail to reach Spitsbergen before the sea ice breaks up. In other words, we could, by cumulative delays, be as much as a full season out of phase and find ourselves in the summer of 1969 drifting on a pan of ice into the Greenland Sea.

There seemed to me to be two solutions: We might, once clear of the fracture zone and on the polar pack, increase our daily mileage by stumbling upon a series of frozen north-south leads; or we might attempt traveling throughout the months of June and July, a period when most polar travelers would prefer to be on dry land. The first of these two solutions would be pure luck, but the second could be prepared for logistically. In the original plan, the Arctic Research Laboratory was to have made the first two resupply drops and the Royal Canadian Air Force the next five. By some adjustment to the dates, but without increasing the number of drops, it would be possible to extend our traveling period. This change of plan was adopted.

Allan, Fritz, and I went off for another long walk on the morning of the fourteenth—Ken having elected to remain at camp in case the floe broke up or a polar bear came on the prowl. It was a convenient arrangement, for neither Allan, Fritz nor I liked staying in camp when there was so much of interest to see and do on a scouting trip. For Ken, on the other hand, it was a good opportunity to catch up on his reading schedule, which had fallen behind over the last few tense days of sledging. He had hoped to set aside a period each day for prayer and the study of the scriptures.

The last hectic days at Barrow and the events of the past three weeks had left little time to get acquainted with Ken on a deeply personal level; I had noticed at Barrow that he would, as often as an opportunity arose, go into Barrow village to share the company of the missionary and his friends, and had guessed then that once on the ice he would miss the company of fellow Christians. How if at all this would affect his relationship with us I could not guess, for I had never (nor for that matter had Allan or Fritz) encountered on a polar expedition a man of such strong religious conviction. Indeed, with the exception of one man, we had never in our collective thirty-four years of polar work met anyone who professed to a faith. We had drawn no conclusions from this, nor did we now do so, but it provoked some thought and discussion between us that day as we picked our way over the jumbled ice.

"Do you think he's wishing he'd never come?" asked Fritz.

"Even if he is I doubt if he'd ever admit it. Too many people are using him as an example—the Army, the Church, his professional colleagues, friends. . . . In any case," I added, "it's a personal challenge he's got to see through."

"I suppose so," said Fritz as he hit the thin ice covering the lead to test its thickness. "I mean, if Allan here decided to jack it in, who'd care? He doesn't know anyone." Allan shrugged but did not take the bait. The conversation petered out and we spread out over the floes, joined up again about a mile further on, and came back together along the edge of a lead.

The fog lifted later in the day and to our amazement we discovered that the floes had tightened up. We made about five miles, mostly to the east, and the next day got some northing in before Bob Murphy found us and landed with some supplies. It was hard to judge how far we traveled after he left us to fly north on an ice reconnaissance, but we found ourselves sledging over some thin ice that afternoon before eventually reaching what looked like either an old piece of polar pack or a piece that had broken off an ice island. We parked ourselves on it for the night and got ourselves our first good night's sleep for eighteen days.

The going was miraculous again on the sixteenth, and apart from a couple of small leads, we had no holdups at all. Our guess at the day's march was fourteen miles and our position fix that evening put us just north of latitude 72°. We were all very tired, but for the second night in succession stood no night watches and slept like babes. We did fifteen more miles on the seventeenth and by setting off early on the eighteenth got in another day's travel. Much of the ice we were crossing was younger than four months; only occasionally did we ride up onto a floe thicker than five feet, but we had evidently got clear of the fracture zone, and were now settling into a new routine of long steady sledging on a course straight up meridian 156°W.

7

The Long Haul

OUR day's toil on March 20 was mostly across thin ice. The next day promised to be as tough. One of our two transmitters was broken. We were four hundred statute miles behind schedule, and 1,170 miles from the North Pole. That day, at the northern axis of the earth, the sun rose for the first time in six months. Each day for the next three months it would be spiraling higher; quickly at first, but slowing down as it approached its highest altitude at the solstice of June 21. It would then start to lose altitude, slowly at first but falling faster as it sank lower in the sky until, at the equinox of September 23, it would set at the North Pole and rise at the South. But not for us the six months' continuous daylight that on March 20, 1968, lit up the North Pole. Even if we were to maintain an average of sixty nautical miles a week in our trudge northward, it would be a few weeks before the sun would remain above our horizon for twenty-four hours a day, and by that time in all probability it would be hidden by fog. Indeed, the only thing we had to look forward to on the evening of March 20 was the prospect next day of crossing the seventy-third parallel, and it was now even beginning to look doubtful if we would reach the Pole before daylight returned on March 20 of the following year.

The shortest possible distance between Point Barrow and Spits-bergen via the North Pole is 1,920 statute miles. The chart showed no features along our chosen route. We could expect to find nothing but ice—floating ice that responds to the winds and currents. Ice that is constantly on the move; five million square miles of it. Not the smooth skin of ice one usually finds in bays, coves and fjords of an indented Arctic coastline, but an irregu-larly broken and ridged skin of ice; an ice cover reduced in the summer by the heat of the sun that circles constantly above the horizon; a monotonous waste of ice. How could we counter the sheer mental drudgery of sledging and drifting across such a god-forsaken desert?

It is a characteristic of the desert traveler that he sets himself imaginary landmarks to take the place of real ones. During our journey from Qanaq to Resolute Bay the previous year we had found no need for such stimuli, for there was enough of interest around us and our targets were real: huts, capes, islands—they were all marked on the map. Had we had no map, or had we been the discoverers of the land through which we were passing, the incentive to push on would have been even greater; I had found this to be so in the Antarctic where I had mapped a total of forty-six thousand square miles of previously unexplored country. But here on the Arctic Ocean we were faced with a problem I had never known on such a scale. It was not enough that I had di-vided the journey into five phases, and arranged for a change of diet and activity. It was not enough that I had reduced the pos-sibility of tension between the men by arranging for each to have his own team of dogs, and writing into the plan a commitment that we would change partners every twenty days. We needed targets. Anything that would break down that enormous distance still further. And the cartographers had provided them, for our chart of the ocean was precisely divided into 360 degrees of longitude with radiating circles of latitude described for each degree.

In time those imaginary lines were to become as real to us as if they had been painted on the ice floes, and the crossing of them more exciting than any round-figure distance from land we calculated we had sledged. We became as impatient on the eve of each new latitude as children on the eve of a birthday—and, like children, dejected the morning after at finding little had changed.

Such was the feeling on the morning of the twenty-second when we woke to find the day overcast and all color drained from the scene. We were fifty-seven nautical miles from our next line of latitude; the sledges were in need of minor repairs, and Fritz, whose hand had been bitten by one of his dogs the night before, was feeling dizzy. In Barrow I had based the size of the teams on the assumption that one dog in ten would either prove incurably neurotic, too old for the journey, or so unpopular that his teammates would kill him at the first opportunity. With patience, a nervous dog can sometimes be reassured, but a dog that bites the hand which feeds it must be shot. Fritz put the biter down that night, and Ken shot the oldest dog in his team the next day. Of the two men Ken seemed the more upset.

We had now lost three dogs since leaving Barrow and dogs of course were the topic of conversation in our camp that night— that is, until the wires connecting the battery to our reserve transmitter snapped off at the socket. We were now without radio—cut off from the outside world. It took Allan the whole of the twenty-fourth to fix it, using a heated clasp-knife as a soldering iron, and for solder what little remained on the pins of the socket. He had performed a similar repair during the Greenland journey which had been equally successful. I joked with him, promising to buy him a new clasp-knife when or if we ever got off the Arctic Ocean. He just shrugged and suggested I have a soldering iron and some solder sent out with the next supply drop.

By the end of March we had had our first change of tent partner, crossed the seventy-fourth parallel, and seemed to have got clear of the last of the dangerous coastal currents; but although we were making better progress, it was not across compacted polar pack as we had expected but mostly extensive areas of young ice. To the surface traveler these areas looked like vast frozen lakes, and the floes like low-lying islands, snow-covered, undulating, and in some places hummocked. The ice of these frozen lakes or polynyas, as they are called, was not dead flat, for along the lines of weakness when pressuring had occurred the young ice had rafted, and slabs of ice four to ten inches thick had formed steps —whole flights of steps laid out horizontally. Nor were these polynyas fast traveling surfaces, for the young ice was salty and the sledges dragged. But there were encouraging signs. Temperatures were still in the minus thirties Fahrenheit and the fractures and leads were healing quickly; old floes were becoming more numerous, and the action of the drifting ice more predictable. We were beginning now to regard as normal situations which three weeks before would have alarmed us: the splitting of floes, the heaving, groaning walls of ice; the sinking feeling of sledging over ice which in the early days of the journey we would have considered too thin to bear the weight of a loaded sledge. "Sea ice is flexible like plastic," we had been told by the Eskimos. We had taken their word for it and ventured out only onto ice that would take three hefty blows of the ice axe—ice about eight inches thick. Now, by holding our breath, we found we could take loaded sledges across ice only four inches thick, which would bend as much as a foot from its normal plane as the sledge, pushing a bow-wave before it, rode the ice like a ship. We now took in our stride pressure ridges that were still working—even the dogs were getting accustomed to scrambling over walls of ice and rubble that was heaving under their feet. The dogs were well fed and very fit; there was power in the teams (the resupply aircraft flying out from Barrow were finding us without difficulty), and we were beginning, consistently, to better our daily target of ten nautical miles a day. In fact, not until April 4 did I record in my log any obstacle to our steady progress toward the Pole of Relative Inaccessibility:

> I got away first and held the lead until noon when I stopped to set up the theodolite. The others drove on. Came up with 74° 45'—only eight miles since yesterday's noon shot. A poor mileage, but I suspect some of the distance we traveled went into westing. No really difficult problems today but the surface

seems to be getting softer. Came upon a lead at 4:30 P.M. that was crossing our line of march; it was running 260° magnetic to our course of 300° magnetic, so we didn't lose much by following it on the south side. Allan wanted to cross it at a point where it was about ten feet wide, but it had a thin elastic cover of ice not much more than two inches thick that wobbled like a jelly when we planted a foot on it. Just couldn't risk a sledge on it, for even though the twelve-foot sledge would have spanned it for a split second, we only needed one sledge to break the skin and the rest of the circus on the south side would have been stuck there until the lead closed.

Saw two-day-old polar-bear tracks this morning. Temperature was minus thirty-one Fahrenheit—wearing nose protectors all day.

The noon fix on the fifth was discouraging. We had made only four miles of northing during the past twenty-four hours, and at camp that evening were still on the south side of the lead, having spent all day following it west in the hope that we would see seals and find a point where the two banks touched, or where the ice cover was thick enough to take the weight of a sledge. The temperature was —35°F most of the day. It was a little warmer on the sixth, in fact a perfect day; but that lead, which at its narrowest point was now sixty feet, just went on and on. We put in another five hours travel the next day and then gave up. We had fallen twenty-three nautical miles behind our weekly target but there was nothing we could do about it. Even the two seals we spotted in the lead that evening seemed to mock us as they poked their slippery heads out of the water.

But evidently we were not the only sledging party on the ice of the Arctic Ocean held up by a lead: I learned that night in a message relayed through Freddie from the Arctic weather station at Mould Bay, NWT, that Ralph Plaisted, who was making his second attempt to take Skidoos across the polar pack to the Pole, had been stopped by open water at latitude 87°N, longitude 75°W, and that it was rumored he was arranging an airlift of his party and equipment over this. Needless to say, the rumor was not taken seriously by us, but it gave us something new to talk about. "Ralph's not that stupid," I said to Allan; we had changed tent partners and he had joined me. "He knows that if he reaches the Pole, his will be the first uncontested claim, and he is not going to throw that away by getting Weldy Phipps to give him a lift across the lead."

"Just depends what the object of his trip is, I suppose," Allan said thoughtfully. "I mean, if he is just doing some sort of publicity stunt for the Bombardier Snowmobile Company, it doesn't much matter if he *is* lifted over a lead, provided he eventually gets the machines to the North Pole. What is it from Ward Hunt to the Pole—seven degrees? Four hundred and twenty nautical miles—say with detours about nine hundred statute route miles? Who would make a fuss about one mile if he had sledged eight hundred and ninety-nine?"

"The same people who are keeping the Cook-Peary controversy alive," I replied. "Remember that telegram we received from the Cook Society just before we left Barrow?—wishing us luck, and saying that they hoped we'd find occasion at or near the North Pole to pause and honor the memory of the intrepid explorer, Dr. Frederick Cook, who was first to reach the Pole. These people won't miss a trick. The Peary supporters are as bad. No, Ralph won't take a lift."

Our position fix that night (April 7) put us at latitude 74° 49′N, longitude 158°45′W—about two hundred and fifty statute miles from Barrow, and one mile south of our position of two nights before. We had been forced some fifteen miles off course to our west by the open lead, and were now in a region where the pack ice was very active. We could not afford delays like this if, by Midsummer's Day, we were to be in the vicinity of the Pole of Relative Inaccessibility, that imaginary point on the Arctic Ocean farthest from land in any direction. It even occurred to us that we might be in the vicinity of Hell Hole, about which the Eskimos in Barrow had warned us. "Maybe their stories are right," Fritz suggested, "and there is at this place a recurring lead directly above some trough in the ocean bed. But then how the devil would they know? None of them has ever been farther onto the pack ice than thirty miles."

Overnight the lead closed to about fifty feet and the thin elastic cover of new ice (nilas) had finger-rafted like a zipper with alternate interlocking thrusts of ice plates from either side. There was still some movement, and, the course being somewhat tortuous, we had a few anxious moments in getting the four teams across; for the technique of maneuvering dogs and sledges in confined spaces or on a sharp zigzag course across fracturing ice was at that time still something of a mystery to us.

Once over this lead, we met no more problems for two days; in fact, not until just before the transit of the sun on the tenth, when I found myself waked out of a very pleasant daydream as my dogs came to a halt at the edge of a vast sea "lake," a polynya covered evenly with a thin mat film of coagulated crystals which gave the surface a soupy appearance—grease ice, the whalers had called it. The polynya appeared to stretch to the horizon east and west. Fritz took over the lead, went west, and about an hour later came upon a floe which at a guess was about a mile in diameter. Like a logjam in a river, this floe would serve as a bridge by which we would get across. It took us over an hour of hard manual labor to engineer a causeway across the touching point onto this floe, for the two floes were not on the same level; but no sooner had we all got safely onto it when the floe gyrated, our causeway collapsed and we found ourselves marooned. We set up camp in the most picturesque spot on the floe and settled ourselves in for another long wait.

I had a successful radio contact that night with the Arctic weather stations at Mould Bay, 730 statute miles away, and with Alert at the northeastern tip of Ellesmere Island, 1,450 miles away. This was very reassuring for Freddie, who had based his communications plan on the assumption that our 15-watt transmitter would be adequate over a range of 500 statute miles. As we moved out of range of Barrow, he had planned to move his station to ice island T-3, which would put him once again within range of the crossing party. It now seemed that Freddie, could, if he wished, stay at Barrow a few more months. He was more use to us there than stuck at T-3, and clearly he would be happier, for he had made many friends in Barrow. That same night I heard from Alert that the Australian, David Humphrey, had changed his plans and was now about to leave by air with light sleds and a few dogs for the North Pole. The message had continued: ". . . as far as we can gather his purpose is to pinpoint the Pole and walk back over the ice. Plaisted is now at 87.8°N and going well. He is using a Collins KWM-2 transceiver and has a VHF beacon. Understand aircraft take photos of ice ahead and drop to him at regular intervals."

We sent both Humphries and Plaisted messages wishing them good luck, and the following morning after a leisurely breakfast set off to scout around. Allan took a movie camera, I took a couple of still cameras, and Fritz a rifle. It was a dead calm, clear day. There had been no movement overnight and the ninety-yard gap between our floe and the floes to the north which the previous day had been loosely packed with ice cakes and brash had now fused together with a thin skin of ice. Picking a way across this ice jam took the three of us a couple of hours. We would no doubt have found a way sooner had the day been overcast or the company been less congenial, but scouting trips like this were a pure delight and too rare to rush. For the first time on the journey the warmth of the sun penetrated our light windproof anoraks and woolen shirts and sweaters. We smoked, chatted, joked and occasionally put a foot through as we covered the ice jam with tracks which found and retreated from one dead end after another. One would never have thought, to have seen us that morning, that we were so far behind schedule: the resolve, the drive, the ambition had evaporated in the warmth of the sun.

We ambled slowly back toward the tents prodding the ice as we went and looking over our shoulders to check which set of footprints we should follow when we brought the dog teams across. What a shambles of ice; it was almost as though someone had dumped five hundred truckloads of alabaster and slates between our floe and the floe to our north: the material for some exotic rock garden which the local authorities had planned, reconsidered, then abandoned. There were flowers growing—iceflower clusters as bristly as cactus, ice leaves and nilas like luxuriant lawns across which our shadows glided like swimmers.

The route we had so carefully chosen we did not take when we returned about an hour later with the dogs and sledges, for the jam of ice blocks had begun to relax and slump; the whole thing was now in motion and we were obliged to cross in a headlong rush, driving the dogs with screams and cracking whips. It was an exciting scramble; tense, dangerous, hot as hell. We were all streaming with sweat by the time the sledges reached the safety of the far bank. We thudded and rattled for a couple of hundred yards across foot-high walls of ice to a safe distance from the now heaving mass of ice—on which, only a couple of hours before, we had been sitting facing the sun, eyes closed, soaking in the tranquility of a perfect polar setting.

We had expected the polar pack to be a thick canopy of giant floes, compacted tightly together, but for the next five days we made steady progress across vast tracts of young gray ice which, judging by its thinness, had formed very recently. Probably as much as seventy percent of the ice cover between latitudes 75° and 77° was less than two feet thick, which at that time of the year, with air temperatures averaging —16° Fahrenheit, would have taken only about two weeks to grow. A good deal of it was less than six inches—which, with temperatures sometimes as low as —42°F, would have formed in only two days. Had we been a week or two earlier in reaching that area we would almost certainly have been stopped by open water—a phenomenal seventy percent of the area, black with exposed sea and overhung by clouds of frost smoke. From the air it must have looked like a gigantic black lake peppered with islands; each island a hummocked floe with clean-cut banks two or three feet high, blueblack in shadow, blue-green in the flood of sunlight. Now it was ice-covered—nowhere was the water visible—and yet six inches beneath our feet was an ocean 3,000 feet deep. It was a fragile, fascinating region through which we were passing. Often we would run onto ice that sagged under the weight of the sledge, or across a clean hairline fracture where the floating ice on each side would move up and down out of phase as first the dogs, then the sledge, transferred weight from one skin of ice to the other. The sledges left inky tracks on this ice which curved in graceful sweeps around floebergs and smaller pieces, or snaked up the center of a long frozen lead behind a team of dogs spread out like a nine-fingered hand that reached for the northern horizon.

We made about seven miles on April 16 before the sun's transit of our meridian. We could get a latitude fix from the sun very easily at that time of the day; all we needed to know was the number of degrees and minutes the sun was north of the Equator at local noon and the amount by which we should correct our theodolite observation of its altitude. I would make my computations on the snow, scratching the figures with the tip of a ski stick in the manner Red Indians planned their ambushes in the mock dust of a Hollywood set. My calculations that day put us at latitude 76° 11.7′; I guessed the longitude at 160°43′W, and as arranged the previous night, switched on the radio at 2:30 P.M.

The resupply aircraft was already on its way out from Barrow, and by 3 P.M. was circling low on the horizon and coming in for its first dropping run. For a second or two we were only a few hundred feet from old friends from the Arctic Research Laboratory. We could see Dick Dickerson at the controls of the Dakota and caught a glimpse of Randy, Frenchy, and Bill Beck as they kicked the boxes out of the door. Two more passes they made of our dropping zone and one low pass of the camp before the roar of the engines died away and we were left once again alone with the Arctic. During those sixteen months on the roof of the world we never did get used to that mixture of relief and isolation which descended over us immediately after an aircraft had gone, or the sight of foreign objects on the floe anchoring parachutes which like spinnakers strained to haul them away from us across the frozen ocean.

We hitched the dogs up to the sledges and drove them out to collect the boxes. The parachutes had by that time spilled their pockets of air and lay like wet sails on the frozen sea. On the boxes in a felt pen had been written a few words of advice, some very rude, some practical. There was a short message of encouragement from Walt Wittmann, the world's foremost authority on the drift of ice in the Arctic basin, who had followed my plan with great interest through the many stages of its development. We had not known he was in the plane, nor did we know what extras, if any, would have been put in by Freddie or our friends at Barrow. What we did know soon enough was that no batch of presents was ever better packed. It was a couple of hours before we could break into the eight boxes and excavate from among the packing the items so vital to our survival in that environment—food, fuel, and extra clothing. We found a few steaks there too, some eggs, some beer, and a little mail.

It took us the rest of that day and half the next to sort the gear into four sledge loads. The progress we made that day was therefore nothing more than a token—an opportunity, without too much inconvenience, to change partners. Fritz moved in with me, Allan with Ken, and, as expected, we talked into the early hours of the morning.

In the Antarctic I had always been against changing partners during a journey; my argument being that not until two tentmates have exhausted their repertoire of jokes and stories and become uncommunicative do they become efficient. It was in fact not a very good argument, and I knew it; but in spite of resolutions at the start of each journey to change tent partners, my companions and I had invariably slipped quickly and comfortably into a routine from which we had not wished to budge, and within a month had formed two cliques. On the trans-Arctic journey, which would last five times as long as the longest Antarctic journey and cross a surface far less stable, it was vital that each man knew the strength and weakness of each of his companions, and that he was freshened every twenty days by a change of partner. Surprisingly the inconvenience of having to accommodate a new man and modify one's routine slightly to compromise his habits proved only a minor irritant. Within a day or two we had grown accustomed to the way our new tentmate moved in the confined space of the fabric shelter, prepared the stew, hung his clothes, served the porridge, rolled up his bedding and broke camp, and told his stories.

We put in a good day's travel on April 18, and morale in the party was high; but the next day, when crashing through some very rough country, my sledge split a runner. The split was about ten feet long. I did a temporary repair on it and we pushed on for another seven hours before camping. We lost a day and a half as a result of that broken runner, for to make a strong repair we were obliged to rig a canvas tarpaulin to protect us from the wind. The ice that had formed in the crack we thawed out with primus stoves. We sealed the crack with Araldite, an epoxy resin, bolted six metal plates across it, and, as an extra precaution, "stitched" the runner in three places with bearded seal hide. We had learned this technique of repairing a sledge from the Eskimos, from whom we had bought the bearded seal hide; the sledges were based on theirs, the shelter we had rigged up was another of their tips, and the harpoons that served as uprights for the tent had been given to us by them. It was ironic that on this day we should learn that Ralph Plaisted had reached the North Pole with machines.

We were pleased for him, and yet strangely dejected; I had felt so sure that the only method by which man at this stage in his technological development would succeed in making a surface crossing of the Arctic Ocean was by combining the basic technique of the Eskimos with air support. From what Freddie told us that night, it seemed Plaisted had reached the Pole from Ward Hunt Island, a distance of 474 statute miles, in forty-four days. We had already been fifty-nine days on the ice and had covered only 368 statute miles. In route miles we had of course covered a good deal more than that—in fact, about 650; but then so too had Plaisted. Their total distance evidently was 825 statute miles, which was most interesting, for it showed our detours as a percentage of our straight-line distance to be almost exactly the same: in Plaisted's case 74 percent, in ours just over 75 percent.

Since this was as I had predicted, it was not necessary to make any corrections to the overall distance of 3,800 statute miles I had calculated we would need to travel; but clearly we needed to increase the pace considerably if we were to catch up with our schedule. We of course sent Ralph and his companions our warmest congratulations—it had been a great achievement and his attainment of the Pole with motor toboggans in the face of so much skepticism had made a lot of so-called experts look silly. But we did not envy him his journey: ". . . how boring it must have been without dogs."

The going was very rough over the next few days. We were now meeting heavier ice, fractured and pressured in tighter fields which from the air must have looked like the shattered windshield of a car. We occasionally broke free onto larger floes or stretches of new ice, but seldom got a clear run of more than a mile before meeting a wall of ice—or, as on the evening of the twenty-fourth, a large expanse of fractured pack ice that was moving across our path at a rate of about half a mile an hour. It was an impressive sight, for unlike the night of the pressure in the Barrow fracture zone, where the moving ice had been grinding against the land-fast ice, here the motion of the two major floes was parallel. Whether the two floes were both drifting in the same direction with one floe slower than the other, or whether they were drifting in opposite directions—or indeed, for that matter, whether one was stationary and the other was drifting—was impossible to tell. One could watch the huge blocks of ice moving past and, by concentrating, switch the movement to the floe on which we were standing. This impression was confused still further by the ice which about every four minutes would shift of its own accord and move in the opposite direction. The sea was a stew of smaller pieces with clear patches of black water directly behind the bigger ice cakes and floebergs. From time to time what the whalers had called a growler of ice, a sizable sea-eroded block, would rise out of the mush ice with water pouring off its slippery green, gnarled root and flop back into the slopping stew of mush. For a while it would heave and plunge as it sought to find its new equilibrium while the mush ice around it, rising and falling on the wavelets, rustled like a riptide retreating from a shingle beach. There were no other sounds. The evening was dead calm.

We camped not thirty yards from all this activity. There was no alternative, for our retreat had been cut off by a new fracture, and the route east and west was a hopeless chaos of smashed floes and icy slop. There was talk of standing watches but we decided against it for we were now getting twenty-four hours of daylight. We did, however, take the precaution of getting the sledges ready for a quick getaway and slept a very shallow sleep. There was still a lot of movement the next morning, but we found a place where the two floes were screwing against each other and crushing up the young ice that had formed between them into a wall of wet rubble; and across this moving wall we managed to get all four teams of dogs before the two floes parted again, leaving a pile of debris on the edge of each floe. Fritz of course was fascinated by all this and took copious notes of everything he saw.

There was hardly a day now when we were not meeting leads, fractured areas, and moving ice, but we were tackling these with more assurance than we had during the early days. We had picked up a few tricks, mostly by accident; no longer did we strain a gut trying to right a capsized loaded sledge unaided, or wait for help to arrive; we would now bring the dogs back and hitch the traces to the side of the sledge a little forward of the halfway point, take the traces over the capsized sledge and drive the dogs hard at an angle of sixty degrees from the line of advance. As they pulled the sledge upright, it would thud onto its unweighted runner and slide forward a few feet. Backing out of impasses had always been awkward until we found that the dogs could be called back, the traces lifted over the sledge so that they lay along the top of the load, and the team driven back along their tracks hauling the sledge out backwards. A refinement of this was to do an about face; this trick, however, could be performed only on a smooth surface. The traces in this case were brought back along one side of the sledge and hooked over a handlebar. The sledge was then run back along its tracks until it ran onto a smooth patch of wind-packed snow. If the traces were then jerked free of the handlebar, and the sledge (still in reverse motion) given a violent swing away from the traces, the sledge, which might be carrying as much as 900 pounds, would spin through 180°. Maneuvering the sledges and teams across shattered pack ice and rocking ice pans, where it was vital that the sledges followed a precise route, would never have been possible had we not discovered that by shortening the traces, or even attaching several dogs to the sides of the sledges, we could zigzag the dogs and sledges through any maze or across almost any broken ice skin that fell across our path.

We were using most of these techniques daily now as we plodded forward wearily into a milky world of shapeless shadows; for we were now in the month of May—the month of mists and snow and overcast skies. Daylight diffused by the multiple reflections between snow and cloud bleached out all contrast, all horizons. All surface features now were vague—their size we could no longer judge. Mountains of ice as we approached shrank into knobbles, and pressure ridges loomed, then faded into ghostly forms. We followed dogs and sledges over hummocks we could not see and fell into holes that were invisible. Gone were all the daydreams, gone those quiet smokes at the back of the sledge when we sat cocooned in fur, soaking in the tepid warmth of a low Arctic sun and counting the diamonds that lay scattered on the snow. We had breathed deeply then, knowing that it would be many months before we would breathe air as clear again; for it was now thick with fog or falling snow, and to us, now acclimatized to the cold, it seemed clammy and close. Our world had become a stagnant mist, a set of tracks, and voices of speakers near but seldom seen.

The radio which Freddie had collected from us on March 28 and repaired in Barrow was dropped by parachute to us on May 5 by the Arctic Research Laboratory. Bob Murphy had on that occasion found us by homing in on our radio beacon and coming down through the cloud ceiling of three hundred feet. Our resupply of food and fuel came a few days later, when the Canadian Armed Forces flew their first mission in a C-130 Hercules staging through Barrow. On that flight they also dropped one of the four Nansen sledges which I had had specially built for use on the Arctic Ocean. My old Eskimo-type sledge had survived in spite of its split runner and probably would have lasted right through to the winter camp; but I felt that here was an opportunity to test out the other type of sledge. The Nansen was built on a totally different principle. The runners were broader, and laminated bridges supported the loading platform. Its weight was about 220 pounds, only a few pounds less than the Greenland Eskimo-type sledge, but it had greater flexibility. Over smooth ice caps, or even on sea ice, provided it is not too rough, the standard 100-pound Nansen is ideal. Whether this strengthened version would survive the tremendous hammering it would take on the pack ice we did not know, and watching it snake and squirm during the twelfth over a surface that the old sledge would have plowed straight across worried me a good deal. In fact, had we not by midday on the thirteenth crossed so many small fractures and finally bogged down in the deep snow which now covered the floes, I would have turned back and collected the sledge I had abandoned.

We were now faced by a lead which barred any further progress north. An alternative route east or west was out of the question, for it would have taken at least six days with such heavily loaded sledges to have carved a detour through four or five miles of the deep sticky snow that had fallen in the last few days. It would be as many days before the ice on the lead was thick enough to bear the weight of a sledge, for the air temperature was now only a few degrees below freezing. The time had come to convert our sledges into boats.

I had secretly looked forward to this moment, for as long ago as 1964 I had drawn up my first design for a sledge that would convert easily into a boat; we were, after all, a maritime expedition. My first designs had been inspired by watching sailing dinghies tacking gracefully across the glass-calm lake in the center of London. From a park bench on the edge of the Serpentine in Hyde Park I had sketched a sledge around which would be fitted a light duralumin frame, over which would be stretched a terylene tarpaulin that had been coated with a waterproofing chemical. The sledge-boat would have a keel, a mast, a sail and a rudder; its overall length would be fifteen feet and its beam ten feet. The sledge-boat I had tested on a frozen lake in Norfolk in November, 1967, however, had been somewhat cruder, and it was this construction that we set about building with enthusiasm on the south bank of a black gash in the skin of the Arctic Ocean at 2 P.M. on May 13, 1968.

We lashed harpoons and skis across the loading platform of an unloaded Nansen sledge; pushed it onto a waterproofed terylene tarpaulin which had eyelets at one-foot intervals around the edge, and stitched it up with parachute shrouds which crossed from one side to the other. Our "parcel" when it was ready for launching looked not unlike a boat; indeed, but for the handlebars of the sledge which stuck up at the stern, it had a certain quaint grace about it. My companions were, I think, surprised how well it floated, but still very dubious about loading it up with boxes. In any case, there was a skin of grease ice on the surface of the lead which had to be broken before we could start ferrying gear and dogs across, so Ken and I made a pioneering voyage to cut a channel through to the far bank. This was a slow job. We had to reach over the bow and break every foot of the way. The second trip was made by Allan and me with the sledge-boat loaded up with three boxes of dog food, two boxes of man rations, and three reluctant dogs. We got across to the far bank without much difficulty, but in the meantime the far floe had shifted off line with the channel we had cut, which by that time was deforming and closing up. There was no choice but to return and wait for the ice movement to quiet down, and in order to get back a little quicker, Fritz and Ken towed us with the line. The three dogs had, during the outward journey, been too scared to move, but on the return they became restless, possibly because their tails and buttocks were getting wet. They shifted their weight and tilted the craft, which by now was being towed at about one knot by Fritz and Ken, who took in line quicker as they saw the boat taking water; and we reached the home shore just as it sank. Allan and I managed to scramble out onto the ice and the dogs we fished out in due course; but the sledge and the gear lashed to it took several hours to fish out. Most of the gear of course was ruined.

Allan, who was a nonswimmer, took the incident very philosophically; Fritz felt the system could stand improvement; Ken felt it was lethal and wanted a rubber boat sent out. I agreed with Fritz that the sledge-boat had a few bugs that needed ironing out before we made another attempt, and we were all agreed that no more boating attempts should be made while there was any movement in the floes, or while there was ice on the lead.

The next day, at a point about a mile to the west of our campsite where the floe to our north had overnight closed on ours, we crossed over in a headlong rush and spent the next seven days chopping our way north through a chaos of moving ice worse than anything we had hitherto seen. We were now in old floe territory. Here was ice that had been drifting around the Arctic Ocean for several years in the circulation of currents known as the Beaufort Gyral; massive floes that had been screwed up and crushed, shattered and forced into huge block ridges rising thirty feet above the flooded ice at their base. We had worked our way north a hundred yards at a time, built causeways, hacked roads, and rafted across fractures on rocking chunks of ice. So tough had been those seven days that the lead we met on the twenty-second, which separated us from an old weathered floe to our north, was a temptation too strong for us to ignore, and we built ourselves another boat. This time, however, we got all the dogs, sledges and gear across the lead without any difficulty, and made another six or seven miles before we met what seemed at the time the final impasse.

There was to our north an open sea from which we were separated by about three hundred yards of floebergs, floating ice wreckage of broken floes and mush ice. The base of the overcast directly above the open water was as black as the blackest storm cloud I have ever seen; everything else was gray-white; even our dark green tents were bleached and shadowless. There was nowhere we could go, nothing we could do. The next day a twenty-five knot wind got up and drifting snow cut the visibility to a few yards, but we at least had the consolation of a wind from the southeast which would drift the pack ice on which we were camped in a direction 28 degrees to the right of the wind, according to Nansen's law. Based on the speed of the wind, we could count on a half knot drift in the direction we wanted to go, which was about the sort of progress we had been averaging under our own desperate efforts the past few days.

We set off in whiteout conditions on the twenty-sixth and soon found ourselves wading in thigh-deep snow. We literally shoveled our way through it and drove ourselves to the point of collapse in a violent effort to break through to a small patch of smooth ice—the only patch that looked big enough to set up two tents and tether four teams of dogs. We had that day made about three hundred yards. Visibility all the next day was like soup. It was no better on the twenty-eighth, but we dug out and broke through a belt of smashed-up floes onto better going and sledged due east in an effort to skirt the open water to our north. For the next two days we threw ourselves at the ice, worked until we dropped, drove the dogs and sledges like maniacs over vicious-looking smashed pack and boiled-up mush ice, and on meeting a lead on the evening of the thirtieth attacked it with demoniacal hatred. We crossed that lead in five hours of ferrying with a sledge-boat built in the form of a barge, two sledges lashed together. The other sledges we just heaved into the water and towed across.

We got up as usual at 6 A.M. on the last day of May intent on putting in a long hard traveling day, but Ken wanted to have a four-man conference before we got going. He told us that he felt we three had formed a clique from which he was excluded; that we had given him little or no encouragement or advice. We spent over an hour, the four of us doubled up in a two-man tent, drinking tea and talking this problem through. We were all under tre-

mendous stress at that time. As a party we were a long way behind schedule and traveling in fogs across some of the roughest
and most broken pack we had seen during the whole journey. As
individuals we each had our anxieties, responsibilities, doubts;
mine were those of any leader whose party is under stress and a
long way behind schedule. Fritz, although he never admitted it,
must have been worried about our position too, but for a different reason. He had left his wife and baby to join the expedition;
if it foundered he would be ridiculed by those of his scientific
colleagues who felt that he had shown himself to be as a scientist
irresponsible and as a husband supremely selfish. He could vindicate himself to them and repay his wife's sacrifice only by completing the journey and bringing back enough scientific data to
justify the sixteen months the journey had lifted from his career.
Allan had the nagging worry of whether his knees would hold
out; they had given him a lot of trouble during the twelve-hun-
dred-mile journey we had made the previous summer. Mine had
been troublesome too, and we had often talked about this. We
had taken a risk by setting off on this journey—but then, prehis-
toric man took a risk when he climbed out of his tree and has
been taking risks ever since; calculated risks are the very essence
of exploration. Ken's problems were social; physically he was in
good shape, professionally he was admired and encouraged by
his regiment for joining the expedition, but it was inevitable that
the difference in training and temperament would set him apart
from the three of us.

Ken was a good officer, a Christian and a gentleman. We were
three seasoned polar men. The many years we had lived in isolated polar camps had left its mark on us; we would no doubt be
regarded by a genteel society as rough, crude, self-reliant and
irreligious. We were obsessed by and in love with the polar setting
and the hard physical challenge of polar exploration. We were
old friends: Allan and I had made a tough journey together the
previous year; Allan with Fritz had made others; the three of us
had gone through the same basic polar training at the same Antarctic base, Hope Bay. There was a close bond between us, a

mutual trust and respect; we spoke the same language. Only a man with precisely the same background would have fitted instantly into such a society; it was therefore no surprise to us that Ken had felt an alien at the start of the journey; but it had been worrying us for some time that he did not appear to be slipping naturally into our way of life. In a normal society, most men seek the companionship of others with similar interests, beliefs, and social status, and seldom if ever find themselves for any length of time confined to the company of men with whom they have little in common. Ken by his own admission was unhappy in our society because he felt we were not "bringing him in," and there was little we could do to improve the situation, for as far as we were concerned we had tried to interest him in our way of life and evidently failed. We could not change characteristics which had been developing in the three of us over the past thirteen years of polar expeditioning—nor could we make a conscious effort to help him without being reminded that he was not comfortably and naturally one of us. But clearly we had to make the effort, not only for Ken's sake but in the long-term interests of the expedition, for we had ahead of us another year—possibly another eighteen months, if we got out of phase with the seasons. While we obviously could come up with no conclusive solutions, the talk did manage to clear the air somewhat, at least as far as Ken was concerned, I felt; and at this point in the discussion we broke it up, packed up, and continued our journey north.

We stopped early that afternoon and turned in, for we had decided that morning to change onto a night traveling routine in the hope of getting some small benefit from the cooler nighttime temperatures, and on June 1 we made ten nautical miles. We had another good day to follow—a wild, windy day during which we must have drifted a couple of miles in addition to the seven for which we worked so hard. It was one of those rare days on the Arctic Ocean when from time to time sunlight would pierce the clouds and explode in small ragged pools on the floes, slide across them rippling over the hummocks and fire the ridges for a second or two before fading again as the clouds closed in. We had been traveling across a badly fractured zone trying all the time to keep a heading north, but we were being driven off course imperceptibly to the east. On the night of the second we met an obstruction to our progress which in the poor light seemed unbelievable. This was a chaos of ice blocks more massive, more grotesque, and more extensive than we had believed possible. We had no choice but to retrace our steps and go east; and eventually, after a scramble across some moving pressure, we sought shelter on a small floe which was, we discovered after camping, split in several places. There proved to be no way off this floe except by the way we had come. We were pinned there all the next day by a blizzard, but on the night of the fourth and fifth we backed off it and sledged east through a whiteout looking for a safer place to rest up. All that day the wind was blowing hard, and all the next as we struggled to find a way through the maze of fractures. Cracks and leads we were now meeting every few hundred yards. The whole vast area was in motion, slowly swirling, eddying— a confusion of currents, countercurrents, and winds which moved the sea ice like brittle scum in a stagnant pool stirred from below.

We found that night, when the sun broke through and we snatched a position fix, that over the past ten days we had been carried eighty miles off course to the east as we struggled in vain to maintain a northwest heading. We were utterly depressed, made hardly any progress the next day, and were stopped again after only three miles by mush ice at 4:30 A.M. on the eighth. Ken, feeling the strain, had another long talk with me the following morning. He had been thinking a lot about the discussion we had had some nine days earlier and was more sensitive than ever about our relationship. We were all feeling worn out, dejected and vulnerable. At no time in the journey had we been in an area so completely smashed up and turbulent. We were averaging only two or three miles a day, there was a radio blackout, the snow was getting deeper and softer each day, soon it would be melting; we had to find a big floe before the end of the month or we would be in serious trouble. Even the floe on which we were camped that morning was groaning under us, and our escape from it was a headlong dash into an area we had had no time to investigate in advance—a gamble which might well have landed us in a desperate situation. This was no time for introspection. Every word, every subconscious thought had to be directed toward getting ourselves out of that mess and onto a safe floe on which we could spend the summer. We found it on the morning of the eleventh—a big floe, the safest-looking floe we had seen for ages—and having found it, carried on.

Our fortunes improved a little over the next few days, and with the extra supply of food and fuel we received on the morning of the twelfth we were provisioned for a further three weeks, during which time I hoped we would reach the Pole of Relative Inaccessibility. But we were hearing the sound of the sea almost every day now as we progressed across the chart, through six degrees of longitude, fighting for every mile; and by Midsummer's Day were still a long way behind schedule.

Four months earlier to the day, we had set out from Point Barrow; four men and four teams of dogs on a journey the outcome of which few even of our friends would favorably predict. Less sympathetic but more shrewd had been those who had remained noncommittal, for the conditions we met and our rate of progress had at times been very disheartening. At noon on June 21 our latitude fix showed 81°18′N, an advance of only half a mile on our position of two days earlier. That fix put us at the same distance from the Pole of Relative Inaccessibility as Shackleton was from the South Pole in 1908 at the time he and his companions turned back: 98 geographical miles. I doubted then that we would get much further, for the old floes were badly split; black sea pools and leads were spreading like a stain; we were traveling on borrowed time.

Our last seven days before setting up summer camp on July 4 at latitude 81°33′N, longitude 165°29′W, were physically the hardest of the whole journey. We drove the dogs out of their depth in wet snow and melt-water pools, and had to drag them out one by one. We put two teams together and drove them through on extended traces with all four of us pushing, stumbling and shouting ourselves hoarse. The ice floes were by that time a shimmering maze of melt-water pools and leads. In places there were cracks every fifteen yards. Each day the pools were deeper and the dogs more reluctant to plow their way through dragging a sledge. We were fighting a losing struggle with the drift— a hopeless effort to travel northwest in search of a safer area in which to sit out the summer melt. We had come a long way. Since leaving Barrow on February 21 we had sledged one thousand, one hundred and eighty route miles.

We had sledged farther from land over the polar-pack ice than any other travelers. We had measured floe thicknesses and snow densities almost every day. We had kept logs of wildlife, and logs on the types and ages of the ice across which we had traveled. We had recorded synoptic weather data which we had coded and then transmitted daily to Freddie Church at Barrow; he in turn had passed it on to the United States Weather Bureau and the British Meteorological Office. Sadly, we had failed to travel far enough, for we were still in the influence of a current circulating to our east; but we had reached our limit and could do no more.

8

Summer Sixty-Eight

SINCE first conceiving the idea of crossing the Arctic Ocean I knew my two most difficult decisions would be the decision to stop and set up the summer drifting camp, and the even more critical choice of a floe on which to establish our winter quarters for the five-months' drift through the polar night.

Both are gambles. You know nothing of what lies ahead. On June 11 for the first time in several weeks we had found ourselves on a big, safe-looking floe but resisted the temptation to call a halt to our misery, hoping that somehow we had reached the southernmost of a nest of giant floes—that here in this area of the Arctic Ocean, by some anomaly in the currents, all the big ones had been herded together. We had been wrong; but finding ourselves once again amidst shattered ice churning itself into a stew, it was impossible to retreat to the big floe we had crossed and left behind. It was lost; our tracks had been wiped out and the floes reshuffled.

On July 3, with only ten traveling days left before the Canadian Air Force would fly out the summer supply drop, our situation was desperate. The sledges were bogging down in slush and the ice across which we were traveling was too thin to survive the summer melt. On that day, on a northwest heading, we ran into an old floe and plowed across it through shin-deep slush. Beyond it was another—an even older floe, judging by its rounded hummocks. We weaved across it, keeping where possible to the crests of waves from which the melt water had drained, and found beyond the next pressure ridge yet another multi-year floe: a giant stretching to the horizon like a vast, dazzling ice sheet. We had seen no floes as big or as solid-looking since latitude 75°. This had to be the summer camp, of that I was almost certain; but we drove the dogs on, at times wading through slush and icy water up to our knees, and at the end of the day, at what seemed to be the end of the floe country, I tripped, went sprawling in the slush, staggered forward dripping icy water and set up camp on a hummock.

The following morning after breakfast Fritz and Ken came over to the tent which Allan and I were now sharing and we talked it out. At the very best we could hope to make only another six or eight miles across the ice rubble which lay to the north of our floe. Fritz, however, still felt we should go on, arguing that "any miles we make now are miles we don't have to make later." Ken thought we should stop where we were; Allan had no strong views either way. The visibility was poor, the wind was blowing hard, driving drizzle against the tent with a soft hiss and soaking the tarpaulins that covered the gear on the sledges. The floes were flooded, vapor was pouring out of the tent vent from clothing soaked the day before and now drying out above the primus stove in the apex of the tent. I weighed up Fritz's argument against the chances of not finding a better floe and decided to stay put. Fritz accepted the decision without further argument and went off to scout around for a site for his micro-meteorological instruments. Ken set to work recharging the radio batteries, while Allan and I spent the rest of the day trying to solve a serious problem.

Our tenuous link with the outside world was a three-foot cable connecting a hand generator to a nickel cadmium battery, the power supply for a remarkable transceiver, the Redifon GR345.

With this portable high-frequency radio, which has a peak power of only fifteen watts, we had been transmitting daily progress reports and weather data which Freddie passed on to the Canadian Forces and the U.S. Naval Arctic Research Laboratory.

Using a Collins KWM2A transmitter and amplifier, with a peak power of about a kilowatt, Freddie also relayed these progress reports to the Royal Aircraft Establishment's Experimental Station at Cove near Farnborough in England; here these signals were received by directional antennae and recorded on magnetic tapes. Within a few minutes the messages would be passed to Sir Vivian Fuchs, the coordinator of the expedition's activities in London, and through his office to the other members of the Committee—who, should we require any replacement equipment not held in reserve at either Barrow or Resolute Bay, would vote their approval of its purchase from expedition funds and arrange for its shipment to the Canadian Forces Base at Edmonton.

A small number of amateur shortwave stations in the United Kingdom, acting as a backup to the Radio Station at Cove, handled the expedition's weekend traffic, while our link to Barrow was backed up in poor radio conditions by other enthusiastic amateur radio operators on the American drifting station T-3, and the Canadian Arctic Weather Stations in the Queen Elizabeth Islands.

Only at the source was the system vulnerable, and it was here, in the three-foot cable which connected the hand-powered generator to the radio batteries, that we discovered a wire had broken.

The consequences of a complete radio breakdown had, of course, been seriously considered as long ago as April, 1964, when the plan for the crossing had first taken shape. But if in London this was a sobering thought, much more sobering was the isolation we felt when faced with the possibility of radio failure on a drifting icefloe eight hundred miles from Point Barrow. Our radio beacons, which in theory attracted aircraft like audible magnets, had a limited battery life, and in the event of a radio breakdown we could afford to switch them on for only a quarter of an hour each day, starting from the fifth day after the last radio contact. Bear in mind that the party was drifting, and the drift unpredictable, even knowing what speed and in which direction the wind was blowing. Consider also the error of an astrofix made from the support aircraft, and the problem of estimating a time of arrival at a point eight hundred miles away without knowledge of the wind along the flight path. The chances of finding the party were, at the very best, even. We would need to drift only about ten miles to be out of the aircraft's target area; and to find us by systematic search, the aircraft would have to cover an area of some 1,600 square miles.

Among the tracery of shadows, fractures, and polynyas, four men, two small tents and thirty-six dogs would be almost impossible to see. There had been occasions during this journey when aircraft had flown within half a mile of our camp without seeing our smoke flares. On other occasions aircraft had been even closer before we heard their engines. What then were our chances of survival?

The Arctic explorer Vilhjalmur Stefansson believed that man could survive by hunting in the Arctic Ocean. We had not been convinced, for Stefansson had not sledged far enough from land to put his theory to a proper test. We had therefore relied not on game but on aircraft support—and it was well we did. We had seen both polar bear and fox tracks frequently during the journey, but the animals themselves kept out of our way; and the total of twelve seals we had sighted in the previous five months, together with four gulls, a little auk, two long-tailed jaegers and a flight of ducks, would hardly have made three respectable feeds for our thirty-six working dogs.

Luckily, we never had to put these theories to a test. The break in the generator cable finally was found and fixed by Allan with yet another home-made soldering iron—and the subject of survival dropped.

Since May 31 we had been on a night-traveling routine in order to take what little advantage there was from a slightly cooler "night" temperature. Now, with the radio fixed, we changed our watches back to Barrow time and eased ourselves into the new arrangement with the luxury of an afternoon's snooze. It was bliss. All the toil was over; tension gone. We stretched out on top of our sleeping bags, and while the primus roared its warmth and the wind drummed the tent and spat drizzle, we drifted north.

"Sun!" Fritz hollered like a doting father calling his offspring. The word penetrated our shallow sleep and jerked us awake.

"Jesus Christ!" Allan muttered. "OK . . . OK!" He pulled on his baggy windproof trousers, pulled his anorak down from the apex of the tent where it had been hanging to dry and wrestled into it.

He grabbed his notebook and dived out of the tent sleeve, kicking off his down slippers as he disappeared. I heard him fumbling with his boots which had evidently been lying in a pool of melt water, for I heard a muttered curse, a splash as the water was emptied, and a few moments later the slithering sounds as he made for the theodolite.

We had set it up on its tripod, leveled ready for situations such as this, and covered with a waterproof bag to protect it from freezing drizzle; the sky was like a gray blanket worn threadbare in a few places through which the sun occasionally broke just long enough for a quick man to snatch a position fix. Allan caught it this time, and with a couple more shots was able to compute our position at latitude 81°32.8′N, longitude 165°29′W.

Over the next two days I devoted my time to assessing our situation, while my three companions went on reconnaissance trips around the floe with the dogs in search of a more suitable site for the summer camp. By the evening of the sixth I had completed the assessment and begun the long job of transmitting it to Freddie over the radio.

During the past two months we had made only two and a half degrees of northing, and, in spite of our efforts to maintain a heading of twenty degrees west of true north, had been carried off course by the drift of ice or driven off course by the nature of the ice conditions. We had made a determined effort to sledge

clear of the influence of the Beaufort Gyral (the clockwise circulation of currents in the western half of the Arctic basin), and
the last four weeks of sledging had countered the current by
sledging almost due west. We had by this desperate action pulled
back five degrees of longitude and got back on course, but we
had finally been stopped seventy-five miles short of the Pole of
Relative Inaccessibility.

From a careful study of the chart and my diary, I found that
since setting out from Point Barrow on February 21 we had
sledged 1,180 route miles; which averaged out at 8.7 statute
miles a day. Affecting that average, however, was the deep snow,
adverse drift and the open water we had encountered during the
last two months—when, sledging with heavy loads, we had made
only 173 statute miles. In the first seventy-three days of the journey we had averaged 11.4 statute miles a day, and it was this sort
of average we would have to maintain if we were to stand a
chance of reaching Spitsbergen ahead of the melt season in 1969.

By July 6 we were 167 statute miles short of the position at
which in the original plan I had hoped to set up summer camp.
We guessed we were still in the influence of the Beaufort Gyral
and would drift northeast about sixty nautical miles (or one degree of latitude) during the next month. We had no idea what
traveling conditions to expect during the months of August and
September, for no man had traveled on the Arctic Ocean at that
time of the year; nor could we predict on what date conditions
would permit a start to the autumn sledging. Assuming, however,
that we set out on August 15 and traveled until September 25,
and that the Canadian Forces would make the winter airdrop on
October 1, we would need to be self-sufficient for a total of forty-
five days—of which forty would be spent in traveling northwest
to get ourselves out of the influence of the gyral currents and
across the date line into the influence of the transpolar drift
stream, which would carry us north during the five months of
winter darkness. By August 15 the dogs should have recovered
from the long haul and be fit enough to survive the autumn sledging period on one pound of dog pemmican a day instead of the

usual one and a half pounds; by this reduction in rations we would be setting out with the same basic weight in dog food as a normal thirty-day load—which we had discovered during the long haul was the maximum we could carry.

With heavy loads, and with the prospect of a lot of open water around in the month of August, we could reasonably expect to average only five or six miles a day. This would put us approximately at latitude 85°N, longitude 175°E by September 25, or 218 statute miles short of the position I had originally settled on for the start of the winter drift. We had hoped to do a geophysical traverse for Lamont Geological Observatory during the winter as we drifted across the submarine Lomonosov Ridge, but by starting our drift from latitude 85°N, we would by March 1, 1969, have drifted only as far north as latitude 88°N—the position at which, in the original plan, the expedition was to have started its winter drift.

However, since the hut in which we spent the winter would continue to drift with the transpolar stream after we had abandoned it and set off for Spitsbergen, why not hand it over to Lamont as a field camp?—so that our winter geophysical program could be extended as the hut continued its drift northward over the submarine ridge. I made this suggestion to the expedition's committee in London in the assessment I sent to Freddie, arguing that the hut would not need restocking; we could also leave behind two small Honda generators, our micrometeorological instruments, and our reserve theodolite—a considerable financial saving for anyone taking over our station, and therefore an incentive, should Lamont need one, for extending our program.

As for the final dash to Spitsbergen: Assuming the crossing party set off from winter quarters on March 1, 1969, from approximately latitude 88°N, longitude 175°E (about 200 statute miles behind my original schedule), I calculated that to make a landfall on the north shore of Spitsbergen on the original deadline of May 31 we would need to make good an average of exactly nine miles a day. This pace we had sustained only during the month of April last. On the final stage, however, we would have the benefit of a stronger and more consistently favorable drift and the experience and incentive to travel harder. In order to travel as light as we had done in the early stages of the journey, we would require two air drops of supplies in addition to the one already planned, and these should be spaced at three-degree intervals along the route: that is, 89°, 86°, and 83°.

In the event of a negative summer drift, a great deal of open water in the autumn (which would stop us from making any appreciable adjustment to our course), and a slow winter drift, all contributing to place the crossing party by the end of the winter no further north than latitude 85°N, we could still reach Spitsbergen before the summer was too far advanced. If this were the case, however, more than likely our final approach would be across open pack ice to a rendezvous west of the island with HMS *Endurance*.

I had also taken carefully into account in making this assessment the drift of the American scientific station T-3. On July 6 it was at latitude 83°09′N, longitude 150°42′W, and although near the northern limit of the Beaufort Gyral it seemed fairly certain it was set for another circuit of the western half of the ocean. As a staging post for any light aircraft operations in September, T-3 would be much nearer to the expedition than any other manned station, and by March 1 would probably be equidistant with Alert from the expedition's winter quarters. In either case the expedition would be out of range of T-3 for light aircraft unless the aircraft made a landing on the pack ice to refuel, and refueled again at the expedition's winter quarters. I therefore made arrangements through Freddie for extra fuel to be dropped to us on the winter supply drop: three drums of JP4 and eight forty-five gallon drums of av-gas. The date at which Freddie should transfer his relay station to T-3 I left open at that time.

The whole assessment of course was only my best-considered guess at the conditions the expedition would meet during the next twelve months, but in retrospect it was very largely as the result of the careful thought that went into this appraisal that the expedition came through.

Over the next six days there was no letup in the wild weather, and by the ninth we had been blown thirty-five statute miles north—an average of seven miles a day. The melt had also really got a grip now. The floes were awash. What few hummocks were still above water level looked now like islands in a vast sea of pale blue water. There was no drainage, no hairline cracks. While this was comforting on the one hand, it was proving damned uncomfortable on the other. I got a message out to Freddie for onward transmission to the Canadian Air Force asking them to waterproof individual loads for the drop they had scheduled for the twelfth, as some of the boxes might be sitting in three-foot deep melt pools for some time before we could drag them clear. Radio conditions were not very good at this time; a tremendous amount of traffic was piling up; Fritz and Allan were busy setting up the scientific apparatus for Fritz's program. Ken had a bit of professional work at this time too; he replaced a huge filling in one of my teeth, and spent a good deal of time in reading up the instructions for a program on a comparative study of wool and synthetic clothing which he had been asked to conduct by the International Wool Secretariat.

We were having to go easy on the rations now, and in an effort to dry out, moved our camp site a couple of hundred yards to a long isthmus of high ground.

On July 12 the Canadian Forces flew out from Resolute Bay with our summer resupply on board, but though from time to time we could hear the sound of engines, the fog by some strange accoustical trick scattered the sound and we could not tell the captain of the aircraft precisely where he was in relation to our camp. It was a desperately frustrating experience; for some reason the aircraft could not pick up a signal from our radio beacon; smoke flares were no use, unless the aircraft could get down under the cloud base, and the base was not much more than two hundred feet.

I picked up the call sign of the aircraft on the radio at 5:45 the following morning and the contented purring of a Hercules was heard at 6:30 A.M. By 6:45 the aircraft was roaring overhead.

It was an overcast day and a pale blue-gray ribbon of light around the horizon created the impression that the low cloud above us was suspended like a false ceiling by unseen wires.

In between dropping runs the captain told me over the radio that radio propagation was so bad that we were the first station he had heard on the radio since leaving Edmonton three days before. I was surprised that in such conditions they had risked the flight:

"You need the food—we get it to you," was his reply.

The drop went off very well. Out of the 9,000 pounds of food, fuel and equipment dropped, the only loss was one batch of jerry cans of kerosene—a loss covered by a 30 percent spillage factor which I had applied in working out the loads. Most of the scientific apparatus required by Fritz had been dropped by the Canadian Air Force on their last resupply, so that Fritz would have to waste no time starting his program should traveling be cut short before the summer supply drop was due. He did, however, receive a few extra items of scientific gear, and for a few frantic hours after the Hercules had climbed into the clouds, my three companions were busy dashing all over the floe checking the boxes and rolling those that had landed in melt-water pools out onto drained ice, while I unpacked those that had been ferried back to the camp. My typewriter had survived the drop as had Ken's rubber boat and wet suit, which we had had sent out so that he could do some underwater photography. There was beer and steaks and mail—even Allan got a letter.

By now Fritz was far the busiest of the four of us. First up every morning and last to bed each night, he worked for seventeen hours a day. He seemed almost continually to be on the move across the floe from one delicate instrument to another, measuring temperature profiles through the four meters of ice below us, and the minute changes in the wind, temperature and humidity in the air column five meters above the melting surface of the floe.

His main object was to study the regional and temporal variation of the ice surface of the Arctic Ocean. This study, while of value for its own sake, would, he hoped, give a further insight into total ice production in the Arctic Ocean at a time when the Arctic Ocean's influence on world climate and glaciation is exciting great interest. By measuring the amount of snow and ice that is melted from the surface of a representative area of the ice pack during the summer, and subtracting this from the amount of new ice that had formed since the end of the previous summer's melt, he was left with a surplus of ice which, if a steady state (or what is sometimes known as a balanced ice budget) is to be achieved, has to be exported from the Arctic Ocean each year. The export figure calculated by this method works out at approximately 4,000 cubic kilometers of ice a year, most of which is exported through the Spitsbergen-Greenland gate into the Norwegian Sea. So much ice is bound to have a cooling effect on the climates further south. Could the climatic balance be deliberately upset by man's interference with nature? In theory it could. By bombarding the Arctic Ocean's ice cover with dark-colored powder, the ice would absorb more solar radiation and melt more quickly. And what of the possibility of the ice melting by natural causes? It has been theorized that an increase in the mean annual temperature of only 2°C would be sufficient in a few years to cause the ice to disappear—and what effect would an ice-free Arctic Ocean have on the world's climates? Clearly Fritz's work was important, but as a scientist he realized that there were many factors to be considered.

Ice does not grow and decay at a uniform rate; Fritz was finding that younger floes were melting more quickly than old ones, and his later measurements were to show that although the old ice covered about three-quarters of the area across which we traveled, only one-third of the ice forming in winter grew at the base of the floes. The remainder formed in areas left open at the end of summer and in fractures that opened during the winter. Every new fracture and pressure ridge had to be taken into account. Fritz had to determine the mean thickness of the ice cover of the Arctic Ocean by drilling through the floes. He had to know what proportion of the ocean was ice-free at different stages throughout the year by keeping a log of the ice cover along our route. He had to know how much of the incoming radiation was absorbed and how much reflected by the many different ice forms and over open water. He had to know the salinity of the surface water of the sea and how the ice of the Beaufort Gyral differed from the ice in the transpolar stream. Some of these questions could be answered by aerial reconnaissance, submarine observations, and precise studies carried out at such stations as T-3, but there were many gaps in man's knowledge of the ice cover of the Arctic Ocean that could be filled only by a scientist crossing it on foot. Only a man on foot could judge whether the profile along the traverse route was truly representative; only a man on foot could measure the slab thickness of the material that went into the building of each pressure ridge and from this deduce what proportion of the total ice production was formed by the refreezing of leads that opened up in the winter and spring. Fritz felt sure he would confound the many detractors among his scientific colleagues if only by the sheer volume of his data.

While Fritz and Allan were doing a set of precise levels with the theodolite across the floe to determine the effect of the melt on the surface profile of the ice pack, I was erecting a work tent, a place where we could sit at table, stretch, stand up, swing an imaginary cat. The frame was made out of skis, ski sticks, tent poles from the mountain tents we carried as reserves, and harpoons. The four main poles, one in each corner of the structure, were guyed and anchored with dog-pemmican boxes. I made a floor platform out of cargo pallets and built shelves and tables out of packing crates and empty boxes. It was rough, crude carpentry, knocked together with nails we had pried out of boxes and hammered straight; but the furniture, although not attractive, was functional. Finally, man-ration boxes were placed around the table to serve as seats, and five of the fifty-odd parachutes that a few days earlier had rained down on us were stretched over the frame and weighted down around the sides with more man-ration boxes. Meltville—the world's most isolated and insecure village—had been established.

For the first time since leaving Barrow, we sat that night at table and ate our evening meal of meat-bar stew in a civilized manner. There was something of a party atmosphere in that bright, airy shelter; it was the first of many pleasant evening meals we took together during the next few weeks. As a work tent it had its limitations; it was big and therefore cold, flimsy and therefore draughty; so I did most of my writing in the polar pyramid tent. Allan had moved out of my tent by that time. Now that the weather was warmer, he much preferred sleeping outside on the sledge. He spent his working day either puttering with his gear, repairing sledges and broken instruments, doing the computations for position and floe gyration, or helping Fritz; his base was the parachute tent but he was seldom in it. Fritz and Ken were still sleeping in the other pyramid tent, but after breakfast each morning, Fritz would go the rounds of his instruments and spend the rest of the day operating from a base in the parachute tent. Ken spent some of his time brushing up on his navigation and sorting out the psychological questionnaires prepared by the department of clinical psychology of the Ministry of Defence. Such data would provide information on the interaction of men in isolation and under stress that would be of great value to the military. There were also interesting parallels between our expedition and lunar explorations that might yield data of use to those responsible for the selection of astronauts for the longer space missions.

There were four occasions during the course of the expedition when we had to answer what seemed several thousand questions: at Barrow, at the summer camp, at the end of the winter drift, and finally on arrival in Spitsbergen. The questionnaires were so arranged that they were convenient to administer and easy to process; a test, so we were told, of our efficiency of intellect and our innate level of intelligence. There were the usual introvert/extrovert questions, and the "likes-and-dislikes" forms which evidently are used in the selection of astronauts. There was another devised to measure "self-disclosure," another to measure social adjustment, and one which highlighted idiosyncrasies. Finally, there was the Minnesota Multiphasic Personality Inventory—a well-known clinical tool for measuring, among other things, depression, both reactionary and endogenous, antiauthoritarian features of psychopathy, masculinity/femininity scale (which we were told reflects what is called by psychologists obsessional traits), and phobias. In order to give the psychologist some idea of how we were responding under the ordeal of a long and arduous journey, some of the test papers were produced for a second time at a later stage in the journey, and this we found irritating, for try as we might we could not remember what we had answered the first time. We were damned if we were going to give the psychologist at the Ministry of Defence the satisfaction of catching us out.

The Englishman's traditional opening gambit, the weather, had long since lost its novelty; it was so predictable in the summer that there was nothing new to say. The absolute range of temperature during the whole month of July was only four degrees Centigrade; often the temperature varied less than two degrees for periods of several days. It was misty, miserable, and very sticky—the relative humidity at one meter was generally above 90 percent. We saw the sun through a screen of drizzle, everything was limp and wet. The dogs lay around on the tops of hummocks yawning with boredom and scratching off their molting fur. They looked around the horizon expecting nothing, and seeing nothing went back to sleep. I envied them as I crept back into the tent after breakfast. Every day was so depressingly similar to the one before. Every day I turned the hand generator for two hours and spent six more writing while the mists closed in and fell back, lifted and fell like some enormous lung in which we were imprisoned, with odors of decay and sodden fabric clinging to us like a film of grease.

My breakfast conversations with Allan in the parachute tent as a rule started with a grunt and became more intelligible with each successive cup of tea. But on July 27 we surprised each other by drifting into a discussion on the navigational problems we would meet at the time of the winter supply drop. On Septem-

ber 25 at latitude 85°N, the sun would be only four degrees
above the horizon at upper transit. We could not expect to see
any stars with the naked eye until the first week in October.
There would be no moon, and the altitudes and azimuths of the
brighter stars we would not be able to precompute without a
reasonably accurate guess at our position. The sun, even assuming it was visible during the week before the air drop, would be
so low that refraction corrections would be way off the scale, and
after a week without an astro check our dead reckoning could
be in error by as much as thirty miles. This led to the problem
of trying to locate the North Pole in mid-March, 1969, when the
sky would be too bright to see the stars but the sun would not
yet have risen. We took it a stage further—to the estimated position at which we would receive our first air drop on March 25,
when we would be at approximately 85°15'N on the Spitsbergen side: the sun would then be only three degrees above the
horizon at upper transit, and in temperatures of minus fifty with
the fantastic temperature inversion the sun would in all probability be split in several strips like a sliced orange. It seemed likely
that on that occasion we would be obliged to rely solely on our
radio homing beacons for guiding the aircraft in to our position.
This was worrisome, for our homing beacons had up to the summer camp worked effectively on only two occasions.

Our breakfast conversation over, we refilled the buckets with
fresh water from one of the nearby melt pools and returned them
to the parachute tent; then took one of our three rifles and went
for a walk. Fritz, reporting on his daily dog runs around the
floe to check the changes in surface topography as the season
advanced, had told us that morning of a new fracture about a
mile from the camp that was in places several yards wide, and
we had wanted to see for ourselves. Allan didn't want to risk
taking his dogs, for the last time he had taken them for a run,
their pads had been badly cut on the razor-sharp ice candles that
now covered the beds of the drained melt streams. Why Fritz's
dogs did not get cut up was a mystery. We had of course tried
protecting the dogs' pads by fitting them up with canvas dog

boots, but the dogs had taken an instant dislike to these and torn them off. I remember that walk as one of the most pleasant diversions I had during the entire summer, for it was one of those rare summer days on the Arctic Ocean when there was a clear sky, and the company of my old sledging companion was relaxing and helpful. The subject as usual came round eventually to Ken, but to the problem of how we might help him to enjoy the environment and the company with which he was stuck we had no solution. Our only consolation was that he seemed to be a man of exceptional determination and Christian charity who harbored no grudges as far as we could judge; we were bound to conclude he would be able to stick it out, provided he could get through the winter. This would be the testing time as it is with all polar explorers. Both Allan and I had seen many winters in the polar regions and knew the telltale signs of deterioration; but we also knew from experience that if a man became depressed during the long polar night, there was little one could do to alleviate his misery. The only real cure is to send him out. To be sent out from a scientific outpost would carry with it no stigma—it happens often enough; to be sent out from an expedition such as ours on the other hand would attract considerable publicity. Ken would need to muster every bit of courage and self-control to see this expedition through; we did not doubt for a moment that he could do it.

The twenty-ninth was the only other day during that summer when the warmth of the sun penetrated our clothing to the skin. It was a perfect day; temperature two degrees above freezing; clear blue sky, not a breath of wind—the sort of day when working dogs with no work to do lay sprawled out like rugs.

Our dogs had fed well the night before on a hungry polar bear and two cubs that had come unexpectedly into camp while I was talking to Freddie on the radio. Ken had been first to notice the bears and in a state of great excitement came over to my tent for a firearm. Two of the three rifles were always kept in the parachute tent, and one on Fritz's sledge; the mother bear, by then about a hundred yards away, was being harassed by one of

Ken's dogs that was loose. Ken was worried that the bear might kill the dog and clearly was in a hurry to go to its rescue. Had his gun not jammed he would have shot the bear; as it was I shot the bear myself.

It greatly upset Ken that we had been obliged to kill that mother bear and her two cubs, but it seemed to me we had little alternative. Clearly the mother was in search of food and attracted by the scent of the camp, and had we driven her away, in all probability she would have returned. We had a talk that night about the whole attitude of the expedition toward what little game we saw: should we whenever possible kill seals and bears to feed the dogs, or should we try to leave behind us no trail of carnage? My feeling at the start of the journey had been that whenever possible we should supplement the dogs' basic diet of pemmican with fresh meat, for we did not then know for certain that the pemmican would be an adequate diet for the dogs over such a long period. The longest period that dogs had ever lived exclusively on pemmican was three months. But by now we had been five months on the Arctic Ocean and the dogs were showing no sign of inadequate feeding. The outcome of this discussion was a policy we were to regard as general for the rest of the journey: we would kill seals for dog food if or whenever an opportunity arose, but would kill polar bears only when it was quite certain that a dog's life was in danger, or if it was coming at a man. Ken meanwhile took personal possession of one of the rifles, and the rifle that had jammed was thoroughly cleaned up and tested.

Dick Dickerson, flying the ARL Dakota, found us on the thirtieth and dropped a new reserve radio to replace our No. 2 set, which had been out of action since March 23. Dick had been captain of the U.S. Navy Hercules that had made the historic flight from South Africa to New Zealand via the South Pole in 1963—the first flight ever made by that route. Many times during his remarkable career he must have flown close to his safety margin, but I doubt if even he had ever flown to a target as small and as isolated as our camp at Meltville. It was very foggy and Dick, finding us by a remarkable piece of astral navigating, told me over the radio that he could afford to make only one pass of our camp because of his short supply of fuel. In fact he was obliged to go into his reserve supply and make five passes in order to dispatch all the cargo. We saw the aircraft for only a few seconds on each run. Freddie Church, who was in the plane, saw nothing of us except a faint split-second outline of the tents.

The 1,700-mile round trip was celebrated by Dr. Max Brewer and his staff at the Arctic Research Laboratory that evening, and good reason they had for the celebration: the Dakota had pushed the limit of its range and had arrived back at Barrow with only five minutes' fuel left in its tanks. We too, that evening, celebrating 800 miles out on the Arctic Ocean, enjoyed an enormous feast while listening to Bach Suites 1 and 2 on a tiny cassette tape recorder sent out to us from London.

Max Brewer had evidently felt that we should have some variety in our diet during the summer period. He was not satisfied that I had arranged for an enormous variety of canned foods, frozen foods, and the basics for more adventurous cookery to see us through the long dark winter. "You mean they're sitting out the summer on the same diet they've been eating for the last five months?" he had exclaimed when Freddie told him how little we needed in the way of luxuries. Now he had really gone to town. The scientific instruments they had flown out for Fritz and the radio had been carefully packed in bread! In addition to the cushioned instruments there were eggs, chickens, steaks, fresh fruit. We felt safer and more contented than we had at any time; the weather no longer depressed us; we had cans of delicacies to empty into the stewpot or slop directly onto our tin plates.

Then at 1 A.M. that night the floe that had carried us steadily north for three weeks split wide open a hundred yards from our camp.

At 3 A.M. it was still opening and gray patches on the cloud base indicated vast areas of open water all around the horizon. Fritz, Allan, and I did not turn in until 4 A.M. on the thirty-first. Every hour we took a walk over to the fracture, for the two parts of the floe, which had split along a jagged line, had offset as they drifted apart, and in places the projecting "capes" were grinding against each other. We were more than a little worried that the floe might fracture at right angles from the points where the two floes were in contact; but no more fractures split our floe that night, and by midday on the thirty-first the noise of pressuring had died down and all again was peaceful.

Among the four of us in that isolated camp, only Fritz was completely wrapped up in his work and seemingly unaffected by the dreary prospect we faced every day. To Fritz the mists, the melting ice, the freshwater layer on the surface of the sea were all of scientific interest and to be measured or recorded; to the rest of us it was an environment that had turned rotten and grown tedious. I seemed to spend the whole of that summer either writing or turning the hand generator to recharge the batteries. Ken, now well-versed in the instructions he had received through the International Wool Secretariat, occupied some of his time measuring and weighing every item of footwear we had with us (seven different kinds) and the weight and thickness of our socks and mukluk liners as part of his clothing research program; Allan's chief summer project was the navigation: Once, sometimes twice a day, if the sun burned its way through the clouds, he would take a sun shot which confirmed an almost monotonously steady drift due north. But our parachute tent, in which he spread out almanac, tables, and forms and, like a boy poring over his homework, computed the fixes, was no longer the cheerful place it once had been; it was now a grimy hovel.

The ceiling by then was sagging around its props. From a web of strings hung socks and gloves. There was an odor of wet wood and stagnant water. Some of the floorboards were submerged; others, pedestaled on slippery ice, were wedged with tins and metal spikes. Two primus stoves roared beneath the table. Sledgeration boxes served as seats. We dressed for dinner in woolen sweaters and windproof trousers, down jackets, gloves, and Wellington boots. We drank beer with our meals and used table napkins. Our conversation was lively but not up to date.

Our two doctors generally did most of the talking until it was time for Dr. Koerner's nap. There would then be the usual ten-minute break, during which Ken would slip away; while Allan, overcome by drowsiness, released the cigarette from between his fingers and dozed off without closing his eyes. Allan used to call this drowsy feeling after a big meal the "bloater's lurg"—it would hang, so he told us, suspended and unseen above him and descend when the plates were stacked. Ten minutes later he would nod and give an involuntary grunt as Dr. Koerner opened one eye like the blind of a bungalow window; then they would get up and go back to work.

By September 2, when the sun found a hole in the clouds and lit the floe for a moment, our shapeless shelter was casting long shadows over a surface that was no longer familiar, for by then the first snow of winter had settled on the squalor and puddles that pockmarked the surface around our camp and had transformed an icescape, wet-green and rotten, into a dazzling wilderness. Each pit and crack was now a trap; each forest of razor-sharp crystals a hidden menace. In five weeks we would lose the sun and sink quickly into winter; but hazardous though the conditions were, the time had now come to move on.

The floe on which we had spent the summer had served us well. In the sixty days we had been camped upon it, we had drifted almost two and a half degrees due north—an average of 2.7 statute miles a day. This was much more than we had expected or even hoped for, and we were now only 92 statute miles from the position where, in my original plan I had calculated we would be at the end of the summer drift. Alas, that difference was mostly in longitude. We were too far east and would, if we were to stay at the summer floe, almost certainly change course sometime early in the winter and start drifting to the east, for we were still in the influence of currents that circulate in a clockwise gyral —the gyral in which station T-3 has been caught for more than a decade and carried four times round the western half of the Arctic basin.

We had to break away from the influence of that current system and correct our course. We had to aim at reaching latitude

85°30′N, longitude 175°E, by September 20, and in that vicinity spend four days looking around for a nest of giant floes on which to set up our winter quarters. On September 25 the Canadian Forces would fly out our massive winter supply drop. If we were lucky enough to reach that position, a strong, steady and favorable winter's drift was assured, for we would be in the transpolar drift stream and heading straight for the North Pole. But that position was 172 statute miles to our northwest; to reach it in fifteen days would mean averaging eleven and a half miles a day over a surface more treacherous than any we had sledged across in the last six months. Moreover, we had misgivings about the dogs.

The animals were well fed—indeed, we had a large amount of dog food left over, for after our experience on the training journey in the spring of 1967, I had made certain that we had ample dog food all along the line—but with the exception of Fritz's team, which had been taken out every day for a two- or three-mile run to check the movement of the surrounding floes, they had been given very little exercise. Because of Fritz's instruments we had not been able to let them off their traces. He required a sterile area for his radiation measurements—and the dogs would have made a beeline for his radiometer, anemometer mast, and every other marker he had carefully placed within a mile of the camp. In theory each dog had a circular territory of twenty-foot radius (the length of their traces), they were tethered in teams, all nine dogs to the same picket. Any one dog could roam around the territory of his own team provided he had the approval of the pack—for, as with most creatures that move around in packs, there was a "pecking order." In practice the underdogs usually stayed well clear of the rest and seldom enjoyed so much as the luxury of a stretch without being growled at or nipped. Thus only the dogs in the upper strata of the pecking order were reasonably fit for a hard haul by the end of the summer. Perhaps we should have persevered with the canvas dog boots, or tried hardening their pads with some form of chemical. There seemed little point now in worrying over it. We had loads of 1,200 pounds on each sledge all ready for them to pull, and 172 statute miles to go.

9

Accident!

AT 1:40 P.M. on September 4 we set off. The melt pools that had "burned" through the floes were now bottomless holes capped with a thin film of ice under a soft blanket of snow; long ice crystals like racks of razor-sharp spears carpeted the beds of drained meltwater pools hidden beneath a thin covering of snow. Old cracks and fractures were dangerously undercut, and intricate snow-covered channels of slush were still knee deep. The sledges stuck in every hollow; the dogs were puzzled and heavy on their feet; every yard we gained was by the whip. Exhausted, we camped after only two miles. By the following morning the sledges had burned their way through the thin crust of snow into the slush and every single item of gear had to be unloaded, the sledges moved forward a few yards onto fresh snow and loaded up again. The temperature was lower than it had been for several weeks, but at $+24°F$ was still nowhere near cold enough to freeze the slush that lay under the snow blanket, and for the rest of that day we waded through it as we chopped a way with ice axes toward the shattered remains of what perhaps once had been a sizable floe. That night I sent a message to Freddie over the radio for onward transmission to the Air Transport Command Headquarters, asking that the big winter supply drop should be made on September 25 instead of October 1 as originally planned. We needed every mile we could get out of that autumn sledging period, but in those conditions it was proving far too dangerous to sledge with heavy loads; by bringing the airdrop date forward a week we could afford to jettison some of the food we were carrying.

We made only 400 yards on the sixth before meeting a fracture in the ice. We inflated the rubber boat and got Allan across to the next floe which he covered quickly on skis. His report was depressing: after about half a mile he had come upon a belt of mush ice; the mush was loose, the belt was about 100 yards wide and stretched as far as he could see east and west across our route. We advanced the sledges about another fifty yards to a better campsite and set up for the night, but during that short move Allan sprained his back when he was wriggling the front of his sledge to loosen it from the grip of the slush. He felt very stiff the next day but managed with the use of a couple of ice axes to hobble over to the fracture with Fritz and me. It had closed up a little overnight, and although it was still working we just possibly could have got across had Allan been fit and we been prepared to take a risk. That evening in conference Fritz offered a suggestion, the details of which I cannot now recall but the gist of which went as follows: We should relay, move the gear forward in easy stages, half a load at a time, for across such obstacles as the one we had before us only light loads could be maneuvered with any degree of safety. This would mean, however, that for the first time in the journey we would be splitting up and would run the risk of getting temporarily cut off from some of our supplies. The day before, Fritz and I had been cut off from the other two for a couple of hours at one stage, but he argued that provided there was a radio with each pair we could keep in touch and reunite a few days later. It was a bold plan—and in Ken's opinion a rash one. An argument flared up between the two men and the conference promptly broke up.

Fritz and I went for a walk back to the spot which we had

tested earlier that day as a possible crossing place. Once again we found ourselves talking about the relationship between Ken and the rest of the party—which was clearly strained. The incompatibility did not manifest itself in dramatic outbursts but in a deep and nagging disapproval of each other's ideas and ideals. It was like a marriage that had failed in spite of efforts on both sides to make a go of it. The big question, not unlike the married couple's, was whether to put an end to the relationship before the winter set in (Ken could be sent out on a light aircraft which Max Brewer, who was supporting Lamont's interest in our geophysical program, would attempt to land about September 25 to deliver the gravimeter and one or two other delicate scientific instruments), or whether, out of respect for the institution of "the polar expedition" (as with couples who respect the institution of matrimony) we should stick it out to the end. Both Allan and Fritz felt Ken should be sent out. To Ken, a devout man, forgiveness and reconciliation were not only basic principles of his faith but a solution he considered dignified and honorable. While I agreed with Allan and Fritz, I felt bound as leader to give Ken the opportunity to see the expedition through to the end for his own sake and for the sake of those whom, in a sense, he represented.

We were determined to make some progress on the eighth and set off in fog, successfully crossed the fracture which had stopped us the day before, and made for a spot about 300 yards from where Allan had turned back. We stopped the sledges alongside a point where the mush-ice belt seemed to be compacting. At that point it was about sixty yards wide. Fritz and I set off across it about fifty yards apart in order to save time—should either of us have found a possible route we would have had a quick second opinion before committing the four sledges to it. That mush-ice strip under compression from the two converging floes was in a highly dangerous state. Most of the bigger blocks were ten to fifteen feet across, but judging by the greasy, green-gray appearance of that ice there had been a lot of movement along the flaw, for every block had evidently been submerged within the last twelve hours. That ice, since it was not floating naturally but being held in position only by the pressure from the floes on either side, would, if the pressure were realeased, capsize and plunge. The flaw would need to open only a few feet to upset the equilibrium of that mass, and the whole lot would have "boiled" the slush and debris. We had been told stories by the Eskimos in Barrow of hunters who had seen a whole party of Eskimos caught on such ice when it had relaxed; they were sucked under and pulverized by the ice blocks. Whether it was to put us off making a journey across mush ice, or merely to warn us of the dangers, I do not know; but I shall never forget their description of the sight and the sounds of that ice as it loosened, crushed their companions, and threw up their smashed bodies amongst a boiling stew of blood-soaked mush. Every now and then as Fritz and I were hacking a place to put our feet on the slippery ice boulders we heard groans—we could not be sure if they were the sounds of the ice compacting or relaxing. Either way it would have been a waste of time chopping a route for the sledges across a belt of mush ice as broad and as rough as that while there was any possibility of movement along the flaw. So we returned to the sledges.

Allan had not felt too bad that morning. The stiffness had worn off and he was hobbling without the use of ice axes for support, but he had not come with us on our short reconnaissance of the mush ice. Now as we were approaching we were surprised to see him sitting on the snow. Ken came out to meet us and said that Allan had hurt his back again and was feeling very cold, and by the time we reached him it was immediately obvious to all of us that he was in a bad way. In the short time that Ken had been away calling us, Allan had seized up—he could no longer move his legs and seemed to be frozen into a sitting position.

I squatted down beside him.

"Sorry, Wal," he said.

"He put his foot in a hole and fell awkwardly back there when he was running beside the sledge," Ken said. "We'd better get the tent up quick, his body temperature is falling fast."

Ken wrapped him up with a couple of wolfskins while Fritz and I went to work erecting the tent. There was no time to move

Allan to a safer spot farther from the edge of the mush ice, and judging by his agony and the difficulty we had getting him into the tent through the sleeve entrance, we had not been a moment too soon. Ken moved in with him, gave him an injection of morphine, and made him comfortable.

Ken had already given me some warning of the seriousness of Allan's injury when we were putting the tent up. The sharp jerk to Allan's back, which was already weakened by the sprain he had received two days earlier, had either slipped a disc or severely sprained a muscle; Ken said he would come over to my tent as soon as he had completed an examination. The news Ken brought was shattering: Allan was in no fit state to continue the journey and should be sent out at the first opportunity. That first opportunity would be that flight on September 25. A second opportunity was a charter flight at about the same time by the *Sunday Times* and the BBC.

It had long been the intention of the *Sunday Times* and the BBC jointly to charter Weldy Phipps, the Canadian bush pilot, to fly out from Resolute Bay in his twin-engined Otter and land at our winter campsite. The BBC crew hoped to take film of the crossing party erecting the winter quarters and of our preparation for the winter sojourn on the ice; the *Sunday Times* crew were to interview us. For my own part, I had always had mixed feelings about this landing, although clearly it would be to the expedition's advantage, should the Arctic Research Laboratory flight be unable to reach us: we could then use the press plane to send out all the exposed film and records and to deliver Allan's delicate scientific instruments. Even before Allan's accident, I had therefore decided to give our sponsors as much encouragement as they might need and as much cooperation as possible.

Fritz and I, deeply depressed by the seriousness of Allan's injury, spent a long time after Ken had returned to his patient discussing the situation. Not only was Allan one of our closest friends and an ideal sledging companion, he was an essential part of our crew. Although he had no academic qualifications, he had spent several years in the polar regions as a geophysical assistant and was, from a practical point of view, eminently capable of running our geophysical program. He was also a man with a talent for improvising, and although most explorers have this talent to some degree, he was a master of the art. We were of course even at that black moment hoping for a miraculous recovery, and felt sure, knowing Allan, that within a couple of days he would be able to tell us whether or not he wanted to take the risk of staying through the winter.

There could be no question now of continuing our journey northwest in an attempt to correct our course and reach the transpolar drift stream. Nor could we cross the mush-ice belt with Allan now bedridden, and the small floe on which were were presently camped was really too vulnerable even for an overnight stop. We had to find a safe place to shift Allan, preferably one that would be suitable as a winter floe. We therefore decided to try to locate the string of floes on which we had spent the summer, and while Ken remained with Allan to minister to his needs and keep an eye on the state of the ice nearby, Fritz and I set off the following morning with two sledges, a radio, sleeping bags and provisions for ten days.

We sledged into a head wind and drifting snow, not back along our outward sledge tracks (for the route had been smashed up behind us), but in what we guessed to be a direct line for the summer floe, and to our surprise found it. Retracing our tracks with difficulty we stuck in marker flags and returned to the mush-ice camp relieved to see that it was still intact, and that Allan was comfortable. I now had to inform Freddie and the committee about the accident and set in motion arrangements for a replacement for Allan in case he failed to recover. Fritz went over to visit Allan, and Ken came over to my tent to report on his patient. I sent a carefully worded message which was marked URGENT AND CONFIDENTIAL—INFO DR. MAX BREWER:

> Distressed to report Gill has badly injured his back. Hedges suspects either acute slipped disc or severe muscle strain, both of which are liable to recur. Found summer floe after search today. Gill will be drugged and man-hauled to summer

floe as soon as possible. If no miraculous recovery within next few days will have to ask ARL to fly him out in the Cessna that brings in the geophysical equipment. Need with the utmost urgency a replacement ex-Falkland Island Dependency or ex-British Antarctic Survey geophysicist. Renner first choice. Please ask him if he will drop everything to join us for ten months.

We had not yet looked for a landing strip in the vicinity of the summer camp—we had been in too much of a hurry to get back to the mush-ice camp before the drifting snow obliterated our tracks—but we felt reasonably confident that a Cessna-180 fitted with skis would be able to find a landing strip somewhere within a five-mile radius of the old summer camp by the twenty-fifth. As for the possibility of a miraculous recovery, I asked Ken for his opinion. He explained that even if Allan did recover, the possibility of a recurrence must be seriously considered, and to my suggestion that we might nurse Allan through the winter he remained adamant that he should be evacuated at the first opportunity.

The two of us made a second journey to the old summer floe the following day, taking on that occasion a small load of expendable stores which we left in a depot about a mile to the south of the old summer campsite. Nearby we found a frozen polynya which had formed after the zigzag fracture had offset and closed. The ice cover on the polynya was about eight inches thick and was fresh-water ice containing only 0.2 parts of salt per thousand (as compared to sea water which shows about 30 parts per thousand). The reason for this is that after a long summer melt the top four to six feet of the surface water layer is water melted from the floes which, if older than a year, will have lost most of their salt. When sea water freezes, the salt concentrates in pockets of brine which "migrate" down through the floe until the brine is released into the water below and sinks. Fresh water is stronger but less flexible—we guessed that eighteen inches of fresh water would hold a Cessna and, provided the polynya ice did not crack up, it should be thick enough in about a week or ten days. The polynya was certainly long enough; there was a good thousand yards of it.

My sked that night with Freddie was on some counts not too encouraging: I received a message from London telling me that Geoff Renner was not available and from Freddie learned that there was still no confirmation that Lamont Geological Observatory were interested in my offer of our winter quarters at the end of our winter drift. I had hoped they would take it over and thus extend our geophysical program. I now had another reason for wanting them to participate in our scientific program: Provided Allan survived the winter without a relapse, he could stay on at winter quarters as the station leader accompanied by one or two of Lamont's men and continue the geophysical program he had directed through the winter months. In this way, he would have some consolation in not completing the journey, for which presumably he would be unfit. What had set me thinking positively along these lines was partly the improvement in Allan's condition (he was no longer suffering acute pain), his wish to remain through the winter and take the chance on a relapse, and a message from Max Brewer saying he did not think it feasible to send a replacement man in the aircraft that might fly out the gravimeters—and in any case this flight was not definite. The only really good news I had that night was confirmation of the extra aircraft fuel I had requested added to our winter supply drop, in order to stock our winter quarters as a refueling depot for Cessnas or twin Otters.

All this I discussed with Fritz in great detail and we both came to the same general conclusion that if Allan was fit enough to get through the winter but not fit enough to travel the following spring, the only way by which the four members of the expedition could complete all the programs was to split up: Ken should stay at winter quarters with Allan until the Cessnas brought in the Lamont crew about March 1, 1969. Allan would remain on the ice through to June as station leader with the Lamont crew and continue the geophysical work he had conducted right through the winter. Ken would either go out on the aircraft that had brought in the Lamont crew or remain with the station until its crew was relieved in June. There was, it seemed to us, no other way by which both the crossing and the scientific work could be completed, for unless the crossing party left winter quarters by mid-February at the latest, we would not make it to Spitsbergen before the summer melt. It would of course be a great disappointment for Ken should this plan be implemented, but far less so than it would be for Allan, who had devoted twelve years of his life to polar work and who regarded the crossing of the Arctic Ocean as the culmination of that career. As for the feasibility of two men completing the journey, Fritz and I had not the slightest doubt. Throughout the toughest part of the journey we had worked together as a pair with Fritz and me sharing the lead. Nansen and Johansen had as a pair survived a tough journey across the Arctic ice pack and they had not had the advantage of supply drops. No, there was no question of whether or not we could do it, and unless Allan by the following spring was fit enough to complete the journey to Spitsbergen we would have no alternative. The only possible complication we could envisage at that time was that Allan might not be sufficiently recovered by the time the BBC and *Sunday Times* crews came out to visit us on September 25, but I had no intention of making a hasty decision on whether or not to evacuate him; I would weigh up the chances of a relapse against its consequences both to Allan's future health and to the logistics problems of getting an aircraft out in winter to evacuate him. But the final factor, and the one which would carry the heaviest weight, as far as I was concerned, was whether or not Allan wanted to be evacuated.

On the morning of the eleventh, Fritz and I set off from the mush-ice camp with three loaded sledges—Fritz in the lead with his own team and sledge, Allan's team following without a driver, and I bringing up the rear with my own team. Not until that morning had Allan been sufficiently recovered to stand the shock of the journey; to save time, therefore, Fritz and I intended to shift as much gear as possible over to the summer floe. It was a journey of only about two miles but exhausting work, for every time Allan's driverless dogs stuck, either Fritz or I had to leave our own team and get the stuck team started again. And yet it was with three teams that Nansen and Johansen had traveled across the polar pack; indeed, they had originally set out from the *Fram* with six sledges—an impossible problem of management even for those two extraordinary men. Clearly, if Fritz and I were obliged to make the journey from winter quarters through to Spitsbergen as a pair, it would have to be with two large teams of dogs and loads as light as possible—say thirteen or fourteen dogs to a sledge. With teams of this size, provided we could keep the weight down, we would have more power with which to negotiate the pressure ridges.

We tethered my team and Allan's at the old summer-floe depot, put up a tent, off-loaded the gear and supplies we had brought over on the three sledges, and returned to the mush-ice camp with Fritz's team. We pulled the tent down around Allan and loaded him, still in his sleeping bag, onto an upturned inflated rubber boat that was lashed to Ken's sledge. Well bolstered and protected from the elements by a rubber groundsheet, he was driven over the two-mile course at a fair pace with Ken giving a running commentary on what was happening and what ice forms he was passing, for strapped in securely as he was, he could see nothing but the lurching sky above him. That night in the tent we used the hurricane lamps for the first time in almost six months. We could expect a shorter transition between day and night at that higher latitude; within three weeks the sun would be gone and the long polar night would have begun.

Ken came over to report on how Allan had withstood the journey back to the summer floe and spent some time explaining to me as he had to Allan just what a slipped disc was and how it could be treated. From what I gathered a man could, provided he was very careful, survive the condition with field treatment. In the long term, a patient treated in the field might not make so satisfactory a recovery—indeed, as a result of inadequate treatment at the time of the injury, he might suffer for years from a weak back; he might even be crippled for life. There was also the possibility of a relapse of the injury during the winter. Ken had evidently made this perfectly clear to Allan. Nevertheless, my general impression from this conversation was that while Allan would certainly receive better treatment in hospital, with care he might well survive the winter without a relapse and without serious long-term consequences. I put this impression to Ken as a hypothetical question, and got the answer I had hoped for—that there was no risk to life, and that should Allan suffer a relapse we had an ample supply of pain-killers to comfort the injured man. The question now revolved (since I knew Allan was prepared to take the risk of staying on the Arctic Ocean throughout the winter) solely on whether or not I as leader was prepared to take overall responsibility.

Fritz and I went over to visit Allan and Ken in their tent the following morning. Allan was now able to raise himself to eat, and the continuous pain, though more widespread, was less intense. It was a great relief to see him looking a little better and after a brew of tea we got onto the subject of Allan's future, and to the astonishment of Allan, Fritz and me it soon became obvious that Ken was determined that Allan should be evacuated if a landing was made at our camp, in spite of the fact that Allan wanted to stay through the winter and that I as leader, having overnight given careful consideration to all the possible consequences of a relapse, was prepared to let him. I asked Ken point-blank what his intentions would be if I proceeded with my plans against his advice. He told me he would resign but remain at his post to continue the patient's care. He later explained to me that his answer had been intended neither as a threat nor a gesture of defiance but as a demonstration against a plan which would in his opinion jeopardize his patient's long-term chances of returning to normal health for returns that could only materially benefit the short-term interests of the crossing party. We all three reminded Ken that Allan wanted to stay and that it was up to him to decide whether or not the risks to him personally were justified. Furthermore, I argued that having been fully briefed by Ken on what he considered to be the nature of Allan's injury, it was now up to me the leader, not the doctor, to decide whether or not Allan should be evacuated, and that this decision would be based not only on Allan's personal feelings about the issue but on a consideration of every possible aspect and consequence.

Our difference of opinion could not be resolved: Ken felt it was his responsibility as a doctor to safeguard the well-being of his patient; my feeling was that if a member of an expedition in the middle of the Arctic Ocean had sufficient distrust in his leader's judgment to resign, then it was better in the interest of the party as a whole that that man's resignation should be accepted and he should be evacuated as soon as possible. Ken's offer of resignation however was hypothetical, for everything depended on whether or not an aircraft could reach us and make a landing at our camp. If there was no aircraft, there could be no formal showdown; but the damage had in fact already been done. Ken's demonstration, sincere though it was and admirable from an ethical standpoint, had shown Allan, Fritz, and me that here was a determined man, a man of the highest principles, but one who was nevertheless lacking in one important consideration: the instinctive acceptance of calculated risk. Every journey we three had ever made had been a calculated risk. We thrived on such risks. The trans-Arctic journey was the greatest and most carefully calculated risk we had ever taken—justified because it was the last great pioneer journey that man could make in the polar regions. To give up while there was a chance of success or to be evacuated while there was a chance of recovery was absolutely out of the question. This was not a case of sentiment over Allan's predicament getting the better of sound judgment; it was the judgment of highly motivated men, men determined to go on.

That night Ken handed me a medical report on Allan addressed to the commandant of the Royal Army Medical College in London via Sir Vivian Fuchs. In it he stated that Allan had an acute prolapsed intravertebral disc, gave details of his examination, and said that he had strongly advised me that Allan should be evacuated if at all possible and should not spend the winter on the Arctic Ocean. He mentioned that Allan wanted to stay and that he as Allan's doctor was under extreme pressure to acquiesce, but that he was most concerned about the outcome should Allan have a further relapse. He asked for advice on the prognosis and on the wisdom of Allan remaining with the expedition even though in a sedentary capacity. This I transmitted to Freddie. That same night I received confirmation that an attempt would be made by Weldy Phipps in the twin-engined Otter to land at our camp with the BBC and *Sunday Times* crews on September 25.

The wind blew all the next day and built up drifts of snow around the tent as I wrote, and that night I transmitted the results of my efforts: a short article for the *Sunday Times* and a message to the committee.

In the latter I reviewed the prospects:

> Because of the unusually open season, a Cessna flight by a direct route from Barrow out to the expedition's position at latitude 84°05′N, longitude 162°W, is not possible. A Cessna flight by the longer route via Mould Bay and T-3 would be almost as hazardous an operation. It may nevertheless shortly be attempted by the Naval Arctic Research Laboratory in order to deliver a small payload of delicate geophysical equipment. In this case, however, no passengers can be carried and no evacuation would be attempted except in a dire emergency for the extra payload of an injured man would decrease the margin of safety and put, perhaps unnecessarily, a considerable burden of responsibility on the pilot in the event of a forced landing. . . .
>
> I am advised that Gill may repeat may comfortably and safely get through the winter by occupying himself with the sedentary aspects of the scientific program and light tasks which would relieve the monotony and be an asset to the party, even if in a bedridden state. Fully aware of the risks and consequences, Gill nevertheless wishes to stay with the expedition through the winter. I realize he would receive better medical treatment in a well-equipped hospital and that the professional advice given me by Major Hedges is in the best long-term interests of Gill's state of health. In response however to Gill's wishes and more especially in consideration of the risks involved in

trying to evacuate him by Cessna in the twilight of an abnor-
mally open summer, I recommend that no attempt should be
made to evacuate him until the condition of the ice improves
or, preferably, until the return of the sun—unless of course he
suffers a relapse.

I also sent a message that night from Ken to the committee
reporting the uneventful progress Allan was making toward recovery, but amplifying the argument for evacuating him. The
message pointed out that Allan had for some months been both-
ered by knee trouble which, when weighed with his recent injury
and an earlier, less obvious episode of back trouble which had
lasted for several days in April, made him a poor physical risk
from the sledging point of view next spring.

I received word that night from Sir Vivian Fuchs saying that
"the Royal Army Medical College states emphatically that Gill
must be evacuated when possible and should not repeat not continue sledging even if recovered as he will remain a danger to
rest of party." This I regarded as a predictable reply to the one
sent by Ken.

During the next three days, Fritz and I made a thorough reconnaissance of the area and I reported to Freddie by radio that
we had found a good site for the winter camp about a mile and a
half in diameter. The whole nest of floes covered an area of about
five square miles, but each floe was separated from its neighbor
by either a pressure ridge or a strip of mush ice. On the polynyas
near our camp I reported that we had found a number of long
level stretches, the best two of which were about half and three
quarters of a mile respectively, but the ice on both needed to
thicken up considerably before they could be used as landing
strips for aircraft.

I was at the receiving end of some good news over the radio at
this time too: Freddie had heard from Air Transport Command
Headquarters that the Canadian Forces would give us the two additional airdrops I had requested as a result of my assessment of
July 6; the first of these drops was to be in March, 1969, the
other two in April and May.

I did not go out with Fritz on his reconnaissance of the floes around us on the seventeenth but spent all day drafting a message to the committee, outlining my two-man assault plan for the concluding stage of the journey and informing them of my decision to let Allan stay with the expedition right through the winter. Evacuation in the unlikely event of a relapse would not be difficult, since the expedition was only one hundred and fifty miles from T-3, which could be used as a staging post. The winter is the normal flying season for air operations on the Arctic Ocean, and an airstrip could easily be lit with candle beacons and marker flares.

The following day I received through Freddie a rumor in the form of a quote from a message from the Foreign News Editor of the *Sunday Times* to Peter Dunn. It said: "Fuchs now definitely decided not to send in fourth man or outbring Gill." Allan of course was delighted, but Ken was puzzled by this message which seemed to indicate that the committee was ignoring his recommendations. We had another long conference between the four of us on the twentieth and yet another on the twenty-first, but without resolving our differences.

Ken drafted another message to the committee for transmission that night, but it was never sent, for no sooner had Freddie made radio contact than he read out a message from London:

> Committee discussed all known factors including communications and beacons. While recognizing Allan's great wish to winter we regretfully decided that on medical grounds and to enable earliest possible start next spring, he must, repeat must be evacuated in Phipps' plane. A three-man party is regarded as the minimum acceptable risk, therefore Wally, Ken and Fritz to winter and complete journey. We appreciate this may mean abandoning geophysical program if spring landing to recover instruments cannot be made before journey resumed. Lamont should be warned of this problem. Letters written yesterday to be delivered by plane will indicate the thinking which prompted committee's decision.

Ken was with me at the time the message came through. I read it out with difficulty for the words stuck in my throat. The *Times* rumor evidently was too good to be true. Ken went back ahead of me to the tent where Allan and Fritz were having a brew; I walked around for a while trying to get a grip on what I suppose was a mixture of anger and the deepest personal sympathy for my old sledging companion—but for whose loyalty, at the end of the Greenland journey, I would never have held the committee's confidence in the plan and subsequently got the trans-Arctic journey under way. I crawled through the tent and squatted on a box at the foot of Ken's bed. Allan and Fritz looked up expectantly.

"You've shot your bolt, mate—they want you out."

Allan had taken fresh air for the first time that day, hobbling around near the tent talking to his dogs. He was out again the next day too for a short walk, and later I took him on a ride on a sledge which we had fitted up with a padded seat over to the polynya. Fritz joined us and together we observed that it had fractured across the middle, reducing its length to about one hundred yards on our side of the water. We could see no way across that fracture—no way of making use of the longer stretch which remained intact. The floe on which we were camped had also split and we were now cut off from the old summer campsite. But it was a dull, depressing day in every other respect. Nor did what I felt find its full expression in the written word. I had put a plan to the committee and expected their support. It had been impossible to give them my recommendations in great detail, for every word had to be transmitted 4,800 miles. But then, there was no need for me to give more than a brief and direct opinion; I was the leader of the expedition, the man in the field, the man directly responsible. Nevertheless it was indiscreet of me on the night of the twenty-second to tell Freddie over the radio (in the relative privacy of a frequency seldom used at that time of day, and in the knowledge that there were very few eavesdroppers with receivers sensitive enough to monitor my transmissions) what I thought of the committee's directive: ". . . they don't know what the bloody hell they are talking about."

For half an hour every day for the last seven months I had spoken on the radio to Freddie. Rarely had I been aware during those conversations of the distance that separated us, for I had grown as accustomed to his radio voice as I had to the mannerisms of my three traveling companions. Night after night for five months he had sat in his radio shack, jamming his hands over his earphones like a man with migraine, listening for my signals through the raucous noise caused by geomagnetic and iono-spheric storms on the off chance that I might have an important message to pass. If all else failed, he would try again later, switch-ing from voice contact to Morse and probing through the ear-shattering crackle to pick up signals so weak at times that he sometimes suspected they were more imagined than real. Freddie and I had passed our traffic and comments on the day's events as between friends who by profession are diplomats, guarding our remarks now and then and on occasions using cipher to protect the interests of the expedition, its committee and its sponsors. On only one occasion did I make a spontaneous and angry critcism—the one I had just uttered. Had the remark been less spontaneous it would have reflected more truly my relationship with the com-mittee, with whom I had worked in harmony for two and a half years and for whom I had the highest regard. Had it been less spontaneous, however, it would no doubt have been less quot-able, and far less often quoted.

It made the headlines of some of the biggest-circulation news-papers in England on September 25: ROW OVER ARCTIC EX-PLORER said the *Daily Mail:*

> A row broke out last night over the four-man British Trans-Arctic Expedition, which is now about three hundred and thirty miles from the North Pole. The organizers in London is-sued the statement saying that the leader may be suffering from "Winteritis." This is a condition "which clouds the judgment and can become a danger," but the leader, Mr. Wally Herbert, whose dog-sledges are now two-thirds of the 3,800 miles be-tween Alaska and the Norwegian Island of Spitzbergen, hit back with fierce criticism of the Organizing Committee. In an interview with the *Sunday Times,* Mr. Herbert said over a radio link: "The Committee are getting completely carried away with themselves sending me directives when they should be sending recommendations."

You are crouched in a tiny tent on an ice floe three hundred and thirty miles from the North Pole. Outside a hurricane rages at 120 mph. Outside you cannot see a yard in front of you in the blinding snow. Outside your dogs in the sledge team bite and snarl at each other. Inside you huddle for warmth against your three companions. One is injured. You are off course, and behind schedule. The eyes of the world are upon you. This is the agony at this moment of Wally Herbert, leader of the British Trans-Arctic Expedition, the loneliest man in the world in the earth's white graveyard. What effect can such appalling conditions have on the mind and morale of a man? Do they explain the terse messages Herbert has been sending back to the Expedition's organizers in London?

These were the opening words in an article entitled IN THE ARCTIC BLIZZARDS, EVEN A MAN'S MIND CAN FREEZE UP by Donald Gomery of the *Daily Sketch* of September 26, 1968.

Or yet another: IF YOU EVER JUST SIT AND STARE BLANKLY AT THE OFFICE WALL . . . THEN YOU COULD HAVE "WINTERITIS." "Wally Herbert, leader of the British Trans-Arctic Expedition, may be suffering from 'Winteritis' says the expedition's London organizers. They describe the condition as one which 'clouds the judgment and can become a danger' " (Peter Pringle, *Evening News,* September 25). With so much drama and so much speculation, it was hardly any wonder that the interpretation of my behavior was at times a little bizarre.

On the twenty-fifth and twenty-sixth we received our massive winter supply drop from 435 Squadron of the Canadian Air Force. The drop was an outstanding success. The two C-130 Hercules, having made their first low pass of our camp in formation, had separated and taken up stations a few minutes apart and systematically peppered our chosen floe with seventy parachute loads of supplies for men and dogs totaling twenty-eight tons— and the only loss was a dozen bottles of HP sauce! We had come to rely on the Canadian Forces not only for our supply drops but also for the moral support and encouragement we needed in order to survive. We sensed this encouragement in the care taken to check our equipment, the many thoughtful gifts—magazines, cakes, fruit, even a bathtub on this occasion—and the shouts of the dispatchers standing in the open cargo door at the rear of the aircraft as they made their final low passes of the camp.

Richard Taylor of the BBC and his filming crew were on board one of the C-130's, and I had taken the opportunity of warning him that the ice conditions were not good for the twin-engined Otter landing. But Richard was most anxious to try and told me they would be setting out from Resolute the following day on the first stage of their long flight to T-3.

The main landing strip had by then badly cracked up and was unsuitable. There was a fracture near the camp with a fresh-water-ice skin eight to nine inches thick; this fracture was about one hundred and fifty yards long and thirty yards wide, but there were walls of pressure on either side of it up to fifteen feet high. The possible landing strip on the floe was covered by a six-inch blanket of soft snow and I estimated it would take several days to clear. I understood from one of Freddie's comments that Weldy Phipps proposed using his twin Otter with retractable wheels, rather than the Dakota wheels he used on occasions in the Canadian Arctic when he was contemplating a landing on either a rough rocky beach or soft snow. Only by using retractable wheels would he have the range to fly in one leg from Mould Bay in NWT to T-3, for he had a heavy payload of men and camera equipment. I sent a message to Freddy recommending that Weldy fit skis to the twin Otter, for he would not stand a chance of landing at our camp otherwise. I also suggested, since we had so much gear to collect from the floe, that Weldy's flight be delayed until September 30 or October 1, and warned Peter Dunn and Richard Taylor that I seriously believed that the ice might crack up at any time and that there was a strong possibility that even if Weldy was able to land he might be unable to get back down to pick up the men landed at our camp.

The *Sunday Times* crew arrived at T-3 on the thirtieth; Weldy Phipps landed on T-3 October first with the BBC crew. An attempt to reach the expedition was arranged for the following day, but radio conditions generally were spasmodic, owing to an auroral disturbance, and the poor weather. The best I could do for them was to oblige with a long radio interview as a safeguard against the possibility that they would be unable to land at our winter quarters. I spoke to Weldy Phipps too, who told me he would need a minimum of two feet of ice before he could risk putting the twin Otter down on a frozen lead. Even at this stage, however, there was still a possibility of a landing, for had Weldy and his planeload flown over us and found a landing site within a radius of three miles of our camp which he considered safe enough, he would have fulfilled his charter and landed. I would then have had to make the vital decision: whether to send Allan out or go against the committee's directive by keeping him on the ice; accepting Ken's resignation and either letting him stay with the expedition, as he had offered to do in order to look after Allan, or sending him out. Allan was by now up and about and carefully active. He had played an important part in helping to erect the hut and apart from the dreadful wait for the final decision was now almost resigned to going out. He made one last effort, however, in cahoots with Fritz: the pair of them came over, rather sheepishly I thought, and suggested that Allan should ski off and hide. Hilarious though the thought of this was when they put it to me, they were dead serious and wanted to know if this would embarrass me. I told them that this would not be necessary, for in confidence I had been assured a couple of days ago by Max Brewer that I had his full sympathy, and that he would mount an airlift should I decide to keep Allan on the ice and should he suffer a relapse during the winter. As for a landing strip, we felt sure there would always be a polynya within five miles of the camp suitable for a light aircraft, possibly even for a wheeled Dakota. Meanwhile there seemed no point in exacerbating the delicate situation with the committee by announcing this intention in advance of a landing, nor for that matter upsetting Ken by offering him the dilemma of whether or not to resign in protest against an action that might not need to be taken.

After a three-day wait on T-3, the attempt to reach us in the

twin Otter was called off. Foul weather at our camp and bad radio propagation had foiled the attempt on October 3, and whiteout conditions on the fourth spoiled the final effort of the press
to get more than a fleeting glimpse of us as they roared overhead
in the Arctic Research Laboratory's Dakota, which had homed
in on our radio beacon about thirty miles out. Peter Dunn got an
interesting, though not entirely accurate story out from Barrow
for the *Sunday Times* about the abortive mission:

> . . . twenty-four hours after receiving the committee's order
> to evacuate Gill, Herbert noticed that the landing strip was
> breaking up around his camp. Even the thicker ice-floe land-
> ing area was becoming unapproachable due to heavy snow-
> falls—"a hell of a job to clear," Herbert said. Out on T-3 we
> heard Herbert report difficulty with his hand-operated battery
> charger which charges his radio batteries. Then his voice faded
> away and further contact was impossible. Nex morning, a
> fairly clear day for observations from the aircraft, we had an
> early radio date with Herbert in which he was to have reported
> on a further reconnaissance around him. Unfortunately, al-
> though we could hear Barrow radio eight hundred miles away
> on the Arctic coast, we didn't hear Herbert who was on the
> same frequency one hundred and fifty miles of the west of us.
> Herbert's radio improved amazingly when the landing became
> unthinkable. He was at that point in excellent form.
>
> Herbert now has everything his own way. Gill stays out
> until he wants him to leave. The scientific equipment which we
> took to T-3 for the expedition's winter program has been
> lugged back to Barrow and will be parachuted to the expedi-
> tion's winter camp by the Arctic Research Laboratory. A par-
> ticularly delicate instrument has been left on T-3 and will prob-
> ably be landed at the camp by one of the laboratory's highly
> skilled bush pilots. The general opinion here seems to be that
> the fuss over Allan Gill got a little out of hand: whatever hap-
> pens this winter, Herbert will not be short of friends on the
> North Alaskan coast and he will not need aircraft support di-
> rected from London.

10

The Long Drift

THAT autumn journey was the shortest and most abortive I have ever made. In the eight days from the time we left our summer camp to the time we returned with an injured man, we had covered only six and a half miles and our farthest north latitude was a mere two miles from the floe on which we had spent the summer. Luck was not entirely against us, however, for by the time we returned to that floe it was about sixteen miles farther north than when we had left it, and the favorable drift continued right through to October 6—the date on which officially we established our winter quarters. On that date our floe crossed the eighty-fifth parallel at longitude 162°W (admittedly by only a few hundred yards); it then drifted back a few miles before changing direction and once again heading toward the Pole.

But grateful though we were for this drift, which in the month since leaving the summer camp had carried us one degree due north, the setback of Allan's injury and the consequences of our failure to correct our course and get out the influence of the Beaufort Gyral was serious. We were now 126 statute miles to the ESE of the position we had hoped to reach when we had set out on

September 4, and 240 miles behind our original schedule. The floe itself seemed safe enough—after all, its four-meter thickness had enabled it to survive the summer melt while the younger, thinner floes nearby had either melted down to a fragile shell or disappeared altogether—but its direction of drift was bound to change. Judging by the drift tracks of station T-3 on its previous circuits of the western half of the Arctic basin, it seemed likely that within the next month we would start a long slow drift ENE, which would put us by the end of the winter even further behind schedule.

It was a depressing prospect, relieved not even by the remarkable drift of October 3 to 5, when the floe was blown NNW almost 30 miles, or by the great amount of activity at our camp during those early days of October, 1968.

Gathering together all the essential tools and sections of the winter hut took much less time than we had expected. It had been dropped in one enormous load about five feet by thirteen feet long with three parachutes; we separated it into individual crates and sledged them to the site. With three of us working hard at the store hauling, Allan occupied himself usefully on repairing the damaged floor-sections of the hut, and in less than eight hours on the twenty-eighth we had laid the floor on the perfectly flat frozen surface of what in the summer had been a fresh-water lake.

The construction of the hut was very simple. The packing boxes themselves we used as a floor and their contents were erected around them. This was basically a frame, covered with padded blankets, which had two windows at each end and one door leading to a small porch. The hut went up very quickly once the floor was laid—in about nine hours as I recall. The floor dimensions were 15 feet by 15 feet, but since the hut was cylindrical in shape the effective area was somewhat smaller. It was of course bare at that time, and we guessed rightly that it would be just a little cramped for four men by the time it was cluttered with furniture and gear. On the other hand we did not want too much space, since it would be too difficult to heat.

The heating arrangement was a Coleman space heater, a kerosene-burning stove which had an exhaust pipe running upward for about five feet before turning through a right angle out of the hut. With the stove roughly in the center of the hut, and the exhaust pipe traveling some fifteen feet inside, we had the benefit of an extra source of heating (in fact, this pipe at times became very hot, the temperature at the top of the hut running as high as 80° or 90°F while on the bare floor it was below freezing).

A corner of the hut had been allocated to each man, who had furnished it according to his needs and temperament. Ken characteristically had been the first to get himself organized. An upturned packing crate served for a few days as a writing desk and, with shelves hammered inside, a storebox for clothes and personal gear. Set up over the foot of his bunk he had constructed more shelves, the backboard of which served to partition off the kitchen alcove.

Fritz's furniture, unsymmetrical and cramped, looked very cozy but somewhat rickety, while my own, covering three square feet of floor more than my share, was a robust-looking piece of carpentry incorporating a writing desk and a set of shelves built around four radios, two tape recorders, cameras, books, and navigational tables. Charts of the Arctic Ocean mounted on plywood boards were strapped to the sloping ceiling of the hut; rifles hung near the door; drying woolens, anoraks, wolverine mitts, wolfskin parkas, and pressure lamps hung from the hut's ribs. It was a hut soon aromatic with the smell of newly baked bread and noisy with the clatter of carpentry; a hut in which there were only three beds, for Allan, in spite of his back, and for some reason which he was never able adequately to explain, preferred to sleep in a tent outside.

On October 8 I transmitted a message to the expedition's patron, HRH the Duke of Edinburgh, informing him that we had established winter quarters on October 6, the day the sun set at latitude 85°00′N, longitude 162°00′W—950 statute miles from Barrow, Alaska, and 550 miles from the nearest land.

. . . During the next five months, while we are fully and usefully occupied with our scientific program, our hut, which is situated on an icefloe at present one mile in diameter and three meters thick, will be drifting and, if our predictions prove correct, will by March 1, 1969, be at latitude 87°00′N, longitude 150°00′W. From that position, providing the crossing party sets out three weeks before sunrise and resists the temptation of trying precisely to locate the North Pole (in the vicinity of which we expect to be on or about the vernal equinox), it should be possible to reach Spitsbergen or a rendezvous with HMS *Endurance* before Midsummer's Day.

At the time of establishing winter quarters, Allan's sleeping habits made good sense for it was still warm—the temperature was about minus 10°F. It did not stay warm for long, but Allan stuck it out, and right through the winter insisted he enjoyed creeping away to his tent each night. It was naturally a great temptation to make use of that corner of the hut in which there was no furniture and no bed, but Allan regarded this as his territory and didn't want anyone else's stuff in it. If it was a shambles, he preferred it to be a shambles of his own equipment. Generally we didn't go in for personal things like photographs; there were no pinups and not a single picture until toward the end of the winter when Fritz put up a colored picture from one of the *Sunday Times* magazines, a Matisse I think. The only other things of a decorative nature were some Christmas cards which Ken had been set in the summertime marked "not to be opened until Christmas Eve." These he had stuck on the door for we had no other Christmas decorations.

We were reasonably squared away by the end of the first week of the winter. In a random scatter around the floe we had laid out five depots totalling 32,620 pounds of food and fuel, which included sledging rations enough for sixty-five days (to cover any emergencies that might occur during the winter and the first stage of the dash to Spitsbergen); four new Greenland-type sledges modified slightly by the manufacturer in England as a result of radio messages giving our comments on the performance of the sledges during the first half of the journey; two new pyramid tents; three new sets of sledging clothing; crates of shirts, sweaters, underclothing, socks; new sleeping bags and bedding; down jackets, headgear, gloves, mitts, mukluks, snow boots; sunglasses in anticipation of the return of the sun six months later; and the eight 45-gallon drums of av-gas and three drums of JP-4, which I had arranged during the summer to have dropped to us as additional items in our winter airdrop to cover any emergency landings during the long polar night. The dogs were tethered downwind of a quadrant of virgin snow reserved for Fritz's micrometeorological instruments and air-sampling apparatus, and all empty crates and boxes were shifted downwind and well clear of the hut as a reserve of timber for later use in the construction of an astro-observation shelter and an extension to the tiny hut porch.

During all this activity Allan was playing quite an active part. He was very careful of course not to lift boxes when anyone was watching, but there were plenty of jobs he could manage: furniture making, puttering in the hut sorting out gear, rigging up the Honda generator and battery bank, doing the navigational fixes and computing them—usually balancing the books on his lap, for there was seldom space on the workshop table he had built, and he did not feel at home in any other part of the hut. He was eagerly looking forward to starting his geophysical program, which would involve three hourly gravity and magnetics readings and ocean-depth soundings. We did not know what sort of readings to expect, but many scientists suspected at that time that the 40,000-mile seismic chain of mid-ocean ridges, of which the mid-Atlantic ridge is an important link, extended across the Polar basin. Soviet scientists have been studying gravity and magnetics in the Polar basin for twenty years; unfortunately very little of their valuable information is released and the Western scientist has to be satisfied with the occasional published interpretation unsubstantiated by data. As many as ten years ago, however, their findings were raising questions about past climates and the wanderings of the poles—subjects which in the last few years have been attracting the attention of geophysicists the world over.*

---

* When Alfred Wegener first proposed the theory of the drifting continents in 1912, he was ridiculed by many eminent geologists of his day. He observed that the continental boundaries, taken not as the present-day coastline but as

Ken had already started his comparative study of wool and synthetic clothing during the summer; now he took accurate measurements and weights of all the various items of clothing that we would wear during the winter, and organized a clothing diary in which all the gear worn by each member of the party would be recorded by the individual together with his subjective comments. Coupled with this log and all of Ken's other measurements was a physical-fitness test which we performed twice a day—before breakfast and last thing at night before turning in. We would take a pulse rate before and immediately after the exercise, which involved stepping onto and off a box about 18 inches high every two seconds for three minutes in time with a beat recorded on a tape recorder. The difference in the pulse rate would indicate an index of fitness at the end of a day's toil and after a night's sleep. Of the four of us, Fritz undoubtedly was the finest athlete; the difference in his pulse rate seldom varied by more than one or two beats in a minute.

Fritz was also the busiest during the first two weeks at winter quarters in getting his scientific program underway, but by October 19 it was operational and we were all comfortably settled in among a concentration of gear so conveniently to hand that we

---

the edge of the continental shelf, could be fitted together almost perfectly like pieces of a jigsaw puzzle. The coincidence of finding geologically identical structures where the continents fit together was too great to be ignored; but over the last few years, gravity, magnetics and paleomagnetics data have proved beyond reasonable doubt that the continental-drift "theory" is a fact. One of the last obstructions to the theory had been the mid-ocean ridges, and in 1964 when I first proposed crossing the Arctic Ocean, the link in the chain of mid-ocean ridges which was attracting the interest of polar scientists was the Lomonosov Ridge. I had proposed to set up winter quarters on the Alaskan side of this submarine ridge and conduct a program of gravity, magnetics and ocean-depth soundings as we drifted over it during the winter night. But as it worked out, we were so far behind schedule that it looked as though we would be drifting over the Alpha Ridge instead—a submarine ridge that by 1968 was exciting the geophysicists at Lamont far more than the Lomonosov Ridge, for the magnetics anomalies there were of a far higher amplitude. Providing we set up the program without delay we could not fail to bring back some exceedingly valuable data, for as a result of Allan's accident we had been obliged to set up our winter quarters in the perfect location for a study of the Alpha Ridge.

needed at no time to go outside into the polar night except to feed
or exercise our four teams of dogs, do a navigational fix, conduct
our research, or check the floe for fractures. It was a convenience
and a routine which, by that evening, we had for the first time in
eight months begun to enjoy. We looked forward to a winter busy
with work and yet with ample time for relaxation and the luxury
of reading.

We established a good working routine. We would rise at eight
A.M and start work at nine; we would carry on, working each on
our individual projects, until ten P.M. and enjoy the luxury of
spare time from ten till midnight—the same routine every day of
the week right through the winter. Each man would take his turn
at cooking: one day on, three off. He would make a fresh batch of
bread rolls every lunchtime, and one loaf a day which would be
eaten during dinner and the following morning's breakfast. The
cook would be expected to show some imagination in his menus.
There was no excuse not to; we had 4,334 pounds of base-store
provisions consisting of 1,540 assorted cans. In addition to this
basic stock, we had freeze-dried foods, frozen foods, vegetables
and eggs that had been fresh on September 24, and of course de-
hydrated foods. The ingredients were there for the adventurous
cook to produce exceptional menus; all one needed was time,
enthusiasm, and patience with the tin oven which balanced pre-
cariously on a primus stove. Our water container was equally
simple—a galvanized trash can balanced on blocks of wood. Under this were fitted two primuses, at least one of which was kept
going all day. Into the tub we would place blocks of snow that
had been sawed out of the drifts around the hut, and it was the
duty of the cook to keep the tub topped up, for the snow melted
quicker if it was put into a tub already half or three-quarters full
of warm water. It was also the duty of the cook to keep a clean
kitchen and keep the Coleman space heater topped up with kerosene—it burned about five gallons a day.

The morning of the twentieth had started just like all the others since settling into our winter routine—a cup of tea delivered
to the bedside by the duty cook, who had by that time warmed

the hut to a tolerable temperature by giving the stove a quick blast and lighting the lamps, whose 250-candlepower apiece gave not only light but a certain amount of warmth. We had then checked our pulse rate, rechecked our pulse rate, and had breakfast—porridge or cereal to start, followed by eggs, bacon, tomatoes, baked beans, toast, and lashings of butter; more toast and butter to follow with marmalade, and three cups of tea. Breakfast over, we had as usual gone our separate ways: Ken to visit his dogs; Fritz to his outside instruments; Allan to his corner to compute the star shots Fritz had taken before breakfast; and I to get some fresh air and untangle my dogs' traces before settling down to work.

It was an overcast day with barely a hint of light to the southeast, even though the sun had set only two weeks before. It was very still—I could hear the creak of each stretching dog, the crunch of each footstep, and each word of the conversation between Ken and his dogs some 150 yards away. In the eerie semidarkness I shuffled around for several minutes before becoming strangely aware of a dark shadow on the floe. As I approached it my worst fears were confirmed—my flashlight caught the clean-cut edge of a fracture which had cut through the camp only thirty feet from the nearest teams of dogs and some seventy-five yards from the hut.

I looked around. There was a light jerking in the direction of Fritz's dogs.

"Hey. . . . Fritz."

"What?" It was uncanny how clear the word sounded; almost as though he had been standing a couple of yards away and just mumbled under his breath.

"Come over here," I said without raising my voice. "Come and see what I've found."

Frost smoke was rising from the fracture, and in places parachutes that had been buried by the recent drift of snow directly above where the crack had run were being stretched across the water gap, which was about twelve feet wide and still opening; beads of water were jumping off the shrouds as they tightened, and the film of grease ice on the water was already developing small clusters of salt-crystal flowers. The crunch of footsteps stopped.

"Christ!" he said in a low voice. "That must have been what I heard about six o'clock this morning—a sort of dull booming sound. Thought I was dreaming."

"I didn't hear a bloody thing."

We soon discovered that we were cut off from two of our five depots of food and fuel and that the floe on which our hut stood, which a few hours before had been the largest in the area, was now reduced to a segment just under half a mile wide.

The Arctic ice pack is an irregularly broken and brittle skin of ice that is in constant motion. It is as liable to fracture, gyrate, and pressure in the dead of winter as it is at any other time of the year. It is totally unpredictable, for the motion of the floes within an area of say twenty square miles—the sort of area that we could keep under close observation from a camp on the ice—is governed not only by the local winds and currents, but by the jostling of floes driven by other winds and currents within a radius of perhaps as much as fifty miles. Nor is it possible to select a site for a camp even on the most massive floe with any guarantee that a fracture will not split that floe directly beneath the tent or hut. The chances of a giant floe smashing up like matchwood are of course less, for its great size and weight would tend to crush the neighboring smaller floes if they converged; but evidently even the biggest sometimes crack up.

By the following afternoon, the segment on which we were marooned had shattered at the north and south ends, and hairline cracks running parallel to the main fracture had further reduced the area of the floe to a strip half a mile by 250 yards. A mile to our southwest there was a fractured area that for several weeks had been in a constant state of movement. To our west and northwest, two major fractures separated us from the partly healed remnants of the floe on which we had spent the summer; a third fracture separated us from the floes to our southeast and east. Only in the northeast did the prospect of finding a floe that was not already smashed up seem promising, and it was in this direction that Fritz and I concentrated our search for an alternative campsite.

It was overcast and almost pitch dark, but by leaving three hurricane lamps on the tops of hummocks at strategic points along the outward course, and a 250-candlepower kerosene-burning pressure lamp suspended from the anemometer mast at winter quarters, we could keep a check on our direction; and the distance we traveled we measured by the watch on the assumption that we were moving at about 2½ miles per hour. We had very little on the two sledges: just a ration box, a couple of boxes of dog food, a box containing pots and pans and a primus stove, a tent, our sleeping bags, ice axes, and a rifle. Hanging from the back of each sledge were two small hurricane lamps, one on each handlebar.

Once beyond the shattered area, and finding ourselves on what seemed to be a sizable floe, we separated and sledged parallel to each other about two hundred yards apart. Our general heading we kept by the luminous aircraft compasses mounted centrally between the handlebars, and by keeping an eye on the lights of the other sledge we were able to judge that the floe had the surface configuration of an old weathered floe, for the lights did not disappear as often as they would have had it been hummocked or broken. By this technique we found, in pitch darkness, a floe about twice as big as the one on which we were camped—an alternative campsite on an ice pack that was drifting at a rate of two to three miles a day and jostling like leaves floating on the surface of a slow-flowing stream. The actual site itself, about two route miles from the first winter quarters, we selected by probing with ice axes until, in a trough between two low hummocks, we found a large frozen fresh-water pool covered with about six to eight inches of snow. Once this was cleared of its snow cover—a job which took us one full day—we had the perfect foundation for our second winter camp; and to this site, in temperature of about —30°F and low-drifting snow, we started relaying the twenty-seven tons of gear that now lay partly buried by the drifts.

The hut we did not start dismantling until after lunch on the twenty-sixth, but so smoothly did the operation go that we had the hut down and shifted over to the new site two miles away by ten o'clock that night; and the following day we moved off in slow procession with our furniture. A stranger sight I have never seen than those four sledges rattling through the night, their hurricane lamps casting weird light on an ever weirder cargo of desks, shelves, beds, tables, stove and stovepipes. We were like the victims of some terrible earthquake, or the refugees from a battle-torn village, our crude furniture symbolic of man's struggle for survival. But like refugees we could not help wondering how many times during the next few months we would be obliged to move on with our sledge loads of furniture, stove and stovepipes, always escaping into the darkness, always the same skeletal rattle, the same pathetic junk worth more to its owner than its weight in gold.

Late into the night of the twenty-seventh we worked erecting our padded tent on the square of fresh-water ice from which its snow cover had been cut, and in a wind with a razor-sharp edge which raised the weals of a whiplash on our faces, we worked all the following day outside securing the guy wires and sorting out the massive pile of gear that had been dumped about in loads. Our position was then latitude 85°34'N, longitude 164°18'W; we had reestablished our winter quarters.

By November 4, the track over which we sledged to and fro in darkness for ten days had become a polished highway and the site of our first winter quarters a desolate spot marked only by a few mounds of wind-packed snow. Ironically, by then the floe from which we had escaped had quieted down, the fractures had frozen over, and snowdrifts covered all the smaller cracks. In the light of the full moon we could see it all and the icescape looked very peaceful, but the muffled booms and pistol shots transmitted through the ice as it contracted with the cold had never seemed more ominous or our camp more vulnerable.

We probably lost about a month's work in our scientific program as a result of that evacuation, for although the move itself was carried out smoothly enough, it took us far longer in the darkness to sort out our depots and reorganize. We built an extension onto the hut with packing crates and the pallet boards on which the parachute loads had been dropped. In this we stored about three weeks' supply of food, from which Allan would restock the kitchen shelves. All the other chores of course we simplified as much as possible, but it was some time before we slipped back into a routine as smooth as the one we had establishtd at our first winter quarters. Some of the simplifications, however, had been built into the system in the planning and equipping stage of the expedition; for example, we had no need to wash our clothes; we had stocked our winter quarters with so much clothing that we could afford to throw away anything that needed washing and replace it with something new. Not only was this hygienic, it saved time and water. As for personal hygiene, we had had a wash in the summer and occasional washes in the winter, but we did not make a habit of this, nor did we indulge in the luxury of baths. We could have had a bath had we wished in the tub dropped by the Canadian Air Force; inside someone had painted a reclining woman whose legs bent through 180 degrees at the tip of the tub and gripped the outside. I am surprised in retrospect that we didn't take a bath at least once during the winter—though once would have been enough, for melting so much snow would have been a major operation. As for the toilet arrangements, we had a freedom of choice. We could either go for a long walk or shelter in the lea of the hut over a cardboard box. The only restricted areas were the quadrant of virgin snow in Fritz's scientific compound and the horseshoe-shaped snowdrift around the hut from which we took snow for the kitchen water tub.

We tried to keep things reasonably tidy. For instance, all the gash, as we called the empty cans and boxes that were to be thrown away, were put in a box and given to Fritz to dispose of when he went on his tours of the floe with his dog team. This he did every day throughout the winter, for part of his scientific program was to keep under close observation the activity of the neighboring floes; the boxes he used as markers around the perimeter of our floe. This tidy habit may seem a little strange, considering it was dark outside and drift snow in any case would soon have covered the rubbish; but this like most of our habits had a sound practical justification, for every object left near the hut that was big enough to create a drift of snow would have helped raise the general level of drift snow and so speed up the process of burying the hut. A buried hut cannot be moved in a hurry. There was another reason for shifting this rubbish; at that time my proposal that the expedition's geophysical program should be extended by the Lamont Geological Observatory was still being considered, and it would have been an embarrassment to us if Lamont took over our winter quarters and the summer melt of 1969 exposed the trash we had left buried beneath us.

Allan's full geophysical program had unfortunately to be cut down. On November 13 Bob Murphy flew out the ARL Dakota from Barrow via T-3, spotted our parachute flares and bonfire from forty miles out, and dropped the gravimeter and oscillograph, several pieces of scientific apparatus for Fritz, and a very generous supply of fresh fruit and steaks—a present from Max Brewer. Bob had dropped the load near a cross we had marked out on the floe with cans in which we had placed wicks soaked with JP-4 aviation fuel. We laid out and fired these beacons so that Bob would drop well away from the hut and dogs; it was a good test of the type of beacons we might use to mark a runway in the event of an emergency landing. Bob seemed suitably impressed with our ingenuity as indeed were we with the accuracy of his drop. The magnetometer, which Allan found to be malfunctioning, he soon repaired; and the oscillograph, which would record the time taken for the shock wave of an explosion to travel to the ocean bed and bounce back, he recalibrated and set up in readiness; but the soundings could not commence until he had the dynamite and caps with which to make the explosions. A thousand pounds of dynamite and detonator caps were to have been flown out to us a week later, but that flight out from Barrow was never made, for the aircraft had been damaged shortly after it returned to Barrow and by the time it was again serviceable the winter was too far advanced. Nevertheless Allan went ahead with the magnetics program and took during the course of the winter a total of six hundred readings as we drifted in zigzags and loops across the Alpha Ridge.

The generators and battery bank were also Allan's department; and with a Tiny Tiger two-stroke generator, kindly supplied by the Arctic Research Laboratory as a standby, we ran the Honda generator for approximately six hours a day to operate the air-sampling apparatus, recharge the radio batteries, the electronic flash and movie lights, and a great assortment of scientific instruments which Fritz was operating.

His program was an extension and a complement of his summer one, for by good fortune from the scientific point of view we were camped near enough to the old summer camp for Fritz to visit it at regular intervals and measure the growth rate at the same points at which in the summer he had measured the rate of melt; he was also able to run theodolite levels along the same lines he had observed in the summer to see how the surface profile of the floe had changed. He wanted to find out if the hummocks and pools were self-perpetuating, or whether over several years the rough surface profile of a floe would level off with several successive seasons of melt in the summer and accumulation in the winter. He found in his daily tours of the floes in our vicinity that differential movement had occurred overnight (or was occurring while he was watching) on the average of one day in four. As we had expected, the polynyas that opened up during the winter quickly froze over now that we were getting temperatures regularly in the minus thirties Fahrenheit, and occasionally as low as minus forty-five. Ice on the polynyas was growing at a rate of about eighteen inches a week. This was thick enough to take a Cessna-180, and there were plenty of polynyas within a radius of two miles of winter quarters. Had Allan suffered a relapse we would have had no trouble in finding a landing strip or in lighting the strip with kerosene beacons, and our bonfires evidently could be seen from a far greater distance than the range of our radio-homing devices. Moreover, the weather on the Arctic Ocean in winter, as expected, was more stable; storms were rare; the average wind speed during the winter was much the same as the rest of the year (about eight or nine knots), but visibility generally was better and there was less cloud than in summer. There was less precipitation, too—most of the winter's snow cover having accumulated in September, when about 75 percent of the snowfall consisted of stellar crystals. During the rest of the winter, although snow fell on more than one day in two, it was generally in the form of minute columns or bullets which added very little to the depth of the snow cover and did not much reduce visibility.

Fritz's program we often discussed, for our interest in it had by now been fully aroused by Walt Wittmann of the U.S. Oceanographic Office (the world's foremost authority on the drift of the Arctic ice pack), who had sent out to us with the summer supply drop a great batch of reprints of scientific papers and various publications concerning the heat balance of the Arctic Ocean. We had selected the most interesting of these and carried them with us on our abortive autumn journey, and our study of them during the winter provided us with many a lively theme for discussion.

Particularly intriguing to me as a layman was the idea that man already possesses the technical ability to upset the balance of the world's climates. We read the proposal of the Russian engineer, Borisov, that a dam should be built across the Bering Strait through which would be pumped water from the Arctic Ocean to the Pacific in order to increase the inflow of warm water from the North Atlantic and thereby remove the ice cover. There were other suggestions for removing the ice cover: the use of nuclear explosions, which would create a more turbid winter atmosphere and reduce the loss of heat from the surface of the Arctic Ocean; many scientists suggested dusting the surface of the ice pack with a dark-colored substance in order to increase the solar absorption and speed up the melting during the months of summer; yet another suggestion was for dispersing the cloud cover of the central Arctic basin. Some scientists argued that if the ice cover of the Arctic Ocean were removed it would reform; others held the view that it would not.

Borisov had based his prediction of the effect of an ice-free Arctic Ocean on world climates by referring back to the ecological conditions that existed in the past. By pumping Arctic Ocean water into the Pacific at a rate of 145,000 cubic kilometers a year, he believes a climatic improvement would occur within a year. The climate would then be controlled according to the quantity of water shifted. By the end of what he called the first stage, the climatic amelioration would have reached a stage similar to that experienced on earth during the tenth century; winters would be less severe, and in the temperate latitude vegetation would have a longer growing season. By the second stage, a level approximating the climate of about 4,000 years ago would be reached. Permafrost would disappear; tundra and forested tundra would be transformed into regions of large-scale cattle raising; water would reappear in the dry riverbeds and dry steppes, and savannas would again spread out over the vast areas of desert. By the third stage, northeast Asia would be liberated from any remaining tundra, and by the fourth stage the world would have become a Utopia. But many scientists disagreed with Borisov on the effects of an ice-free Arctic Ocean on world climates; the opinion most generally held being that the atmospheric depressions would consistently follow a more northerly path, with the result that there would be *less* moisture in the lower latitudes of the northern hemisphere, deserts would advance, and over Canada and Scandinavia heavy precipitation would fall as snow which would eventually build into ice sheets and glaciers.

With man's present state of knowledge of the dynamics of climate, it might well be disastrous to interfere deliberately with climatic factors which might trigger off another ice age; but in the more heavily populated northern hemisphere the ice cover of the Arctic Ocean is the key to its climate and a sensitive lever about which much more must be known.

Fritz's aim was to measure the various heat sources—principally radiation, for not only does it account for the largest turnover of energy, but its variation also influences the pattern and size of the other processes taking place at the surface. His radiation levels, wind and temperature profiles, sea temperature and sea salinities were all different from those he had recorded during the summer, thus making the program far more difficult to conduct from a practical point of view. The cold caused instrument failures and snapped cables; hoarfrost formed on the sensing elements and encrusted the anemometer cups. The work was easily doubled by these exasperating problems, but Fritz kept at it, seldom working less than fifteen hours a day. In addition to his heat-balance program he operated a program of air sampling, sucking air through a filter by means of a vacuum pump. Any solid particles caught by the suction were held captive. Fritz exposed some fifty of these filters during the course of the winter for Wayne Hamilton to analyze at the Institute of Polar Studies, Ohio, where Fritz had worked before joining us. Each filter was carefully boxed after an exposure of from six to twenty-four hours, and all fifty packed in an airtight container in readiness for their long journey to the laboratory. With the analysis complete, these filters should show the rate of particle fallout over the central Polar basin, and the composition of these particles falling into the earth's atmosphere from outer space. Already, with the study of these filters as yet far from completed, Hamilton has found on several of the filters colorless glass spherules, the optics of which would seem to suggest they might have originated on the lunar surface. In addition to this and several other side studies, such as snow-pit stratigraphy and ice crystalography, Fritz took over a hundred auroral observations during the course of the winter. The only data we had time to transmit was one synoptic weather observation a day, which was transmitted via Barrow, and Cove Radio in England, to the British Meteorological Office, from where it was fed into the world meteorological circuit. The rest of the synoptic observations and all of Fritz's other data he copied out in note form and, as extra security, recorded on magnetic tapes which I would carry on my sledge when eventually we continued our journey.

One of these synoptic records noted a breeze from the southwest. It was entered in Fritz's meteorological log at 1900 hours GMT on November 1, 1968. At the time he made the entry I do not recall his offering any comments, nor did Allan, who had at that time (9 A.M. local on November 1) crawled out of his sleeping-bag, shaken the hoar frost out of his hair, dressed, and staggered across from his cold tent to our warm hut for breakfast. Nor did it occur to me later in the day, while I was driving my dog team back along the tracks to the site of our first winter quarters, two miles to the southwest that the cutting breeze in my face was not the breeze of movement but a change in direction of the wind which signaled the start of our drift to the east. Our position was then latitude 85°48'N, longitude 164°20'W, our farthest north in a drift that for four months had been consistent almost to the point of being monotonous as it steadily closed on the Pole at a rate of two and a half miles a day.

On November 9, Fritz, Allan and I had set off with two teams of dogs to check the state of the ice to our north, while Ken, whose turn it was to do the cooking, stayed at base. We had expected to find the neighboring floes smashed up or badly fractured, and we had taken with us two hurricane lamps on each sledge and enough equipment and supplies to keep us going for a few days.

As an extra precaution we had added to what otherwise was a light load a radio, a theodolite and a set of navigational tables, but the precaution on that occasion had proved unnecessary, for to our surprise all the floes were tight and all the cracks healed. Even the belt of loose mush ice we had been trying to cross at the time Allan injured his back was by November ninth well-knit and offered no obstruction. We crossed it in moonlight and continued on a northly heading until we were some ten miles from our winter quarters. We turned for home at latitude 85°54'N, convinced that we would not better that northing until we abandoned our winter quarters, and resigned ourselves then to the certainty of being blown a lot farther to the east before the winter was through.

By November 27, our position was latitude 85°00′N, longitude 149°24′W. We had been carried exactly one hundred miles to the southeast in the past twenty-six days, and the wind was still blowing. The American scientific drifting station T-3 was now only 103 miles to our east-southeast. We were slowly closing in on it all the time, in spite of evidence from the "shadowing" effect of our track and theirs that both stations were caught in the same general weather system.

We brooded on how the adverse drift of the last three weeks might affect our chances of reaching Spitsbergen before the ice broke up. There were still three months of the winter to go; would we drift still further off course? If on March 1, 1969, we were still south of latitude 85°, or delayed in setting out; or if we were slowed down by bad ice conditions, or caught by adverse drifts, our approach to Spitsbergen would not only be late but extremely hazardous.

Every night I would lie in bed gazing up at the chart of the Arctic Ocean that was pasted on a board hanging from the sloping ceiling of our hut and fret over the adverse drift that was robbing us of the bonus miles I had planned on collecting from the transpolar drift stream. Now we were drifting south, helpless to counter the drift, helpless even to ignore it. I went for walks alone along the thin ice of a fracture which had split our floe at the end of November. It was a black lane, boulder-strewn in places, with high ice hedges on either side: an English country lane, petrified, dark, magical in the swinging yellow light cast by the hurricane lamp, crowded with moving shadows and faces that disappeared a fraction of a second before I looked in their direction. I imagined bears, like moths attracted by the light, creeping stealthily toward me, and hazards as yet unreal. I would climb out of the black gully and from the slippery summit of the tumbled walls look out across a black floe toward the hut: my base, afloat in the center of an ocean, its one light like a yellow jewel piercing the darkness of polar night.

On December 14 I sent out an assessment from latitude 85°13′N, longitude 147°42′W:

> The arrangements as they stand at present are as follows: there are three airdrop loads at River Air Despatch School, Manitoba, plus a 15-day reserve consisting of 13 dog-ration boxes, four man boxes and five jerry cans of kerosene—a sum total of 100 boxes of dog rations, 19 boxes of man rations and 23 jerry cans of kerosene.
>
> The three airdrops scheduled for 1969 are spaced at three-degree intervals along the route from the Pole to Spitsbergen: March 25, latitude 89°; April 17, latitude 86°; and May 10, latitude 83°. Assuming we set out from latitude 85°, we will have fifteen degrees of latitude to cover, and on last season's performance we would not reach Spitsbergen until well after our scheduled date of arrival—the thirtieth of May. This contingency has been foreseen: there is enough dog food at the Canadian Forces Base at Rivers to take 33 dogs on full rations through to July 23, and enough man rations to take four men through to July 4. As for extending the traveling period, we can if necessary either spread out the scheduled drops, or ask the Canadian Forces for another airdrop—I am loath to do either; we will instead travel harder.

I had every intention at this time of setting out from winter quarters on March 1 at the latest. Aircraft would have to land at winter quarters during the last week in February to bring in the Lamont relief crew, and take out the instruments, film and records. If this landing was made, Allan would stay on at winter quarters as station leader until the station was relieved in June; if no landing was possible until late March, Allan and Ken would remain at winter quarters, thus enabling Fritz and me to set out at first light of dawn in a bid to reach Spitsbergen ahead of the melt. If no landing was possible we would all four of us set out, with as many instruments as we could afford to carry and all the film and records, in anticipation of an aircraft reaching us from T-3 and making a landing to collect the instruments, film and records. It would pick up Allan in this event only if he had in the meantime suffered a relapse, or if it seemed unlikely that a rescue aircraft could evacuate him from a higher latitude should he suffer a relapse later in the journey. He was at that time in excellent condition, and with Ken's supervision enthusiastically working hard at a set of special exercises.

The fracture which had split our floe fifty yards from the hut at the end of November had been so quiescent that we had long since disregarded it as a potential hazard; indeed, it had become my favorite feature and a place of meditation for me. But this secluded, frozen rift in the floe became active on December 17, and for the rest of the winter incessantly the ice around us creaked and groaned. There were times in our hut when even the roar of three primus stoves and four pressure lamps could not drown the crunching, creaking sounds of advancing ice ridges, and in the still of those starry midwinter nights after all the stoves and lamps had been turned out, when only the flicker of a flame in the tray at the base of the Coleman stove gave any light, I would lie awake for hours listening to the sounds of pressuring ice. Sometimes I would get up, pull on a pair of windproof trousers and my wolfskin parka, shuffle across the hut in my down slippers, open the door quietly, cross to the door of the porch and let myself out into the night. I would climb the snow steps and stand on the mound of drift snow downwind of the hut and listen. Waves of sound came and went, and on clear nights I could see the ridges around the horizon like monstrous breakers chewing up the floe on which we drifted helplessly.

The Christmas period was a time mark in our winter. On that day I finished building a snow house that was to be our workshop, and over the next few weeks, while the floes around us worked against one another and ate away the platform on which our hut lay purring with the noise of petrol engines, we each took turns in that cramped quarter to construct our heavy sledges. It was a period I remember with great nostalgia—that snowblock room with its tarpaulin roof and its false ceiling of parachutes held up with skis; its sledge like some strange creature growing in a glistening womb above the vortices of warmth that rose from the primus stoves on the floor; those fine plumes of drift snow that formed great snow warts on the walls; those cassette tape-recorder concerts—Bach Suites 1 and 2, Berlioz' *Symphonie fantastique,* and the Swingle Singers, the only three pieces of music we had, for our 48 hours of taped classical music had been lost or stolen somewhere between London and the central Polar basin. I remember those days wrapped up in fur, hands gloved in white evening-dress silk, in that morgue where breath vapor hung in a swirling cloud below the false ceiling. Twenty degrees Fahrenheit—but outside it was minus fifty, and ground drift was slithering like snakes across the floe and licking the walls of the shelter.

On January 2, 1969, in the light of a moon, we noticed what appeared to be a water sky to our east and northeast and on investigating found that the floes had relaxed and drifted apart— a vast expanse of open water now separated us and our first winter quarters. Fritz and Allan, who had gone off with their dog teams on a circumnavigation of the floe, came back reporting excitedly that we were an island floe, and that on the eastern side water stretched to the horizon. They had evidently been profoundly moved and shaken by what they had seen. We quickly hitched up the dogs and shifted two of our depots nearer to our hut, which was now situated only fifty yards from the edge of the floe in one direction. The floe's greatest width was now less than half a mile.

I went for a long walk with Allan the following day. We completely circumnavigated the floe and found that the neighboring floes had converged on us a little over night, and the vast areas that had been water the day before were already frozen over with about four inches of ice, which would just about bear our weight. We lost some more of our floe on the seventh; then for a while the floes around us settled down. Our preparations for the dash to Spitsbergen were beginning to take shape by this time; my sledge was ready; Allan had his sledge in the snow morgue, and we were all four of us making the occasional harness and in our spare time sorting through our gear. The drift no longer worried us. We were in the eighty-five forties and once again slowly climbing north—we were even beginning to feel there was a chance we might be north of latitude 86 degrees by the time we were ready to set out; and an awareness of what lay ahead was by now beginning to tighten the muscles. I was sensing this most in the evenings after I had turned in for the night; it was an exciting feeling which I knew from past experience would build until by the eve of departure I was practically screaming inside for action.

Fritz was now working even harder than he had done in the early part of the winter. He wanted to finish more scientific work than it was humanly possible for one man to do. Allan and I gave him a hand from time to time but there was not much we could do to help, for by February 1 we were all completely wrapped up in the seemingly massive amount of preparation necessary for the journey ahead; and Allan, in anticipation of going on to Spitsbergen—in spite of the committee's directive that he was to be evacuated in the spring, and in spite of Max Brewer's plans to get his Cessnas out to T-3 by the first week in March and fly out to us from there—was now taking his dogs out every day as part of his training.

On February 3 at midday the temperature was —47°F. Vapor from the chimney was rising vertically and feeding a thin canopy of mist which hung above the hut, partly buried by the drifts of snow in spite of our efforts to keep it clear. To the southeast, and low in the sky, Venus was like a pearl. To the north the moon was full and cold, and directly beneath it a brilliant burst of silver light spread out across the floes. The whole icescape was awash with light: cold, weird, winter light. But overnight the weather changed; the sky clouded over, a strong wind got up, and at 4 A.M. the floe split in two.

By the next day we had been carried eight miles south, and our winter quarters, which the day before had seemed relatively safe in spite of being only fifty yards from the nearest flaw, were now dangerously situated on a wedge-shaped floe between two fractures which might at any time pressure and crack the ice between. The moon, hidden behind a curtain of cloud, slipped below the horizon. We would not see it again until February 21—the date, a year before, when we had set out from Point Barrow, Alaska, and driven four teams of dogs onto the Arctic Ocean at the start of a sixteen-months' journey. We had then been in high spirits, confident that if we survived the first hundred miles of treacherous young ice off the Alaskan coast, we would, by the first melt season, have pulled back the distance lost in setting out three weeks late. We had been stopped well short of that first target by deep slush and vast areas of open water. We had been stopped short again in the autumn when Allan had injured his back while we were attempting to put ourselves in a better position for the start of the winter drift, and had in consequence, during the winter been carried by an unfavorable drift 120 miles off our course to the east.

We were now 350 miles behind schedule and only halfway to our destination. The journey ahead seemed formidable. To reach Spitsbergen, we would have to travel as far in one hundred days as the distance we had to date covered in just two weeks short of a year.

On the seventh, Freddie told me that he had had word from Dr. Hunkins at Lamont Geological Observatory that for reasons of logistics and shortage of staff they were obliged to decline my offer of the station, complete with Allan as its station leader and one of its geophysical observers. Although disappointed, I had foreseen this possibility a few weeks before and already discussed with Max Brewer via Freddie the feasibility of a Cessna landing at some point north of our winter quarters. The earliest Max could get his Cessnas out to T-3 was March 10; as far as range was concerned, he again assured me that we would never be out of range of the ARL Cessnas if they were needed to evacuate Allan (whom the ARL still regarded as one of their own men). The Cessnas could be flown to within 200 miles of T-3, land on the pack ice, collect drums of fuel dropped from the Dakota that would be flying cover, refuel, take off and continue. This technique could not have been used during the winter had the Cessnas or the twin Otter of Weldy Phipps been called out on a rescue mission; but then, T-3 was only 150 miles from our winter quarters and refueling would not have been necessary, even if the Cessnas or the twin Otter had failed to locate us and had to return to T-3—an unlikely eventuality, considering the fact that our bonfire on the occasion of Bob Murphy's winter flight had been seen at a range of 40 miles. With this assurance from Max I informed the committee the next night that we would abandon our winter quarters on or about the twenty-fifth and set off, all four of us, for the Pole. Setting out that early would mean traveling with maximum loads at the coldest time of the year, for the Arctic Angle Squadron of the Canadian Forces was not scheduled to make the first of the three resupply drops during the final stage of the journey until March 25. We therefore set about carefully selecting and packing several scientific instruments which would need recalibrating, eighty pounds of exposed film, and a massive accumulation of micrometrical, glaciological, psychological, and geophysical data collected during the eight months' drift, on the assumption that they would have to be carried all the way to Spitsbergen. Meanwhile Max went ahead with his plans to get his Cessnas out to T-3, for the laboratory had work for them to do in the vicinity for the University of Alaska. Any assistance he might be able to give us would be a side operation, but Max I knew was still very concerned about the records we were carrying, and anxious to relieve us of them if possible.

We had begun to feel by that time that there was some obstruction along the imaginary line which describes a circle around the Pole at a radius of 260 miles—a hump perhaps, over which ice drifting north could not pass! No less than four times since the end of October we had drifted toward latitude 86°N (coming at one time within an hour's walk of that imaginary obstacle), only to slip back again to latitude 85°30′N. Now at last our long drift was almost over. The polar night was being rolled back almost too quickly for eyes grown accustomed to the continual darkness, and the sky to the south seemed brilliant at midday. The sun was climbing faster than man and dogs could run; we knew it would start melting the thin skin of ice which covers the Arctic Ocean long before we caught sight of our destination. We had one hundred days in which to sledge 1,700 route miles. What possible hope was there of covering such a distance?

By February 23 there was a hard-packed route winding five miles toward the retreating gloom on the northern horizon—a blazed trail that crossed the crests and troughs of the hummocked ice floes and swept gracefully over frozen sea lakes to the chaos of ice beyond. We were almost ready to leave that camp, to break free from the protective shell which had suddenly become a prison. Every instinct by then was straining for freedom, every fibre tense, every dog harnessed, every sledge ready to receive its load.

11

Lodestone and Morning Star

THE alarm rattled irritably on the bare floor of the hut until it ran out of energy and with a final pathetic spasm stopped. It was six o'clock on the morning of February 24, 1969. I had already been awake for about an hour, thinking about the journey that lay ahead.

I had slept on the floor that night; so too had Allan. I had been obliged to smash up my bed with an axe the night before to get at the reserve radio and the homing beacon that had been locked into an apron of frozen condensation at the base of the wall. Allan for the first time during the winter had slept in the hut that night—I suppose out of curiosity. The hut was in a shambles. Half-packed boxes and bags lay everywhere, the dining table was sagging under the weight of gear, the hut was cold—the only light a flicker from the kerosene stove in the center. Fritz's flashlight threw a beam across the hut and darted uncontrollably around for a second or two until the flashlight was slapped down on the table while Fritz lit the lamp and the primus stove. Five minutes after the friendly roar had started up, Allan, Ken, and I crawled out of our bags and rolled them up, and had just started breakfast when a whole salvo of twangs vibrated through the hut.

We all dropped our cutlery, struggled for the door across a pile of gear, and tumbled outside to find the floe splitting and opening all around us. One crack, the nearest to the hut, was about twelve feet away. We were dressed only in hut gear, woolen shirts, windproof trousers over long johns, down slippers—not the gear for outside work in —40°F with a stiff breeze blowing, but we had to move fast. We scrambled up the snow bank and scattered. I leaped the fracture just after Fritz—I don't know where the others went. The whole floe seemed to have cracked up like an eggshell. I could reach three of my dogs by leaping another crack but the others were cut off; so too was my sledge. Fritz yelled something, I turned and made it back to the crack which had just missed the hut, leaped it and looked around. It was still fairly dark but I could see that we were all on the same small floe. Fritz had got his dogs across just in time, Ken's dogs and sledge were safe; Allan's and mine were cut off. The whole jigsaw of ice was relaxing and opening at a rate of several feet a minute, and within less than a quarter of an hour one of the fractures near the hut was forty-five feet wide.

Meanwhile, the whole area had started to gyrate. Pressure was building in some places and leads were opening in others. What we feared most was that the floes on either side of the jagged fracture would shift out of alignment, close where two points projected, and set off a series of cracks at right angles which might drop the hut, sledges, or dogs into the sea.

"Hey, have you seen the tent?"

"It's collapsed into the water—it's just bloody well lying there."

"Christ, if a bloke had been in there he wouldn't have stood a chance."

"We wouldn't have stood much of a chance if it had gone under the hut either. In fact, the sooner we get away from this place the better."

We were all feeling frozen to the core by that time, but dared not all go into the hut together. Allan stood watch while the rest of us slithered back into the dungeon and pulled on some warm clothes, grabbed what each of us felt to be the most vital possessions, and hurled them outside in piles. Allan came in and struggled into some gear. I don't know to this day what the others took as their top priority; I just grabbed a big waterproof bag and stuffed it with anything that came readily to hand: the almanacs and HO-214 tables off the shelf, the Kern theodolite, cameras, radios, bullets, film—all the loose stuff I had been intending to pack carefully after a leisurely breakfast. Our four breakfasts were still sitting on the table in a space which had been cleared by Fritz with one sweep of a forearm, but they were now cold and greasy and we had lost our appetite. All the time we were in that hut we were vulnerable and on edge. We kept our sheath knives ready in case we had to cut our way out, I found that the radio co-ax cable was frozen into the ice and had no alternative but to take the hand axe to the set of desks and shelves I had taken so much trouble to construct and hack it out.

It was still fairly dark outside, so every time someone left the hut he had to take one of the lamps and those left behind were plunged into semidarkness. All the time we could hear the noises of the pressure grinding the floes, and the relief when once we got outside was fantastic.

"That hut's a bloody tomb. How much more gear have you got to get out?"

"Dunno; I suppose I've got most of it," Fritz said as he fished among the heap of bags and boxes.

What a waste! All that expensive gear we were going to leave for ARL to pick up with the Cessnas. And all those good intentions of leaving the hut spick and span: "Do you know, I'd even thought of scrubbing the floor!" I muttered as an afterthought as I pitched a bag of clothing in the general direction of my pile.

"It would have served you right if you had."

"Well, you never know where this hut might end up or who will find it—I mean, it's a bit like wearing clean underclothing in case you get knocked down by a car, isn't it?"

"This hut's certainly going to be crushed if a ridge builds when these two floes come together."

"Sad really."

"Eh?"

"Sad!" I shouted.

But Fritz was already twenty yards away now, making for his sledge.

The sledges already had been partly loaded a couple of days before with dog food, fuel, and man rations. The two new tents were there, and some of the personal gear; in fact all we had left to load were the more delicate instruments, logs and records— stuff which we always kept near at hand and which now, be- cause of the emergency, was crammed into bags and boxes lying in four piles outside the hut. Ken's and Fritz's dog teams and sledges were near at hand, but the other two dog teams were widely scattered, and in the semidarkness the sledges we guessed to be about a hundred yards away. We were separated from them by a mass of moving ice, and leaping from one small floe to an- other we eventually got across to our respective teams and hitched them up to the sledges. But the route we had taken out had by then been broken up and the dogs were not easily persuaded to venture onto ice cakes that rocked or tilted under their weight. We took the whips to them and drove them across screaming at them, reached the hut, quickly loaded up, and took one last look at our old winter quarters with the vapor from the chimney still pouring past the flag. We had left an old lamp burning on the roof of the small extension we had built, but by the time we had worked our way across a quarter of a mile of broken floes, that light and the hut had disappeared into the gloom.

We sledged north toward the darkest part of the horizon with only Venus as a guide—a wilderness in monochrome through which the sledges weaved and rattled along a trail already blazed; and by the time we camped we had covered the first five miles of the 1,700-mile, 100-day journey that lay ahead.

Allan by now was in pretty good shape. Apart from his back he was probably fitter than any of us. He had been doing between forty and forty-five jump press-ups a day and had worked at his exercises until the sweat poured off him, usually outside in the cold so that he could keep his body temperature down. He, Ken, and Fritz would run on the spot until I felt quite tired. For myself, I hardly ever do exercises. I much prefer to set off and suffer during the first few weeks of the journey than to suffer for several months in preparation for it.

At the time of abandoning our winter quarters we were 322 statute miles from the Pole and soon found ourselves on very active ice. We had to make several detours to get round new cracks and leads, and on the second day found ourselves in among pressure fields. There were only about four hours of twilight and we made little progress. The temperature was —40°F.

The first real crisis occurred on the third day out when we noticed that Allan's sledge had split along the whole length of the runner. That night we stopped to camp and make repairs—a miserable job as the temperature was about —45°F. We had to rig up a shelter as a windbreak and use two lamps, since it was too dark to see. The following day Fritz's sledge cracked, then mine, and within a period of a week all four sledges had major splits along the full length of the runners, caused no doubt by a combination of the tremendous hammering they were receiving and the very low temperatures which had made the wood brittle. These new sledges had been dropped to us at the beginning of the winter drift, along with the hut. They were of a slightly different design, with much broader runners than the previous season's sledges, nearly four inches wide. The type of temporary repairs we now carried out had proved successful the previous season and we felt reasonably confident they would hold. We bored holes right through the runners, fixed metal plates, inserted bolts, and lashed them up with rawhide which pulled the edges of the cracks together. All four sledges were treated thus. In fact they lasted for the rest of the journey.

There was a fantastic amount of pressuring going on around us. A lead would open, come together again, and form a pressure ridge; then the floe would split in the opposite direction, come together again, and build another pressure ridge at right angles to it. Judging by the chaos this had been going on all through the winter. In places there were blocks about thirty feet high, a jumble of ice through which we were averaging only two miles a day. At that rate we wouldn't have stood a chance of getting anywhere, and after one week of this I was worried. In due course, however, traveling conditions improved and we started to pick up a few more miles each day.

We were still navigating on Venus; the stars had all faded and neither the sun nor the moon was up, but by March 9 clouds were catching the sunlight. The temperature then was about —55°F. We were traveling eight hours a day, which meant that we actually spent about ten hours of each day working outside, and the fatigue was crippling.

The alarm would wake us at six o'clock and the man whose turn it was to make breakfast would ease himself out of a frozen shell of warmth and fumble in the dark for a match. A sharp scratch, a spurt of light, and a flame would grow at the end of a stick that would snuff itself out as it reached the lamp and moved under the glass toward the wick. At the second or third attempt it would catch and the tent fill with yellow light. A burning match would light the fuel in the priming cup of the kerosene stove, then the cook would shrink into his bag. Hoar frost and ice glazed the head of the bag and coated the walls like fungus. Hoar frost like fleecy beards hung from the clothing in the apex of the tent, and trembled as breath vapor floating in curls drifted up among them on a rising draft of warmth. A leg, stiffened with morning cramp, would shake loose a cascade of delicate crystals that would float down on the two men and settle like spiders' webs on the face of the one who was watching the priming fuel licking the burner tubes of a grimy stove. He would release two arms from the warmth of the bag and with grubby hands wipe the melting hoar frost evenly over his face and poke his fingers into his ears. His morning ablutions done, he would pump the stove, which would splutter and fire. The pot, which the night before had been filled with water and which now was frozen solid, he would place on the stove, and while the flame cupped the pot like a blue-fingered hand and the ice contracted with pings and cracks, the cook would wriggle once more into his cozy cocoon.

Few words were passed at that time of the day, for not until the stove had been burning for half an hour would the temperature in the tent have risen from —45°F to a tolerable —35°. We started each day with a cup of tea and followed it with porridge, with as much butter as we could afford chipped off its frozen block and buried in the simmering goo. Sugar and milk were added, but, at that stage in the journey, never enough. Two more cups of tea would complete the meal and we would pack up and go. The walls of the tent by then were wet, and the clothing that had been hanging in the apex overnight limp and damp.

We moved around outside with lamps and fumbled through the twilight, breaking camp and loading the sledges, untangling the dogs and hitching them up; and by 8 A.M., with our wolfskin parkas frozen solid as suits of armor, we were on the move, cutting through the cold with each footstep jarring the body back to the misery from which it had been released by sleep only eight hours before.

It would be eleven hours before we could take another drink, eleven hours of sustained physical stress which would wear down our resistance to the cold and the very will to move. We were at that time on a well-balanced but inadequate diet of 5,200 calories a day. There could be no question of carrying more food or fuel; already the dogs were hauling maximum loads of 1,300 pounds and we had four and a half weeks to go before the first resupply drop. We could keep warm only by moving, but the harder we worked the more hungry we became, and the hungrier we became the less resistance we had to the cold. There was no alternative; we had to suffer for our miles and had known as much many months in advance.

We had taken what precautions we could; we had fed and rested well during the last days at winter camp and given the dogs as much food as they could eat every day during the last month. With the exception of our wolfskins all our clothing was brand new and we had plenty in reserve; we had new down-filled sleeping bags made up of an inner bag, an outer bag and a heavy-duty shower-proof cover; and new sheepskins and foam rubber mattresses for the tent floor. Each man was wearing on his upper half a thin woolen vest, a thick, long-sleeved, long-tailed woolen shirt, and a thick woolen sweater; on his legs, two pairs of woolen long johns and a pair of down-filled full-length underpants and lightweight windproof trousers; on the feet, two pairs of thick woolen socks, two pairs of duffle socks, and mukluks; and on the hands, two pairs of woolen mitts and a pair of soft leather outer mitts. Each man had two anoraks, a lightweight single-lined anorak and a double-lined one with the hood trimmed with wolverine fur; a down-filled jacket which had been specially designed for the expedition; and of course the wolfskin. But in spite of all this clothing, after an exposure of several hours the body temperature would gradually fall off, and by the end of the day it would be practically impossible to hold a knife in the hand, for by then the hands would have lost all sense of feeling and the mitts would be frozen solid. It was difficult to do anything with the hands in this state, and with the mitts frozen in the shape of boxing gloves from holding the handlebars of the sledge. Take the mitts off and you strip the hands of what little protection they had from the wind, and at that time of the day, when a man is fatigued and very cold, his hands would be frostbitten in minutes. But replacing those hands into the mitts was an even greater agony, for by then they would have chilled off and one would have to cup the hand in a half-clench and work it into the mitt as if both the mitt and the hand were the fossilized extremities of a human limb— not one's own, for the hands no longer had feeling.

There were other states of detachment; I had experienced them before on previous expeditions when I had been under sustained stress and weakened by hunger and fatigue. The soul would seem to wander from the tired body and drift out ahead. Effortlessly floating backward, my spiritual self would observe the shell of myself struggling pathetically forward and urge the body on. This was no mere subconscious thought—it was for me very real. I was not talking to myself from within but actually watching myself. How long this state of duality lasted is impossible to say, for a man suffering from hallucinations is not a reliable timekeeper

—a few seconds perhaps, maybe several minutes; but for as much as twelve hours a day I would be sledging in a dream, shuffling alongside the sledge on skis inside a protective skin of windproof fabric which would become part of me, as real as my own cold flesh. They were with me again. I recognized them as symptoms of severe fatigue but welcomed them for they were company in the solitude of physical suffering.

During this period Ken had a lot of difficulty in sleeping. He used to wake up about five times each night, and feeling too cold to go back to sleep, would light the primus and make himself a brew of tea. The cold for him was a dull, ever-present misery, relieved only superficially and for a few minutes by the roaring warmth of the stove and a hot drink of cocoa or tea. So cold did he feel some of those mornings during the early days out from winter quarters that only with the greatest of difficulty was he able to dress himself. Starting the day cold like this was the worst of all agonies, for it was practically impossible to sustain any warmth created by exercise, and without that initial warm start a man stood little chance of getting through the day without the risk of frostbite. Of the four of us, Allan seemed to have the greatest resistance to the cold; whether he was physiologically better acclimatized or just simply regarded the physical suffering as so much a part of his way of life that it was not worth discussing, I do not know. It was nearly always Allan who was called on to help Ken or Fritz pull their mitts on at the end of the day, when their hands (which they had pulled out of their protective shells to massage or to untangle a dog) had seized up and lost their feeling. Allan, like the Eskimos, could work bare-handed for long stretches; even touching bare metal did not seem to burn his horny fingers. He had less trouble with his face than the rest of us, too. He seldom wore any protection on his nose; Ken and I were obliged almost continually during this period to wear nose-bands which covered the cheeks as well and left only the nostrils exposed. The eyes were protected with sunglasses, and our helmets came down the forehead to within an inch of the eyebrows.

Apart from the fatigue which we were all suffering as a result of the relentless struggle for miles across heavy pack, I had on only one day during the first two weeks been really worried for myself, and this had been very early on—the day after Allan's sledge had split a runner. That night he had spent a long time outside repairing the sledges while I had been in the tent writing dispatches for the *Sunday Times* and working on assessments of our progress. That long spell in the tent with what surely must have been a fuming primus had given me one of the most severe headaches I had ever experienced—and, more seriously, blurred vision. Throughout the whole of the traveling day of March 1, the moon through my eyes had been quadrupled, with moons overlapping each other by 20 percent of their diameter in the horizontal plane and 40 percent in the vertical plane. It was the same with all other objects—four of each dog, four of each man. That same day I sprained a knee. It was a mystery to me that Allan survived this period without a sprain, for in a fatigued state one is so much more vulnerable to injuries of this sort. Had I not been so relieved when my eyes went back to normal vision on the second, I would probably have worried a great deal about that sprained knee, for any injury which might handicap the party at that stage of the journey was serious. Fortunately it came right again after about a week, and by March 10 we had started to overhaul the records of some of our greatest predecessors. We had passed Nansen's, Cagni's, and Peary's 1909 farthest-north positions and were approximately at latitude 87°15′N.

The 110 nautical miles we had made good since leaving winter quarters fifteen days before had been hard-won. On three occasions we had to break camp in a hurry and escape as the floes cracked up, and the strain was beginning to show in the relationship between Fritz and Ken, who at that time were sharing a tent. We needed only to run into a twenty-mile pressure field or felsenmeer, as Fritz called them, and we would be set back so many days that our chances of reaching Spitsbergen before the ice melt would have been lost. Any delay at all was serious: an overturned sledge, a broken runner, an argument. On the third, Ken, who was at the back of the column, had had an overturn in an awkward spot with not enough room to maneuver the dogs to right the sledge. We were at that time well spread out with Fritz and me sharing the leading. An overturned sledge that cannot be righted without unloading it completely is one of the most frustrating and irritating experiences, and Ken was in a black mood when I eventually off-loaded my sledge and went back to see if I could help. He felt, quite rightly, that we should not have been so spread out and that we should be helping each other more than we were. Still, I decided that from then on either Fritz or I would take the rear position with Ken in second place and Allan in third.

Allan, the emotional anchor man of the party, was himself very miserable at this time, for the arrangement still stood that a relief operation would be carried out by the Cessnas from ARL as soon as they could get out to T-3, and we expected this relief shortly after the return of the sun. Every day now the sky was flushed rose and the high clouds lit by a sun which was creeping nearer to the horizon. But he did not complain openly, even after we had learned from Freddie that Geoff Renner, who had been flown out from London on March first to replace Allan should the evacuation prove possible, was at this time in Barrow with Freddie. Ideal as Geoff was as a replacement, it was upsetting Fritz almost as much as it was Allan that the evacuation plans were still afoot. On the seventh Ken and Fritz had an argument over this. It was by no means the first nor the last argument on this subject, and again I racked my brains in vain to find some acceptable solution.

On March 12 we saw the sun for the first time since October 6. It was a blood-red, beautiful sight after five months and seven days—a living, pulsating thing it seemed to be, slowly drifting on a sea stained red with the blood it released. I was at that time out in the lead with Fritz bringing up the rear. I could see three sledges coming toward me across a colored sea, streaming breath vapor from the dogs; they left a weaving trail as they followed my tracks through jumbled ice and over cracks and small fractures, a plume stained pink in the low rays of the sun. As they drew up to me and stopped, the plume of vapor dissipated, then grew again as we continued. Those vapor trails were a common sight during the month of March and one of the most beautiful sights we saw during that hard, bitter haul toward the Pole. Sometimes they would hold together long after we had created them, sometimes in a crosswind there would be a sharp-cut image of a man, sledge, and dogs on one side and a stream of vapor pouring off them on the other like a diaphanous veil laid out across the purple surface of the ice.

The sixteenth was such a day. I was then at the rear of the line with the others out of sight. What made me look around I am not sure; I heard no sound, there could be nothing behind me but the tracks of our four sledges weaving through the rough ice pack; but I sensed something following me, and sure enough there was a polar bear heavily shuffling along the tracks about 200 yards away. Between the four of us we had three rifles, but at that time only one of them was in perfect working order, that one was on Fritz's sledge at the front of the column. The rifle on Ken's sledge had a broken firing pin; the one on my sledge had not been adequately degreased and in temperatures below —30°F had a tendency to jam. During the bear season we always kept the rifles loaded, but we had seen no bears since the previous summer and had not expected to see any for another month; nevertheless I always carried a few rounds in the pocket of my anorak and in the bag which hung from the handlebars at the back of the sledge. On that day, however, I was not wearing my anorak under the wolfskin—it was buried in the front of the sledge load under the tarpaulin.

I screamed at the dogs and drove them as hard as I could in the hope of catching up with the rest of the party, but the polar bear was closing on me all the time. I dared not stop and unload the front of the sledge to get my anorak out, so I kept the dogs going while I lay along the top of the moving sledge and unfastened the load. By the time I had fished the anorak out, the bear was less than 50 yards away, and sitting astride the load I fed four rounds into the rifle and rammed one up the spout. But the rifle would not fire, and the bear, his curiosity now excited, was evidently intent on getting an even closer look. My dogs had not yet become aware that there was a bear following but cast glances over their shoulders from time to time to see what I was doing and, on a couple of occasions, stopped! I must confess it was an exciting five minutes I spent wrestling with the bolt of that rifle and snatching the trigger before, in frustration, I hit the bolt with the palm of my hand and the rifle fired. It was not at that time aimed at the bear but up in the air. However, to my surprise and relief, the report stopped the bear in his tracks, and by the time we had extended the gap to 100 yards he seemed to lose interest and ambled off to one side, in among the pressure blocks along which we were making a detour.

Bear sightings so close to the North Pole are rare I suspect only because the visits of man to these regions is rare; polar bears after all are far better equipped for survival in the pack-ice environment than the men who sight them. They are inveterate wanderers, capable of going for long periods without food, moving freely across the floes, taking to the water only when they have the need. They don't as a rule dive beneath the ice; they can stalk their food, the ringed seal, on the surface—or, if it is basking on the edge of a floe, approach it by swimming under water. Though we had seen few during the journey, in the first eight hundred miles we had crossed many tracks, and from these and the spores had learnt a great deal about their habits. Often we had seen the tracks of a bear that had climbed a pressure ridge or hummock to get a better view around the horizon, the skid where it had slid down from hummock and continued its slow, shuffling stroll or rested in the snow. Occasionally we had come across the signs of a stalk where the bear, using the pack as cover, had closed on a seal dozing fitfully on the ice near a breathing hole. The trail retold the story of the bear moving forward, freezing (the instant the seal awoke), and bursting forward from a range of ten or fifteen yards to fall upon its prey. What it had not eaten had been cleaned up by the foxes. We had seen fox tracks frequently up to latitude 81°N, but none since the summer of 1968, and no polar bears or tracks of bears and only one seal, since August 10. Nor was it for the want of looking. We concluded that Stefansson's "friendly Arctic" presumably applies only to the summer, and even then does not extend much beyond 200 miles from land.

Our camp that night was in an area that had been working only a few hours earlier, and we set up camp with misgivings on the only floe that had survived the pressure. Ken and Fritz had another argument that night. I suggested we have a change of partners to split them up, but the floe shattered even while we were discussing this and we had to scramble the dogs and sledges over to another part of the floe. The move temporarily broke the tension, and Fritz and Ken decided, against my advice, to try to stick it out until the airdrop, which was due on the twenty-fifth. By the following morning, after a sleepless night as the ice around us churned itself into mush, all we wanted to do was get clear. We worked hard that day for the two miles we made good, and on the eighteenth after another five miles of hacking were still not clear of that dangerous area. In an effort to postpone Allan's evacuation and gain time in which to convince my London committee that he was in good shape and no longer a serious risk, I sent a message over the radio to Max Brewer:

> It occurs to me that it now seems unlikely that the Cessnas will be on T-3 for several days and since we are making fairly steady progress we could be as far north as latitude 89 or even 89°30' by the time you are ready to make the attempt to relieve us of a man who, more than anyone else I know, deserves at least to reach the Pole. Why not therefore delay one week more and make the relief operation from the Pole itself? Allan is in splendid condition. Only you of course can judge whether the extra 40 or 50 nautical miles are feasible but I would be more than grateful to be the object of the Naval Arctic Research Laboratory's second North Pole flight with light aircraft. At present very cold, wet, tired and hungry. Dogs are slowing down as the result of hard work and long hours in minus 40 temperatures.

Max agreed to this.

The most important logistics problem was now to prepare a

contingency plan to cover the final stage of the journey, and this
I sent out on March 22 to my London committee:

> Should we fail to reach Spitsbergen north shore before the
> summer melt it will be impossible to airlift us off the ice and
> far too risky for us to sit out the summer for we may drift
> into the Greenland Sea. Furthermore, we have not enough dog
> food in reserve at the Canadian Forces Base at Rivers, Mani-
> toba, to see us through the summer and it would in any case be
> almost impossible to travel by dog sledge during this period.
> I propose therefore should we be faced with this situation, to
> man-haul the final stage of the journey. Only in this way can
> we counter the drift and make a landfall.

I then specified our requirements: two full-length Nansen man-
haul sledges complete with harnesses; one inflatable rubber boat;
one PVC-coated terylene tarpaulin; six to eight weeks supply of
sledging rations and kerosene—ready to be flown out to us if
necessary about June 5.

Three days later we received the first scheduled airdrop of
supplies of the 1969 season from the Canadian Air Force. This
resupply drop provided us with enough food and fuel to last
twenty-five days. There were 23 boxes of dog pemmican, five
man-ration boxes, and six jerry cans of kerosene, plus 20 pounds
of potato powder and 24 pounds of chocolate. Our approach
to the campsite at which we received that supply drop was made
in fog across a broken-up area and a good deal of young ice.
There was a cutting wind, and Fritz, who for several days had
been in a bad way, was that day colder than he had ever been.

Fritz's symptoms were strangely similar to those we had experienced during the worst part of the training journey two years
before when Roger, Allan, and I would wake up with splitting
headaches, feeling dizzy and sick, and at times even drunk. We
had thought at the time that we were suffering the cumulative
effects of carbon-monoxide poisoning—the result possibly of con-
taminated fuel in the primus stove—and have yet to be given
an alternative diagnosis that would fit as exactly all the symptoms
of that insidious form of poisoning. The general lassitude, the
apathy, the marked physical weakness, the light-headedness, fa-

tigue, cold—Fritz had them all. True, we had in the last thirty days experienced prolonged exposure in temperatures of —50°F, but at the time we left winter quarters Fritz had been in superb condition. Another mystery was that apart from the fatigue and cold, Ken, who was sharing a tent with Fritz at that time, was not suffering any of these symptoms. He sent a message to the Royal Army Medical College in London informing them of Fritz's condition, offering a diagnosis and asking for advice. A message came back: "Your diagnosis of hypothermia [subnormal temperature of the body] and exhaustion probably correct. . . ."

Our approximate position at that airdrop was 88°40′N, 128°W. The temperature was —48°F, but the sun was now above the horizon for twenty-four hours a day, and with all the extra items of food we now had, the extra kerosene and the prospect of slightly warmer temperatures, we hoped Fritz would soon start to improve. We increased our rations to approximately 7,000 calories a day and pushed on.

It had become customary for the Canadian Air Force crews to shout to us from the open rear door of the Hercules as they made their final low pass of the camp after all the resupply had been dispatched—a friendly shout we always looked forward to. It was usual for the captain to pass over the radio to me his impressions of the ice ahead along our route. On that occasion he told me it did not look too good; but as we got into the territory which he had described we found it was passable, and our relief was far greater than if he had given us a glowing report. In fact, the ice conditions got better and better all the time.

With the sun now warming us and with a diet adequate to our tremendous appetites we were now able to put in much longer days. The surface was improving too; we were finding for the first time during the journey that we were consistently traveling across hard wind-packed snow and seeing "sastrugi" from time to time. Sastrugi is caused by the wind which packs down the snow, polishes it, then starts chiseling it into sharp-edged waves. The sastrugi, while not quite as regular as a plowed field, nevertheless was a perfect surface across which to sledge—in fact, the sledges hardly left a track at all. Following the others it would be hard to see where their sledges had cut through the crests, or to see the claw marks of the dogs where they had scratched the surface. A man's footprints could not be seen at all, for we were wearing soft-soled mukluks at this stage in the journey.

Allan had promised that he would never lift or heave anything, that he would always wait till we came up and gave him a hand; but he could quite often be seen on the horizon struggling and heaving and tugging at his sledge. On a few occasions I had gone up to him and asked why he hadn't waited for me. Sheepishly he would tell me that he was managing all right, that he had developed a technique of shoving and pushing and that he did not feel any pain and was quite sure it was doing his back no harm. In fact, he never had the slightest hint of a twinge. Even his old knee trouble, which he had had for years, did not recur. On that training journey all three of us had suffered from sprains, twists, knee trouble and the sledgers' "ryg"—a back ache which at first we had all put down to creeping old age (I remember at one time being at the back of the column when all three of us were limping; a comical sight it would have been had it been less painful—we were all going along like old men).

Long and distinct shadows were stretching out ahead of us at local noon by the time we had reached the eighty-ninth parallel as we trudged toward the Pole; but the sun directly behind the column no longer set alight the breath vapor which poured from the dogs and men; it was too high. Our wolfskins were much heavier now for they were matted with frozen condensation, as were our beards within half an hour of setting off each morning to hack our way northward. We were on the move now for ten hours of each day, by the end of which time we were always dead beat. But there was no longer the agony of doubt about Allan. He had come through the hardest and coldest part of the journey, and we were now steadily trudging up the final slopes toward the summit of the world.

It was during these long, smooth, steady days that Fritz, fit again and relaxed now that he was sharing a tent with Allan, saw the return of his "crowds." They were the same crowds that had followed him all his life, imaginary crowds that had seen him win every Olympic gold medal at one time or another, and every Nobel Prize but the one for peace. In his daydreams, as he strode along beside his sledge, he would be conducting a great symphony before an audience that stretched to the horizon—for a chaos of ice could, in an instant, become a million people. Never were they hostile or tactless; they would disperse, just fade like a mist warmed by the sun as soon as Fritz stumbled or was approached by a companion. He could summon them up any time he wished; they were at his beck and call. They were his delight during the day and ours each evening in the tent, when we would get him to tell us what medal he had won since last we were together eight, ten, or twelve hours earlier. I envied him his crowds; for my days were spent in a maze of problems to which there seemed no answers, and in mentally drafting messages and articles which, by the time we camped, I had forgotten. I no longer had my "other" self to go out ahead of me, for my body was now fed and fit and needed no spiritual company. My amusement I would find in singing aloud or in dreaming shallow dreams as one does when driving a car alone for ten hours at a stretch on a long, empty, monotonous road.

It had never been my intention at any time to bypass the Pole on the Greenland side. That would have been the shortest possible route from our winter quarters to Spitsbergen. But the most favorable current in fact starts on the Siberian side of the date line, passes the Pole, and goes into the Greenland Sea, so we had to get to the Pole in order to pick it up. In other words, if we were going to make a detour round the Pole, it had to be on the eastern, the Russian side, rather than on the Canadian side. Since leaving winter quarters, I was determined we should go to the Pole in any event. Bypassing it on the Canadian side would have put us too close to the Greenland Sea, which we were trying to avoid. This was the real danger spot in the whole Arctic Ocean: It is the exit point for about eighty percent of the ice of the Arctic Ocean, which, as it gets closer to the Greenland Sea, moves faster and spews out into the North Atlantic.

Just before leaving winter quarters we had been told that

Dr. Hugh Simpson, with his wife Myrtle, and Roger Tufft who had accompanied Allan and me on the training journey for the trans-Arctic expedition, were about to attempt an expedition to the North Pole from Ward Hunt Island, off Ellesmere Island (the same route taken the previous summer by Ralph Plaisted). But we did not know what date he was setting out, what weight he was carrying on the sledge the three of them would be hauling, or when he planned to be at the Pole. We felt no dismay on getting this news, just a certain mild irritation. But these uncharitable first reactions soon wore off and we sent them messages wishing them luck and giving advice on certain items of gear based on our own experience of the last year on the ice. As Freddie sent through more information, it did seem to us that we were going to have to hurry if we were to beat my old sledging companions. Admittedly they were starting from a point 160 statute miles to our south, but it was quite possible that we would run into problems—Allan might have a relapse or we might meet open water or a pressure barrier. And, sure enough, during those first few days of the journey after leaving winter quarters we had been averaging only two miles a day. All Hugh, Myrtle, and Roger had to do was average about ten miles a day and they would have overhauled us in the vicinity of latitude 86°. Our objective was of course the crossing of the Arctic Ocean, not the attainment of the Pole, and to achieve this objective we had to travel as fast as we possibly could. It would nevertheless be untrue to say we were not rattled by the prospect of being beaten to the Pole by a trio of man-haulers who had only recently come on the scene, a prospect that became an added incentive to travel even harder. We put in an extra half hour's traveling each day, not knowing where Hugh and his party were or how fast they were going. But then, as we climbed to within a degree of the Pole, word came through that they were having a hard struggle in the pressure ice off the coast of Ellesmere Island and had progressed only twenty-seven miles, and we breathed a sigh of relief.

12

The Honor to Inform

OUR position at the end of a hard day's travel on March 30 was latitude 89°14′N, longitude 123°W. The following day was even harder. By the time we camped, not one of us had any feeling left in our hands or feet, nor energy enough for another step. That day we had covered about twenty route miles —been on the move for eleven hours, plodding wearily across a curdled sea beneath a dome of frosted glass through which the sun shone without warmth, or light enough to cast a shadow. The temperature was —38 degrees; the icescape colorless and without form or texture. In a daze we broke camp again ten hours later, and at a great barricade of pressured ice, after two hours of frustrated effort during which Fritz and I had been trying to catch up with the leading sledges as they swung in error farther and farther off course to the east, I took over and drove the dogs due north in an anguished and desperate hunger for miles. Fritz relieved me after four long hours, and steering on a hazy sun went on until stopped by exhaustion. April 1 had been a poor day; only twelve route miles—probably less than six minutes of latitude made good.

The rattle of the alarm, the thick coating of frost on the walls of the tent, the nagging misery of crawling out of the warmth and into the armor of my wolfskin now seemed all part of a recurring dream from which I had just awakened. Day and night were fused together. There was no longer light, shade, subtlety; no longer any humor; only that one obsessive ambition to reach the Pole.

Fritz led off on the morning of the second and we found ourselves for a while making steady progress across cracked and pressured floes in strong but diffuse lighting. Ken took the lead after five hours and went on for about an hour before he ran into trouble when a fracture across which half his team had jumped widened and swallowed five of his dogs. I was at the back of the column about a mile behind the leading sledge, and by the time I had caught up, Fritz had gone to Ken's assistance and together they had fished the dogs out of the water and were reorganizing. Ken was still a little shaken by the incident, for until Fritz arrived there seemed no way he could save the dogs from drowning. Had the fracture been clean cut and the water clear there would have been no cause for alarm, for huskies like most dogs can swim, and with their thick coats for protection could survive for several minutes in icy water; but this particular fracture choked with ice debris was like a thick soup of sludge in which the dogs in their panic were soon locked together in a fight. By the time I arrived, however, they seemed none the worse for their dipping, so I went ahead, whipping the dogs across the fracture at a point where it was a little narrower and drove them hard for the rest of that day—a good day's travel; at a guess, about 24 route miles. Fritz led off again the next day into thick overcast and plowed a way north across rough country into an area of fractures which took us three hours to pick a way through. The frustration of this, so close to the Pole, was almost unbearable; and by the time we had broken through to a floe at about 3 P.M. the wind had got up from the east-southeast and was lifting the snow.

All that night and right through to 2 P.M. the next day, the wind drummed the tents and flying snow reduced visibility to a few score yards. We guessed it was averaging about fifteen knots; there was no question of breaking camp, for with that wind behind us we might have overshot our target.

This seemed as good a time as any to change over to Greenwich Mean Time. Since setting up summer camp we had been on Barrow time, which was eleven hours behind GMT for the convenience of keeping in phase with Freddie. Now, almost at the northern axis of the earth and only a few miles from the spring of all meridians in the Northern Hemisphere, it seemed more sensible to use GMT, to which we were obliged to convert our computations (in fact, Allan's chronometer had for several months been keeping Greenwich Mean Time for timing astro-observations). At 1 P.M. on our old time routine my three companions turned in to bridge the eleven-hour time difference with some sorely needed sleep, while I stayed awake poring over figures in an effort to determine our dead-reckoning position.

Our last position fix had been five days before. Our position then had been 89°14′N, 123°W. We had seen the sun well enough to steer by on March 31 and on the first and second of April, but had not seen it at all on the third. In the four traveling days since that last fix, I estimated we had sledged about 74 route statute miles—or in nautical miles, which was the way we usually worked, about 65. To this figure I applied a correction to reduce the nautical route miles to minutes of latitude made good (our detours as a percentage of the straight-line distance we had found in practice to be 75 percent; Plaisted's figure was 74 percent). In the estimated total of 65 route nautical miles I had allowed for one mile of drift on April 1 when we had picked up a southerly breeze; there had been no other winds to take into account up to the time we pitched camp on the third. The route nautical-mile distance I calculated out at a gain of 37 nautical miles (or minutes of latitude), and this, added to our last position fix, put us by dead reckoning at the time of pitching camp on the third at latitude 89°51′N—nine nautical miles short of the Pole.

But by 2 P.M. on the fourth, by Nansen's empirical law of drift, we had drifted 6.9 nautical miles on a true bearing of 328 degrees, which had given us in northing a bonus of six minutes of latitude, putting our position at approximately 89°57'N. At that time the wind had changed direction and was for the next six hours blowing from the south-southwest at ten knots, and by 8 P.M. local Barrow time on the fourth (0700 hours GMT on the fifth), I estimated the drift track had curved and we were at 89°58.2'N on the meridian 125 degrees west. There was also surface current to be considered. The colossal influx of water into the ocean from the Gulf Stream, the Barents Sea, and through the Bering Straits must be balanced by outflow. How much to add by way of a bonus from the currents I was not sure, but guessing at a quarter of a mile a day put my calculation of our position at latitude 89°59.4'N—some six tenths of a nautical mile from the Pole. The calculation was the best I could do by dead reckoning, and it seemed we would have to be satisfied with this, for a blizzard was raging and we had no sun to provide us with a more accurate position fix; our objective after all was not the attainment of the Pole but the first surface crossing of the Arctic Ocean. (It is interesting to note how many factors I had been unable to take into account in these calculations: The ice drift depends to some extent on the compactness of the ice cover, the size of the ice floes in the neighborhood, the "sail" area, the irregularities on the surface of the floes presented to the wind, the bottom profile that is offered to the currents, and the amount of jostling from the neighboring floes. Without a bicycle wheel in tow behind the sledge to measure off the route miles—and on the Arctic pack ice it would have buckled at the first encounter with a pressure ridge—the only way to keep a check on one's position on drifting ice pack is to do regular position fixes with a sextant or a theodolite using the stars, the planets, or the sun as objects of reference. If the sky is overcast for several days, the best one can do, as I did on this occasion, is make an inspired guess.)

In point of fact, while my companions were sleeping the sky cleared with the change of wind and between 0200 and 0600 hours GMT on the fifth I was able to get five observations. These I had been unable to compute at the time as Allan had all the tablēs in his tent and I had not wanted to wake him—there would be time enough later that morning to confirm our position, and if necessary sledge the extra mile or so to that exact point on the Earth's surface known as the North Pole.

At six o'clock I woke up Ken and told him the results of my dead-reckoning calculations and we had breakfast. It was a very relaxed occasion, almost festive. I switched on the radio in the hope that propagation was good enough for me to make contact with Freddie direct. I wanted him to be first to know; but it was not to be. Instead I passed my messages via John Belcher, an electronics technician with the U.S. Navy stationed on T-3. The first of these was to Her Majesty the Queen:

> I have the honor to inform Your Majesty that today, April fifth, at 0700 hrs Greenwich Mean Time, the British Trans-Arctic Expedition by dead reckoning reached the North Pole 407 days after setting out from Point Barrow, Alaska. My companions of the crossing party, Allan Gill, Major Kenneth Hedges, RAMC, and Dr. Roy Koerner, together with Squadron Leader Church, RAF, our radio relay officer at Point Barrow, are in good health and spirits and hopeful that by forced marches and a measure of good fortune the Expedition will reach Longyearbyen, Spitsbergen by Midsummer's Day of this year, thus concluding in the name of our country the first surface crossing of the Arctic Ocean (signed W. W. Herbert, Expedition Leader)

I sent only three other messages on that occasion: one to our patron, HRH the Duke of Edinburgh, one to the chairman of our committee, and one to the editor of the *Sunday Times* our sponsoring newspaper—the other messages announcing our arrival at the Pole had been passed to Freddie a few days earlier and held by him until the time was right to send them on.

Allan came across to my tent with the computation results just after I had finished transmitting and switched off the radio. There was a strained expression on his face as he poked his head through the tent door.

"Aren't you coming in?"

"No . . . er, well you see, we're not quite there," he said apologetically.

"How far short are we then?" I asked.

"About seven miles. . . ."

"Seven miles!" I exclaimed. "That's bloody impossible—the DR can't be that far out." But our dead reckoning had been further out than that many times in the past thirteen months—what a damn silly thing to announce that we had reached the Pole by DR; it was just asking for trouble. It was now 0900 hours GMT. We had several hours to go before the GMT date changed.

"Well . . . maybe I've made a mistake. Do you want me to check it?"

"What? No. . . ." I hadn't really been listening. "Let's get going," I said wearily, "we can do another fix when we've gone six miles."

I suddenly felt very weary as I crawled out of that tent for the last time at that camp, loaded my sledge, hitched up the dogs and moved off across the polished snow surface in pursuit of Ken. We were leaving behind us a trail of vapor but scarcely a mark on the wind-packed snow. Was it not the same with this expedition, I wondered: *What mark are we leaving on history?* The rewards of priority had already gone. The Pole no longer meant anything to me. I had in a sense left it behind, for I had already had that moment of pride, the personal and heady moment of glory. Whatever happened now was nothing more than a chore, a formality.

Navigation in close proximity to the Pole is filled with possible errors. If your calculation of the longitude is slightly out, or if, as in the case of Peary, you didn't take one during the whole journey, then the time you calculate the sun will cross your meridian—in other words, the time at which you think the sun is due north—is wrong. Blindly you head in the wrong direction, and as you do so the error in the dead-reckoning longitude increases, your azimuth is thrown still further into error, and these errors increase progressively until, confounded by the mystery of it all, you set up your theodolite once again and do a precise observation.

We had set off in high spirits, hiding any secret embarrassment we felt at having already announced that we were by dead reckoning at the Pole, and after traveling what we estimated to be seven miles were stopped by an open fracture. It was a perfect day, and there seemed little point in putting up the tent for shelter from what was then only a slight breeze while Allan set up the theodolite and did a quick check on the latitude.

"There's something very wrong," he muttered, looking more forlorn than I had ever seen him look before.

"How do you mean?"

"Well . . . we are still about seven miles from the Pole."

"What! That's crazy, we've just sledged seven miles toward it from a point seven miles back from where it was seven miles away in this direction."

"Well, we're definitely seven miles from it, so I suppose we must have been passing it and cutting 89°53′ in a chord."

We concluded there must have been something very wrong with the direction taken from the position we had computed that morning; so we set up a tent, threw in a few boxes to sit on and went into the computations again. The error was in the longitude. We did another series of observations, all of which took time, then set off. We traveled hard for three hours, set up a theodolite yet again, and found that we were three miles south of the Pole on the Greenwich Meridian. With Spitsbergen as our goal and being still three weeks behind schedule, it was a temptation to abandon that search for an imaginary point; but we could not do so with a clear conscience, especially since we had told Her Majesty that by dead reckoning we had reached it. How close does one have to be to the North Pole to say one has been there: one mile, half a mile? The ice is drifting all the time.

We set off yet again and traveled on a precise azimuth. We chopped through every pressure ridge that came our way, cutting ourselves a dead-straight road due north. But it was slow progress and the drift was against us. We were, in fact, hardly making any progress at all, and after about four hours had come less than a mile.

In desperation, we off-loaded the sledges, laid a depot and took on with us only the barest essentials, just enough for one night's camp. It was a risk, the only time during the whole journey that we took such a risk. But it paid off. With the lighter sledges we made faster progress, and after about three hours estimated that we must surely be at the Pole, possibly even beyond it. So we stopped, set up our tents, and did a final fix which put us at 89°59′N, one mile south of the North Pole on longitude 180°. In other words, we had crossed the Pole about a mile back along our tracks. The time was 0345 GMT on April 6, 1969. We crawled into our sleeping bags and fell asleep.

By the time we awoke, the pad marks of thirty-five Eskimo huskies, the broad tracks of four heavy Eskimo-type sledges, and the four sets of human footprints which had approached the North Pole and halted one mile beyond it on the morning of Easter Sunday, 1969, no longer marked the spot where we had taken our final sun shots. For even while we were sleeping, our camp had been slowly drifting; and the Pole, by the time we had reloaded our sledges a few hours later and set course for the island of Spitsbergen, lay north in a different direction.

It had been an elusive spot to find and fix—the North Pole, where two separate sets of meridians meet and all directions are south. Trying to set foot upon it had been like trying to step on the shadow of a bird that was hovering overhead, for the surface across which we were moving was itself a moving surface on a planet that was spinning about an axis beneath our feet. We were dog-tired and hungry. Too tired to celebrate our arrival on the summit of this supermountain around which the sun circles almost as though stuck in a groove.

We set up our camera and posed for some pictures—thirty-six shots at different exposures. We tried not to look weary, tried not to look cold; tried only to huddle, four fur-clad figures, in a pose that was vaguely familiar—for what other proof could we bring back that we had reached the Pole?

13

Longitude Thirty East

THE first two miles of the journey south was back along our tracks. We were heading straight down the Greenwich meridian—and you can't aim more precisely for London than that; but so weak did I feel through lack of sleep and the emotional exhaustion of the last few days that all I can remember of that day is a blurred impression of ice hummocks and ridges moving toward me and sweeping past as I lay slumped on the sledge. I vaguely recall stopping at the place where we had left most of our gear, reloading the sledge, staggering alongside it, leaning for support against the load, and coming to a halt at the place where we had set up a tent the day before to check our computations—the second seven-mile camp. The wide fracture was now frozen over but the ice still not thick enough to take the weight of sledges and dogs, and in a daze I moved about helping to set up camp for the night. Over dinner I fell asleep. I fell asleep again later over the messages I was trying to draft in time for the radio sked with Freddie, and was not waked from this trance until Fritz stuck his head in through the sleeve door to say the other tent had caught on fire.

"What's the damage?" I asked without moving off my back.

My body seemed too heavy to raise; I wanted nothing more than the bliss of ignorance, the release of all obligation to think, to speak, to move. . . .

"The top three feet has burnt out. Al's sleeping bag's a write-off, and most of the clothing that was hanging up in the apex has gone," Fritz said in a flat, tired voice.

"Any chance of repairing it?"

"Could do; it'll take a while, though."

I crawled out of the tent and slithered across the polished wind-packed snow with my hands tucked under my armpits to protect them from the breeze. Allan was scratching amongst the charred remains of clothing that lay scattered around; the tent's four blackened ribs projected from the hole at the apex like the bones of a carcass from which the vultures had been disturbed during their feasting on the flesh. The snow all around was streaked black with soot that had been trodden in.

"What happened?"

"Dunno. I was drilling a hole in the ice over there; Al was testing the balance of a whip he had just finished making; next thing we knew, there was smoke pouring from the apex. We dragged out as much stuff as we could; beat the fire out. . . . That's about it."

"Something must have dropped onto the primus as I got out," Allan added sheepishly.

"Surprised more tents don't burn down, really." I shrugged, shivered, and went back to my warm tent and switched on the radio. Freddie I could hear quite well and from time to time he could hear me, but we were now at the farthest stretch of my range with a 15-watt transmitter. Within a few days he would be moving his station out to the ice island T-3; meanwhile we relayed our traffic as we had done the day before through John Belcher. There was a message from Her Majesty The Queen:

> I send my warmest congratulations to you and the other members of The British Trans-Arctic Expedition on reaching the North Pole. My husband and I are delighted that you are well and wish you the best of luck for the rest of your journey.
> signed ELIZABETH R

There was a message too from the Prime Minister, Mr. Harold Wilson:

> . . . Yours is a feat of endurance and courage which ranks with any in polar history. My colleagues and I send you our heartfelt congratulations and our best wishes for a safe and triumphant completing of your journey.

We were to receive many messages of congratulation over the next few days from friends, professional associates and politicians; but on that night the sked was not a long one and the only message I sent out was a short note to Freddie asking for the reserve tent—the one Allan, Roger and I had used during our journey two years before—to be added to the list of items scheduled for the next airdrop. Fritz and Allan came over just after I had switched off the radio, and over a brew of tea the four of us chatted, mainly about the burnt tent and Allan's sleeping bag. The tent could be patched crudely with bits of tarpaulin and cuts of material taken from the snow valance. It was doubtful, however, if it would survive a strong wind, but neither Fritz nor Allan seemed particularly worried; they had been intending to sleep outside in a few days' time, going onto what we regarded as our summer routine of using the tent only as a shelter in which to do the cooking. Allan's sleeping bag was a more serious problem with the temperatures still in the minus thirties. The four of us had a sort-out of spare clothing and for a few days Allan used our wolfskins for bedding. One of the garments I donated Allan was a heavy crew-necked sweater which was in very good condition. It was characteristic of Allan that he never wore this during the day, preferring to use his own which he had salvaged from the fire and which now had three enormous holes in the sleeves and front. My sweater he used at night to wrap around his feet.

By the morning of April 7, the fracture which had stopped us was covered with five inches of ice and we took the sledges across it without much risk. We met many more fractures of about the same age during that day and on the eighth, none of which caused us any trouble; but at camp that night we were still more than two degrees of latitude behind schedule and had only sixty days left in which to cover an absolute minimum of six hundred nautical miles. Men and dogs were run down as a result of the grueling sledging of the last six weeks in temperatures of —40° to —50°F on a diet that was insufficient. We could not, I told the committee in a radio message of that day, possibly maintain an average of ten nautical miles a day, which in route statute miles would mean covering just over twenty miles a day, unless we could arrange to receive on each of the next two Canadian Air Force resupply drops five hundred pounds of red meat for the dogs and supplementary rations for the men to increase their calorie intake to approximately 6,500 calories a day. I had therefore made arrangements to meet these needs, and in order to compensate the extra weight would jettison all unessential instruments and gear. I assured the committee that we would not jettison film or any of our records, and informed them that we would proceed to Spitsbergen with Allan in company.

I sent a message to Max Brewer that same night:

> . . . it is with the very deepest sense of gratitude that I recognize your offer made some time ago to assist this expedition by sending out two Cessnas with R4D cover to relieve us of our scientific instruments, exposed film and records. However, in view of your many logistic problems in supporting T-3 and the great distance we expect to be from that station by April 16 (450 nautical miles), the urgency with which we must press for Spitsbergen, and the relatively small payload of film and instruments that would be collected from us (the Lamont equipment was left at winter quarters on the authorisation of Dr. Hunkins), I feel that the complex and costly operation of sending out two Cessnas with R4D cover is no longer justified. It will of course be a great disappointment to Geoff Renner who has so patiently and sympathetically held himself in readiness at Barrow to join us as a replacement for Allan. Geoff has followed our progress with great interest and no doubt a little envy as we struggled those last few miles to the Pole. . . .

At latitude 89°17′N, longitude 09°00′E, we were spotted by a U.S. Air Force weather reconnaissance aircraft. They had come up on our frequency on the Barrow side of the Pole, and asked if we had any smoke flares. "I can do better than that," I told them. "I'll switch on the Elliott homing beacon." We had a very pleasant chat—which cost us an extra hour's work on the hand generator—and I was surprised and delighted to hear that Colonel Joe Fletcher was on board. The American drifting station T-3, otherwise known as Fletcher's Ice Island, is named after him; he was the first pilot to spot and to land on the ice island in 1952.

The weather aircraft flies the route once a day: from Europe to Alaska via the North Pole one day, and returning along the same track the next. Their ETA at the Pole is generally within a few minutes of the same time every day. This set me thinking. With the poor radio propagation we were experiencing at that time, and the prospect of more difficult radio conditions as we increased our distance from Freddie, it might be prudent to come to some arrangement with the U.S. Air Force.

Instead of shifting his radio station to Spitsbergen, which would have left us during the period of his move without a service officer to coordinate the air-support operations, he proposed to move his station to T-3 and remain there until we made radio contact with HMS *Endurance,* the Royal Navy's ice-patrol ship that was to be on standby in Spitsbergen waters between May 21 and June 21 in case the crossing party was caught in a fast current and carried into the Greenland Sea. But our radio contact with Freddie at T-3 was proving less reliable than we had expected, and I was worried. I had to be able to keep Canadian Forces Headquarters regularly informed of our progress, so that if we went off the air a few days before a scheduled airdrop they could make an inspired guess as to our position (within fifteen nautical miles) to give them fuel enough to carry out a square search of the area and spot our flares. If they could not find us, once we had run out of our reserve rations we would have to eat dog, and feed dog to dog—an eventuality for which we had been prepared at the outset, and indeed one of the reasons why I had chosen to take dog teams rather than mechanical vehicles.

The approach to Spitsbergen required some careful thought and as much up-to-date information as I could amass before I would commit the party. Meanwhile, we changed course slightly and moved over to longitude 30°E, which at that latitude was no great distance. We found it more convenient from a navigational point of view to choose a longitude and stick to it, and over the next few days I sent out several messages seeking the predictions and latest weather and ice reports for the north shore of Spitsbergen. I had of course made a very detailed study of the ice conditions in the Spitsbergen area many years ago as part of the basic plan; but ice conditions vary considerably from one year to the next, indeed from week to week at that time of the year when the ice starts to loosen up.

Bernt Belchen, who had been with Amundsen in Spitsbergen in 1926 when Amundsen had made his transpolar flight in the dirigible *Norge* and was with Byrd as pilot on the first flight to the South Pole in 1929, had been in Norway recently and picked up some information which he sent me via Max Brewer: "The ice has been against the north coast of Spitsbergen since last September and now extends well to the south. It's pretty rough; sounds like seasonal ice that has been badly broken, and sounds as though it might still be much in evidence when June 21 arrives. . . ." And from Colonel Fletcher, who had flown over us a few days before: "Along longitude 30°E, a system of refrozen leads, apparently of some age, oriented ENE/WSW extends from Pole region to below 86° north, with leads wider and more regularly spaced below 86, with narrow crossings fewer. General travel conditions appear progressively more difficult farther south over highly fractured younger ice. Good luck."

For information on our immediate vicinity I came to an unofficial arrangement with the weather reconnaissance crews to call them up on the radio every second day and get from them a bird's-eye description of the ice conditions immediately to our south. From these regular flights along our route, from flights of the U.S. Navy ice reconnaissance, from weather-satellite information supplied by the U.S. Oceanographic Office, and from the predictions of specialists in the subject of ice concentration and movement, I decided that on our approach to Spitsbergen we would follow a track that would take us parallel to the major leads, give us a respectable margin of safety in case we were halted by the conditions or by injury in the closing stages, and head directly for Phipps Island, the largest of the Sjöuyane Group (the northernmost offshore islands, twenty-odd miles from an unoccupied but well-stocked Norwegian hut at Depotodden on Northeast Land), and make a landfall, probably on Phipps Island, on or about June 4.

On April 12 I had tuned my No. 2 radio off our operating frequency of 6544 kilocycles to try and pick a time check from Station WWV on 10 megacycles, and had failed not only to get a time check but also to get the transmitter back onto our frequency. We had been two days without radio contact through bad radio propagation, and over the next two days there was no improvement. We were at this time in tremendous traveling form and the big question now was whether we could afford to push on and make more miles than anyone would be expecting of us— for if we failed to make radio contact before the scheduled resupply flight of the sixteenth we would be so far to the south of where we were expected that the aircraft would not find us. On the fourteenth we had three days' food left on full rations; we cut down to half rations and pressed on.

At 0515 on the sixteenth I switched on my No. 1 radio and rattled off a few call signs to test the set. "Traction, Traction calling Arctic Angel—how d'you read?"

"Loud and clear," came back the reply, to my complete surprise; it was my first radio contact for six days.

"This is Captain Ronning speaking; we've been looking for you for the last forty minutes up near 89. Where are you?"

"88 north, 30 east," I said.

"Congratulations! We'll be over you shortly." They had, I learned later, taken off from Thule Air Base in northwest Greenland some three hours earlier, in poor weather. Radio conditions had been atrocious. My voice had been the first intelligible sound they had heard on their radio since setting out. About twenty minutes after that contact we heard the sound of the engines and lit a red smoke flare. It was spotted and the drop made smoothly in three passes of the camp. There were the routine supplies—twenty-three boxes of dog food, five boxes of man rations, twenty-four gallons of kerosene—plus a few additional items I had requested: Our reserve tent, four new heavy all-metal ice axes to replace those that had been broken during the cold weather of the last few weeks; twelve steaks, twenty-four cans of beer, fresh fruit, potato powder, porridge oats, chocolate—all of which would help to boost our daily intake of calories and give us more miles through added strength. Finally, a Nansen sledge to replace Ken's Greenland-type sledge which had taken a tremendous battering on the journey to the Pole. Had we more Greenland-type sledges in reserve I would have called for one, for even though all four of the Greenland-type sledges with which we had set out from winter quarters had split their runners, and were now held together with metal plates, bolts, rawhide and parachute shrouds, they were undoubtedly tougher than the Nansen type. Captain Ronning took the Hercules up to 900 feet to make this last drop; the sledge came down beautifully and landed on its runners facing south.

We had our customary feast that night, made the more memorable through having been on short rations the last few days; and the following day, the weather being more inclement, we rested up. It was on that day, with radio propagation now improved slightly, we heard the news that Hugh Simpson's party had abandoned their attempt at the Pole. They had evidently had a tough time getting back to land, but the details of this we did not receive until some time later.

On the eighteenth I was able to get our position to Freddie by relaying through the U.S. weather reconnaissance aircraft, but I had no contact over the next two days and our position by the twenty-first came as a surprise even to us; we were by then at 87°23′N on longitude 33° east. The ice conditions we were now meeting were quite different from those we had grown accustomed to in the Beaufort Gyral. Here in the transpolar stream the ice was younger and faster flowing, the floes smaller, and the pressure ridges more numerous, but the ridges were not the huge twenty-foot walls we had had to hack a way through in our first year's travel; few of the ridges we were now meeting were bigger than eight or ten feet, and by picking our route carefully we were able to avoid those long and frustrating delays.

But our rate of progress was not entirely due to better ice conditions. By this stage we had had more sledging experience on the Arctic Ocean than any of our predecessors. We had spent fourteen months on the ice pack and grown accustomed to the sights, sounds, and movement of ice. We had survived four seasons and, in spite of the many setbacks and frustrations, had reached the North Pole by the longest axis of the Arctic Ocean. The weather was getting warmer; we could work the dogs more comfortably, and could put in more hours as we ploughed through the misery of the last few hours of each day toward a target time we set each morning while we were still warm and eager. But with each degree the temperature rose, and with each sign indicating the advance of the season, there grew an anxiety which only miles and more miles could alleviate. It had become a race with the season, a race in which we were handicapped out of all reason and which we could win only by driving ourselves and our dogs to the limit of our physical endurance. We were now on the move and exposed to the weather for fifteen hours a day, and made progress by working for it across country where good progress was possible only for men with a greater incentive than the enticing hope of success. We made miles to save our skins.

In the fifteen traveling days since leaving the Pole, we had made good three degrees of latitude. Given the same traveling conditions over the next fifteen days, it would not be unreasonable to expect that we would be at latitude 84°N by the next and last scheduled resupply drop of the Canadian Forces on May 10; and continuing this same rate of progress we would make a landfall on the north coast of Spitsbergen on schedule. For the first time in the last twelve months I felt we stood a very good chance of reaching land before the melt season, but optimism is only a state of mind; plans must be based on something more solid. For sev-

eral days while plodding along beside the sledge I had been working out a contingency scheme which could be put into operation
should the weather or ice conditions deteriorate rapidly. This I
put to the Chief of Defence Staff at Canadian Forces Headquarters in the form of a letter transmitted to Freddie on April 22:

> . . . we intend making every possible effort to reach Spits-
> bergen on June 4, but in spite of the favorable drift of ice from
> which we hope to benefit during the final two hundred nautical
> miles of our journey, it would be unrealistic to expect travel-
> ing conditions to remain as good throughout the month of
> May as they were in early April; indeed, reports from the U.S.
> weather aircraft flying daily along meridian 30°E indicate
> that the ice conditions deteriorate south of latitude 86°N, and
> reports from Norwegian sources state that the pack ice is badly
> broken off the north coast of Spitsbergen.
>
> It is essential therefore that a contingency plan is laid. The
> plan calls for an airdrop on or about June 4 which would equip
> us with lightweight man-hauling sledges and an inflatable rub-
> ber boat, and food and fuel enough to keep us going for about
> thirty days. Details I will transmit in a separate message via
> Sir Vivian Fuchs and your air attaché's office in London. May
> it suffice here to say that I am confident that with one addi-
> tional airdrop we would meet the contingency and make a
> landfall and our rendezvous with HMS *Endurance* safely about
> Midsummer's Day.

The rubber boat we had dropped to us in the summer of 1968,
and which served as a mattress for Allan when we shifted him
after his injury, we had been obliged to jettison along with all
other weighty items of gear for which we had no immediate use
in order to get more speed out of the dogs. We had known then
that we would not need the boat until June, and there seemed little point in carrying it over fifteen hundred miles when a replacement could be dropped later if needed. And we now needed one,
plus six lightweight-alloy waterproof boxes which would fit on
two lightweight Nansen man-haul sledges. In these we could stow
all our bedding, film, and records; and since they were buoyant,

we could tow the sledges and loads behind the rubber dinghy across any water obstacles we should meet.

We were now seldom meeting each other during the day, for the traveling conditions were so much better than we had found the previous year. The pack ice in the Pacific Gyral had been more massive and the pressure ridges, though fewer in number than now, had been bigger in all dimensions. Where the previous season we had spent days hacking our way across vast areas of smashed-up pack, or plodding wearily across giant floes and over hummocks smoothed by the warmth of several summers, the sledges were now rattling along across younger floes and over smaller and more angular hummocks and ridges.

Being spread out across the floes (alone but for the tracks of the sledges that had gone before, and for the howl of dogs one sometimes heard a long way off when one had stopped to untangle traces) was for each of us a new experience in polar travel. The whole vast expanse of ice one could imagine was deserted; only Allan's cigarette ends which I passed at regular intervals along the trail, the chocolate wrappers dropped by Ken or Fritz, and the deep yellow stains in the snow were signs that men had passed by, for the sledge tracks and the sprinkle of dogs' pad marks seemed to blend into this environment as naturally as the ice floes which lay tightly packed on the surface of the sea. No longer cold and exhausted I would lope along beside the sledge, or toss a leg over the load and for a while puff at the short fat stem of my pipe, which I had snapped off so that the warm smoke had less distance to travel before it reached my mouth—less time in which to condense and freeze. The short-stemmed pipe is the sign of a polar smoker; the consoling joy of the Eskimo hunter. They have a special pocket in their polar-bear pants where they keep the pipe and baccy and their American Zippo lighter—a sort of inner sporan. Natural, relaxed travelers, the Eskimos; I thought of them a lot in those times when I was alone and relaxed. Then I would once again become a European and my mind would wander over every possible disaster which might befall the expedition in the closing stages of the journey and try to formulate some plan which would leave no chance for error.

Since latitude 89°N on the other side of the Pole, I had been averaging only five hours sleep a night and traveling in a kind of dream, clearing obstacles that came my way by somnambulistic instinct. At the end of each long traveling day there was an hour's hand-generating to provide battery power for the radio transmission of messages, assessments, and plans I would stay up late to write. It went on like this through to the end—there was no other way. Every contingency had to be anticipated by a plan; we could not stop to rest or write; I could not write while on the move, although often enough I tried; the evening was the only time, after my tentmate had turned in. That's when I put on paper what during the twelve-hour marching day I had formulated in my mind.

The assessment I started transmitting to Freddie on the evening of April 26 had been put together in this way; our position then was 86°12'N on longitude 30.6°E. It ran to almost a thousand words and took several long sessions to transmit. Many other messages were appended to it; some of it was repetition of what I had said in messages to the committee before, parts of it were in the form of action memoranda. It was in fact an operational instruction that would coordinate the efforts of everyone who had an active interest in the concluding stages of our journey to Spitsbergen.

We were to maintain a course down longitude thirty east as far south as latitude 83°N. There we would alter course for the northwest tip of Northeast Land, and all being well we would make a landing in that vicinity about June 3, locate the Norwegian hut at Depotodden, and rest up for two days before continuing the journey to a rendezvous with HMS *Endurance* in Tempelfjord after an overland journey. A message I had sent to my old friend Tore Gjelsvik, the director of the Norsk Polarinstitutt, asking for information on the hut and its food stock, was to be appended to the assessment, together with his reply and maps which he would supply; and this was to form part of the brief for the captain of HMS *Endurance*. I listed our target dates and course coordinates for each degree.

I stressed that if the crossing party made their landfall as planned, or if the helicopters from HMS *Endurance* could get within range or lay a depot of food and fuel in our line of advance, then the additional airdrop requested of the Canadian Forces should be canceled. I asked for information to be sent to me immediately on the range and payload of the helicopters aboard HMS *Endurance;* and for the captain's opinion on the feasibility of the helicopters relaying fuel along the north coast of Spitsbergen in order to extend his helicopter range from the ship; and asked that all dates should be coordinated between the crossing party and the ship and be based on my sitreps dating from May 10 onward. In this way I hoped the *Endurance*'s sea time could be kept to a minimum. I asked that Geoff Renner should be taken on the expedition's strength and take passage aboard *Endurance* as the expedition's liaison.

Should it appear fairly certain that by May 25 the crossing party was unlikely to make a landfall or come within range of the helicopters from HMS *Endurance* by June 4, a resupply of food and equipment would be required; provided we were then within striking range of Spitsbergen, it should consist of thirty days' supply of sledging rations, six jerry cans of kerosene, all the remaining dog food held in reserve at the Canadian Forces Base at Rivers, Manitoba, and a supply of equipment (part of which I had already ordered) which would give us the capability of converting to a man-hauling party if necessary. The final decision on which technique we would adopt for the final scramble across broken ice pack would depend on many factors: the position of the crossing party in relation to the landmass, the weather, ice conditions, strength of drift, direction of drift, and the position of shipping in the Spitsbergen area. We had the choice of three basic techniques. We could make our final approach as a dog-sledging party with full teams plus man-hauling equipment in tow; as four reduced dog teams hauling man-hauling sledges; or as a man-hauling party with the capability of boating. Needless to say, if there was the slightest possibility of completing the journey with all the dogs we would do so.

The area across which we had been sledging during the last few days was not altogether without interest or the occasional more dramatic diversion. On the afternoon on which I had started transmitting my assessment, for example, we had run into an area of violent ice movement and come closer than at any time during the journey to losing a sledge and a team of dogs. Allan was at the time in the lead. He and Fritz had hacked a way through a pressure ridge onto a strip of rubble and mush ice which, although wet, was quiet. There was another ridge on the far side of the strip of mush which started to groan the moment Allan set foot upon it. I went over with him and gave him a hand negotiating the ridge on the far side, but we had no sooner got the dogs safely onto the far bank than the mush ice started to slacken and boil and the floe on which we were standing to tilt up to an angle of thirty degrees. An immediate choice had to be made between my sledge and Allan's. Mine carried a radio, Allan's geophysical records, a duplicate set of Fritz's records, one of two sets of navigational gear (the other set was on Allan's sledge), tables, the theodolite, and half the exposed and unexposed film stock. Allan abandoned his sledge and the remainder of exposed film, cut his dogs loose and made for the safety of the floe to the north, while I scrambled back across the bucking slippery blocks and mush to save my own team. The whole floe was splitting up and heaving. With some frantic maneuvers, Ken, Fritz, and I managed to get our three teams away from the immediate danger and leaped across several fractures to a slightly bigger floe to our south. Allan, left on his own, meanwhile had discovered that he was cut off from the floe beyond by a fissure in the ice; it was at that time some fourteen feet deep and the bottom compacted slush. I went back to give him a hand while Ken and Fritz looked around for an alternative route by which the four of us could reunite. The mush ice was in constant movement. Several times I was about to set foot on the crossing when it would suddenly boil up; green blocks the size of bungalows would rise out of the stew of ice debris and collapse with a dull thud back into the mush. By the time I rejoined Allan he was once again collecting his dogs together for one final and desperate attempt to haul his sledge clear. We threw every ounce of energy we had against the back of that sledge and with the help of some dog power shifted it in jerks, a foot at a time, to the top of the tilted slab of ice. From that precarious perch we lowered it into the fissure. The slab of ice by now had slumped a little and the drop was only about twelve feet, and its floor of compacted slush so weak in places that we put a foot through it. Had the walls of that fissure relaxed six inches while we were struggling the sledge along it, or suddenly closed, I doubt that we would have survived. As it was, we got out at a point some thirty yards along the fissure where the north wall had crumbled and formed a ramp up onto the floe. It was several hours before we reunited all four sledges, but from there, at least for a few more miles, we made good progress south.

The leads and fractures by this time were becoming a problem, and many long diversions were necessary to make any progress south. It was by now taking many days for newly opened leads to freeze over. There were many indications that the summer was coming early. Thin ice on the larger leads was darkening and becoming soft. The sledges broke through to slop several times a day, but it was about this time nevertheless that we put in our best mileages, for the country kept rolling ahead of us and every minor obstacle opening the way to more floes and minor detours. We made twenty-three nautical miles on May second (in route miles, at least twenty-seven nautical miles). We were putting in sometimes as much as twelve hours of sledging and at the end of each day were dead tired and very hungry.

By May tenth we were at latitude 83°N—the point on our course at which we were to turn and head for land. On that same day we received what was to have been our last airdrop from 435 Squadron—a brilliantly executed mission. At an altitude of 15,000 feet they picked up our beacon at a range of fifty miles but lost it on their descent and, as usual, we brought them in by listening for the sound of the engines and passing them directions over the radio. They descended to 250 feet in fog and, roaring over us, dispatched their load in two passes. We could not have seen the aircraft for more than five seconds of each pass. The captain of the aircraft caught only a split-second glance at his target, but the chutes all landed within one hundred yards of the dropping zone.

There were fogs from then on almost every day, for we were now into the month of mists. We stumbled across pans of ice that seemed at first as limitless as oceans on a compass course past misty shapes which grew, then shrank and faded away. Through the mist on the fourteenth I saw what I thought to be a man standing alone about 300 yards off to the east. An uncomfortable feeling ran through me. I knew it could not be one of my companions, for the sledge tracks, all three sets, swept away slightly to the west. Even through the telescopic sights of my rifle the object still looked like a man, for it was too dark to be a bear and I could think of nothing else it might be. Not until I got within a hundred yards could I make out a log, ice-crusted on one side and sticking out of the floe at an angle of fifteen degrees from the vertical in the direction of my approach—which is why it had seemed to be standing erect.

It was about 4 feet 6 inches high and 2 feet in diameter; a more incongruous looking sight I have never seen. The log only could have come from one of the Siberian rivers that drains into the Arctic Ocean. Caught up in the transpolar drift stream, it no doubt had been already two years on its passage toward the Greenland Sea. The shores of Spitsbergen are littered with great logs that have drifted across the Polar basin—the southeast and southwest coasts of Greenland, too. In Julianehaab on the southwest coast of Greenland some pieces of equipment, a pair of oilskin breeches and some papers, were found frozen into the ice that had been washed ashore in 1884—relics from the *Jeannette,* commanded by De Long, which had been crushed in the ice three years earlier. It was these relics that inspired Fridtjof Nansen to construct a ship that would ride clear of the ice pressure that squeezed its hull and be carried by the ice across the Polar basin. Both Nansen and De Long failed to reach the North Pole. That log, that solitary ice-encrusted object foreign to the environment, seemed to me a tilted tombstone to the memory of those two men who had been my inspiration. On it I scratched with the point of my knife the names De Long and Nansen.

By the sixteenth we were 110 miles from a landfall in an area where there were many pressure ridges and cracks. We were from time to time finding what seemed to be a growth of fungus in dirt patches on the ice, and tiny clusters of shells. We had seen nothing like this on any other part of the ocean and excitedly collected samples. We were flown over by a little auk that day, and the following morning when we awoke saw a snow bunting pecking around in the snow among the sleeping dogs. All these signs of the nearness of land were heartening, but at the same time a little worrying for we knew from the ice reports that the final stage of our journey would be across ice that was very broken. The sky was now our surest guide. On the cloud base of the overcast were reflected the dark streaks and patches that indicated the open water directly beneath; it was like a mirror suspended above us. By staying on longitude thirty east as far south as latitude 83°N, I had judged that we would be making our final approach parallel to the major fractures. This the sky confirmed —we were sledging beneath a striped canopy which indicated the presence of major leads on either side of us. This the satellites confirmed when on rare occasions the cloud cover broke and the satellites transmitted photographs to Washington of the breakup of the ice—information which I had arranged should be passed on to us.

Rising at 1500 hours, we had for several days now been traveling through the night and sleeping outside on the sledges during the heat of the day when the temperatures rose to about +20°F. By the twentieth the ice was slushy; for the first time since the summer of 1968 we could smell the sea. Wildlife suddenly became abundant: twenty-seven birds of five different species—little auks, fulmars, ivory gulls, king eiders, and terns. Perhaps this smell and this abundance of wildlife had something to do with the upwelling of water near the edge of the continental shelf; perhaps we were on the southern dispersal edge of the ice pack—we did not really know, but the excitement we were now beginning to feel was intensified by all this life. We saw birds, a seal, and a school of six narwhales the next day, and on the twenty-second, polar bear tracks—the first we had seen for 870 miles. With a good day's travel on the next day, by my calculations we ought to sight land—fifteen months to the day after losing sight of Point Barrow on the other side of the Arctic Ocean. Several times that night I rechecked my figures and climbed an ice hummock to scan the horizon through the telescopic sights of my rifle. I could see nothing but a jagged ice horizon.

The sky began to clear after we had been on the move for about half an hour on the morning of May 23, but the area across which we were traveling was very badly fractured and Allan and I at the back of the column about a mile or so behind Fritz and Ken found ourselves at about 1800 hours halted by a new fracture, which evidently had opened and offset by about ten yards since our two companions had crossed that spot. We were held up there for about an hour before the two floes came together again at a point about one hundred yards to the east of their tracks—by which time the day was brilliant, absolutely still, and very warm. The sky was empty now except for a few wispy cirrus, and a roll of cloud low on the horizon directly on our heading.

"They've got to be land clouds, Al—you wouldn't get that kind of orographic cloud over a flat surface. See that curve and the vertical development; they've got to be clouds directly above a landmass with a fair amount of warm rock exposed."

"Sure they're land clouds." There was a long pause while I waited for another comment. He lit a cigarette, took a couple of draws and moved up to the front of his sledge, leaving behind him a swirling pall of blue smoke above where he had been standing.

"Shall I go on then?"

"Yeah, see you tonight." I leaned back against my sledge and watched him give the front of his sledge a wriggle to loosen it from the grip of the sticky snow and wake up his dogs by shaking their traces. He moved off in his characteristic, slightly flat-footed shuffle which broke now and then into a trot and within five minutes was lost to sight.

For a while I listened. I could hear him calling to his dogs and as the sounds grew weaker and a perfect silence settled over the area I pushed myself upright, woke up my team and set off in a slow, steady plod along the tracks. After about half an hour I stopped the dogs and climbed a whale-backed hummock. There was nothing ahead but the dazzling frosted surface of the ice pack; no sign even of my three companions, for they were lost in the maze of ice hummocks, boulders and ridges that scattered the light. At fifty minutes past the hour of ten that night I climbed another great hummock past which the tracks of the other three sledges had swept without stopping. Into the summit I stuck a harpoon against which I steadied my aim on the cloud base directly ahead and peered through the telescopic sight of my rifle. Land climbed out of the horizon into the cloud rolls—a gray-and-white wall of land, hazy with distance, hostile-looking, bleak, spanning several degrees. I lowered my aim very slightly to the pack ice; I could now see all three sledges in line ahead but widely separated. They were dead on course.

I sent out a message that night which, although curt, had the ring of jubilation:

> . . . 240644Z, Herbert to Church—A.1080: Land sighted directly ahead 2055 GMT 23 May 459 days out from Barrow. Present position 81°13′N, 22°00′E—29 nautical miles NNE of Phipps Island.

14

Land!

I HEARD HMS *Endurance* calling me on 6544 kilocycles on the morning of May 24, but they had been unable to
hear me or Freddie. Their position at that time was "Norwegian
Sea—estimating northwest tip Spitsbergen twenty-seventh." Our
position at that time was a patch of ice only sixteen inches thick.
There were many cracks in it and a lot of movement round about,
and not surprisingly we had felt little inclination for a celebration. At camping only the most casual of comments were passed
on the great events of the day: sighting land, Fritz's narrow escape
when two polar bears had come to within a hundred yards of him.
With the warmer weather and with a new firing pin dropped to
us on the last resupply, we now had three rifles in working order;
but on this occasion, the first face-to-face encounter of any member of our party with bears since my solitary encounter with one
on March 16, Fritz had had only two rounds in the magazine.
And he was far out ahead of the rest of us. Fortunately the bears
had lost interest and ambled off, but the incident had put us
on edge.

I thought a good deal too about the message I received from
the U.S. Naval Oceanographic Office via Freddie that morning

regarding shearing and piling at the north shore. "A moderate thirteen-knot wind has been from the south for last six days and shearing believed to be minimized. . . . Regarding buildup of pressure about the Sjuöyane Group, satellite of area obscure but guess there would be moderate buildup of ice pack covering about six-eighths of the water surface. Regarding Hinlopen Strait: in the extreme north portion satellite reveals lead approximately 45 miles long extending south through strait."

We slept through the heat of the day on the sledges and in spite of the thinness of the ice on which we were camped, the noises all around us, and the strong wind from the northeast which had come a few hours earlier than forecast, we awoke refreshed and eager to push on for land with all the speed we could muster. On the strength of the forecast and ice report I had received a few hours earlier I decided to go for the nearest group of islands. Six-eighths ice pack sounded a little slack, but provided we countered the drift by keeping over to the east of the group, I guessed we would be able to scramble ashore at some point along the coast as the ice drifted past. It would be risky, but it would be worth it, for, once the landing was made, the crossing of the Arctic Ocean would be historic fact. Fail to make a landing and it would be a journey that did not conclude, but merely petered out. In terms of exploration, in terms of personal satisfaction, a landing was essential. We would spare no effort to make that landing and, if necessary, spare no risk.

Once that landing was made, we would as soon as possible get back onto the ice pack and sledge due west, passing the open water at the northern entrance of Hinlopen Strait well to the north, and try for a second landing somewhere in the region of Gråhuken on the northern tip of Andree Land. My original intention of sledging all the way to Longyearbyen by the overland route (down Wijdefjorden and up over the ice cap) I now was reluctantly obliged to abandon. Clearly the ice conditions were not good enough; the ice breakup was earlier than usual; it would be difficult enough making a landing on the Sjuöyane Group.

We were soon in trouble on the twenty-fourth and spent several hours chopping a way out of an area where the ice was shattered and heavily ridged. The whole mass of ice was gyrating and each move from one patch to another had to be made in a headlong rush once a way had been hacked through the rubble. Several times we ran into dead ends where there was no possibility of continuing—where the way ahead was blocked by a chaotic and turbulent field of churning ice, or by fractures too wide to cross but too full of loose ice to launch a boat—and after all our effort to cut a way through we would have to turn the sledges and pull out. It was on one of these occasions early in the traveling day that we were visited again by an inquisitive polar bear—a disconcerting experience, for we were at that time fully occupied in trying to maneuver the sledges over a hazardous stretch of ice. It went away after sniffing around for about an hour and did not return until after we had camped on a small floe around which the pressure was building. The wind had by then changed to northwest and was blowing fifteen knots; the cloud base had descended to a couple of hundred feet and snow was falling. Indeed there was so much noise all around us we did not hear Allan's dogs break loose of their picket and chase off after the bear. They drove it into the rough-ice pack where they had tangled their traces around an ice knobble, and the bear, presumably realizing they were caught up, came back to take its pick. By this time, fortunately, Allan realized what had happened and he, Fritz, and Ken drove the bear off and brought the dogs back. We moved the sledges into the center of the camp area and repicketed the teams so that they guarded us on the perimeter, but it was a shallow sleep we had on the sledges that day with loaded rifles lying ready.

We left that small floe in overcast at six o'clock on the twenty-fifth and were into broken pack and struggling within a hundred yards. Two hours later we had advanced half a mile. Fritz was halfway across an awkward channel of compacted mush, Ken close behind him in a safer but equally awkward position in which to maneuver, and Allan and I close behind Ken, when a polar bear appeared directly ahead of Fritz's team and came straight for it. At a range of ten yards it was dropped in its tracks by Fritz and Ken. Within just over one hour we had chopped up the bear, fed it to the dogs, had a smoke, and were on the move again; but the going from there on was through very rough ice and many times the sledges got stuck. In places now we were wading through slush and melt water up to our shins and it was becoming increasingly obvious that the last few miles were going to be not only one of the most uncomfortable but probably one of the most hazardous stages of our journey. Unlike the fracture zone off the coast of Alaska, we had here no air cover; the fractures that opened up could not freeze over, and unlike the ice we had met in June, 1968, here the free drift of the ice was obstructed by the nearby islands and set in turbulent motion. Moreover, the ice was drifting faster, too fast to be effectively countered. But our target still was Phipps Island and at camp on the morning of the twenty-sixth, by compass resection on the mural of islands which lay spread out across a gray backdrop of sky, fixed our position at sixteen miles for the nearest point of land.

The sky looked promising when we crawled out of our bags at 3 P.M. but by the time we got going had closed in again and drained all color from the broken-ice pack across which we were struggling. Nevertheless we made three miles before meeting a fracture which deflected our course almost due east. I was again at the rear of the column—the vulnerable spot on this occasion, for it was along our tracks that the polar bear came. In the flat lighting where every ice feature was a shade of gray, that huge yellow bear was as conspicuous as it looked menacing. My dogs, once they had sight and scent of it, were uncontrollable; but as they charged the bear they spun the sledge against an ice boulder and it jammed. The bear kept coming, seemingly without fear, its huge, powerful body rippling as each heavy pad pressed the snow. I fired two shots over its head at a range of twenty-five yards, and the third at a knobble of bare ice two feet to one side of the creature. It lowered its ratlike head, sniffed the spot where the bullet had struck, came on another five yards, then turned and ambled off. From time to time throughout the rest of that day it stalked us. Only when the mists closed in did we imprudently forget it and concentrate on the problems of the ice. By the end of that day we had advanced only five miles and the twenty-knot wind that had been blowing all day from the southeast backed sixty degrees and increased to thirty knots.

While we were sleeping fitfully on our sledges, that wind had blown us almost six miles northwest, and by 1630 on the twenty-seventh we were still about fourteen miles from land. In the flat lighting, Phipps Island seemed no nearer than it had three days before. We should have been closing that last fourteen miles from a position east-northeast of the most easterly island in the group, but our slow progress over the last few days and the adverse drift had robbed us of a fighting chance of landing on Sjuöyane.

Fritz came over to my sledge when we were all ready to set off. We looked at the map and up at the gray, miserable land that lay before us.

"Well," he said, in a tone which announced he had already given the matter a great deal of thought, "we could make faster progress if we went with the drift due west. Why don't you forget about these islands and make a try for the north shore of Spitsbergen? We might find once we get away from the influence of this group that the ice is less disturbed. Mind you, we'd have to keep well clear of the tail of this lot, say north of 80°25′. What do you think?"

"No; the ice will be as broken along the north shore of Spitsbergen as it is here, probably more so since by the time we get there the melt season will be further advanced. We must have one last go here. Let's go due south; aim to the east of the most easterly island and let the drift carry us toward the center of the group."

"Well, it's your funeral," he said jokingly; adding, as if after some reflection, "and mine too if you're wrong."

Allan and Ken had loaded up and hitched their dogs and were just waiting for the decision. Fritz passed the word, and one by one my three companions moved off across the floe on which we had camped into the jumble of ice beyond. After an hour of hard going we found ourselves on a vast smooth field, sledging alongside a wide black-water fracture, and for the next three hours met no obstruction on our course. We changed direction slightly, left the floe and struck out across a long string of polynyas. We were now weaving a tortuous track around small cracks, fractures and ridges, but none of them slowed the steady rhythm of the dogs. The cloud cover had thickened and hung like a heavy, wet, sepia blanket about a thousand feet above us in a frontal system that ended in a line just short of the Sjuöyane Group. Beyond the sky was clear and of the deepest blue; warm sunlight soaked the islands—there was never a sight more beautiful to men who had been so long at sea, nor a blue-gray field of ice more smooth than that across which we glided toward our final triumph.

At about midnight we came upon a huge barrier ridge which stretched east-west across our line of advance. There was another ridge beyond an open polynya. Beyond the second ridge we could not clearly see, nor did we bother to investigate, but went to work immediately to hack a way through. An exciting discussion had developed against a background noise of ice axes shattering, bursting and picking at the wall that barred our way. I believed those two ridges were the demarcation boundary between the pack ice to the north and the landfast ice which I presumed lay beyond the next ridge. Fritz was not so sure; he thought it unlikely that there would be any landfast ice around a group of islands so exposed to the fast drift of ice. There could be no other topic of conversation—we were only eight miles from land. With eight miles of landfast ice the success of the expedition was assured. We got the dogs over the first ridge, skirted the polynya and on reaching the second ridge found a trail of blood running from the edge of the polynya where a polar bear had presumably killed a seal and dragged it up to the ridge and over. The ridge at that point was about fifteen feet high. With such a spoor, we needed little chopping to prepare that ridge for the dogs, and once over this found ourselves on a vast floe which seemed to reach right to the very base of the land ahead. For four miles we passed

not a hummock or a ripple in the surface, and the longer we
sledged the more convinced I became that we were at that very
moment breathing the air of success. Allan was in the lead, Ken
behind him; two tiny specks in the distance. Fritz and I were
sledging alongside each other about twenty yards apart. We were
both sitting on the sledges chatting.

By 0235 on the twenty-eighth everything had stopped. We had
caught up with Allan and Ken at a low pressure ridge, beyond
which was a belt of mush ice and brash, and beyond that open
water which as far as we could see went right up to the coast of
the island. There was nothing we could do but turn our teams
alongside the ice edge and follow the floe west.

However, we soon discovered the edge of the floe was converging on the northwest corner of Phipps Island; and after sledging
for about two miles, it seemed (from what we could see from the
summit of a ridge at the edge of the floe) that at this region the
mush ice was compacted in a wedge between the coast line of
Phipps Island and the edge of the floe. In among this mush ice
were several ice cakes and small floes, none of them any wider
than 150 yards but at least offering us a slight chance of getting
across by leaping from one ice cake to the next. We took a vote
on whether we should take such a risk. The decision was unani-
mous to turn the sledges into what undoubtedly was one of the
most dangerous belts of active ice we had ever set foot upon.

At the point we chose to cross that compacted field of floebergs, ice cakes, and brash, it was about three miles wide; and
within a few hundred yards the full measure of the risk we were
taking had become apparent. Our route back to the floe was cut
off. The whole floating mass of ice rubble was simmering like
some vast caldron of stew. We rushed from one sledge to another as each in turn jammed in the pressure, or lurched as the ice
which was supporting it relaxed or heaved; at one point my sledge
turned completely turtle as the sledge ran awkwardly over a six-
foot drop from one block of ice to another. It landed upside down
in a three-foot-deep pool of melt water. In a box strapped to the
top of the sledge were two cinecameras and two still cameras,

plus all the unexposed film and some of the exposed stock—now under three feet of water with the full weight of the sledge on top of it. I had been carrying this box on the top of the sledge so that should the sledge at any time break through the ice, I could cut the box free and swim with it to the ice edge. A complete overturn into a three-foot melt pool had never seemed even a remote possibility. Fortunately, we had taken the precaution of sealing the box with rubber, and all the contents were in polythene bags; nevertheless, I was lucky to get the sledge out of that particular situation without loss.

Committed irrevocably to spending our rest period in that wedge of mush ice, we concentrated all our efforts in getting onto the biggest floe we could find. This floe on which we set up camp, was not much more than 150 yards across; but we took the precaution of making everything ready for an emergency evacuation, and set up stakes in the ice in line with certain features on the island in order to judge the rate of drift. We ate a meal of meat-bar stew and turned in—sleeping as usual on the sledges to be able to move more quickly in an emergency. Even by the time we had eaten our evening meal, it had become alarmingly obvious that we were drifting at something over half a knot past the island.

Several times during that rest period I woke up. Each time we were closer to the towering black cliffs and adjacent to a part of the coastline I had not seen before. In the eight hours between dinner and breakfast we drifted almost four miles and closed on the island. We were now about half a mile from the rocky coast but not quite at the closest quarters. Between our small floe and the coast there was now a broad strip of open water; there was no way off the floe in any direction, for the ice all around us had slackened.

At the rate we were drifting we estimated that we would come closest to land at 10 P.M. on the twenty-eighth, and anticipating some turbulence at that time, or some jostling of the floes, we made ready and moved the four sledges over to the far side of the floe. We drifted to within a quarter of a mile of the northern tip of Phipps Island, then the direction of drift changed and we started shifting slightly northwest. There was no pressuring effect on the floes when we passed the island at the closest point, and finding that we were still marooned on the floe we set up camp again.

This camp we broke a second time at 0300 hours on the twenty-ninth, for by then it had become evident that we were about to drift between Phipps Island and a small rocky island some 2.5 statute miles to its NNW. We had been wrong on our first assumption that on passing close to the northern tip of Phipps Island we might expect a shaking up as the floe hit a submerged rock or was jostled by another floe; but this did not deter us from making a second assumption—that on passing between the small island and Phipps Island there would be a tightening up in the floes as they were constricted through the gap. We shall never know if that second assumption was right, or if it was a coincidence that at the precise time we were dead in line with the small rocky island and the northern tip of Phipps Island there was tidal influence on the floes. The fact is, at that precise moment the floes did tighten up and we got clear of the small floe on which we had spent an uncomfortable twenty-two hours, and made rapid progress toward the small island to our NNW.

Fritz and Ken had led off, Allan followed, but in loading the cinecamera, I got left behind, and by the time I had caught up with Allan we found we were separated from our two companions by several new fractures. These were not clean fractures. Each was a line of weakness that over perhaps several weeks had been opening and closing; consequently they were full of pressure debris and mush ice. Shifted by the current, this mush and brash would drift along the fracture at about two knots, stop after about thirty yards, then all drift back again. The floes themselves were also gyrating, but relatively slowly. It was some five hours before Allan and I were able to reunite with Fritz and Ken; in the meantime our two companions had tried but failed to reach land. They managed to get to within fifty yards of it but had been stopped by a shore lead, kept open by a tide race that was shifting the smaller pieces of ice along at three knots. There they waited for quite a while in the hope of making a landing. Eventually

Allan and I took a chance on going across the compacted mush ice by stepping on small patches when they tightened up under pressure—a "safe" period that lasted about two seconds, seldom more.

The island itself is a rugged granite rock about one thousand feet high; a spectacular rock from some angles. At first I had not been in the least impressed by its profile. But that had been from the east; from the west its aspect is less sinister.

While we had been sleeping the previous day we had drifted something like three or four miles, and there was every reason to believe that we would do the same thing again. So we set up camp at 0700 hours GMT, and I reported by radio that we had at one time got to within fifty yards of land and were now two hundred yards from the island. We couldn't make it, I told Captain Buchanan on the *Endurance,* and by the following morning we would probably have drifted about five miles to the west of the island; there was no chance of getting across Northeast Land as our route south was barred by a great stretch of open water east and west of the Sjuöyane Group. We would therefore head straight for the ship, which would take us possibly a week or more to reach.

We slept out on our sledges as usual, and when we awoke we found that an eddy had held the ice in tightly to that small rocky island and that we had one more chance of getting across. We had moved hardly more than a couple of hundred yards during the past eight hours, and certainly not alway from the island. We had moved, if anything, slightly closer to it.

The island was slightly under a mile away from the camp itself. The mush ice had widened since the previous day; it was now three quarters of a mile, I would guess, and moving all the time, vacillating, shifting, churning. I loaded up all the cameras—two Nikons, a Rolleiflex, and two 16-mm Bell and Howell cine-cameras—and set off after Allan and Ken. At that moment the ice was fairly quiet, but I could see slight signs of movement. The whole thing was delicately poised; held together by the floe pushing the ice rubble against the land, just sufficient pressure to hold it tight; just tight enough to bear the weight of a man. It needed only to slacken off a couple of inches and it would be impossible to cross.

Fritz elected to stay on the edge of the floe, in case we needed the rubber dinghy. I went after Allan and Ken who had spent some time trying to chop steps down a steep ice drop onto another pan of ice. It then occurred to me that someone ought to stay somewhere near the middle of that belt of mush ice to keep an eye on it. I wanted Ken and Allan to have the satisfaction of reaching land so I told them to go ahead. All during the time they were away I patrolled the ice from the halfway point to where Fritz was standing and was actually with him when we saw Ken and Allan climb onto the land. We could just see two figures scrambling up the rocks. I set off across the ice to meet them and noticed some movement in the ice: a faint groan, a slushy sound—the ice was treacherous and the risk of making a second trip to the island to take some pictures seemed too great. Just as Allan and Ken rejoined me Fritz started yelling that the ice was beginning to move. We had a scramble to get back onto the floe. The gyrating pans were all sloppy by that time and no sooner did we reach the floe than the whole area slackened off.

It was some moments before the full significance of what Allan and Ken had done got through to me, and when it did, it was through a small chunk of granite Ken pressed into my hand.

"Brought you a small bit of the island," he said.

I went into the tent and drafted out a message for Freddie to pass to London. It rang with all the triumph I felt:

At 1900 hrs GMT 29 May, a landing was made by Allan Gill and Major Ken Hedges RAMC on a small rocky island at latitude 80°49′N, longitude 20°23′E, after a scramble across three-quarters of a mile of mush ice and gyrating ice pans. This landing, though brief, concluded the first surface crossing of the Arctic Ocean—a journey of 3,620 route miles from Point Barrow, Alaska, via the North Pole. The four members of the crossing party on their 464th day of drifting ice are now heading across broken ice pack toward a rendezvous with HMS *Endurance*.

15

Endurance, Endurance

IN fifteen months we had grown accustomed to the sounds and the sight of drifting ice, and had developed habits of survival which required no conscious thought. The adventure was no longer the novel situation, but the journey as a whole; and its climax not the sight *of* land, nor even the landing, but the sight *from* land of the ice across which we had come. I had for several days sensed this distance at my back, sensed the tiredness of all those miles in my limbs, the longing for land and the release of my burden—that total commitment to success, without which six years of my life had been wasted.

My three companions did not share this attitude; their motives for making the journey, their attitudes toward the pack-ice environment, their personal feelings on that day when we reached our objective, were all sightly different.

For Allan it was a private adventure, and very personal. He was attracted by the idea not so much because it was a first surface crossing of the Arctic Ocean, but because it was an opportunity to spend sixteen months with dog teams in an environment he loved. He wasn't interested in any broader significance that the journey might have; indeed, he had his doubts that there was any. For Fritz, on the other hand, it was a sort of monument, a monument of achievement in life of which he was proud. He would not have come if it had not been a first—nor if he had been unable to conduct a scientific program. Ken had joined the expedition with an open mind, not knowing really quite what to expect; although he confessed to having vague ideas going back to the historic and romantic times of Shackleton and Scott. But the expedition for Ken had been a struggle, not only with the elements, but just to keep going in an environment and in the company of three men with whom he had little in common. He had at times felt very lonely—not the loneliness of being among so few other people but the loneliness of being the only Christian in the group. I remember him telling me during the winter that his Bible was often a source of comfort to him and always a personal challenge—a general guide and in special circumstances a means of strength. I believe his faith was more real to him as a result of his experiences in the Arctic Ocean; but his dilemma now was to find a niche into which he would fit happily and usefully. In this Ken would probably have less difficulty than Fritz, Allan or I, for doctors are more useful and in far greater demand than polar travelers and glaciologists. Ken had often talked about the alternative to remaining within the medical corps—of working in an area where there are very few doctors and very many patients (although even the Ministry of Defence would admit that sometimes the Army puts a doctor in that position). Fritz's dilemma over what job to take at the end of the journey he would have to discuss with Anna, but his work would almost certainly take him back to the Arctic. Allan's needs were more simple—a bit of loafing around, then back to the polar regions, either north south, T-3 perhaps, or on another journey with me if I could think one up.

On the morning I had been transmitting the messages announcing our landing, Fritz and Allan had gone off together on a reconnaissance to try and find a way out of the broken-ice pack west of the small rocky island and had come back with encouraging news of a way which led onto a sizable floe. We had now to make for HMS *Endurance* with all possible speed; she was at that time about 105 miles to our southwest. Captain Buchanan for his part was trying to drive the *Endurance* through the pack toward us and close the gap so that the helicopters could be employed; but although the ship had made 35 miles on a north-easterly heading on the twenty-ninth, progress looked more difficult from there on. On the thirtieth he told me over the radio that we were within range of his helicopters and he could get to us in an emergency provided we left behind us all our sledges, dogs, records, everything. Fortunately this was no emergency.

We made about five miles when we got going that day, most of which was across the floe Allan and Fritz had found on their reconnaissance. The rough ice into which we hacked our way later in the day was as badly broken as anything we had seen in the last 1,400 route miles, and very active. Polar bears were becoming a serious problem. It was difficult to scare them off, and with only thirty rounds between us, we could no longer afford to fire warning shots over their heads. At a rate of three rounds a bear our supply would last only five days, and without weapons the hazards of sledging in that area would be greatly increased. We were now trying every method we could think of to drive them off: throwing ice axes at them; banging shovels and approaching the advancing bear. Once was enough to teach us that advancing on a bear only closed the gap faster; on one occasion Fritz threw one of my snow boots at a bear who promptly tore it to shreds.

We made no progress on the thirty-first, for the ice around the small floe on which we had set up camp slackened while we slept and marooned us. We were still drifting, however, and by the time I called *Endurance* at 0730 on June 1, the gap between us was ninety nautical miles. Brad, the radio operator aboard *Endurance,* told me that morning that the helicopters had flown the day before to Biskayerhuken on the north coast of Spitsbergen, where a depot of food and fuel had been left in a trapper's hut for us during the summer of 1968. My plan had been to have three depots spread out along the north coast of Spitsbergen and one at Depotodden at the northwest of Northeast Land, so that at whatever point on the coastline we made a landing we would be within thirty miles of a depot with a ten-day supply of food and fuel for four men and four teams of dogs. But the Norsk Polarinstitutt, which had very generously offered to lay these depots for us, had in fact been able to lay only one, for their survey ship had encountered heavy pack off the northwest of Spitsbergen and been unable to penetrate farther east of Biskayerhuken all season long.

The helicopter crews, sent in to Biskayerhuken to collect the supplies and hold them in readiness on board in case we needed them, found that the hut had been broken into by bears, and all our dog food and man rations eaten. Now I had no alternative but to call for the special flight I had requested as part of my contingency plan, for although we were within range of the helicopters for emergency operations, they had no dog food on board for us. All the extra gear that was part of my contingency plan was packed and ready at the Canadian Forces base at Rivers, but there was no need for the man-hauling equipment—lightweight sledges and the rest—nor a full resupply of food, since at the most we could be only ten days from the ship. I therefore sent a message to Air Transport Command Headquarters of the Canadian Forces asking for only two loads to be dropped at our position and the remainder on a floe near *Endurance*.

Over the next two days we made very little progress. We spent a total of sixteen hours during those two days maneuvering the sledges over pans of ice and hauling them out of mush, only to find ourselves in a more precarious spot than the one from which we had escaped. By the morning of the third we were on a very small floe surrounded by slop and loose brash ice. Messages of congratulations had been pouring in over the last few days—we received messages from Her Majesty the Queen, the Prime Minister, and many friends, professional colleagues, and learned institutes. I learned that I had been awarded the Livingstone Gold Medal of the Royal Scottish Geographical Society and had been invited to lecture before the Royal Geographical Society in London; and we gathered that preparations were afoot for a homecoming reception in Portsmouth—the home port of HMS *Endurance* where we were scheduled to arrive on June 23. But in a situation as dangerous as any we had been in during the past fifteen months, we were not at that time in any position to relax.

The airdrop to us on June 3 went off perfectly, and our emergency gear and the rest of our food and fuel was dropped near the *Endurance*. That combined operation was the first break in the monotony of battling with the ice pack for the officers and men of *Endurance,* and was in a sense their first real contact with the expedition. *Endurance* was at that time stuck in ice that was compacting over an area of thirty miles; we were in an area where the ice was slackening. Neither of us could move.

The four of us discussed this situation. Ken agreed with a comment by Captain Buchanan made a few days earlier that the helicopter could be regarded as "an extended arm of the ship," and that as soon as we were close enough for all the gear and dogs to be airlifted off the ice by helicopter we should accept the offer, rather than try to push on and physically close the gap by our own efforts. But the range at which the helicopters could pick us up with all our equipment and dogs was forty miles; for the time being we had no choice but to continue.

So we kept up our struggle and threw every ounce of remaining energy into the obstacles that came our way, and were for this rewarded. We broke away from the chaotic, smashed ice in which we had been drifting helplessly in loops and zigzags and on the fifth made ten miles. *Endurance* that day made nine miles in our direction, and with the drift carrying us west we made another seven the next day with a bonus from the drift of about two miles. We were now fifty-five miles from the ship. Captain Buchanan was delighted with our progress and very encouraging. By the ninth we were almost within range for a full airlift off the ice, but I felt we should go on and if possible reach the ship by sledge, a feeling strongly held by Fritz and Allan. Ken felt, and rightly so, that we were under some obligation to cooperate with *Endurance,* and that we should not ask Captain Buchanan to wait one day longer than he really felt he could afford. We made very little progress that day and were eventually stopped by a wide lead running north-south. How far north it extended we could not tell.

On the morning of the tenth I tuned up the radio. Propagation was very poor, but I could just make out the now familiar voice of Brad. "Traction, Traction, this is *Endurance, Endurance.*" They had been unable to move in the last forty-eight hours. We were forty-two miles from the ship. Captain Buchanan's voice came over the air: "Wally, I know how you feel, and I really would like to see you come right up to the ship, but there's a lot of broken ice around here now and it looks very bad." Not knowing fully our capabilities for traveling, he did not want to be too firm about a date for pickup; but he added that there was bad weather coming up with a snowfall forecast in twenty-four hours. The helicopters could not operate in a snowfall without great risk; however he promised to wait as long as he possibly could.

In order to return to Portsmouth by the twenty-third he had to back out within the next two or three days. If it was going to take *Endurance* as long to get out of the ice as it had taken to get to their present position, Captain Buchanan should have started working the ship free on the morning of the ninth. Clearly he was giving us more than our fair share of opportunities; it was equally clear to me now that we were not going to reach *Endurance* within the next three or four days by our own efforts. I acknowledged his message, but radio conditions were by then so poor that I was obliged to use Morse code. With my high-frequency single-sideband equipment, the Morse signal was no stronger than the voice signal, but it was more penetrating, and through the static I was able to tap out a message saying that in view of the weather situation and the possibility of snowfall the two helicopters should be sent out as soon as possible to pick us up.

As soon as it was confirmed that the two helicopters were on their way, I crawled out of the tent and gave the news to Allan, Fritz and Ken. This announcement for them meant the end of the expedition. Within a few hours they would be off the ice; within a few days they would be going their separate ways. We had come through some hard times together, and through some long periods of uncertainty about the outcome of the expedition—but then it would not otherwise have been a great adventure. Without their loyalty and their complete trust in my overall plan, without their optimism and their endurance, we could never have got through. We had had differences of opinion, but this was to be expected. We were four individuals, four strong characters; had we been men content to be ordinary and to live out our lives in the crushing cities of the civilized world, we would not have made this journey.

The first load would be a cargo load; for the second load one helicopter would take Fritz and his dogs and the other helicopter, his sledge. Each sortie would take one man and his dogs. I would be the last to go.

The helicopters were operating at the very limit of their range, and all they had on board were an observer and one photographer. The photographer stayed with us while the helicopters went back to the ship to off-load the gear before coming out again. It was a mad rush. There was perhaps an hour to spare between the visits but in that hour not a minute was wasted; there were boxes to be packed and gear to be sorted into piles. The huskies were put loose into the helicopter. Dogs don't seem to mind being put in an airplane providing the engines are not running, but try putting dogs on a helicopter when the rotors are whizzing around and the whole machine is shaking! We literally had to wrestle them in and stand at the door fighting them back until eventually, overcome by their fear, they cowered on their bellies and started dribbling all over the floor.

The first couple of flights were awkward because we didn't know how many dogs we could put into each helicopter. The helicopters could remain on the ground for only a maximum of about five minutes. For some reason I never fully understood they couldn't switch the engines off; the temperature wasn't very low at that time but presumably they felt safer if they kept the blades turning. They were of course burning up fuel all the time, kicking up a wind and making a hell of a noise. Everything was panic and flap and bustle, everyone was rushing around shouting.

I must admit feeling a little hostile toward the first man that greeted me. He wore a bone-dome helmet and a satanic beard, and his name I discovered was "Beest." Later on board ship we were to become great friends, but on the ice he wanted me to rush. I didn't want to rush. I hadn't rushed for eighteen months, but his helicopter was sitting there, whirring away, kicking up an awful racket and blowing everything about.

Fritz, Allan, and Ken were carried away and I was left with only a sledge, a tent, and my team of dogs. I got busy packing up my gear, getting it ready to put in the helicopters, knowing they would want to be away in a hurry. When everything was ready, I sat on the sledge and had a smoke. It was a wonderful feeling being all by myself out there. For the first time in sixteen months I was further than five miles from the nearest man. This was something to be savored, and I was overcome by a sense of sublime contentment—neither sad the journey was over nor excited about what lay ahead.

The helicopters came back and the stillness and purity of the Arctic was shattered with noise and tainted with evil smells of engines. People were screaming at me, yelling, laughing. I had to rush. I had to lift dogs, push them into the helicopters. Lift sledges. Crawl in after the dogs and pacify them during the flight —poor little bastards, wondering what the hell was going on. But they would be all right; two teams were to stay on Spitsbergen with a couple of resident miners, the other two teams were to go to a ski resort in Norway.

Occasionally I would glance out of the window; the ice below was really broken up, an absolute mess. I doubted now that we could have got to the ship in less than ten days. The helicopter banked and I could see the ship framed in the window. It looked very small. The hangar on the flight deck was crowded with sailors.

We hovered over the deck for a second or two, then settled. The doors were flung open and the noise flooded in. Wind from the rotors was whipping the film of water on the flight deck, beating it slippery. I was pushing the dogs out of the helicopter door. Their legs were kicking before they hit the deck and they took off as soon as their claws scratched the steel; sailors grabbed them up. I jumped down onto the flight deck. Bloody hell, it was hard —the thud resonated all through the ship.

There was a great sea of faces directly ahead—a huge crowd of strangers. So much wind from the rotors and noise from the engines. I could hear congratulations and feel my hand being shaken. I was confused, dazed, swallowed up in a crowd: everyone was speaking now, but I no longer heard what they were saying.

"The ice and the long moonlit polar nights," Nansen had written not long before his death, "seem now like a far off dream from another world." And so, I suspected, it would seem with me.

Nine years had passed since my fateful meeting with the hunter in the deserted mine of Moskushamn, and the journey which then I had thought not feasible was done.

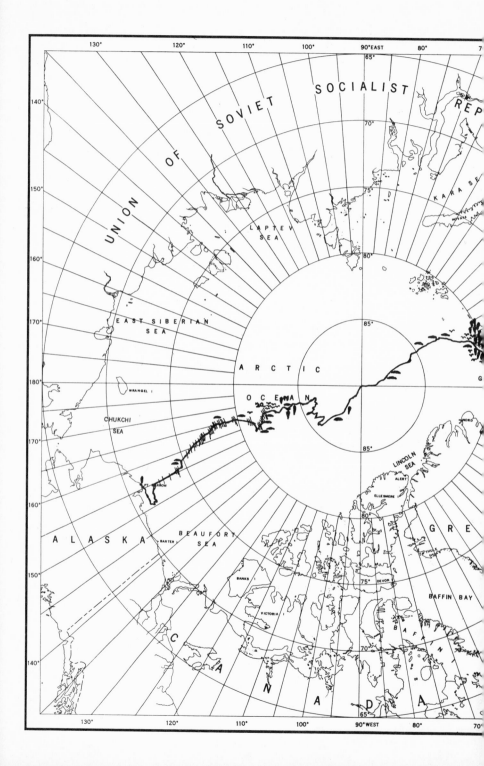

WILDLIFE OBSERVED DUR–
ING THE CROSSING OF THE
ARCTIC OCEAN BY THE BTAE.

POLAR BEAR: On the oceean, 1 fe-
male, 2 cubs, 3 males. On Spitsbergen approach, 19 bears in final
18 days.

SEAL: Total of 20 seen during the
journey.

BIRDS: First summer (mid-ocean),
20 birds of 5 species.

TRACKS: Foxes and polar bear all
the way to latitude 80.

Appendix I

Preliminary assessment of the expedition's
scientific observations

Dr. R. M. Koerner

FRIDTJOF NANSEN in 1893–96 was the first to conduct detailed scientific observations on the Arctic Ocean, and his work remains a classic in the annals of scientific and geographical exploration. His ship the *Fram,* which he intentionally beset just north of the New Siberian Islands, served as a laboratory and a base for three years while it drifted in the grip of the ice across the Arctic Ocean toward the Greenland Sea. Following Nansen's example, other ships were frozen into the ice, notably Amundsen's *Maud* and the Russian *Sedov,* from both of which scientific observations were made. Since 1937, however, when the Russians set up a drifting station at the North Pole, much of the scientific research in the Arctic Ocean has been conducted from semipermanent stations set up on the ice. The Russians have supported several ice-floe stations (the British Trans-Arctic Expedition passed within 60 kilometers of the Russian Station NP-17 in April, 1969), whereas the Americans have generally preferred the greater stability of ice islands. Ice-floe and ice-island stations provide the scientist with a mobile platform where the motive power is nature's and from which oceanographic and geophysical profiles can be obtained at relatively low cost. The Russians are currently maintaining their eighteenth drifting station. This technique has been associated with airborne surveys. Aircraft land on the ice and spend only sufficient time to take basic oceanographic and geophysical measurements. In this way an extensive network of scientific measurements can be set up over a period of a few years. The Americans have conducted a similar but more modest program since the early 1950's.

By the mid-1950's the overall pattern of ice movement in the Arctic Ocean was known. It was discovered that the circulation between the US/Canadian coast and the North Pole is a clockwise gyral in which ice drifts for several years before reaching the gyral's outer edge. From there the ice enters the stream of ice (the transpolar stream) heading for the Greenland Sea. One American station, T-3, has been circulating for eighteen years in this gyral, which is known as the Pacific or Beaufort Gyral.

It was from a knowledge of these ice-drift patterns that Herbert planned the route of the BTAE, which was to benefit by about 4 degrees of latitude from ice drift during the summer and winter, and from Nansen's empirical law that the ice drifts at 1/50th of the wind speed in a direction 28° to the right of the wind, we estimated our drift between star shots.

Despite the impressive amount of information gathered about the Arctic Ocean by the Norwegians, Americans and Russians (see Fig. 1, p. 40), there were still gaps in the knowledge that a trip such as ours could help fill. How could this be? How could an expedition using an old-fashioned method of transport and unable to carry very much scientific equipment gather information that heavily backed national expeditions had failed to gather? There are two answers to this. Firstly, Herbert planned two major static periods during summer and winter when we could conduct research in precisely the way purely scientific expeditions had done. The equipment could be para-dropped by the Canadian C-130s or the NARL R-4D, and all we had to do was to set it all up, observe, and record. Secondly, the only trained scientist who had crossed extensive regions of the pack was Nansen, and although he kept a detailed diary his main objective was to achieve a record northing. With air support we were able to plan to cover much more of the pack than Nansen and Johansen and, moreover, we would straddle both the Pacific Gyral and the transpolar drift stream. Although floe stations drift across extensive areas of the Arctic Ocean, the observers see only the same pieces of ice the whole way. Airborne surveys such as the U.S. "Birdseye" flights are specifically designed to record the details of the ever-changing surface of the Arctic Ocean. However, the observers are looking from 1,000 ft. and traveling at

180 knots. Skilled as the observers are, they miss many details and can record only the gross features of the surface. Nuclear submarines have crossed the Arctic Ocean several times and each time they record invaluable data on the ice. Unfortunately, a lot of this information is restricted because of its apparent military value. Even today, though, many details of the pack cannot be recorded by submarine-borne instruments.

To avoid tedious descriptions of our results, these are shown in tables (see p. 320 ff.), although a lot of the results are still in the raw form and await analysis. This information can be applied in many ways, but perhaps its chief importance is in helping to solve the ice-balance equation in the Arctic Ocean. In simple terms, the ice balance is the difference between the amount of ice and snow forming each year in the Arctic Ocean and the amount that either melts or leaves the Ocean—mainly by drifting through the Greenland-Spitsbergen gate into the Greenland Sea. To maintain what we may term a *steady state* (a balanced budget), the ice and snow gain each year must equal the amount lost. Over a period of a few years this is approximately the case. As we recorded the area covered by ice less than a year old and took several thicknesses through this ice, we can calculate the total amount of new ice formed along the line of the journey. We also measured the amount of snow and ice melt in summer. By subtracting the amount of snow and ice melt from the winter's new ice and snow we are left with the amount of new ice remaining at the end of summer. To achieve our *steady state* the same amount must be exported from the Arctic Ocean each year. The export figure calculated by this method turns out to be 4,000 km³ of ice. Spread evenly over the whole Arctic Ocean it would form a layer about 40 cm thick. This means that about 10 percent of the ice in the Arctic Ocean is exported each year.

The ice export is in many ways an unwelcome one, as it serves to bring cooler weather to the centers of civilization farther south. Scientists have shown that in the past few centuries spells of warmer weather have coincided with a retreat of the Arctic pack-ice edge northward. In cold periods the floating ice edge advances and in the early nineteenth century the edge was just to the south of Iceland. Which is the cause and which the effect is not known, but it has raised the question of what would happen if the Arctic Ocean ice cover were removed and whether man himself could cause its destruction. Various methods have been seriously suggested by American and Russian scientists and these include building a dam across the Bering Strait and by pumping out water, drawing in more warm Atlantic water by the Spitsbergen-Greenland gate. Another suggestion is to spread a dark-colored powder on the ice surface to absorb more solar radiation and promote greater ice melt. It is generally assumed that the ice cover is very unstable and it is theorized that an increase in the mean annual temperature of only 2°C would cause the ice to disappear in a few years.

Tied in with some of these theories is another that relates the ice ages to the presence or absence of ice in the Arctic Ocean. This theory argues that an ice-free Arctic Ocean would release more moisture to the atmosphere. This, in its turn, would cause much heavier snowfall in Siberia and Canada and lead to the establishment of continental ice sheets. However, recent research on the sediments on the ocean bed suggests the Arctic Ocean has been ice-covered for over a million years. If this is true then the ice cover is much more stable than hitherto believed.

Important to many of these arguments and theories is the total amount of ice in the Arctic Ocean. It was originally thought that the mean thickness of ice in the ocean was 3 m—about the same as that of old floes. Later, several thickness measurements indicated a figure closer to 2 m. Following this, nuclear submarines using topside-mounted fathometers measured a mean thickness between 4 and 5 m. This much higher thickness figure took into account the large amount of ice that has been fractured and piled into ridges, 90 percent of which lies below the waterline. Our data was all collected from surface observations. Over 200 thickness measurements have given a good idea of the thickness of the old ice and of the many areas of sea ice we crossed (Table 2). From our measurements of the surface profile of ridges and a knowledge of the density of sea ice and seawater, the amount of ice in a pressure ridge can be calculated. Combining all these observations and calculations, the mean end-of-winter ice thickness turns out to be 4.6 m in the Pacific Gyral and 3.9 m in the transpolar stream. Summer melt reduces this mean figure by 60 cm. Our observations, therefore, only partly substantiate the submarine measurements.

It will be noticed that we found that the ice in the gyral is an average of 70 cm thicker than ice in the transpolar drift stream. We found other differences as well. The ice production per unit area in the gyral is only about 65 percent of that in the transpolar stream where there is presumably more divergent (or opening) movement in the ice. The ice topography is more massive in the gyral, and the pressure ridges, though fewer in number than in the transpolar stream, tend to be higher. The gyral floes are thicker, and instead of the small, angular hummocks on the transpolar stream floes we found solid, smooth hummocks rounded by the melt of several summers. These observations fit the observed and theoretical consideration of drift patterns in the transpolar stream and the gyral. The transpolar stream carries ice in a relatively direct line to the Greenland Sea, and ice as a result is seldom older than 3–5 years. In the gyral, on the other hand, ice may circulate for as many as 20 years before it reaches the Greenland Sea.

During our static periods in summer and winter we measured the decay and growth of the ice. In summer the 3–4 m-thick ice floe on which we were camped was reduced to $2\frac{1}{2}$–$3\frac{1}{2}$ m in thickness. Younger floes nearby were reduced by a greater amount and large holes tens of meters across were melted through the ice. The curious thing about sea ice is that when melting occurs, almost-fresh water is released. Salinity measurements of this water (which, because its density is much lower than that of sea-water, forms a 1–2 m-thick surface layer) showed that it contained only 0.2 parts of salt per thousand. Seawater shows about 30 parts per thousand. We therefore had a ready supply of fresh water throughout the summer. When freezing temperatures returned in late August, the fresh water layer refroze with a structure almost the same as that of lake ice. So we were presented with the phenomenon of lake ice right in the middle of an ocean.

During summer, ponds of meltwater form on the surface and in June they cover nearly three-quarters of the ice surface. Surface travel then becomes impractical. After about a week of these conditions drainage holes form and the ponds diminish in size until they cover only a quarter of the ice surface. They begin freezing over in late August but do not freeze completely until December. As the ponds gradually freeze the water in them is put under increasing pressure as the newly forming ice takes up more room than the water. In November, if the ice drill penetrated these water reservoirs, the water gushed up through the drill-hole to a height of 2 m, like a miniature oil strike. It froze on contact and sheathed the driller in a thin armor of ice.

Although the average temperatures in September, October, and November were −8°C, −18°C and −31°C respectively, ice growth under the old, thick floes was not detected until December (Table 3). In fact, from our measurements we find that although the old ice covers about three-quarters of the area we traveled over, only one-third of the ice forming in winter grows at its base. The remaining two-thirds forms in the areas left open at the end of summer and in fractures that open during winter. In terms of heat loss from the ocean this means that two-thirds of the Arctic Ocean heat loss comes from only one-quarter of its area.

During the winter of 1968–69 an area around the hut measuring about 10 km by 5 km was examined every day. Some differential movement was observed on an average of one day in four. In late December enormous areas of open water formed and covered at least one-fifth of the study area. At this time of year ice forms quickly on open water—11 cm in the first day, 30 cm in five days, and over 70 cm in a month. So by the time we left the winter hut on February 23, the December polynyas were covered by 1m-thick ice.

During the Arctic Ocean crossing we had many opportunities to observe ridges forming. Generally it is a slow process where blocks of ice are forced up the ridge at a rate of about 2–3 feet a minute. Therefore ridges can be crossed while they are forming. Most of the ridges form from new ice 30–40 cm thick. As old floes either side of the thin ice come together, the broken ice forms a ridge of increasing dimensions where about 90 percent remains below the waterline. Frequently the slabs of ice pile up on the thick ice either side, overload it, and fractures form near the edge of the old floe. By the time pressuring stops the ridge is usually 1–2 m high and 2–4 m wide. (Table 4). Underneath the water, though, we calculate it extends to 6–10 m below the waterline and is 16–32 m wide. We crossed over 21,000 ridges—an average of 5–10 a mile.

Weather observations were taken throughout the journey and a summary is shown on Table 1. The coldest month was March 1969 when a very low sun made it bright enough to travel round the clock but did very little to alleviate the low temperatures. In each winter visibility was usually exceptionally good except during the occasional storm when snow from the surface was blown into the air; then conditions became very unpleasant. Fortunately, the Arctic Ocean is not a windy area and in our worst storms we never had winds in excess of 40 mph. During the winter there were no more than two or three days when storms reduced the visibility so that it was risky to go far from the camp.

The heat-balance studies in summer and winter took up more time than any other single program. The aim of this work is to determine the relative importance of the various heat sources and how this heat is used up. Heat sources include short-wave and long-wave radiation, sensible heat, and the ocean. Some of the radiation is reflected back into space, but the remaining heat can be used to warm and melt the ice, heat the ocean, or cause evaporation of the sea, meltwater, or ice. We used radiometers and solarimeters to measure the amount of radiation incident on the snow or ice surface and the amount that was reflected and reradiated. Ice temperatures were measured by freezing electronic thermometers into the ice. Temperature, wind speed and humidity were measured at different levels between the surface and 5 m. Because the surface is almost white, a large amount of the sun's radiation is reflected back into space. Our measurements showed that more than 80 percent was reflected back over snow, 74 percent from snow-free hummocks, and 20–40 percent from ponds. The level areas in midsummer reflected 65 percent of the sun's radiation (Table 5). As a large part of the energy available for melting the ice is from this type of radiation, the old hummocks did not melt as much as the level areas. The ponds, although they melted a lot under the water, refroze in winter and the change in ice level was much the same as on the hummocks. We found this by precise leveling in mid-July and again in mid-August, and if our measurements are representative it means that the floes do not become smoother with age.

The heat-balance program ran without many hitches in summer but during winter the effect of the cold caused several exasperating instrument failures. Cables snapped and hoarfrost constantly formed on sensing elements. The hoarfrost could not always be brushed off so that the instrument had to be brought into the hut, the frost melted off, and the instrument thoroughly dried out. These problems more than doubled the amount of time we had to spend on this program.

The air-sampling program, once we got it running smoothly, took very little time, but setting it up took a lot of patience and effort. The equipment consisted of a vacuum pump from which we ran a long tube to a filter. Air is sucked through the filter and solid particles are left behind on its surface. The pump was driven by an induction motor and, although our small generator was capable of turning the motor once the motor was running, it could not start the motor unaided. The system we gradually developed was this: with the generator running at full revs, we switched on the vacuum pump, blew into the pump intake, and flicked the motor in the right direction with a small screwdriver. After a second of hesitation it hummed to life. All this had to be done outside, and if the switching, blowing, and flicking were not done in the right split-second sequence, the generator would stall. Then would follow a 70-yard dash back to the pump to try again. Occasionally, the flick went the wrong way and the pump, instead of sucking, blew. You couldn't tell this by sound alone, but when the filter and its holder were clamped in place at the end of the tube, the filter would be blown into several pieces. The only solution was to go back into the hut, replace the filter, and start all over again. The apparatus filtered out a lot of foul language as well as particles.

Once all the motor problems were solved, over 50 filters were exposed for 6–24 hours each. These filters should show the rate of particle fallout in this remote area. It is also hoped to measure the ratio of terrestrial to cosmic fallout. Microscopic examination of the particles will indicate the composition of the particles falling into the earth's atmosphere from outer space. W. Hamilton, who is studying these filters at the Institute of Polar Studies at Ohio State University, reports that he has already found colorless glass spherules on several of the filters. A photo * shows one of them, taken between partly crossed polaroids. The spheroid is oblate, measures about 60 by 40 micrms, and is optically anisotropic. The "cross" undulates when the stage is rotated. (The spherule is embedded in epoxy and stuck on a glass fiber in the photograph). Hamilton knows of only two environments that could produce this anisotrophy, both of which are also environments where spherules are formed: the upper atmosphere and the lunar surface. The ablation droplets of meteors *may* be cooled quickly enough in the cold upper atmosphere to be quenched. Also, there is experimental evidence that vacuum quenching of glass droplets produces this effect. So the lunar surface is a real possibility: provided that spray ejecta reaches escape velocity on occasion.

We planned to do seismic sounding and gravity measurements dur-

* See photograph section, facing page 128.

ing the winter, but as winter gear could only be para-dropped the equipment for this work could not be made available to us. So we had to be content with a geophysical program consisting of magnetometer readings taken every two hours. Nevertheless, these readings promise to be of great interest, as our winter drift carried us along the Alpha submarine ridge. The data is being processed at the Lamont Geological Observatory, New York.

Our final program consisted of visual aurora observations. We took over 100 of these and they are being studied at the National Research Council in Canada.

The entire program kept two of us very busy during the summer and winter and occupied my "evenings" during the traveling period. Many of the results still have to be studied, but from those already processed it is clear that the expedition, although planned primarily as an adventure, was very valuable from the scientific standpoint.

TABLE 1: Summary of the meteorological log of the British Trans-Arctic Expedition, February, 1968 to June, 1969.

	temp (°C)			wind		vis (miles) % total			total (oktas)	cloud % total			precip (days)	drifting snow (days)
	mean	max	min	direction	speed (knots)	<2½	2½-10	>10		1	m	h		
Feb*	-32	-23	-41	ENE	6	0	0	100	3	36	14	50	?	?
March	-26	-9	-42	ESE	7	12	26	62	4	64	9	27	13	7
April	-27	-16	-41	E	7	3	6	91	3	14	2	84	14	6
May	-10	0	-28	SSW	10	31	40	29	6	69	9	22	25	5
June	-3	+2	-9	WSW	8	41	46	13	6	76	11	13	9	3
July	+1	+3	-1	SSW	8	75	10	15	7	74	17	9	16	1
Aug	-1	+2	-5	SSW	8	61	17	22	7	66	25	9	23	2
Sept	-8	0	-22	ESE & WNW	7	55	31	14	7	74	15	11	19	14
Oct	-18	-6	-34	SSE	9	38	28	33	6	76	13	11	16	13
Nov	-31	-17	-39	W	8	4	33	63	4	69	3	28	15	7
Dec	-36	-15	-44	WNW	9	7	37	56	5	54	13	33	22	11
Jan	-37	-25	-44	ESE	7	8	16	76	4	30	33	37	21	5
Feb	-36	-21	-47	WNW	7	4	27	69	4	53	16	31	14	6
March	-39	-29	-47	SSE	6	12	6	82	2	6	44	50	6	4
April	-26	-7	-39	—	8	26	6	68	4	56	7	37	13	6
May	-9	0	-21	—	8	45	18	37	6	81	7	12	14	2
June*	-4	-1	-9	—	7				7	85	5	10		

* The averages for February 1968 and June 1969 are based on observations of 7 days and 8 days respectively.

TABLE 2: Ice thickness mainly through ponded areas of multi-year floes. 258 measurements.

cm	% total
150–200	10
200–250	27
250–300	19
300–350	12
350–400	10
400–450	9

TABLE 3: Ice growth (in cm) in the central Arctic Ocean September, 1968, to February, 1969.

Month	Sept	Oct	Nov	Dec	Jan	Feb
From open water, first 5 days	10–18	21	?	?	26–36	32
From open water, first 30 days	54	56	62	?	84	74
200–300cm-thick floe, monthly rate	−5	0	0	5	10	?

TABLE 4: Pressure-ridge height (m) and slab thickness (cm) between 89°N and 81°N along longitude 30°E.

Height (m)	0–1	1–2	2–3	3–4	4–5	>5	
Percent of total	29	27	20	19	3	1	

Slab thickness (cm)	0–10	10–30	30–50	50–100	100	MY*
Percent of total	9	57	15	3	1	13

* MY: Ridges composed of old ice.

TABLE 5: The albedo of Arctic Ocean pack ice: measurements taken on the British Trans-Arctic Expedition, July and August, 1968.

		%
Multi-year floe	old hummock	74
	old, drained pond area	57
	recently drained pond area	51
	pond	41
	level, clean area	65
	dissected, dirty area	62
First-year floe	pond	24
	pond (almost through to sea)	20
	lead (open water)	8

TABLE 6: Ice type, expressed as percentage of distance covered between 90°N–81°N along approx. 30°E.

	% total
Hummocked or ridged ice	9.0
Open water	0.6
Ice 1–150 cm thick	17.0
Ice 150 cm thick	73.4

TABLE 7: Floe size, 89°N to 81°N along longitude 30°E.

size (yards)	0–300	300–600	600–1200	1200–1760	>1760
% of total distance	37.0	20.0	22.6	17.0	3.3
% of total number	79.3	11.2	6.3	2.7	0.5

Appendix II

Glossary of Ice Terms

Sailors' tales fired the imagination of Shakespeare, Milton, Keats and Coleridge, all of whom added their poetry to the imagery and terminology of floating ice. But the great wealth of descriptive terminology that passed into naval documents came from rough, ruthless, greedy mariners who were caught in the grip of the whale-oil rush in Spitsbergen waters in the early seventeenth century.

In time, a standardized ice terminology was suggested for international use; and in 1956 an operational terminology was produced by the World Meteorological Organization. When it proved to have many imperfections, a revised draft was eventually approved and adopted by the World Meteorological Organization in March 1968.

This internationally accepted terminology is the basis for the following sea-ice terms, many of which occur frequently throughout this book. Only where no word in the official terminology describes an ice form frequently encountered by the expedition have I used the word or words we coined during the journey. These are italicized in the alphabetical listing. Words italicized in the definitions are themselves defined elsewhere in the glossary. The symbol BTAE refers to the British Trans-Arctic Expedition.

ABLATION: All processes by which snow, ice, or water in any form are lost from a *glacier, floating ice,* or snow cover. These include melting, evaporation, *calving,* wind erosion, and avalanches. Also used to express the quantity lost by these processes.

ACCUMULATION: All processes by which snow, ice, or water in any form are added to a *glacier, floating ice,* or snow cover. These include direct precipitation of snow, ice or rain, condensation of ice from vapor, and transport of snow and ice to the glacier. Also used to express the quantity added by these processes.

ANCHOR ICE: Submerged ice attached or anchored to the bottom, irrespective of the nature of its formation.

BARE ICE: Ice without snow cover.

BELT: A large feature of *pack-ice* arrangement; longer than it is wide; from 1 km to more than 100 km in width (cf. *strip*).

BERGY BIT: A large piece of floating *glacier ice,* generally showing less than 5 m above sea level but more than 1 m and normally about 100–300 square m in area (cf. *iceberg, growler*).

BESET: Situation of a vessel surrounded by ice and unable to move.

BIGHT: An extensive crescent-shaped indentation in the *ice edge,* formed either by wind or current.

BLOWING SNOW: An ensemble of snow particles raised by the wind to moderate or great heights above the ground. The horizontal visibility at eye level is generally very poor (cf. *drifting snow*).

BRASH ICE: Accumulations of *floating ice* made up of fragments not more than 2 m across, the wreckage of other forms of ice.

BREAKABLE CRUST: See *crust.*

BROKEN AREA: See *fracture zone.*

BUMMOCK: From the point of view of the submariner, a downward projection from the underside of the *ice canopy;* the counterpart of a *hummock.*

CALF: BTAE term for small cake of ice that breaks off a floe and drifts clear (cf. *ice raft*).

CALVING: The breaking away of a mass of ice from an *ice wall, ice front* or *iceberg.*

COMPACTED ICE EDGE: Close, clear-cut, ice edge compacted by wind or current: usually on the windward side of an area of *pack ice.*

COMPACTING: Pieces of *floating ice* are said to be compacting when they are subjected to a converging motion, which increases ice *concentration,* and/or produces stresses which may result in ice deformation.

CONCENTRATION: The ratio in tenths of the sea surface actually covered by ice to the total area of sea surface, both ice-covered and *ice-free,* at a specific location or over a defined area.

CONCENTRATION BOUNDARY: A line approximating the transition between two areas of *pack ice* with distinctly different *concentrations.*

CRACK: Any *fracture* which has not parted.

CRUST: A hard snow surface lying upon a softer layer. Crust may be formed by sun, rain, or wind, and is described as *breakable crust* or unbreakable crust depending upon whether it will break under the weight of a turning skier.

DARK NILAS: *Nilas* which is under 5 cm in thickness and is very dark in color.

DEFORMED ICE: A general term for ice which has been squeezed together and in places forced upward (and downward). Subdivisions are *rafted ice, ridged ice,* and *hummocked ice.*

DIFFUSE ICE RIDGE: Poorly defined *ice edge* limiting an area of dispersed ice: usually on the leeward side of an area of *pack ice.*

DIVERGING: *Ice fields* or *floes* in an area subjected to diverging or dispersive motion, thus reducing ice *concentration* and/or relieving stresses in the ice.

DRIED ICE (or *DRAINED ICE*): *Sea ice* from the surface of which melt-water has disappeared after the formation of *cracks* and *thaw holes.* During the period of drying, the surface whitens.

DRIFTING SNOW: An ensemble of snow particles raised by the wind to small heights above the ground. The visibility is not sensibly diminished at eye level (cf. *blowing snow*).

FAST ICE: *Sea ice* which forms and remains fast along the coast, where it is attached to the shore, to an *ice wall,* to an *ice front,* between shoals or grounded *icebergs.* Vertical fluctuations may be observed during changes of sea level. Fast ice may be formed *in situ* from sea water or by freezing of *pack ice* of any age to the shore, and it may extend a few meters or several hundred kilometers from the coast. Fast ice may be more than one year old and may then be prefixed with the appropriate age category (*old, second year,* or *multi-year*). If it is thicker than about 2 m above sea level it is called an *ice shelf.*

FAST–ICE BOUNDARY: The demarcation at any given time between *fast ice* and *pack ice* or between areas of *pack ice* of different *concentrations.* (cf. ice edge).

FAST–ICE EDGE: The demarcation at any given time between *fast ice* and *open water.*

FINGER RAFTING: Type of *rafting* whereby interlocking thrusts are formed, each floe thrusting "fingers" alternately over and under the other. Common in *nilas* and *gray ice.*

FIRN: Old snow which has recrystalized into a dense material.

FIRST–YEAR ICE: *Sea ice* of not more than one winter's growth, developing from *young ice;* thickness from 30 cm–2 m. May be subdivided into thin first year ice/white ice, medium first year ice, and thick first-year ice.

FLAW: A narrow separation zone between *pack ice* and *fast ice,* where the pieces of ice are in chaotic state; it forms when pack ice shears under the effect of a strong wind or current along the *fast-ice boundary* (cf. *shearing*).

FLAW LEAD: A passageway between *pack ice* and *fast ice* which is navigable by surface vessels.

FLAW POLYNYA: A *polynya* between *pack ice* and *fast ice.*

FLOATING ICE: Any form of ice found floating in water. The principal kinds of floating ice are *lake ice, river ice, sea ice,* which form by the freezing of water at the surface, and *glacier ice (ice of land origin)* formed on land or in an *ice shelf.* The concept includes ice that is stranded or grounded.

FLOE: Any relatively flat piece of *sea ice* 20 m or more across. Floes are subdivided according to horizontal extent as follows:
Giant: Over 10 km across
Vast: 2–10 km across
Big: 500–2000 m across
Medium: 100–500 m across
Small: 20–100 m across

FLOEBERG: A massive piece of *sea ice* composed of a *hummock,* or a group of *hummocks,* frozen together and separated from any ice surroundings. It may float up to 5 m above sea level.

FLOODED ICE: *Sea ice* which has been flooded by meltwater or river water and is heavily loaded by water and wet snow.

FRACTURE: Any break or rupture through *very close pack ice, compact pack ice, consolidated pack ice, fast ice,* or a single *floe* resulting from deformation processes. Fractures may contain *brash ice* and/or be covered with *nilas* and/or *young ice.* Length may vary from a few meters to many kilometers (see also *lead*). Subdivisions as follows:
Very small fracture: 0–50 m wide
Small fracture: 50–200 m wide
Medium fracture: 200–500 m wide
Large fracture: 500 m +
Note: To the surface traveler, "very small" means 0–1 m and small means 1–5 m.

FRACTURE ZONE: An area with a great number of fractures.

FRACTURING: Pressure process whereby ice is permanently deformed and rupture occurs. Most commonly used to describe breaking across *very close pack ice, compact pack ice* and *consolidated ice.*

FRAZIL ICE: Fine spicules or plates of ice, suspended in water.

FRIENDLY ICE: From the point of view of the submariner, an *ice canopy* containing many large *skylights* or other features which permit a submarine to surface. There must be more than ten such features per 30 nautical miles (56 km) along the submarine's track (cf. *hostile ice*)

FROST SMOKE: Foglike clouds formed by contact of cold air with relatively warm water, which can appear over openings in the ice, or leeward of the *ice edge,* and which may persist while ice is forming.

GLACIER: A mass of snow and ice continuously moving from higher to lower ground or, if afloat, continuously spreading. The principal forms of glacier: inland ice sheets, *ice shelves, ice streams, ice caps,* ice piedmonts, cirque glaciers, and various types of mountain (valley) glaciers.

GLACIER ICE: Ice in, or originating from, a *glacier,* whether on land or floating on the sea as *icebergs, bergy bits,* or *growlers.*

GLACIER TONGUE: Seaward-projecting extension of a *glacier,* usually afloat. In the Antarctic, glacier tongues may extend over many tens of kilometers.

GRAY ICE: *Young ice* 10–15 cm thick. Less elastic than *nilas* and breaks on swell. Usually *rafts* under pressure.

GRAY–WHITE ICE: Young ice 15–30 cm thick. Under pressure more likely to *ridge* than to *raft.*

GREASE ICE: A later stage of freezing than *frazil ice* when the crystals have coagulated to form a soupy layer on the surface. Grease ice reflects little light, giving the sea a mat appearance.

GROUNDED HUMMOCK: Hummocked *grounded ice* formation. There are single grounded *hummocks* and lines (or chains) of grounded *hummocks.*

GROUNDED ICE: *Floating ice* which is aground in shoal water (cf. *stranded ice*)

GROWLER: Smaller piece of ice than a *bergy bit* or *floeberg,* often transparent but appearing green or almost black in color, extending less than 1 m above the sea surface and normally occupying an area of about 20 square m.

HOARFROST: A deposit of ice having a crystalline appearance, generally assuming the form of scales, needles, feathers, or fans; produced in a manner similar to dew (*i.e.,* by condensation of water vapor from the air), but at a temperature below 0°C.

HOSTILE ICE: From the point of view of the submariner, an *ice canopy* containing no large *skylights* or other features which permit a submarine to surface (cf. *friendly ice*).

HUMMOCK: A hillock of broken ice which has been forced upward by pressure. May be fresh or weathered. The submerged volume of broken ice under the hummock, forced downward by pressure, is termed a *bummock.*

HUMMOCKED ICE: *Sea ice* piled haphazardly one piece over another to form an uneven surface. When weathered has the appearance of smooth hillocks.

HUMMOCKING: The pressure process by which *sea ice* is forced into *hummocks.* When the floes rotate in the process it is termed *screwing.*

ICEBERG: A massive piece of ice of greatly varying shape, more than 5 m above sea level, which has broken away from a *glacier,* and which may be afloat or aground. Icebergs may be described as *tabular,* dome-shaped, sloping, pinnacled, weathered or glacier bergs.

ICE BLINK: A whitish glare on low clouds above an accumulation of distant ice.

ICE BOUNDARY: The demarcation at any given time between *fast ice* and *pack ice* or between areas of *pack ice* of different *concentrations.* (cf. ice edge).

ICE BRECCIA: Ice pieces of different age frozen together.

ICE CAKE: Any relatively flat piece of *sea ice* less than 20 m across.

ICE CANOPY: *Pack ice* from the point of view of the submariner.

ICE CAP: A dome-shaped *glacier* usually covering a highland area. Ice caps are considerably smaller in extent than *ice sheets.*

ICE COVER: The ratio of an area of ice of any concentration to the total area of sea surface within some large geographic locale; this locale may be global, hemispheric, or prescribed by a specific oceanographic entity such as Baffin Bay or the Barents Sea.

ICE EDGE: The demarcation at any given time between the open sea and *sea ice* of any kind, whether fast or drifting. It may be termed *compacted* or *diffuse* (cf. *ice boundary*).

ICE FELSENMEER: BTAE used this term to describe a frozen chaos of ice blocks and boulders frozen in irregularly. Sometimes called a *pressure field.*

ICE FIELD: Area of *pack ice,* consisting of *floes* of any size, which is greater than 10 km across (cf. *ice patch*).

ICE FOG: A suspension of numerous minute ice crystals in the air, reducing visibility at the earth's surface. The crystals often glitter in the sunshine. Ice fog produces optical phenomena such as luminous pillars and small haloes.

ICEFOOT: A narrow fringe of ice attached to the coast, unmoved by tides and remaining after the *fast ice* has moved away.

ICE FREE: No *sea ice* present. There may be some *ice of land origin* (cf. *open water*).

ICE FRINGE: A very narrow ice piedmont, extending less than about 1 km inland from the sea.

ICE FRONT: The vertical cliff forming the seaward face of an *ice shelf* or other floating *glacier* varying in height from 2–50 m or more above sea level (cf. *ice wall*).

ICE ISLAND: A large piece of floating ice about 5 m above sea level which has broken away from an Arctic ice shelf, having a thickness of 30–50 m and an area of from a few thousand square meters to 500 square km or more, and usually characterized by a regularly undulating surface which gives it a ribbed appearance from the air.

ICE JAM: An accumulation of broken *river ice* or *sea ice* caught in a narrow channel.

ICE KEEL: From the point of view of the submariner, a downward-projecting ridge on the underside of the *ice canopy*; the counterpart of a ridge. Ice keels may extend as much as 50 m below sea level.

ICE LIMIT: Climatological term referring to the extreme minimum or extreme maximum extent of the *ice edge* in any given month or period based on observations over a number of years. Term should be preceded by minimum or maximum (cf. *mean ice edge*).

ICE MASSIF (or *RECURRING ICE FIELD*): A concentration of *sea ice* covering hundreds of square kilometers, which is found in the same region every summer.

ICE OF LAND ORIGIN: Ice formed on land or in an *ice shelf*, found floating in water. The concept includes ice that is stranded or grounded.

ICE PATCH: An area of *pack ice* less than 10 km across.

ICEPORT: An embayment in an *ice front*, often of a temporary nature, where ships can moor alongside and unload directly onto the ice shelf.

ICE PRISMS: A fall of unbranched ice crystals, in the form of needles, columns, or plates, often so tiny that they seem to be suspended in the air. These crystals may fall from a cloud or from a cloudless sky. They are visible mainly when they glitter in the sunshine (diamond dust); they may then produce a luminous pillar or other halo phenomena. This hydrometeor, which is frequent in polar regions, occurs at very low temperatures and in stable air masses.

ICE RAFT: BTAE expression for *ice cake* that is used for getting across a fracture (cf. *calf*).

ICE RIND: A brittle shiny crust of ice formed on a quiet surface by direct freezing or from *grease ice,* usually in water of low salinity. Thickness to about 5 cm. Easily broken by wind or swell, commonly breaking in rectangular pieces.

ICE SHEET: A mass of ice and snow of considerable thickness and large area. Ice sheets may be resting on rock or floating (cf. *ice shelf*). Ice sheets of less than about 50,000 square km resting on rock are called *ice caps*.

ICE SHELF: A floating ice sheet of considerable thickness showing 2–50 m or more above sea level attached to the coast. Usually of great horizontal extent and with a level or gently undulating surface. Nourished by annual snow accumulation and often also by the seaward extension of land *glaciers*. Limited areas may be aground. The seaward edge is termed an *ice front*.

ICE STREAM: Part of an inland ice sheet in which the ice flows more rapidly and not necessarily in the same direction as the surrounding ice. The margins are sometimes clearly marked by a change in direction of the surface slope but may be indistinct.

ICE UNDER PRESSURE: Ice in which deformation processes are actively occurring.

ICE WALL: An ice cliff forming the seaward margin of a *glacier* which is not afloat. An ice wall is aground, the rock basement being at or below sea level (cf. *ice front*).

LAKE ICE: Ice formed on a lake, regardless of observed location.

LEAD: Any *fracture* or passageway through *sea ice* which is navigable by surface vessels.

LEVEL ICE: *Sea ice* which is unaffected by deformation.

LIGHT NILAS: *Nilas* which is more than 5 cm in thickness and rather lighter in color than *dark nilas*.

MEAN ICE EDGE: Average position of the *ice edge* in any given month or period based on observations over a number of years. Other terms which may be used are mean maximum ice edge and mean minimum ice edge (cf. *ice limit*).

MULTI–YEAR ICE: *Old ice* up to 3 m or more thick which has survived at least two summer's melt. *Hummocks* even smoother than in *second year ice*, and the ice is almost salt-free. Color, where bare, is usually blue. Melt pattern consists of large interconnecting irregular puddles and a well developed drainage system.

MUSH ICE: BTAE used this term to denote closely packed pulverized ice and pressure debris in a *fracture* or *flaw* (cf. *brash ice* and *ice breccia*).

MUSH–ICE BELT: Broken zone of *mush ice*.

NEST OF FLOES: BTAE used this expression to indicate a cluster of several sizable ice floes that were frozen together.

NET BUDGET: The difference between accumulation and ablation; usually expressed in terms of volumes of water equivalent per unit area.

NEW ICE: A general term for recently formed ice which includes *frazil ice, grease ice, slush,* and *shuga*. These types of ice are composed of ice crystals which are only weakly frozen together (if at all) and have a definite form only while afloat.

NILAS: A thin elastic crust of ice, easily bending on waves and swell and under pressure, thrusting in a pattern of interlocking "fingers" (*finger rafting*). Has a mat surface and is up to 10 cm in thickness. May be subdivided into *dark nilas* and *light nilas*.

NIP: Ice is said to nip when it forcibly presses against a ship. A vessel so caught, though undamaged, is said to have been nipped.

OLD ICE: *Sea ice* which has survived at least one summer's melt. Most topographic features are smoother than on *first-year ice*. May be subdivided into *second-year ice* and *multi-year ice*.

OPEN WATER: A large area of freely navigable water in which *sea ice* is present in *concentrations* less than 1/10. When there is no sea ice present the area should be termed *ice-free*, even though icebergs are present.

PACK ICE: Term used in a wide sense to include any area of *sea ice*, other than *fast ice*, no matter what form it takes or how it is disposed.
    Compact pack ice: Concentration 10/10; no water visible.
    Consolidated pack ice: Concentration 10/10; floes frozen together.
    Very close pack ice: Concentration 9/10.
    Close pack ice: Concentration 7/10 to 8/10; floes mostly in contact.
    Open pack ice: Concentration 4/10 to 6/10; many *leads* and *polynyas;* floes generally not in contact.
    Very open pack ice: Concentration 1/10 to 3/10.

PANCAKE ICE: Predominantly circular pieces of ice from 30 cm–3 m in diameter, and up to about 10 cm in thickness, with raised rims due to the pieces striking against one another. It may be formed on a slight swell from *grease ice, shuga,* or slush, or as a result of the breaking of *ice rind, nilas,* or, under severe conditions of swell or waves, of *gray ice.* It also sometimes forms at some depth, at an interface between water bodies of different physical characteristics, from where it floats to the surface; its appearance may rapidly cover wide areas of water.

POLYNYA: Any nonlinear-shaped opening enclosed in ice. Polynyas may contain *brash ice* and/or be covered with *new ice, nilas,* or *young ice;* submariners refer to these as *skylights.* Sometimes the polynya is limited on one side by the coast and is called a *shore polynya,* or by *fast ice* and is called a *flaw polynya.* If it recurs in the same position every year, it is called a *recurring polynya.*

POOL: An accumulation on ice of meltwater, mainly due to melting snow, but in the more advanced stages also to the melting of ice. Greater than 5 m in diameter.

PRESSURE FIELD: See *ice felsenmeer.*

PRESSURE RIDGE: A line or wall of broken ice forced up by pressure. May be fresh or weathered. The submerged volume of broken ice under a ridge, forced downward by pressure is termed an *ice keel.* Subdivisions are as follows:

New ridge: Ridge newly formed with sharp peaks and slope of sides usually 40°. Fragments are visible from the air at low altitude.

Weathered ridge (*young*): Ridge with peaks slightly rounded and slope of sides usually 30° to 40°. Individual fragments are not discernible.

Very weathered ridge (*mature*): Ridge with tops very rounded, slope of sides usually 20°–30°.

Aged ridge (*old*): Ridge which has undergone considerable weathering. These ridges are best described as undulations.

Consolidated ridge: Ridge in which the base has frozen together.

PRESSURING: See *ice under pressure.*

RAFTED ICE: Type of *deformed ice* formed by one piece of ice overriding another (cf. *finger rafting*).

RAFTING: Pressure processes whereby one piece of ice overrides another. Most common in *new* and *young ice* (cf. *finger rafting*).

RAM: An underwater ice projection from an *ice wall, ice front, iceberg,* or *floe.* Its formation is usually due to a more intensive melting and erosion of the unsubmerged part.

RIDGE: See *pressure ridge.*

RIDGED ICE: Ice piled haphazardly one piece over another in the form of ridges or walls. Usually found in *first-year ice* (cf. *ridging*).

RIDGING: The pressure process by which *sea ice* is forced into *ridges.*

RIME: A deposit of ice composed of grains more or less separated by trapped air, sometimes adorned with crystalline branches, produced by the rapid freezing of supercooled and very small water droplets.

RIPPLE MARKS: Corrugations on a snow surface caused by wind (as on sand).

RIVER ICE: Ice formed on a river, regardless of observed location.

ROTTEN ICE: *Sea ice* which has become honeycombed and which is in an advanced state of disintegration.

SASTRUGI: Sharp, irregular ridges formed on a snow surface by wind erosion and deposition. On mobile *floating ice* the ridges are parallel to the direction of the prevailing wind at the time they were formed.

SCREWING: Process whereby sea ice is forced into hummocks while one or both floes are rotating.

SEA ICE: Any form of ice found at sea which has originated from the freezing of sea water.

SECOND–YEAR ICE: *Old ice* which has survived only one summer's melt. Because it is thicker and less dense than *first-year ice,* it stands higher out of the water. In contrast to *multi-year ice,* summer melting produces a regular pattern of numerous small puddles. Bare patches and puddles are usually greenish-blue.

SHEARING: An area of pack ice is subject to shear when the ice motion varies significantly in the direction normal to the motion, subjecting the ice to rotational forces. These forces may result in phenomena similar to a *flaw.*

SHORE LEAD: A *lead* between *pack ice* and the shore or between *pack ice* and an *ice front* which is navigable by surface vessels.

SHORE POLYNYA: A *polynya* between *pack ice* and the coast or between *pack ice* and an *ice front.*

SHUGA: An accumulation of spongy white ice lumps, a few centimeters across; they are formed from *grease ice* or slush and sometimes from *anchor ice* rising to the surface.

SKYLIGHT: From the point of view of the submariner, thin places in the *ice canopy,* usually less than 1 m thick and appearing from below as relatively light translucent patches in dark surroundings. The undersurface of a skylight is normally flat. Skylights are called large if big enough for a submarine to attempt to surface through them (120 m), or small if not.

SNOW BARCHAN: Horseshoe-shaped *snowdrift,* with the ends pointing downwind.

SNOWDRIFT: An accumulation of windblown snow deposited in the lee of obstructions or heaped by wind eddies. A crescent-shaped snowdrift with ends pointing downwind is known as a *snow barchan.*

STANDING FLOE: A separate *floe* standing vertically or inclined and enclosed by rather smooth ice.

STRANDED ICE: Ice which has been floating and has been deposited on the shore by retreating high water.

STRIP: Long narrow area of *pack ice,* about 1 km or less in width, usually composed of small fragments detached from the main mass of ice, and run together under the influence of wind, swell, or current.

TABULAR BERG: A flat-topped *iceberg.* Most tabular bergs form by *calving* from an *ice shelf* and show horizontal banding (cf. *ice island*).

THAW HOLES: Vertical holes in *sea ice* formed when surface puddles melt through to the underlying water.

TIDE CRACK: Crack at the line of junction between an immovable *icefoot* or *ice wall* and *fast ice,* the latter subject to rise and fall of the tide.

TONGUE: A projection of the *ice edge* up to several kilometers in length, caused by wind or current.

WATER SKY: Dark streaks on the underside of low clouds, indicating the presence of water features in the vicinity of *sea ice.*

WEATHERING: Processes of ablation and accumulation which gradually eliminate irregularities in an ice surface.

WHITE ICE: See *first-year ice, thin.*

WHITEOUT: A condition in which daylight is diffused by multiple reflection between a snow surface and an overcast sky. Contrasts vanish and the observer is unable to distinguish the horizon or any snow-surface feature.

WORKING: BTAE used this term to indicate ice that was in the process of *pressuring, screwing,* and *shearing.*

YOUNG COASTAL ICE: The initial stage of *fast-ice* formation consisting of *nilas* or *young ice,* its width varying from a few meters up to 100–200 m from the shoreline.

YOUNG ICE: Ice in the transition stage between *nilas* and *first-year ice,* 10–30 cm in thickness. May be subdivided into *gray ice* and *gray-white ice.*

Index

Index